Honest Betrayal

Dara Girard

ILORI
Press Books, LLC

Books by Dara Girard

Duvall Sisters

The Glass Slipper Project

Taming Mariella

A Reluctant Hero

The Black Stockings Society

Power Play

A Gentleman's Offer

Body Chemistry

Round the Clock

Return of the Black Stockings Society

Playing for Keeps

After Hours

A Private Affair

Just One Look

Private Lessons

The Main Attraction

Ladies of the Pen

Words of Seduction

Pages of Passion

Beneath the Covers

Henson Series

Table for Two

Gaining Interest

Careless Rapture

Dangerous Curves

Familiar Stranger

It Happened One Wedding

Unexpected Pleasure

Midnight Promise

Sweet Temptation

Always and Forever

Truly Yours

Say Yes

Picture Perfect

By My Side

Clifton Sisters

The Sapphire Pendant

The Amber Stone

The Emerald Ring

Fortune Brothers

A Tempting Proposal

A Seductive Arrangement

An Unforgettable Moment

Novels

Honest Betrayal

The Daughters of Winston Barnett

Remember My Name

Illusive Flame

Winterwood Lane

Promise Me

This Changes Everything

Sparks

Piece of Cake

Best Laid Plans

Her Tender Touch

To my many loyal readers.

Prologue

The Present

"You don't love him."

Brenna let the words linger in her mind like the sensuous feel of the forbidden kiss on her lips. She could blame the champagne for the kiss or the party or the man, but she wouldn't. Brenna always took responsibility for her actions and this time wouldn't be any different. She looked at the handsome man—her would be lover—as he stood under the lights of the balcony.

He caressed her cheek and again said, this time with more certainty, "You don't love him."

"Him." Her husband. He had a name, but she didn't want to remember it right now. It made him too human, too real and nothing about their marriage was real. It was a business transaction, a partnership that was no longer working.

"Leave him," her would be lover whispered, his words as tantalizing as his cologne. "You don't need him anymore."

No, she didn't need him. Not like she used to. Not like the early stages of their marriage when his money and status were all that mattered. No, she didn't need him, but did he need her? Had the roles changed? It wasn't something he would admit; he was too proud a man. But was it right to leave him now? To set them both free?

She gripped the railing.

"When will you admit your marriage is a sham?"

"I've already admitted that," she said.

"Then admit that it's over."

Brenna turned away, not sure she had the courage to do so. Yes her marriage was a sham—everything about it was false and no amount of time had changed its artificial sheen. How could it? From their first meeting it had all been a game...

Part One

Only when we are no longer afraid do we begin to live.

Dorothy Thompson

Chapter One

The Past

Brenna Garrett was afraid of two things. A large man with the habit of barging into rooms unannounced was not one of them. She watched the intruder settle himself in front of her desk, without any attempts at civility, such as introducing himself or explaining why he was there. Instead he took off his sunglasses and pushed them in his jacket pocket. Brenna glanced at her assistant, Pauline, who hovered in the doorway. Her wispy brown hair surrounded a pale round face, reflecting an expression of dismay.

Brenna sent her a reassuring smile. At Love by Design, her match making service, she had been forced to deal with all types of people (desperate virgins, melancholy widows, impatient bachelors) and had become skillful at handling a large number of situations. Undisciplined men, while not a specialty, presented yet another challenge. Pauline nodded, acknowledging Brenna's smile. She glared at the back of the man's head, making her thoughts of him clear then shut the door.

Brenna returned her gaze to the large figure who sat before her. He boldly stared back. A shiver of awareness raced up her spine as she looked into the piercing darkness of his deep-set brown eyes.

Arrogant, cocky and incredibly sexy, she thought. Brenna was used to quickly assessing potential clients, but didn't like the direction of her thoughts. Unfortunately, a man like this seemed to resist typical hackneyed adjectives such as 'good looking' or 'handsome'. He looked as though he'd been raised from the earth. His skin the color of a dust storm, his eyes the center of a whirling abyss, his lips too soft for such masculine features while his eyelashes curled as though a sculptor had taken special care with them. He was--in a word--trouble.

He stretched out his legs, crossing them at the ankles. Brenna watched as the fine material of his black trousers moved against his thighs. She was certain that trousers shouldn't fit a man that well. Legs were a fascination to her because her left leg was deformed. His were, no doubt, as well formed as the rest of him. Large shoulders diminished the back of the chair, while long elegant fingers gripped the arms. She redirected her attention to his face ready to deal with the matter at hand.

"I take it you're upset about something," she said in an ironic tone.

His jaw twitched, but he remained silent.

She resisted a sigh. He was going to be difficult. She had hoped that today would be as peaceful as the spring afternoon outside her window, spreading a ray of sunshine on her carpet, while she listened to her favorite Caribbean station on the radio. She glanced at the Jack Russell terrier puppy as he played in the corner, his leash tied to the closet door handle. She was looking after the puppy for Pauline, who planned to give it to her niece as a birthday gift later that day. She pushed the remainder of her chicken pattie and potato chips aside and leaned towards him. "Your rather grand display makes it clear you're upset, but I'm afraid I am not a mind reader, so you'll have to tell me the reason why." She turned the radio off.

"I'm Hunter Randolph." His voice was low, deep and smooth, moving about the quiet of the room like a serpent. There was no anger in his tone, an unnerving contrast against the fire in his eyes.

Hunter Randolph. She repeated the name twice in her mind. She knew about the Randolph Medical Supply Company, but his name didn't register. She raised a brow. "Yes...okay, and I'm Brenna Garrett. If we've met before I'm afraid I don't remember." If they had met before, she was certain she would have.

He glanced around the office with a guarded expression that gave no indication what he thought of her office's peach colored walls with abstract paintings of embracing couples. The wind gently toyed with the petals of the white and yellow tulips on her windowsill, their fragrance lightly scenting the air. It was disconcerting that a man who was evidently so angry could look so calm. "No, we've never met." He straightened his gray sports jacket then met her eyes. "You have, however, met my fiancée, Janice Brinkton."

Brenna widened her eyes, but quickly controlled her features before her mouth dropped open. Janice was his fiancée? "That's impossible. Janice is engaged to Michael Peterson."

"She was engaged to me first."

Brenna stared at him as the pieces finally came together, but all she could say was, "Oh."

He folded his arms. "Now you understand."

She nodded. "Yes, she dumped you."

His arms fell. "She must have been suffering from cold feet. That's the best explanation I can come up with. Why else would she come here? Maybe she was just curious." He shifted in his chair, his eyes accusing. "Don't you check your clients' backgrounds to see if they are in relation-ships first or do you also provide married women with boy toys and married men with mistresses?"

Brenna kept her tone level, refusing to let him upset her. "Janice made it clear she was not involved with anyone."

His voice was low. "She lied."

"Well, liars make poor wives, Mr. Randolph. Consider yourself lucky."

He tapped the arm of the chair. "That's not the point."

"What is the point?"

"She was engaged to me and you encouraged her to run off with another man without giving me the chance to win her back."

Brenna could understand why Janice would choose to run off. Hunter's name fit him perfectly. There was a calm, watching quality about him that would make a person cautious. He was too patient; too calculated. If Janice had given him the opportunity to win her back, he would have. The only way to escape him would be to catch him off guard and run into the arms of another man. But would another man be a strong enough defense? An uneasy thought flashed through Brenna's mind.

"Did you hurt him?" she asked.

"Who?"

"Michael." She couldn't help assessing his form again. He made Michael's slim build appear almost boyish.

"Why? Do I have blood on my knuckles?"

She was not amused by his sarcasm. "It's not funny. With your passionate nature I know you must have been upset and perhaps not yourself for a few moments."

He looked offended. "I do not have a passionate nature, Ms. Garrett. However, I can assure you that had I taken the liberty to make my dissatisfaction clear, I wouldn't be sitting here."

"Where would you be?"

He didn't reply, inviting her to create an answer.

Brenna nodded, seeing no need to elaborate. "Let's look at this from another angle. Are you certain you were engaged or had that been your plan?"

"It was understood."

"By whom? You?"

"I told her I would marry her when I returned from New York. Our families have known each other for years. I was only gone for two months. If she had any misgivings she could have come to me and I would have been able to allay her fears and assure her how appropriate our union was."

"Perhaps she didn't come to you because she didn't want her

fears allayed? Maybe she knew you would convince her to marry you."

He looked blank. "Exactly."

Brenna bit her lip trying to choose her words carefully. Unfortunately, she found nothing that would be subtle, so she decided to be blunt. "Mr. Randolph, she didn't want to be won back because she didn't want to marry you."

He straightened clearly perplexed. "Why not? I would have made an excellent husband. I'm successful, organized, dependable--"

"Do you love her?"

"Considering you own a company called Love by Design, I am sure you recognize that emotions such as 'love' can be manufactured. I believe that common interests and backgrounds are the basic needed components for a lasting relationship such as marriage."

A slow smile spread on her face. "You're an excellent businessman, Mr. Randolph. Very skillful at giving vague answers to direct questions. However, let me make this easy for you. I only require a yes or no response. Do you love her?"

For a moment, Hunter looked uncomfortable. "I've known her since we were kids. I would have grown to love her."

"So the answer is...?" She trailed off giving him the opportunity to finish the statement. He stared at her. She glanced past him unable to stare back, briefly wondering what it would be like to be loved by a man like him. Would it be a blessing or a burden? "So the answer is no," she finished lamely.

"I would have treated her like a queen."

"Being a queen is a tiresome and scary prospect. Perhaps all she wanted was to be a wife."

"So she chose some lowly computer programmer?"

His tone of disgust forced Brenna to look at him. "Who will make her happy."

Hunter tugged on the cuffs of his sleeves, his voice smug. "If he can afford it. She is used to a certain standard of living that I was more than willing to provide." He sat back, his voice softening as he looked out the window. "She told me she wanted a man to sweep her off her feet like Prince Charming."

Brenna raised her brows. "And you're Prince Charming?"

He returned his gaze to her face. "No, and I wasn't suggesting I was or am. However, as an eligible bachelor I know my worth."

"Then you have plenty of other women to choose from."

"Women don't know what they want."

"Yes, they do. Janice made her choice clear."

Hunter stood abruptly, Brenna expected him to leave, but he began to pace instead. The activity made the room feel smaller. She discreetly lifted the window higher, hoping the air would dampen the tantalizing scent of his cologne.

"Do you know how she told me about her change of heart?" he asked. "With this." He tossed an envelope on the table. Brenna didn't need to look at it. She'd received a similar lace envelope in the mail. "A wedding invitation. I go away on a business trip and come back to that. She didn't call me or consult with me. We could have had a reasonable discussion, but she didn't give me the chance. She just ran away. Do I look like an ogre to you?" He pointed a finger at her. "That's a rhetorical question."

Brenna closed her mouth.

"We could have gone over the pros and cons of such a decision." He rubbed the back of his neck and sighed. "When I finally had an opportunity to meet with her, I asked her to explain."

Brenna leaned back in her chair. "You didn't demand?"

Hunter shook his head. "I never demand. I try to be very considerate of others."

She glanced at her half eaten pattie and bit the inside of her cheek to keep from smiling. "Of course."

He continued, not recognizing her sarcastic tone. "She told me a lovely woman at Love by Design," he sent her an unflattering glance. "I suppose that's you."

Brenna rested her chin in her hand and fluttered her eyelashes.

He scowled. "Matched her up with Michael. She said that it was love at first sight. As if there is such a thing." He clasped his hands behind his back. "She said that she didn't want to hurt me. She tried to convince me that she would have made me a dreadful wife." He suddenly fell silent then raced across the room. Brenna sat stunned by his odd behavior until she saw him crouch down in the corner where the puppy was.

"What's wrong?"

"Just give me a minute," he said in a brusque tone.

Brenna stood and saw that the puppy had the leash wrapped tightly around his neck. She let out a gasp.

"He's going to be alright," Hunter said removing the limp puppy from its death trap.

"But he's not breathing," Brenna said with rising panic. "I should have been more alert. I didn't even see..."

Hunter breathed into the puppy's mouth and rubbed him and soon his shoulders relaxed. "He's fine." He returned to his seat with the puppy cradled in his arms. "See?"

Brenna fell back into her seat relieved. "Thank god."

He winked. "You're welcome."

She laughed. "You don't know anything about humility do you?"

He shook his head.

"What did you say?" Brenna asked, curious in spite of herself.

He blinked. "What did I say?"

"Yes, to Janice."

He leaned back and the revived puppy squirmed in his arms and started to lick his face. "I wanted to say she was being rash and impulsive." The puppy started to walk around his lap as if he'd found his new favorite playmate, Hunter didn't appear to mind. "That she had no right to destroy the five year plan I had worked out for us."

"Yes, that's what you wanted to say, but what did you say?"

He looked down at the puppy then mumbled something.

She turned her ear towards him. "Excuse me?"

Hunter set the puppy on the ground then moved his chair closer to her desk then sat. He looked directly at her, his eyes like woodchips aflame, the heat in them reaching out to scorch her. Brenna swallowed, wishing she could glance away, but feeling mesmerized. "I wished her joy." His gaze fell; she sat back in her chair relieved. "I only said it because she looked so unhappy and she used tears. She knows I hate tears. I said 'I wish you joy and happiness'," he repeated, his voice a whisper.

"That was kind of you."

His eyes captured hers amazed. "Kind? I had no other recourse." He dropped his gaze to the ground where the puppy was pawing at his leg and whimpering. He lifted him up and settled him in his lap. "What else could I have done?"

The fact that he didn't know was encouraging. Other men wouldn't have been as understanding. Brenna merely shrugged amazed at the ease in which he handled the puppy.

"Can you imagine what it was like for me to say, 'I wish you joy' while I had her ring in my pocket?" he said playfully tugging on the puppy's ears.

Brenna shrugged. "It's for the best."

Hunter ignored her. "She threw her arms around me and kissed me on the cheek. She told me how happy she was that I understood, that I didn't fly into a jealous rage or something. She knows me better than that. I never get jealous and I do not rage."

Brenna raised her brows and glanced at the door. "Really? You did a pretty good imitation."

Hunter dismissed her comments with a wave of his hand. "That was nothing."

"So what happened next? Did you return the ring?"

"Then I met Michael. I admit to wanting to rip out his teeth." He raised his hand. "Not because I was angry, but purely because he kept smiling at me with a smugness I found annoying. I find that kind of attitude with most computer programmers. They're experts in one finite area and consider themselves geniuses."

Brenna grinned. "You're beginning to sound jealous."

Hunter picked up a framed picture of her holiday in England

from her desk. She felt the urge to slap his hand away, but resisted. It would be as useless as a flea trying to fell a brick wall. "Nonsense. I should be applauded for maintaining my composure." He groaned. "Two years of planning the perfect proposal destroyed due to impulse."

Brenna licked her lower lip. "Yes, well. While I understand how therapeutic this little 'chat' must be for you, it doesn't explain why you are here."

He set the photograph down. "I need a replacement. I have an event coming up in three weeks where I'd planned to announce my engagement. The company I work for strongly encourages management to be married. It shows stability. I've assured everyone, my grandfather included, that I would introduce my fiancée there. It's expected and would be humiliating for me to show up without someone."

"But wouldn't they be expecting Janice?"

He lifted his shoulders in a casual shrug. "No, I never made it clear to them specifically who I was going to marry." The puppy rolled onto it's back exposing its tummy. Hunter scratched it and the puppy wiggled in delight.

"But you were dating Janice long enough to want to marry her?"

"I told you we had an understanding. There were others, but they didn't suit me."

"You dated other women while seeing Janice?" Brenna asked trying to keep her disgust hidden.

"I wasn't cheating on her," he said annoyed. "We never dated exclusively. I dated others because I wanted to make sure Janice was the right choice."

Brenna briefly covered her eyes trying to understand his logic. "Then how could you be angry with Janice for choosing Michael?"

"I'm upset because she decided to marry him, that's the whole point. I need a fiancée." The puppy climbed up to his shoulder and began to lick his face. "Stop that," he said in a kind, but firm voice. The puppy took the hint and slid back into his lap.

Brenna watched the exchanged baffled by the man before her. He seemed so arrogant, demanding and cold, but treated this helpless puppy with such considerate tenderness. "Don't you want someone you love?"

"I've explained that," he said impatiently. "It's not essential."

Brenna straightened in her chair and handed him a brochure. "Sorry, but you've come to the wrong place. This is not an escort service. My clients are looking to start long term relationships, and certainly not the type you and Janice were engaged in."

Hunter scanned the brochure with disinterest then closed it. "I don't want one of your clients."

She furrowed her brows. "I don't understand."

"I want you." He stuffed the brochure inside his jacket. "Since you ruined my life, I expect you to fix it."

Chapter Two

Hunter watched Brenna's face change from polite disdain to anger. He feigned a cough to keep from smiling. He was enjoying himself. He hadn't expected that.

"No," she replied her voice quiet but firm.

He blinked. He'd expected more than that. A burst of temper, perhaps even a slap. Not such a cool refusal. "Why not? You have nothing better to do with your time."

Her lips thinned. "How do you know that?"

"Do you think I would come up with such a proposition without being prepared? It would be stupid of me to suggest such a thing if you had a husband." Actually it was her ringless hand that gave him the cue and after looking at the pictures on her desk he noticed there was no man present. Taking her as Janice's replacement had been inspired on the spot. He hadn't come here to do that. He came to tell her off, but when he walked into the room his carefully prepared speech left his mind and for the first time in his life he had no words. He could only stare.

He had expected a romantic, meddlesome wallflower. Not a

striking woman in a blue power suit. She wasn't beautiful, but he liked how her light brown hair framed her high dusky cheekbones, giving her face a haughty look as if she were a goddess offering a lowly servant her attention. When he finally did get his tongue back in order, he scrambled to think of how to gain her sympathy and come up with a reason to see her again. He liked a woman who challenged him.

She intrigued him. Few things did, he had to find out why. "You're currently not seeing anyone steadily."

"How--"

Hunter nodded relieved that he was right. "Do I know this? There are very few secrets in this world if you're willing to pay for it."

Brenna shook her head. "The answer is still no."

"And you still haven't answered my question: Why not? Isn't that what you do, match people up? I want a match and that would be you."

"No."

"Why wouldn't you want to spend one evening pretending to be my

fiancée?"

"Perhaps for the same reason Janice refused to marry you."

Something unreadable flashed in his eyes, before he lowered them. "I see."

Brenna cringed. She hadn't meant to hurt him, although she wasn't sure what emotion she had seen. He was definitely overbearing and arrogant, but he had cared for Janice in some odd sort of way and it was obvious that her rejection had bothered him. "I'm not much of an actress," Brenna said trying to soften her refusal.

Hunter nodded, but his eyes remained lowered. "That's understandable."

Brenna tucked a strand of hair behind her ear unsure whether she wanted him to look at her or not. Both prospects made her nervous. Yet, she didn't like not knowing what he was thinking. She lightened her tone, hoping to come up with a compromise. "I may be able to find a woman willing to pretend to be your fiancée for this important event. You are an eligible bachelor and an evening out with a handsome man such as yourself is always a treat."

His eyes captured hers. "You think I'm handsome?"

Her stomach fluttered at the intensity of his gaze. Very. "Does it matter?"

"I'm curious."

Brenna toyed with a pen on her desk. "I'm sure you're well aware of your attributes."

"It's not the same as a compliment. Humor me. I've just been dumped. My ego is a little shaky."

"You'd need a sledgehammer to shake your ego."

"That's a matter of opinion." He rested his arms on the desk and offered his profile. "Well?"

"I wouldn't have said so if I didn't mean it."

Hunter turned to her, his eyes teasing. "Sure you would. Women always say things they don't mean. I could have spots all over my face and you would have said the exact same thing. Women are trained to be kind so they throw out compliments that make men feel better. I want to know if you mean it."

She picked up a potato chip and bit into it. "You're just curious?"

"No," he said slowly, the attempt deepening his tone. "I find you attractive. It's only fair that you find me the same."

Brenna choked on the chip and grabbed her drink. After a large gulp, she slammed the drink down and glared at him. "Don't say things like that."

"Why not?"

"Because it's not appropriate."

"It's the truth."

"I doubt that's something you say often."

He paused, the teasing gone from his eyes. "You're not used to compliments. Pity. You should be."

"Why?"

"Because there's so much to compliment." Hunter rested his chin in his hand his gaze sweeping over her in admiration. "Your eyes, your face, your intelligence, your sense of style. You know you could hurt someone with that letter opener."

"Yes, I know. Why do you think it's aimed at you?"

He seized her wrist and snatched the opener then dropped it on the ground. "Okay, I'll stop. I'll teach you how to accept compliments another time." He snapped his fingers. "Wait. I have an idea. Give me a compliment and I'll show you how it's done."

Brenna raised her eyes to the ceiling. "You're hopeless."

"That's not a compliment."

"That's the best I can come up with. You barge into my office, ruin my lunch break, insult my business, accuse me of ruining your life, and then make fun of me and you want a compliment?"

Hunter's voice was soft. "I wasn't making fun, I was being sincere. I find you very attractive."

And he meant it. That's what bothered her. She turned to her computer and placed her hands on the keyboard annoyed that they were shaking. "Now let's see who I can find for you." She forced a smile. "Perhaps whoever I chose will end up being your perfect match and turn from a fake fiancée into a real one. Of course I will have to charge you for my services."

Hunter picked up the letter opener and laid it on the desk. "We could discuss this over dinner."

"You plan to eat me?"

The corner of his mouth kicked up in a quick sexy grin. "That's a tempting thought."

Brenna cleared her throat, feeling heat steal into her cheeks. "You can either do this now or schedule an appointment."

"You need to finish your lunch. When do you close your office?"

"Six."

"Good we'll have dinner tomorrow. That will give us a perfect opportunity to sort out any details."

"We're not going to dinner," she said, punctuating every word.

She expected him to argue. He didn't. Instead he sat on the edge of her desk, the puppy again cradled in his arms and began to whistle.

"What are you doing?" she demanded.

"Can you guess the tune?"

"Get off my desk."

Hunter shook his head. "No, that's not right. Listen." He whistled again.

"The theme to Gone with the Wind?"

"Very good."

She stood. "What does that have to do with anything?"

"You remind me of Scarlett. You look like you want to throw something."

"Yes, throwing you out would give me the greatest pleasure."

"Why won't you have dinner with me? I know you enjoy a good meal." He measured her rounded figure with masculine appreciation. "Don't get upset. I'm complimenting you. Skinny women can be dangerous. Their bony elbows are lethal in bed."

"Get off my desk."

He did. For a moment she wished he hadn't. She was afraid her head would fall off from looking up at him. "Fine. See you tomorrow."

"I'm not going to dinner with you."

He grinned and handed her the puppy. "Don't worry. You have all night to change your mind."

Once the door closed, Brenna put the puppy on the ground and rested her forehead on the desk, resisting the urge to bang it.

Pauline entered the room. "Are you all right? I am so sorry, I couldn't stop him."

"You could no sooner stop a hurricane. Which is exactly what he is--unrelenting and destructive."

"What did he want?"

"Me."

Pauline fell into a chair. "What?"

Brenna lifted her head. "Relax, it was nothing like that." Though that would have been nice. She'd never been wanted like that before. She was sure it would be a thrilling experience. She brushed the thought aside. "He was engaged to Janice Brinkton, but she won't have him because she's fallen for someone she met through us. So he wants me to act as his fiancée at an event he's going to in three weeks."

Pauline shivered. "I couldn't imagine anyone marrying him. There are some men who should remain single."

Brenna shrugged and glanced at her briefcase, there she saw the worn copy of Gone with the Wind she'd finished reading. "Clever jerk," she muttered.

"What?"

"Nothing." She bit the end of her pen.

Pauline recognized the telling habit. "What is it?"

She sighed and set the pen down. "I like him," she said, simply. "I know it sounds absurd. He's ridiculously arrogant, doesn't even understand his own nature, is domineering, controlling..."

"And you like these traits?" Pauline asked uncertain.

"No, I like him." For some reason she couldn't get out her mind the sight of him saving the puppy from choking and then rubbing it's tummy and letting it play with his fingers and lick his face.

"I think you're just in shock. Don't get ahead of yourself. True he is good looking." She paused. "Okay gorgeous, but as we both know that is not enough."

"It's not his looks. It's...he's so alive. So sure of himself. And he's ambitious. I find that very sexy." She held her chin in her hand and watched the puppy return to its corner. "He even saved your puppy's life," she said gesturing to it.

"Really?"

"Yes. The poor little thing was being strangled by its leash and Hunter saved it. And he was so sweet with him after." She sighed. "Unfortunately, he's completely unsuitable for me."

Pauline looked at her alarmed. "You'd actually consider him a match?"

Brenna raised a brow. "I am single."

"But he's all wrong." Pauline wagged a finger. "Remember whirlwinds can disorient us."

"Don't worry. I'm too practical to indulge in a passing crush. Anyway he doesn't fit my list of requirements."

Pauline leaned back recalling her requirements. "Considerate--definitely not. Sense of humor--no way."

"I think he has a sense of humor. He thought I was attractive."

"You are attractive."

"Yes, until I walk. That usually alters their perception. It's amazing how easily men lose interest," Brenna said the words without regret. She knew it as fact and didn't let facts bother her. "It was nice to fool him though. I stayed planted behind my desk, meeting him eye to eye as though I were normal."

"You are normal," Pauline said defensive.

Brenna waved a hand annoyed. "You know what I mean. He thought I was attractive and I didn't want to disappoint him. It doesn't matter anyway, I have the perfect woman in mind for him and then this little glitch in our schedule will be over. I'll make sure to double his fee for this unusual service."

"Real men wouldn't care about your limp."

"Real men are in short supply."

"Are you sure you can find Hurricane Man a match?"

"Yes, everyone has one." For some reason the thought made Brenna smile.

"Who's Brenna Garrett?" Miles Almquist asked, glancing over Hunter's shoulder.

Hunter quickly closed the notebook where he'd been writing notes about her. "The owner of Love by Design."

Miles sat at his desk, curving his lean body into his swivel chair. It squeaked against the concrete flooring of the office. Although in his mid thirties, his dark hair was already graying at the temples, and his face, always set with the distinguished British air of ennui, hid a clever mind. "Brenna Garrett Randolph," he said. "That sounds like a dignified name."

"It's not like that."

"When a thirty-four year old man starts writing down a woman's name with his own, it is."

Hunter clasped his hands behind his head. "She fits all my qualifications."

Miles sat forward intrigued. "For what?"

"To be my wife. I plan to present her as my fiancée in three weeks."

"And how long have you known this woman?"

Hunter opened his notebook and jotted down another note. "About an hour."

"An hour?"

He nodded.

"Are you feverish or just mildly insane?"

"I'm fine."

"While I recognize that Janice's behavior must have been upsetting, it's not like you to be hasty. I would say impulsive, but we are talking about you."

"What appears to be impulsiveness is really just a quick assessment of a situation ripe with opportunity."

Miles rested his chin in his hand and shook his head. "That sentence only makes sense to you."

"When you meet her, you'll understand."

Miles narrowed his green eyes. "What does she look like? Describe her."

"She was wearing a blue power suit with silver hoop earrings."

"And?"

"She has light brown hair that just brushes her shoulders and her eyes are brown like oatmeal."

Miles' hand fell to the desk. "Oatmeal?"

"I like oatmeal."

"Try not to write any sonnets." Miles glanced at their secretary. "What is Lynn wearing?"

Hunter opened a drawer and grabbed a highlighter. "A dress."

"What color?"

He slammed the drawer shut. "I don't know. Why would I?"

"Look."

Hunter turned in her direction. What he saw was a slender woman wearing a black and pink polka dot dress with a red lace collar. He winced. "Shouldn't we have a dress code?"

"You can't prohibit bad taste." Miles sat back and drummed his fingers on the desk. "I have a theory."

"Enlighten me," Hunter said without interest.

"Your notebook is an attempt to rationalize a very basic reality. In other words, you want to sleep with her."

Hunter stared at him stunned then clapped his hands together. "Perfect."

"What do you mean by that?"

"If I'm able to convince you of this, then I'll have no problem activating my plan to introduce her as my fiancée."

Miles frowned, shaking his head. "No, I think this is the real thing. Infatuation at its most destructive."

He rubbed his chin. "I wonder if Ruby will be as easily fooled."

"Mothers aren't easily fooled and neither am I. Hunter, you like her."

Hunter shrugged, finding no reason to deny it. He hadn't felt this good in years. "I admit that I find her attractive, fascinating."

"The last thing you found fascinating was a gastro scope. She must be some woman. Be careful my friend, many a stronger man has fallen victim to the disease."

"What disease?"

"It starts out as infatuation then turns into lust then if you're not careful you'll become infected with it."

"What?"

"Commitment. It's something women call love. It has the same affect. A state when all rational thought disappears. You'll sleep with her and it won't be enough."

Hunter ignored him. He routinely blocked out information he deemed illogical. He opened his notebook and tore out the page, staring at it a moment. Yes, she definitely fit all his qualifications. Now he'd have to convince her that he fit hers.

"Code red," Miles warned in a loud whisper. "Here comes the golden boy."

The golden boy, Daron Randolph, sauntered into the room dressed in gray trousers and a tan shirt. He held a manila folder tucked under his arm. He flashed a grin as welcoming as a shark's. "Hello, ladies."

Hunter crumbled the paper in his fist, glaring at his cousin and nemesis. They both wanted the Director position for Marketing and R&D that would be announced after the banquet. Daron seemed to be the first choice since he met all of the company's requirements. He'd married well, risen quickly in his division and possessed all the external qualities of good leadership. He was physically striking, polished and ruthless.

Daron shook his head as he stood between the two desks. "It's unfortunate you won't be able to attend the banquet, Hunter, but I realize public humiliations are not your forte."

"I'll be attending," Hunter said in a quiet tone.

"Without a fiancée to present? You are bold."

"My fiancée will be with me."

"No, she won't. Janice is marrying Michael Peterson. Someone she met through some dating service. Hadn't you heard? I was sure you'd received an invitation."

Hunter's tone hardened. "Since Janice is to be married, obviously it's not her. I thought you would have made that simple deduction yourself."

"It won't work, you know."

Hunter tossed the crumpled paper in the trash bin.

Daron leaned on the desk looking down at him. "I know you. You'll plan something, but it won't work. Producing a fiancée conveniently for one night is so cliché, it's ridiculous. Do you honestly think we won't see through the smoke screen when things don't work out in a couple of days? Face it, your little two-year plan failed. Concede. You're second best." He shrugged. "But that's nothing new. You've always been one step behind me."

Hunter rubbed his hands together, his gaze never wavering. "No. Not always."

Daron straightened, his voice turning to ice. "I have a wife and child now. Uncle Curtis has invited us to the ranch and will hold a party to celebrate my ten year wedding anniversary." He grabbed the folder from under his arm and flipped through its contents. "He may be your father." He lifted his eyes. "But everyone knows who's his favorite."

Hunter tapped his fingers against the desk, bored.

Daron tossed the folder on the table. "Sales are up thanks to my introduction of the Wells walker. Don't worry. When I'm promoted, I'll let you move into my old office. You two look a little cramped in here."

Miles spoke up. "I wouldn't be so sure about your promotion. Hunter's record is as impressive as yours, plus he developed the Trandor cane."

"And what do you call something that nobody ever uses?" Daron stopped, his eyes darting between them. "Oh, that's right. Useless. Nearly a year later and the thing still hasn't sold."

"And I've met his fiancée," Miles added.

Daron paused. "What's her name?"

"Brenna Garrett."

"How long have you known her?"

"A few months."

He began to smile certain he'd catch them in a lie. "What does she look like?"

Miles glanced up at the ceiling as though lost in thought. "Very attractive. When I met her she had on a blue power suit that complimented her light, brown hair and eyes. You'll agree when you meet her."

"That's a little too vague. Tell me something specific."

Miles glanced at Hunter. "She's the one who fixed Janice up with Michael. She took one look at Hunter and wanted him for herself."

Daron stood momentarily speechless. "I don't believe you."

"You don't have to believe me, but do you think I'm clever enough to make up a story like that?"

"I think you're clever enough to make it up. So the real question becomes is Hunter clever enough to pull it off?"

Miles nodded. "True. We'll see. Fortunately, your mouth is big enough for your foot."

"I will be looking forward to meeting her."

"We'll make sure she gets her rabies shots first."

Daron snatched his folder and left.

Miles swayed back and forth in his chair. "He'd be quite likable if he didn't have the habit of being a jackass."

Hunter shut the door. "We wouldn't recognize him otherwise."

"Well, my friend. I've set the stage. Brenna Garrett is your fiancée. Now you have to convince her."

Hunter sat on the desk and grabbed a paperweight. "You shouldn't have added the last part."

"Sounded more dramatic, plus it's partially true. The more unusual, but credible something sounds, the more people will suspend disbelief."

"He didn't believe you."

"Giving you more reason to prove him wrong."

Hunter tossed the paperweight up in the air. "Thanks for your help, an-way."

Miles suddenly frowned. "I hope you say the same thing if this scheme blows up in our faces."

He set the paperweight down. "It won't."

"How do you know?"

"How else would I know?" A devilish look entered his eyes. "I have a plan."

Chapter Three

Brenna groaned at the sight of bright lights coming from her second story apartment window. She lived alone, it should have been dark. She leaned against her cane then headed inside.

"Your mother is here," her neighbor and friend Tima Rees said as Brenna checked her mailbox.

Brenna looked at the tall, stately woman with dismay. "Yes, I know."

Tima put her mail in the large purple handbag she carried. It matched the scarf around her short curly hair. "Would you like to stop by my place before heading to yours?" She closed her box and headed for the stairs. "I doubt she saw your car."

"No, I might as well get it over with," Brenna said following her.

"Whatever she's cooking smells good."

"Would you like to come over?"

Tima grasped her chest in mock horror. "And interrupt a mother-daughter argument, I mean, moment? I wouldn't dare."

Brenna laughed. "I wouldn't mind."

"Maybe next time," she said then disappeared into her apartment.

When Brenna opened the door, the sound of a gun battle from a police show boomed from the TV. She lowered the volume. "Hi, Mom."

Diane Garrett poked her head out of the kitchen where rich smells of a tomato based stew permeated the air with spices.

"Oh, you're here."

"Yes, this is where I live," she muttered as her mother disappeared into the kitchen. Brenna raised her fists to the ceiling in a silent plea of mercy from her mother's meddling. She quickly hid the action when Diane came out of the kitchen with a pitcher of freshly squeezed lemonade. She set it on the table.

Brenna saw herself twenty some years from now, still round with wisps of gray hair and fine laugh lines. Unfortunately, she hadn't inherited her mother's beguiling smile. It made you forgive her anything. She could torch your house, demolish your car then flash a smile that would make you forgive her. She flashed one now. "It's so good to see you."

Brenna's grin was more forced. "Yes." She set her briefcase down as her mother returned to the kitchen. The phone rang. She waited a moment then picked it up. "Hello?"

"Hi," her brother Stephen said. "I just wanted to warn you that Mom's thinking of stopping by."

"Too late."

His voice rose in surprise. "She's already there?"

"Yes."

"That woman moves at the speed of light."

"Or you're just too slow."

"At least I tried."

Brenna drummed her fingers on the couch. "You could have called me at work. You always wait until the last minute. No wonder I was born before you."

"Did she cook something?"

"Doesn't she always?" She rested her elbow on the couch. "Do you want to stop by?"

He hesitated. "What face is she wearing?"

"Her 'I'm here because I care' face."

"Hmm. I think I'll pass."

"Coward."

He laughed and hung up.

When her mother came out of the kitchen again, Brenna said, "Now how do I ask this delicately?"

"You've never been delicate. Always blunt and straight to the point. That's probably why--"

"I don't have a boyfriend." Brenna sighed, finishing the familiar phrase. "I suggest that every couple of months you change that statement."

Diane untied her apron. "What do you want to know?"

She kissed her mother on the cheek to soften her words then whispered, "What are you doing here?"

"Visiting you of course. I have a key."

"I know that. I didn't envision you picking the locks." She tossed her mail on the table.

"You're limping."

Brenna headed for the kitchen, raising her eyes instead of her fists to the ceiling. "I always limp, Mom. I have a bad leg."

"Yes, but some days you limp more than others. How can you expect to get a man when you look like a ..."

Brenna stopped and began to smile. "Like a what? A broken horse, a maimed giraffe? A cripple? Don't leave me hanging."

Diane waved the comment away. "You know. Have you been doing your exercises?"

"Every day. Why do you think I live on the second floor? I'm forced to climb stairs." She rested a hand on her hip. "So why are you here?"

"You already asked me that."

Brenna grabbed a plate. "Yes, and if I ask enough times you might tell me the truth."

"Fine. Today I went to the grocery store and met a man in produce--"

Brenna held the plate to her chest like a shield. Horror crawled up her skin. "Tell me you didn't give him my number." The look on her face said everything. "Oh Mom!"

"Your grandparents are coming for your cousin Trina's wedding next month. She's three years younger than you."

"That's because she was born later."

Diane didn't smile. "Do you know how hard it is for me to say you're still unmarried? That you're still unattached? You're thirty. There's no reason why you should still be single. My generation, the women of the 70's, made it easy for you. You can meet men on the same playing ground."

"Field," she corrected.

"You don't have to perform all the schemes we had to. You don't have to wait for a man to come to you. You need to be more proactive. Instead you spend your time fixing other people's lives."

Brenna briefly thought of the handsome bully who had interrupted her lunch break. "And in some cases ruining them," she muttered.

"And not your own," Diane finished.

Brenna ladled some stew into a deep bowl. "If it ain't broke..."

Her mother rested a hand on her shoulder. "I worry about you. Ever since--"

Brenna sat at the dining table and shook her head. "Don't mention his name. I warned you that your tongue might shrivel up one day."

"He was a wonderful man. He cared about you."

Yes, he did. Her mind whispered his name, although her heart wanted to forget it. Byron Suncliff. Her true love. Her first everything. Byron was a considerate and kind man. Hunter's complete opposite. He'd always been attentive to her needs, easy going, generous.

Yes, he was a wonderful man. He didn't exactly love her, but he was devoted. Nevertheless, she hated his pity. No matter how he looked at her she always saw that emotion in his gaze. He imagined her as a damsel in distress that he could rescue, but she didn't need rescuing; she'd lived with her deformed leg all her life. She'd endured ridicule in elementary school through high school and had attended parties where she stood by the wall all night because no one would ask her to dance.

She had survived with a sense of humor and confidence that should be applauded not pitied. But his pity was such a tiny flaw for an almost perfect man that she forgave him. He had rescued her from a life buried in books and music. She'd met him in the college library her junior year. A man as beautiful and romantic as the poet with the clubbed foot whose name he shared. She didn't remember what he said or what he did just that he'd spoken to her when no one else would. She'd looked straight into his eyes and thought she'd found her soul mate. They'd talked about a number of subjects and soon became inseparable.

"I don't know what went wrong," Diane said.

"We just grew apart."

"I still don't understand."

Brenna would never explain it to her. It was a private pain she couldn't share with her mother, although she remembered it clearly. Remembered how startled he'd looked as they sat in the dining room of his condo. "You want to marry me?"

She bit her lip. "Yes."

His gaze slid away. She wasn't worried about the hesitant expression. If he needed time to think she'd give him plenty. She'd wait for him as long as he needed.

"Brenna, I'd love to really--"

She gripped his hand. "Then there's no reason to worry. Just say yes."

"But I want to have kids."

She sighed relieved that he wanted the same thing. "Don't worry, so do I."

He met her eyes. "It's genetic though, isn't it?"

Her smiled dimmed. "What are you talking about?"

"Your leg. It was a birth defect, right? A gene passed down from your father. So you could pass it to your child."

She swallowed as she tasted the bitter crumbs of rejection. She finally understood the point he was trying to make. She didn't want to hear it. She wanted to pretend that it wasn't a problem. But she could tell by his look that he considered it a big problem. "There's only a small possibility."

"Of course we could adopt, but I'd really like to have a kid of my own."

She lowered her gaze, trying to keep her voice steady although she knew she was losing him. "My brother was born okay."

"And you weren't. I don't want to take that risk. And I don't think you should either. It isn't fair to bring a child into this world with a mark already against it."

"So only perfect babies should be born?" She fought not to sound angry although inside her heart both broke and burned. "Was I a mistake?"

His voice was patient, indulgent as though he were trying to calm a child. "No, your parents decided to take a chance."

She lowered her voice and stared at the ring she'd bought for him. One that held all her dreams. "So you're ashamed of everything that I am?"

He came around the table and rested his hands on her shoulders. "I've always been honest with you and you with yourself. Your life hasn't been easy because of how you were born. I don't think it's fair to bring a deformed child into this world."

Deformed. It was the first time he'd used that word with her. The first time a hint of disdain tinged his tone. She didn't blame him, she'd always admired his honesty even though at that moment his words crushed her.

She wished he'd see beyond that. Didn't he see that she was still very much a woman? Didn't he know that her leg was only a part of her existence? That she had worked her entire life not to be the disappointment her father had expected? That in one day he'd shattered her with his honesty? That he'd made her feel foolish?

"I have the same needs and desires as any other woman." Her words sounded feeble, selfish. She knew he couldn't understand the choice he was taking away from her.

He kissed her cheek and gave her shoulders a squeeze. "Of course you do, but you're not like other women and the reality is no man is going to want to take the risk that his heir will be deformed. I care about you." He held her close but inside she felt hollow. "But I can't marry you."

They managed to part as friends and he went on to become a top criminal lawyer. From that day, Brenna promised herself never to be that vulnerable or foolish again. She was resigned to her decision and had no regrets. She'd buried herself in her work and made it very successful. She found no need for a man's company.

Brenna sighed, pushing the memory away. "It just wasn't the right match."

Diane looked sad. "You're not in the position to be picky."

She shrugged. "Well, I am."

The phone rang before Diane could reply. Brenna picked it up, relieved at the interruption. "Hello?"

"Hi, I'm Tony. Your mother--"

Brenna made a face then sweetened her voice. "I'm sorry, but my mother made a mistake. I've decided to become a nun. God bless." She hung up.

Diane stared at her outraged. "Brenna!"

She calmly returned to her dinner. "I don't need you to find me a man."

"I wouldn't have to if you had one of your own. Why can't you at least date?"

"I do date."

"Then how come I never get to meet them?"

"Because I keep them in little jars in my room."

"Brenna, until you find yourself a man, I will continue to do so."

"Mom, the truth is I've given up on men. Completely. I'm happy with my life and that's the way it will be."

Diane hesitated then said, "I want you to be happy."

Brenna smiled. "I am." But for the first time in years, she wondered if that was true.

Brenna glanced at her watch with mounting dread. Ten minutes to six. Her heart raced as she chewed the top of her pen into a flat sheet of plastic. She wanted to run, but she wouldn't. She would stay with her plan. Everything was set. She would leave five minutes early. When Hunter arrived, Pauline would give him the name of his date then he, in turn, would give up his ridiculous idea of wanting her and leave. Then she'd be rid of him and he'd never know anything about her. She took a deep breath. Everything would be fine.

Brenna jumped when her buzzer rang. She put her pen down then answered.

"He's not coming," Pauline said.

"How do you know?"

"Because I know."

"Fine." She sat back and glanced at her watch. Pauline was right. He wasn't coming. She told herself she was relieved not disappointed.

Pauline came into the room and sat down resigned. "Well."

Brenna nodded. "Well."

"He didn't show up."

"Nope."

"Perhaps he changed his mind."

"I hope so." Brenna glanced at a file she'd set up for him. "Although he did waste my time."

Pauline snorted. "He's inconsiderate, remember?"

"Yes," she said quietly. "I remember."

"So you're no longer attracted to him?"

Brenna began to smile. "Is that what you're worried about?"

She nodded.

"It was a passing infatuation, you needn't have worried. I know how to handle men."

"This one flustered you."

Brenna raised a mocking brow. "He flustered you too."

Pauline shrugged. "At least he's gone. That's the good news. The bad news is Helen's last date was a disaster."

Helen was a client who'd been on four other disastrous dates. "How?"

"Same story. She scared him off."

Brenna picked up her pen then set it down. Back to work. From Hunter to Helen. Life was back on track. "I'll call her tomorrow."

That evening when Brenna got home, she puttered about trying to reorganize her thoughts. She didn't care that he hadn't shown up. She admired his ambition but had recognized an impulsiveness in him that made him unpredictable. She found unpredictability an undesirable trait in a man. Were she to choose her perfect match, he would be a stable, grounded, financially successful man with no wish for children. Simple in his desires and not in the need of a pseudo mother or hooker, but rather a companion. Hunter wouldn't make a good companion. There was something a little too wild about him, uncontrollable and diverting. He probably had decided to choose someone from his undoubtedly thick black book. Good luck to him. At least he was out of her life.

Brenna walked over to the bookshelf, wondering what book to bury herself in. She stared at the rows of books that lined the far wall then turned away. She wasn't in the mood to read. She actually wanted company, which was rare. Books or a good selection of songs usually provided enough company, but tonight they felt like an empty activity. Since Tima wasn't home, she decided to visit her brother who lived in a reddish-brown high rise apartment twenty minutes away. She pushed back a bit of envy when she saw a couple playing tennis and an older man jogging the pristine grounds. Two activities she could never do. She walked to her brother's apartment and knocked.

Stephen opened the door, filling the doorway as he looked down at her. He pulled on his goatee and scowled. "Hello?"

"Hello. I came for a visit."

He playfully narrowed his dark brown eyes. "Do you have the entry fee?"

Brenna held up a pot of stew.

He nodded and stepped aside.

Her brother lived well for a single man. She loved the authentic Peruvian rug that took up most of his living room, the faint scent of cedar from a chair he'd made years ago and the overstuffed gray couch sitting squarely in the living room. But it was the lighting that gave the simple room unmitigated elegance. Her brother was a lighting genius, although he'd never admit it. He could make the smallest, dullest room look beautiful. She never understood why he didn't leave the company he worked for and strike out on his own. Unfortunately, he didn't have her drive.

They ladled their stew into small white ceramic bowls then went into the living room. Brenna sat on the couch. Stephen sat on the floor. He'd always preferred that position although no one in the family could understand why a six foot four inch person would choose the ground.

"So what did Mom have to say?" he asked.

She shot him a glance. "Can't you guess?"

He raised his voice and imitated her tone. "Why aren't you married?"

Brenna laughed. "Very good." She glanced around. "I should invite her to come here."

Stephen shook his head. "Won't work. She can't say anything to me. I'm still married."

"Separated."

"Which means I'm still married."

"Fiona shouldn't count."

He turned to her. "What do you mean she shouldn't count?"

"There should be a law against marrying a bore."

He frowned. "A bore?"

"Yes, she has no ambitions, no interests."

He shrugged. "Not everyone is as career driven as you."

"She doesn't even have a hobby."

Stephen flashed a grin. "I wouldn't say that."

"I don't consider sex a hobby."

He sent her a sly look. "Then you're not doing it right."

"The problem with you is that you don't want anyone to take you out of your comfort zone."

He pointed his spoon at her. "And your problem is you try to fix everyone else's life but your own."

"My life is fine."

"What was the name of your last date?"

"Ignatius Istobol."

"Liar." He set the bowl down. "You should get back into the dating pool."

"I don't like to swim."

"Then at least tread water."

She made a face. "You've been speaking to Mom."

"She has a point."

"What's the name of your last date?"

He hesitated then said, "Fiona."

She paused. "What?"

"You heard me."

"I thought you said Fiona."

"I did."

Brenna shook her head, her voice firm. "No."

His eyes widened. "What do you mean 'No'?"

"As your older sister I forbid you to get back with her."

"Forbid me?" Stephen laughed then went and got more food.

"I'm not joking."

He returned to the carpet and pretended to ignore her.

Brenna wouldn't let him. She tapped him on the shoulder. "She's all wrong for you."

"And who is right for me?"

"You're going to spill your food."

He set the bowl down. "And who is right for me?" he repeated. He suddenly waved his hands before she could speak. "And don't say it."

"Say what?"

"Don't say that woman's name." He pointed a finger at her. "I've told you before I'm not interested."

Brenna sighed. "I don't know why you won't give her a chance."

"And I don't know why you would want to match me up with your crazy next door neighbor."

She stiffened. "Tima is not crazy."

"Does it escape you that her name sounds like a skin disease? You have psoriasis and Timandra."

"I think she has a beautiful name."

He picked up his bowl. "And she paints walls."

"She occasionally creates murals, but she also--"

"I don't care."

"Stephen--"

"I'm not good with women anyway."

Brenna briefly raised her eyes to the ceiling. "The ultimate cop out answer."

"Fiona knows me and understands me. It works."

"You've been married four years and separated twice. This last time is your path to freedom. You need to get a divorce. If you want to stay in touch, then be friends."

"The sex is nice too."

"Forget about the sex."

He shook his head. "I don't think I can. It's too good."

"There must be something else you can do to occupy yourself."

"Not much. Or nothing I'd want to discuss with my sister."

"You shouldn't be in a relationship just for sex."

He began to grin. "Oh, I get it now."

"What?"

"Ignatius Istobol is the name of your vibrator."

Brenna playfully hit her brother on the back of the head. "No, it's not."

"It has another name?"

"It doesn't have a name."

"So you do have a vibrator?"

Brenna resisted placing her hands around his neck. "We're not talking about that. We're talking about you and women."

He shook his head. "No need. I have one. That's fine with me."

"Are you afraid to get divorced?"

"Not afraid. I just want to work on my marriage a little more than our parent's did. I don't want to be part of the statistics if I can help it."

"But it's not working."

"I can make it work in time."

"And if you can't?"

He shrugged.

Brenna stirred her stew then set it down. She couldn't understand why such a handsome man would settle for a woman so wrong for him. "You're a good looking guy and you have a lot to offer."

"A lot to offer?" he scoffed. "I'm an electrician. That doesn't seem to impress a lot of women."

"You're more than an electrician. You are a lighting artist. You should try starting your own company."

"I don't want the hassle. What do you have against Fiona anyway? I thought you liked her."

"I do like her except..." She stopped. "Forget it."

"Tell me."

Brenna shook her head. "No. You'll get upset."

Stephen put his plate aside and sat on the couch. Brenna knew that was a bad sign. It meant he was in his stubborn mood. "Tell me."

"She's safe."

"What's wrong with safe?"

Brenna chewed her lip. "You're getting angry."

"I'm not getting angry." Stephen's tone dropped. "What's wrong with safe?"

"It's just that you don't exert any effort in your life from your job to your social life. You don't take risks."

"And you do?" He sniffed. "Byron didn't seem very risky to me. You couldn't choose any safer than him."

"I'm different."

"Why?"

She stood and grabbed her handbag. "Never mind. I'd better go."

"You think your feelings are more fragile because you have a lame leg?"

She walked to the door.

He followed, "I'm right, aren't I?"

She swung the door open. "No, what you are is a jerk."

"Why?" He slammed the door closed. "Because I don't let you use your leg as an excuse?"

"Because you refuse to believe that it is." Her voice broke. "You don't understand--"

"Oh I understand big sister, more than you give me credit for. You think I didn't hear the taunts? Hell, I got them too. Sometimes I was embarrassed of you. For you. You were the kid people tripped in the hall, the freak, the outcast."

His words caused a tender wound to bleed a little as the memories came forth in her mind. "I'm sorry my existence was such a burden to you," she said in a cool tone. "However, you weren't the only one. Mom and Dad weren't too thrilled with me either." She opened the door again.

Stephen grabbed her arm. "Wait a minute."

Brenna snatched her arm away. "No. I'm ready to go."

He grabbed her from behind and held her. "Stop."

She struggled against him. "Let me go."

"I'm sorry," he said, his voice deep with regret.

"I don't care."

"I didn't mean to hurt you."

"So what? Let me go."

"Not until you believe me."

Brenna stopped struggling, feeling the weight of his strength; the weight of his remorse. "You're going to make me cry."

"Then cry. There's no shame in it. I don't think you let yourself cry enough."

She let her gaze fall.

He kissed the back of her head. "I didn't mean it, Brennie," he said using her childhood name. "I--"

"Yes, you did," she said, steeling herself against his gentleness for fear that he would know how much it hurt. "I don't blame you. I was embarrassed of myself."

He released her. "I want you to sit down so that we can start again."

She opened the door. He closed it. She scowled up at him; he smiled. "You're not very smart if you actually think you'll win this."

"The day you were born I knew you'd be a pest."

He jerked his head towards the couch. "I suggest you take a seat over there."

Brenna met his eyes then spun away. "You're just like him," she said disgusted.

"Who?"

She folded her arms and sat. "Nobody."

Stephen sat beside her. "Brenna, I was angry and my words were foolish."

"It's okay." She moved restlessly tired of the topic, the past was over. She was a success now and knew what she was talking about. "I'm not sorry about what I said about Fiona." She shook her head. "I don't think she's good enough for you."

The corner of his mouth quirked in a cynical grin. "She's pretty, sweet and smart, but she's not good enough for me? However, that Amazon woman with the weird name is?"

Brenna took a deep breath, trying to be patient. "Yes, I'm a matchmaker."

"Your computer is a matchmaker."

That was true, but only partially. A large part of her success also depended on her intuition, a skill she'd developed over the years. At times she didn't even need the expertly designed computer program, but it made her clients feel comfortable. "I know about these things. Take a risk. You're feeling lonely that's all. Don't fall into the same trap just because Fiona is there."

Stephen lowered his head a moment then met her gaze. "I love her."

Brenna hesitated then said, "I think you're afraid not to. Would you risk not loving her?"

Stephen's voice became quiet. "What risks have you taken?"

She didn't reply for a long moment then said, "I asked Byron to marry me."

His eyes widened. "I didn't know that."

"Nobody did because he said no."

"Why?"

"Why do you think?"

He thought for a moment then nodded. "Oh yea, I know. He's a stupid prick."

"That's not true. He's not stupid."

Stephen smiled. "So you're over him?"

"Doesn't matter, the point is I took a risk."

"So that means you'll never take a risk again?"

"We're not talking about me."

He slid to the floor and grabbed his bowl. "Right. Your life is off limits, but mine is open to advice."

"All I'm trying to say is that I went after what I wanted."

"You always do."

"And so should you."

"Why? I basically have what I want whether you believe it or not." He looked down at his stew, trying to look innocent although his words were not. "So what's the name of the guy I just reminded you of?"

She stiffened. "I told you, it's nobody."

He turned to her. "I know his name isn't Nobody so what is it?"

She sighed. "Hunter Randolph. A strange man who stormed into my office yesterday and wanted to use me as a fake fiancée."

"Why?"

"Because he was high on hallucinogens." She threw up her hands. "How would I know? He thinks I ruined his life because I matched up a woman he'd planned to marry." She waved a dismissive hand. "The story is ridiculous. Besides he was suppose to come back today and he didn't so I think he came to his senses."

Stephen narrowed his eyes. "And you wish he hadn't?"

Brenna shifted , feeling awkward. "Doesn't matter what I think."

He raised a brow. "I think you liked him."

"He was a very attractive man." She paused thoughtful. "A man like him on my roster would certainly help business."

"Business had nothing to do with your interest in him." Stephen adjusted his position and patted her on the knee. "You're a matchmaker. When are you going match yourself up?"

"I don't have a match."

"It's not like you to sound cynical."

"Practical. I have high standards."

"Standards you set so high on purpose to make sure no mortal man can reach them."

"Nothing wrong with waiting for a god."

"And as you wait I hope you'll meet a man who'll shoot you down to Earth."

ONCE BRENNA REACHED HOME, she pulled a book down from the shelf hoping to drown out her brother's hurtful words. She knew she'd been an embarrassment to her family. That was why she'd worked so hard to become somebody. And she had. Love by Design had been written up in Essence and Caribbean Times as a great alternative to online matchmaking services and speed dating. It was a classic hands-on approach to finding love. She was performing a great service and making a lot of people happy plus earning a decent income. She traveled, ate wherever she wanted and bought clothes when the mood struck, however these were limited luxuries because she had to stay within her budget. But beside these small treats, there were those few moments of loneliness. And when they descended, she'd slip into the lives of one of the fictional heroines in her books and life would return to order.

She was halfway through a delicious suspense novel when the phone rang. It was her friend, Bette. They'd recently become reacquainted two months ago thanks to her mother. They'd grown up in the same neighborhood before Brenna's parent's divorce forced her to move away. After a few letters they'd lost touch. Until now. Bette was great company, very affectionate and kind.

"I need a break," Bette said.

"Me too."

"We could go to the Ride Club."

Brenna frowned. "I'm not much of a dancer."

"That's okay. They have live entertainment and great food."

"Sounds perfect," Brenna said ready for a diversion although she wasn't a club person. She'd talked about taking risks; she might as well take one now. "Come by tomorrow."

THE NEXT DAY Stephen came to her office as she put things away. "I thought I'd take you out to dinner," he said.

Brenna knew he was feeling guilty about their last discussion.

She patted him on the shoulder. "That's okay. I'm going out with Bette."

"Oh, yea. How is she doing?"

"She's still single. Very cute. You might like her."

His eyes hardened. "I'm with Fiona."

She held up her hands in surrender. "Okay. Okay."

"So where are you going?" Pauline asked curious.

Brenna snapped her briefcase shut. "The Ride Club."

Stephen's lip twitched.

Pauline stared. "The Ride?"

Brenna nodded. "Yes."

Stephen burst into laughter. Pauline bit her lower lip. "Oh, Brenna."

She looked at them confused. "What?"

"The Ride." Stephen fell against the wall doubled over in laughter.

"What is wrong with you?"

Pauline touched her sleeve looking worried. "The Ride is a lesbian club."

"No, it's not."

Stephen said, "I dare you to go and find out. Or 'come out'."

Brenna wadded up a ball of paper and threw it at him. "Be quiet." She turned to Pauline. "Are you sure?"

She nodded.

"But why would Bette invite me to a gay bar? We've been going out for over two months, having such a great time. She said Mom gave her my number and...Oh no. She wouldn't."

Stephen saw her face and burst into fresh peals of laughter.

"Shut up!"

"What?" Pauline asked.

Brenna picked up the phone. "Let me make sure. I may be wrong."

"I don't think you are," Stephen said, wiping away tears.

Pauline looked at them confused. "Wrong about what?"

Brenna picked up the phone and dialed. She waved a hand for quiet as her mother picked up. "Hi, Mom. Yes, I'm fine. I have a question for you. Did you know that Bette was gay? Uh, huh. I see. Yes, yes. Right. No. Bye." She hung up.

Pauline and Stephen stared at her.

"She knew Bette was gay. She said she wanted to cover all bases and if you start laughing again little brother I swear I'll write your name and phone number in the first gay bar I see."

Stephen straightened his face.

Brenna fell into her chair. "This is awful. What am I going to do? She's so nice."

Stephen smiled. "You could take a risk. You never know."

She glared at him. "I may just risk murder charges."

"You'll have to tell her," Pauline said.

She stood and grabbed her briefcase. "Follow me home," she told Stephen.

"Why?"

"Because you're going to help me come up with something."

Chapter Four

"Will you relax," Brenna said as Stephen looked around the apartment corridor. "I'm the one with the problem."

"I hope that woman doesn't come out of her cave."

Brenna gritted her teeth. "Don't worry. I didn't see her tiger outside." She stopped in front of her apartment and searched for her key. When the door next to them opened, Stephen moved to Brenna's other side.

Tima popped her head out and smiled at them. "Hello you two."

"No time to talk," Brenna said. "I have a mini crisis."

"What is it?"

"She's dating a lesbian," Stephen said.

Tima blinked. "Oh, I didn't know--"

"Apparently neither did she."

Brenna nudged him. "I'm not a lesbian. There was a slight misunderstanding."

Tima nodded. "I see. Would you two like to come in and discuss options?"

Stephen took the keys from Brenna and opened the door. "We're fine thanks."

"Are you sure?"

He gently pushed Brenna inside. "Very sure." He closed the door.

"That was rude," Brenna said as he tossed her keys aside. "She was trying to be helpful."

"We don't need her help."

"I think we do."

"If you invite her over, I'm leaving."

She put her hands under her arms and made chicken noises.

He frowned. "Do you want my help or not?"

She let her hands fall. "Fine, fine. Do you have any ideas?"

He pulled on his goatee pensive then snapped his fingers. "I could chaperon."

Brenna narrowed her eyes.

"Or tell her you had an emergency."

"Maybe. Let's think some more." They sat at the table trying to come up with various ideas. A few moments later, the doorbell rang. They stared at each other.

Brenna glanced at her clock. "She's early."

"Make her wait."

"For how long?"

"Until we come up with something."

"That could take a while." She went to the door.

He grabbed her arm. "Wait."

"What?"

"Ask who it is. It could be Amazonia."

Brenna sent her brother a look of disgust then opened the door. Bette stood there with a ready grin, dressed in a short black skirt and paisley blouse that complemented her petite build.

Brenna opened the door wider. "You look great."

"Sorry I'm early," she said. "But I thought we could drive for awhile too. I love the spring. It's a soft feminine season."

Stephen folded his arms. "And you like all things feminine, right?"

"You remember Stephen," Brenna said, giving her brother a sharp look.

"Yes, you're all grown up." They shook hands.

"Do you mind if I just use the bathroom before we go?" Bette asked.

"Sure."

Stephen watched her leave then said, "You should go out with her."

"Why?"

"She's cute. Of course you'd be the butch in the relationship."

Brenna's response was a silent one, but when Bette came out of the bathroom, she saw Stephen hopping around on one leg. "Is something wrong with him?"

"He walked into my cane," Brenna said without sympathy. "Could you sit for a moment? We need to talk."

"Sure." She sat on the couch.

Brenna smoothed out her trousers. "I'm not the best at being subtle. I try, but fail many times." She paused. "I've really enjoyed the time we've spent together."

Bette's face fell. "You're breaking up with me. I can tell."

Stephen grinned. "She didn't even know she was dating you."

Brenna turned to him and whispered. "One more word and I'll aim higher than your knee."

He sat.

Brenna turned back to Bette and said carefully, "The truth is I like you very much."

"But it's not working, right?" She nodded. "I knew there was something missing. I didn't want to believe it because I like you too. But something has to click and it didn't with us." She stood and went to the door. "It's been fun."

"Yes."

Bette stepped outside and saw Tima putting a picture on her door. A watercolor of a spring scene. "Hi," Tima said.

Bette stepped closer to the painting. "That's beautiful."

"Thank you, this is my favorite season."

"Mine too."

But since you two are heading out, don't let me keep you." She winked at Brenna. "Have fun," she said then went back inside.

Bette widened her eyes, her voice in awe. "She's gorgeous. You are so lucky to live next door." She smiled. "I get it now. You want a chance with her. I saw that special look you gave her."

Brenna started. "No, it's not--"

"Don't worry, I'm not upset. Wish me luck tonight."

Brenna watched her skip down the stairs. "I don't believe it. She thinks I'm a lesbian and attracted to Tima."

Stephen draped an arm on her shoulders. "That makes Tima a little more interesting."

"What does?"

"That she attracts lesbians. Though I'm not surprised."

Brenna elbowed him in the ribs. "You'd be a lot more attractive if you kept your mouth shut."

He rubbed his side not offended. "You know that was one of the best breakups I've ever seen. I wish I could break up with women like that."

She looked at him hopeful. "You could practice."

His face grew serious. "Do you want me to pay for dinner?"

"Yes."

"Then shut up."

* * *

HUNTER STARED at his grandfather across the fine china plates and sterling silver cutlery as they sat at a large dining table in his grandfather's estate near Maryland's Eastern Shore. He could hear the wind rising up from the bay and the rain hitting the roof. He hadn't had a choice in attending. The dinner invitation was--in fact--a summons. Orson Randolph, a hulky man of eighty with sharp eyes and a booming voice, expected everything he said to be obeyed. "Doran's already made me a great-grandfather," he stated once the main entree was served.

Hunter nodded.

"When are you planning to?"

"In due time."

"I don't plan on living forever."

"That's a surprise."

"Hunter," his grandmother warned. It was the first time she'd spoken since they'd been seated. A quiet woman with refined features and few opinions, Audrey Randolph liked to blend into the background.

"Oh, let the boy talk," Orson said, his Georgia accent penetrating his words with more country crass than Southern charm. "He isn't one to keep opinions to himself." He pointed a fork at him. "It isn't a close tie."

Hunter frowned. "Tie?"

"Between you and Doran. Doran's certainly ahead of you. It isn't fair, but business isn't about being fair. He projects the right image. And business is all about image, isn't it Lewis?" he said to his butler, a solidly built black man of indeterminate years who stood quietly in the corner.

"Yes," Lewis said.

Hunter glanced at the man he'd known most of his life and winked. Lewis ignored him. "I know, Grandfather."

"Then why aren't you married yet?" Orson demanded.

"Things haven't gone quite as I'd planned."

"Hmm. Yes, you make a lot of plans. I like that, but you don't have time for that right now. Get yourself a woman. There are plenty of them out there. Good ones too. Get yourself a good, sturdy woman that will give you some babies. Don't be too particular." He leaned forward dropping his voice. "You're not looking for love are you?"

"No."

He sat back relieved. "Good. You couldn't afford that."

"I know."

The remainder of the dinner conversation dipped into mundane chatter then soon ended. It usually did once Orson had said his peace. He didn't like to sit around and chat. Fortunately, neither did Hunter. Orson walked him to the front entrance, his arm on Hunter's shoulder. "You realize you can have a woman on the side as long as nobody knows."

Hunter slipped into his jacket. It was against his nature to cheat, but he wanted to be in an agreeable mood. "Yes, sir."

"The board wants to see you married."

"I know."

"You know, but you haven't done anything about it. What are you going to do at the banquet?"

"I have a woman in mind."

"Is that right?"

"That's right."

His grandfather's face spread into a grin. He gave Hunter a hearty slap on the back. "Why didn't you say so?"

"I hoped it would be a surprise." Hunter opened the door.

"You've made an old man happy."

Hunter shook his head. "Don't try to fool me. We both know you plan to live to a hundred and thirty."

Orson laughed. "Hundred and fifty."

"You'll outlive us all." Hunter nodded farewell then raced to his car, huddled against the rain. Orson watched him drive away then suddenly turned and marched down the hall leaving Lewis to close the door and keep the rain from soaking the foyer. He joined his wife in the sitting room. He clasped his hands together with pride. "So he has himself a woman."

"You sound surprised."

"I am. I have to keep my eye on him."

"You've kept an eye on him his entire life. Hasn't he proven himself to you yet?"

"Don't speak in code Audrey. If you want to say something say it straight out. The good Lord won't strike you dead for being honest. "

"He's a good man. Don't be too hard on him because of...circumstance."

Orson's voice became harsh. "Are you going to sit there and tell me what to do? Who's the head of this family, woman? I know what I have to do. I've always known. My gift is knowing what to do and who to watch. He's a dark horse. Got some of his mother still left in him. Enough to cause damage if I'm not careful."

"He's a Randolph first."

"No harm in reminding him of that every once in a while." He poured himself a drink. "I wonder what this woman is like."

"I'm sure she's fine."

"Do you?" He looked at her. Really looked at her. He hadn't done so in so many years he was surprised to see how much older she looked. The fine lines of her brown skin, thinning gray hair expertly curled, even the gaze looked older. He didn't usually feel the years creeping up on him; he only felt them when looking at those around him like his wife, his sons and grandchildren. They reflected that time was running out for him. He had to make sure things went smoothly in his absence. That his bloodline and all he'd built continued to live on. He turned away from his wife's simple face. "Yes, you would." However, he wasn't so sure. The banquet would prove to be interesting.

BRENNA STARED at the woman in front of her with a sense of hopelessness she hadn't felt in years. Helen Voltanz had wide gray eyes that could be considered attractive if the look of desperation had been replaced by a more serene expression. Nervous fingers tugged on the strap of her handbag. She seemed harmless, except she was so desperate to get married and start a family that she terrified every single man who crossed her path. Unfortunately, Margaret O'Hanson, Brenna's on-call dating consultant, had pegged Helen as a lost cause and refused to do anymore sessions with her.

"Just give me another chance," Helen begged. "I know where I went wrong. I'm thirty-two years old. You're my last hope. My fertile years are whittling away. I've already passed twenty-five, which is a woman's peak fertile years and now my eggs are shriveling up and most of the men my age are dating younger women and--"

"That's the attitude that is getting you into trouble," Brenna cut in. "You want to get married now. So you're ready to marry the first guy that looks at you. That's not healthy. I'm thirty and feel there's time."

"But you're different."

Brenna let the comment pass. She clasped her hands together and rested them on the table. "If you want a baby there are many ways--"

"No," she said firmly. "I want to get married."

"Marriage is a partnership. You're thinking about all that you want, but what do you have to offer?"

"I'll be a wonderful mother."

"How about a wife?"

Helen nodded quickly. "Yes, that too."

Brenna bit back a groan. She wasn't sure of that anymore. "I don't think I'm the right agency for you."

"Oh, but you are. I didn't mean what I said about you being different."

"Listen, Helen, it's nothing personal, I assure you. I just think you deserve a service that will address your needs. Think about it. There is certainly an agency out there that can help you and will see you go down the aisle in no time." Brenna doubted it, but wanted to offer her hope. "I'll see where I can refer you."

"Thank you." Helen jumped to her feet and shook her hand. "Thank you. Thank you so much."

Brenna smiled, relieved the meeting was over. She discreetly pulled her hand away flexing the fingers that had been enthusiastically crushed. "Yes, you're welcome."

Once Helen left, Pauline entered the room. "Did you drop her?"

"I don't drop clients. I end consultation."

Pauline wasn't in the mood to worry about semantics. "Did you drop her?"

Brenna picked up a pen. "Yes."

"She'll go to your competition."

Brenna bit the end. "I know. I plan to recommend her."

"Why?"

"I had to think of a way to let her down gently. I'll recommend her with reservation."

"The owner of Perfect Match is getting married."

Brenna set her pen down Perfect Match was one of her main competitors. "I know."

"Clients may start wondering why you aren't married."

"Clients worry about their own social lives not mine."

Pauline went back to the front desk. Brenna cleared up her desk ready to leave. The buzzer rang. "Yes?"

"You're 5:59 appointment is here," Pauline said resigned.

Brenna glanced at her calendar confused. "My what?"

The door swung open; Hunter appeared in the doorway. Her spirits fell as her heart accelerated. He was still gorgeous. She had hoped she'd imagined it.

He held up a flyer. "I didn't know you were sponsoring a Spring Single's Party. Why didn't you tell me about this?"

She tapped her finger against the desk. "Are you extremely slow-witted or do you just enjoy being insulted?"

Unperturbed, Hunter folded the flyer and tucked it inside his jacket. "Are you ready for dinner?"

"I told you I am not going out with you."

Hunter nodded. "Yes, I remember you mentioned that." He rested a hand on his chest. "And since I am a considerate person, I decided that we'll eat in." He stepped into her office and opened the door wider. Two waiters dressed in black tuxedos entered, respectively pulling and pushing a table draped in a royal blue tablecloth with red and golden candles sitting among two covered plates, a basket of wheat rolls, and chilled lemonade.

Hunter said a few words to the waiters before they left. He turned, his eyes clung to hers. "I forgot to say hi."

"Hi." She cleared her throat annoyed with how breathy she sounded. "This is ridiculous."

He shut the door and closed the blinds. "No, it's not." He glanced around the room. "Where's the puppy?"

"He's not mine. I was only looking after him for a short while."

"Oh," Hunter said sounding a little disappointed. "I got this for him." He set a chew toy on her desk. "Would you like a puppy?"

"No," she said quickly in case he got any ideas.

"Okay." He took out a lighter and lit the candles. Then he turned off the lights letting the flames cast shadows on the walls. "Won't you come and join me?"

"I don't work after hours."

"This is called eating." He held out his hand. "Want me to show you how?"

"I know how to eat."

His hand remained stretched out to her. "Good."

Brenna was hungry, but was trying to think of the best way to reach the table without him seeing her walk. It would be awkward otherwise since she wasn't the woman he thought she was. "I'm a little chilly. Could you get my sweater, please? It's in the hall closet."

"I'll loan you my jacket."

He would be chivalrous. "I'd prefer my sweater."

"This is better."

"Here." He draped the jacket around her shoulders. It encompassed her in its warmth and musky scent. "There. Now come on." He grabbed her hand and pulled her to her feet. She landed on her bad leg and stumbled into him.

He looked down at her concerned. "I'm sorry. I didn't mean to pull you so hard."

"It's not you, it's me. I have a bad leg." She glanced at her cane hidden under the desk. "I use that to walk."

"Oh. Good." He grabbed her chair then set it at the table.

She stared at him. "Good?"

"Yes, I'm glad I didn't hurt you. Now come on. I'm hungry."

Brenna only stood there. Good. That was it? No, 'I'm sorry', or other such platitude? No pity, no sadness, no disgust? He didn't care? Her relief nearly made her laugh. Instead she grabbed her cane and folder then sat at the table.

Hunter lifted the covers off the plates and revealed grilled chicken, seasoned basmati rice, tomato and feta salad.

He poured the lemonade as she bit into the chicken. Outside they heard cars passing by and the quick pattering of footsteps as people headed home.

Brenna searched her thoughts for something to say, but her mind seemed to be experiencing sensory overload. A room usually familiar to her now seemed strange, smaller more intimate, tinged with the scent of cologne and brushed cotton mingling with the taste of spices.

She watched Hunter bring his glass to his lips. They really were incongruous with the rest of him. They should have been stern not so sensual.

"I do find you handsome," she said.

He choked and began to cough.

"Are you all right?"

He set the glass down. "I'm fine."

"Is that how you accept a compliment?"

Hunter sent her a playful glare. "You surprised me."

"I thought you'd be used to them." Brenna began to grin. "There's so much to compliment. Your eyes, your body, your mind."

He leaned forward the flickering candlelight dancing in his dark eyes. "Thank you."

Her gaze fell. "This meal is delicious."

"Brenna--"

"I've found her."

He hesitated. "Who?"

"Your fake fiancée. It wasn't very nice of you not to come by the other day."

"I was hoping that absence would make your heart grow fonder."

"It didn't. It only annoyed me." She opened her folder and handed him a picture. "She's attractive, educated, works in advertising, volunteers with numerous organizations, has never married but hopes to."

Hunter glanced at the picture then set it aside. "I'm not interested she--" He stopped then stared at the picture again. Brenna wasn't surprised. Sara always warranted a second glance, especially from men.

"I know her," he said.

"Oh, then this should be easy."

He looked at her horrified. "Are you kidding? I'd never go out with her again. I admit she's attractive both in real life and on paper, but she needs a caution sticker: Men Beware."

"She's very sweet."

"Saccharine. Took me two months to break up with her."

"Why?"

"I didn't want to hurt her feelings. Do you know how hard it is to break up with someone because they're too sweet?"

Brenna opened her folder pleased she'd come up with a plan B. "Then there's Carlotta Willington. She's--"

He shook his head. "Completely unsuitable."

"Why?"

"Too flighty. She has absolutely no common sense to keep her grounded."

"Barbara Jason--"

He shook his head. "Her name should be Barbiturate."

Brenna closed her folder and glared at him. "Is there a woman in this city you haven't gone out with?"

"Yes. You."

Brenna cut into her chicken with a short, determined motion.

"I'm not going." She chewed a moment then pointed a finger at him. "I've got the perfect woman."

"Is she medium height, brown hair, wearing a nondescript jacket?"

She frowned. "Yes. How did you know?"

"The wicked grin pulling on the corner of your mouth alerted me that you wanted to dump one of your rejects."

"Helen is not a reject."

"Helen." He nodded. "So the creature has a name."

"First, Helen is not a creature and second how do you know her?"

"I met a woman who was leaving the building. She looked at me well...let's just say a man usually gets such open invitations on street corners."

"Do you frequent street corners?"

"I don't have to."

Brenna glanced at the ceiling. Poor Helen couldn't even get a desperate man like Hunter interested.

Hunter was quiet a moment. "What kind of man are you looking for?"

"None of your business."

"I bet you have a list hidden somewhere."

Brenna felt her cheeks getting hot, but managed to keep her features neutral. "No, I don't."

He tapped the side of his head. "All up here I suppose."

She scooped her rice.

"He'll have to be in good shape."

"Who?"

"Your perfect match. Since you won't tell me your type, I'm forced to guess." He tapped his finger against the table. "He can't be too tall. You'd like to be able to look him in the eye. Equality is very important to you. He must have nice teeth because smiles are essential. He must think with his heart, not his head." He sipped his drink. "An artistic type, perhaps, with or without money and have lots of charm."

"I don't go for artistic types. He doesn't need to make as much as I do, but I would like him to have a steady income."

"And he must be kind, handsome and love your mother."

"No."

"No? You don't want a kind--"

"I want the first two, but he doesn't have to love my mother. I love her dearly, but she'd drive any man insane."

"There's no father in the picture?"

"He left for other reasons, but her habit of driving men batty may have been one of them." Brenna concentrated on her food, feeling his eyes on her. "Stop that."

He glanced away. "I can't do anything about my height, however I do have a stable job, I am in line for a promotion, and I'm handsome, charming and kind. I think I'll do."

She pointed her fork at him. "You forgot something."

"What?"

"I haven't seen you smile yet."

To her surprise he looked embarrassed. "I'm afraid that's not my strong point."

"Are you missing teeth?"

"No. It just doesn't suit me."

"Your smile doesn't suit you?"

"That's right."

"That's not possible. Everyone's smile suits them in some way."

He shook his head. "Okay, so there are two strikes against me, but I make up for them by getting along with parents, especially mothers. They love me."

"You have to..." She stopped and fell forward. "What did you say?"

He began to repeat himself. "Okay, so there are two strikes--"

She waved her fork. "No, no about mothers."

"They love me."

She stared at him as a devious idea formed in her mind. She quickly shook her head. "No, I couldn't."

"Couldn't what?"

It was a terrible, but tempting idea. If she could present Hunter as her boyfriend her mother would finally leave her in peace. Unfortunately, then she'd have to go to the banquet as his fiancée. She grabbed a roll and began to butter it. "Forget it."

"Brenna--?"

"It's nothing. So what are you looking for in a woman?" She expected a prompt reply. He surprised her by leaning back in his chair and closing his eyes.

"Medium height, healthy build, light brown hair." He opened one eye. "I like a little imperfection, limps are nice."

She stared at him stunned then laughed. Her limp was something people tried to ignore, he made it part of her appeal. Her heart swelled.

"The banquet is in two weeks so we'll--"

"I didn't say I would go."

"I'll pick you up in my Porsche."

"I don't care what car you drive."

His expression turned serious. "A Porsche isn't a car. It's a driving experience."

She bit her lip. "I beg your pardon."

"Her name is Rhonda Goodnight."

"That sounds like a porn star." She shook her head before he could reply. "I don't want to know."

"It's an interesting story."

"I don't care."

He shrugged. "There will be a champagne waterfall, a spiraling staircase".

Brenna clicked her tongue in pity. "And you standing there all alone."

"I'll buy your dress."

She set her utensils down, feeling herself weaken. "Why me?"

"You fit my qualifications."

She picked up her fork as her thoughts of romance disintegrated.

"Besides they'll be expecting you."

"They'll be expecting me?"

"Yes."

"Why?"

"I already described you and gave them your name."

"That was presumptuous."

"I was being optimistic."

Brenna nodded. "Well, since it will be a night of lies you can find someone to pretend to be me."

Hunter stared at her in consideration. "Why won't you come?"

"Because the idea is ludicrous and second I'm not sure I like you."

"Of course you do. You're here."

"I stayed for the food not the company."

He glanced down at his chest.

"What are you doing?"

"Since you've just stabbed me through the heart, I thought there might be blood."

Brenna reached out and patted his hand. "You're made of stronger stuff."

"I'm not so sure. So why aren't you married?"

"Usual reasons."

"It seems odd that a matchmaker isn't matched herself."

"You're in medical supplies. Do you use bedpans or walking frames?"

Hunter fell back, covering his heart. "Withdraw your sword madam."

Brenna laughed then bit her lip as her idea grew stronger in her mind. He would be perfect. Absolutely perfect. He could easily fool her mother. Stephen was right. She couldn't tell him to take risks if she didn't take any of her own. She decided to ignore caution and said, "If you do me a favor, I'll go to the banquet with you."

Hunter rubbed his hands together prepared for the task. "Yes. What is it?"

"I want you to meet my mother."

His enthusiasm crumbled. "The one that drives men insane?" He lifted a brow. "You really don't like me very much."

"You'll be able to handle her. I just need a man to take to dinner so she'll see that I have a social life."

"But you don't."

"And you don't have a fiancée, but you're willing to produce one." Brenna waited, hoping she hadn't asked too much. He had every right to say no.

He poured more lemonade into his glass and took a long swallow. He looked at her pensive. "Dinner with your mother."

"That's it. One night."

Brenna could almost see his mind weighing the pros and cons. "Is she a good cook?"

"Yes."

"Okay."

She was so happy she leaped out of her seat. She quickly recovered herself and sat back down. "Great."

The corner of his mouth kicked up. "Were you going to give me a hug?"

"No."

Hunter held out his arms. "I don't mind."

She ignored him. "You'll need a crash course."

"In what?"

"How to survive a night with my mother."

He stood. "I'm sure I'll be fine."

"You need to be prepared," she insisted, hoping to convince him to stay a while longer. She liked having him there.

"Fine. We can discuss it another time. Here's my card." He reached down and then realized he wasn't wearing his jacket. He looked at her then reached over, opened the jacket covering her shoulders, and retrieved a card. His hands brushed her side. "Here."

Brenna took the card and slipped out of the jacket as though it were crawling with spiders. It suddenly felt far too intimate. "I'll call you."

He stood and opened the door. "I'll have people come by early tomorrow and clear the table," he said then left.

She blew out the candles, the sunlight casting strips of light across the floor.

Hunter suddenly reentered the room. "I forgot something."

"What?"

Without warning, he brushed his lips against hers. "There. Now our bargain is sealed," he whispered then as quickly as he'd arrived he disappeared.

Brenna sat behind her desk trying to dismiss the kiss even as it lingered on her lips. It was no big deal, she assured herself. She sat staring at the phone. She finally picked it up and dialed. When her mother answered she said, "I have someone I want you to meet."

"It's a terrible idea," Pauline said once Brenna told her.

"What's a terrible idea?" Tima asked entering the office.

Brenna stared. "What are you doing here?"

"I called her for backup once The Hurricane entered your office," Pauline said.

"I'm able to handle him on my own."

"That's why you're agreeing to this ridiculous idea?"

"What idea?" Tima asked. Brenna told her and Tima grinned. "I think it will be fun."

Pauline scowled, raising her forefinger in the air. "This one act is sending feminism back generations."

"I'm not doing this for feminism," Brenna said. "I'm doing it to get my mother out of my life. At least temporarily."

"There are other ways to do that," Pauline said.

Brenna rested her elbows on the table intrigued. "How?"

"Just tell her truthfully to leave you alone." The two women stared at Pauline amazed. She blushed. "Okay, I know that isn't completely realistic but it's better than being deceitful."

"Be deceitful," Tima said. "It might be fun."

Pauline shook her head. "You haven't met this guy. He's egotistical, demanding, annoying--"

Tima shrugged. "This is a ploy not a proposal."

Brenna nodded. "Exactly. Now if I could only get my brother to take a risk."

"Get a fake date?"

"No, try something unlike him."

"What's wrong with him?"

"He's seeing his wife," Brenna said annoyed.

"Home wrecker," Pauline teased.

"They're supposed to be getting a divorce."

Tima shrugged. "They're trying to make the marriage work."

"They're trying to save a sinking ship."

Pauline nodded. "Brenna's right. I've met Fiona and her brother could do better."

Brenna flashed Tima a sly grin. "Actually, I'd love to pair you two."

Tima shook her head. "No way. I like my men fully grown."

"He's twenty-five."

"So? Men mature slowly. They don't even start ripening until they reach their mid-thirties."

"But you can teach younger men things," Pauline said.

"Things they'll turn around and use on younger women. Forget it."

Brenna looked pensive. "If he were older would you be interested?"

"No."

"Why not?"

"You're my friend, so I'm not going to tell you."

"Fair enough." Brenna sighed defeated. Stephen wasn't interested in Tima or she in him. Perhaps her instincts were wrong.

Stephen smiled to himself thinking of his mother's phone call as he drove home. He wasn't sure what Brenna was up to, but it seemed she'd managed to snag a man. Good for her. He wiped his brow, suddenly feeling the weight of his exhaustion. His last job had finished early and he'd helped a colleague move a large poster bedroom set up two flights of stairs. All he wanted to do was go home and shower. Then he'd go visit the Alandale Theater and see how the production was coming. He parked his truck and jumped out then caught a glimpse of the local stray--a gray and brown cat. He opened his lunch bag and tossed it some leftover chicken. The cat snatched it and ran off.

"Hey sexy," a female voice said.

He spun around and smiled at Fiona. "Hey babe. Stay away I'm all sweaty. Let me change my shirt." He turned and grabbed an extra one he had in his truck then pulled it on.

"I came to have a little snack with you. I packed some food." Fiona lifted a bag.

"Good. Why don't we eat it here? It's a nice day."

She wrinkled her nose. "In the truck?"

"It's clean. Come on." He grinned. "We've done a lot more than eat back here."

"All right."

Stephen lifted Fiona onto the flatbed then climbed in behind her. He watched her spread out the food, her long hair falling around her slender shoulders that always seemed to cower from the weight of the world. He felt fiercely protective of her, determined she would always feel safe with him. He grabbed a sandwich. "What is this?"

"Turkey."

He looked at the other sandwich. "What's that?"

"Turkey."

He didn't like turkey; she always forgot that. He took a bite anyway, appreciating the effort. "Hmm, delicious."

She smiled.

Her smile erased the bland, rubbery taste of turkey in his mouth.

Stephen leaned back against the cab feeling good. Fiona was like his truck--comfortable and reliable. She didn't want anything more from him. He knew that in a few months he'd probably ask her to move back in with him. Getting a divorce would be a mistake. He couldn't do better than Fiona. Her deep brown eyes and calm presence were nice to come home to. She was content with her life and her job as a clerk at The Bath Shop. It was his fault the marriage had hit rough spots. He hadn't given it enough time. He hadn't been there as a husband. He'd grown restless, but he wouldn't this time.

They ate in silence. Neither of them were great conversationalists. This trait had drawn them together as high school seniors. He remembered asking her out after months of practice and staring at her across the aisle in Chemistry class. She said yes, to his surprise and relief, and things progressed from there. At times he wished they had more to say to each other, but he didn't want to bother her and it wasn't really that important. Fiona was definitely someone he could see himself growing old with.

He put his arm around her waist. "What are you doing after this?"

"Visiting my mother. You?"

"Nothing much." It wasn't true, but he hadn't told her about the theater. Stephen didn't want to let her know that for two seasons he had been sneaking back stage to watch the set being built and the lighting production. But perhaps keeping it a secret was keeping a part of him from her. If he wanted their relationship to be different he'd need to be different. This was something they could talk about. He cleared his throat. "Actually, I was thinking of going by the Alandale Theater. They're going to start production on a new play."

Fiona reached for a pear. "So?"

"So, they may need some help with the set design. I could perhaps help with the lighting."

She took a bite then held the pear out to him. He shook his head. "That theater has been having performances for over twenty years. I'm sure their lighting director knows what he's doing. You wouldn't want to upset him by telling him what you think he's doing wrong." Fiona took another bite, quickly wiping some pear juice flowing down her chin before it stained her blouse.

Stephen felt his enthusiasm falter. "Yes, well I thought if I could help... Give them some new ideas."

"The director might hate them." She set the pear aside. "You know how those artistic guys are. They like to run the show. Just stick to what you know." She cupped his chin when she saw his face fall. "Oh, I'm sorry. I didn't mean to discourage you. You have such a kind heart. I know you want to help, but think of something else. Something you're good at."

"I'm good at lighting."

Her hand slid slowly up his thigh and her voice turned seductive. "I wasn't thinking about that." She began kissing him and pushed all thoughts of the theater away.

"Let me understand this," Miles said as he and Hunter sat at their desks. "You're going to meet her mother?"

Hunter tapped his chin. "It does sound a little absurd."

"Sounds brave."

"It's my part of the bargain. I meet her mother and she meets--"

"The entire Randolph company and their family and friends."

"It's not that bad."

Miles leaned forward. "And your grandfather."

"I'll handle him."

"Does she know how big this event is?"

"Won't matter." Hunter clasped his hands behind his head. "I'm thinking of seducing her."

"Can she be seduced?"

"Any woman can be seduced."

"You'll get in trouble with an attitude like that."

Hunter lifted a brow. "That's good. I can handle trouble."

Chapter Five

Two days later, Brenna and Hunter chose Whalton Park for their crash course lunch meeting. Brenna sat on a bench and stared at her list, too absorbed to hear the squeal of children at the playground or the zip of bicyclists passing by. Everything had to work out or the whole plan would fail.

"I see you brought your cane," Hunter said, glancing at the object that took up most of the bench. "Do you usually allow it to have its own seat?"

"It keeps me from getting hit on."

"Do you whack potential suitors with it?"

Brenna glanced up then frowned at the picnic basket in his hand. "We're here to work."

"Yes, I realize that. Come on. I know a spot that will suit us."

"Where?"

He pointed. "Over that hill."

She sighed. "Great. Go ahead and I'll follow you."

He glanced at her cane. "You can't make it?"

"I can if you promise not to watch me."

He squatted in front of her. "Get on my back then."

Brenna stared at him. "What?"

Hunter glanced at her over his shoulder. "You heard me."

She looked around. "You can't do this."

"You don't know unless you try."

Her curiosity overrode any doubts. She wrapped her arms around his neck. He easily rose to his feet and began to walk.

"You've never done piggyback before," he said after a few steps.

"No. Why?"

"You usually don't try to strangle your carrier."

Brenna loosened her grip. "Oh, sorry."

"Thank you. Now I can breathe."

She rested her chin on his shoulder. It was dangerous being this close to him. Close to his scent, his warmth, his vitality. She could feel the inherent strength of his back muscles. He was so strong, yet he didn't use it as a method of intimidation. She felt safe with him.

Hunter stopped under a large maple tree. In the distance, a pond glimmered with the light of the sun. Brenna jumped down stumbling a bit but quickly regaining her balance.

She watched him spread out the blanket a blue cotton/linen mix. "May I help?"

"No."

She glanced towards the pond, watching people feeding the swans. Not since she was a girl had she sat in a park to relax. She usually walked through it to get somewhere. Not to enjoy it as she did now, sitting with someone else. Not talking, just being. Strange that he'd be someone she felt comfortable with. He was too patient and very cunning. She should feel cautious, instead she felt at ease.

He handed her a plate piled with potato salad, grilled fish and green beans. "So what should I know about you so I can impress your Mom?"

"First of all, you and I met in a greeting card shop. You were shopping for your mother." Brenna took a bite of the fish.

"Impossible."

"Why?"

"I don't know where she is."

"I'm sorry."

He shrugged. "Don't be. My stepmother did a wonderful job."

"Okay, so you were picking up a card for your stepmother and asked me for my opinion. We started talking then you asked me out. Our first date was at the Thai restaurant on the corner of Mistleton Road. Our next few dates were scattered because of your hectic schedule. That's why you're only meeting her now. Do you think you can remember that?" She asked as Hunter finished his first helping of potato salad and went for a second.

Hunter leaned against the tree. A piece of bark fell on his shoulder. He picked it up and stared at it. "I'm sure you have it all written down for me."

"For the sake of consistency we will use the same story for your banquet."

He threw the bark aside. "All right."

"Now about me. I have a BA in Sociology, I've never married, I don't smoke, I am thirty and--"

Hunter held up a hand. "That won't work. You're not filling out one of your questionnaires. I need to know something personal."

"I floss my teeth every evening."

He scowled.

"We've only dated a few times. I wouldn't have told you any dark secrets."

"No, but I would know more than what you'd put on a survey. For example, you could tell me about your childhood. The name of your best friend or your first kiss. What do you plan to do in five years? Do you want to get married?"

"I'm not sure."

He looked surprised. "You're not sure?"

"I'm not sure I'm suited for it."

"If the right man comes along you'll--"

"He won't," Brenna said with a certainty that made her heart ache. She brushed the feelings aside. "My childhood was painful and my first kiss was unremarkable. Now that you know something about me--"

Hunter set his plate aside. He drew up a leg and rested his arm on it. "Your answer's too vague. What's the real reason?"

"Tell me something about yourself."

Hunter lowered his voice. "Was it a college sweetheart that made you unsure?"

"That topic is closed."

"But it's so interesting."

Brenna looked at a passing runner.

"Someone will change your mind," he said certain.

She rolled her eyes. "How like a man. I bet you think all women dream of having a husband and lots of children."

"No, I don't. My mother left me to pursue her career. I don't blame her for her choice. She was miserable as a wife and mother." He glanced up at the sky then her face. "I know firsthand that not all women are made for a domestic life, but you are. You're giving, compassionate and you believe in marriage or you would not have opened Love by Design."

Brenna shifted feeling awkward. She hated how right he was. "I saw a money making opportunity."

"You can't convince me of that. You're not greedy enough." Hunter lifted his plate. "Now let's talk about me. I'm thirty-four."

She waited. "And...?"

"You fill in the rest."

"I'm not as presumptuous as you are."

"Of course you are. After meeting me for one hour, you already thought you had found my perfect match. Why is that? I hadn't filled out anything. You didn't know what I did, if I'd been married before or not. I revealed little about my tastes, yet you thought you knew who would make a good match."

"You gave me plenty of clues. Janice was my first. She gave me an idea of your taste in women. Second, because you carefully selected her, I guessed it would be your first marriage."

"I'm divorced."

She paused. "Oh."

"I was twenty at the time and thought I was in love so I married her. Unfortunately, we were too young. However, we were clever enough to discover that before we had kids. After my divorce, I enacted The Plan."

Brenna furrowed her brows. "The plan?"

"The schedule I live by. It's served me well until recently. Unfortunately, it doesn't incorporate irrational human behavior."

"What was she like?" Brenna asked, wondering what kind of woman would convince Hunter he was in love.

"Who?"

"Your first wife."

He grabbed a blade of grass and twirled it. "I don't remember."

"You're lying."

He tossed the blade away. "No, I'm sitting."

"Hunter."

"Yes, I'm lying."

"Was she like Sara?"

He glanced towards the pond. "Who?"

"The woman you said was too sweet."

He shrugged. "Wouldn't know." He sent Brenna a mischievous glance. "I've never met her or the others. I lied because I didn't want anyone else but you."

She scowled. "I should be furious."

Hunter lifted her chin, his fingers warm and smooth as they grazed her jaw. "Try being flattered instead."

She swallowed. "Okay so you were married before and wish to remarry to promote yourself."

"Plus I'd like to have some kids."

Brenna's heart sank. Of course he'd want kids. "That's nice." She looked at him. For the first time she could read his eyes clearly. She saw his attraction burning, mirroring her own. "I can't do this," she said.

"Don't worry I can."

Like a bird of prey, his lips swooped down to capture hers. Leaving no time to retreat or think. After a few moments she didn't want to--she couldn't. The feel of his gentle lips on hers persuaded her to push away all apprehension. She wrapped her arms around him as though he were an anchor against the very storm of emotions he created inside her.

Hunter's feelings were even more tempestuous. He'd wanted to kiss her briefly, sweetly, but there was nothing sweet about her mouth right now. It was intoxicating and he loved it. His hands trailed a sensuous path up her arm.

She abruptly pulled away and began packing the basket.

"You're angry with me," he said surprised.

"No, I'm angry with myself."

"Why?"

"Because I'm giving you the wrong impression of me. You'll think I'm attracted to you."

He grabbed her chin forcing her to look at him. "And you're not?"

Brenna slapped his hand away. "I'm presently experiencing a strong emotional response."

"Is that a yes or a no?"

"I have no desire to marry. This isn't real, remember? We have a bargain that's all. You will not convince me to marry you even if I do fit all of your qualifications."

His eyes brightened with humor. "A challenge. I love a challenge."

"No, it's a warning."

Hunter opened his mouth to reply, but stopped when a familiar voice called out his name. He turned and gritted his teeth as he watched Daron climb up the hill towards them.

"I thought it was you," Daron said, stopping in front of them. His eyes darted between them, his smile grew. "My, my having a lover's quarrel all ready?"

Hunter kept his voice level. "Brenna, this is my cousin Daron."

She shook his hand. "Nice to meet you."

Daron gave her hand a gentle squeeze. "Likewise. I just hope you two can last until the banquet. Sometimes little arguments turn into big ones."

"We like the big arguments," Brenna said.

"Why?"

She slipped an arm around Hunter's waist. He did the same to her, his grip both possessive and reassuring. "Because making up is so much fun."

Hunter drew Brenna closer. "So if you'll excuse us..." He let his sentence trail off as a polite dismissal.

Daron hesitated, unsure if he should believe what he saw. Eventually, he nodded and left.

Brenna let out a breath. "I'm glad that's over. You can let go now."

When he didn't, she looked at him.

Hunter stared back. The intensity of his gaze weakening her resolve, tearing at the wall that kept her heart safe. Yet a delicate thread tied her to him, preventing any urge to look away. She didn't even realize he'd picked up a buttercup until she felt its tender petals against her cheek, against the curve of her neck. He brushed it against her forehead; her nose then pressed it against his lips before setting it against hers. The gentle act made her entire body tingle.

When he tucked the flower in her hair, she knew what he was up to. That didn't stop goose bumps from forming on her arms. He kissed her mouth then moved to nibble on her ear.

"Your seduction technique needs some work," she said.

He stared at her stunned. "Work?"

"You are trying to seduce me, aren't you?"

"Do you think I would admit to it after what you just said?"

"So the answer is yes?"

Hunter scowled.

"All women aren't the same."

"I know that."

"If you'd known that you would have realized that ear nibbling is a risky tactic. Not all women like it. I, for one, find a tongue in my ear revolting."

"I see. How about elsewhere?"

Brenna blinked. "Elsewhere?"

"Yes, how do you like the feel of a tongue elsewhere?"

"I think that's fine."

He adjusted her earring. "That's good to know."

"You're a very good kisser that's why I'm helping you."

His voice cracked. "Helping me?"

"Yes. Let's take your hands for example. You have very nice hands, but I'm sure you know that. If I had hands like yours I'd do this." She touched the sensitive part of his ear and gently caressed it. "Feels good doesn't it?"

It did, but he was too offended to agree with her. He merely stared.

"Your lips are nice too. I'd like to feel them here." She kissed a path down his neck to his shoulders, gently touching him with her tongue each time. She'd never thought of men being edible but this one came close. She undid a button. "And then—"

Hunter pushed Brenna back and held her down, amazed. "You're trying to seduce me."

"Is it working?"

He narrowed his eyes. "I won't say."

Brenna moved against him, feeling the hard bulge in his trousers. "I'd say it was."

"You're right." His eyes dipped to her chest. He licked his lips.

"Don't you dare."

"Getting nervous?"

The look on his face sent a shiver of unease. "There are children playing."

"So? Unless they've all been bottle fed they'll know what I'm doing."

"I'll scream."

"I hope so." He surveyed her face. "Admit you want me."

"No."

He bent down and used his teeth to gently pull down her blouse.

"All right."

"You smell good." He rested his nose between her breasts.

"Hunter?"

"Hmm?"

"I said I want you."

"I want you too."

"That means stop."

He lifted his head and frowned a little dazed. "That doesn't make sense."

"Get up and I'll explain it to you."

He let her go. Brenna sat up and glared at him. "That wasn't fair."

"I suggest you don't try seducing me in public places."

"You were trying to seduce me first," she countered.

He folded the blanket then said with all seriousness. "I'll be careful next time."

* * *

"So how was it with Hurricane Man?" Pauline asked when Brenna entered the office.

"It was fine."

"I want to know more."

"There's not much to say." She hung up her jacket in the closet then shut the door. "We ate, we talked about 'The Plan,' he kissed me then we talked some more and then ended the meeting."

"Oh," Pauline said disappointed.

Brenna went into her office.

Pauline rushed in a few moments later. "What do you mean he kissed you?"

Brenna rested her chin in her hand. "You know what kissing is, don't you?"

Pauline fell into a chair. "But with him?"

"It was nice." It was more than nice, but she wouldn't go into the details.

"He's just trying to seduce you."

Brenna winked. "I don't mind. I tried to do the same."

"Why?"

"He might prove useful."

Pauline blinked. "Useful?" she pulled her chair in closer.

"Yes."

"I'm not sure I like this."

"It's just two nights. What could happen? I need a man to get my mother off my back. You wouldn't understand. You're married."

"I don't have kids yet. Should I go to a playground and buy a kid for a day to please my mother?"

Brenna smiled. "If it makes you feel better."

Pauline made a face. "You know the point I'm trying to make."

"Yes, and I'm doing my best to ignore it."

"It's not like you to be irrational."

Brenna leaned forward. "Let me give you the true definition of irrational. Irrational is a woman who offers a telemarketer a bonus purchase if he agrees to go out with her daughter. Irrational is a woman who gives her daughter's phone number to men she meets in the produce section of the grocery store. Irrational is a woman who then gives her daughter's number to a lesbian friend just in case her daughter swings the other way. Irrational is a woman who constantly hounds her daughter about how her cousins are getting married while she's still single. Irrational is--"

Pauline waved her hands. "Enough, enough. I get the picture." She let her hands fall. "I just wish you didn't have to pretend that's all."

Brenna thought about the time with Hunter, a sense of wistfulness descending. "Yea, me too."

"Fifteen minutes," Miles said.

Hunter glanced up from his desk. "What?"

"You haven't moved for fifteen minutes. Is there something wrong with The Plan?"

"No, The Plan is fine." He was the one in trouble. He couldn't stop thinking about Brenna. He wanted to kiss her and hold her and tease her and talk to her and... She made him tell her things only a few people knew. He hadn't talked about his first marriage in years. There were so many things he wanted to tell her. Unfortunately, although she fit his qualifications, he knew he didn't fit hers. But he would. He just had to figure out how.

Then again he wasn't sure he wanted to. He didn't like what he was feeling. He didn't like not being able to concentrate. Not being in control of his emotions. His emotions were what had lead him to his ill-fated marriage in the first place. He couldn't afford to be careless again.

He jumped when Miles patted him on the shoulder. "You're in phase two."

"Phase two?"

"Lust."

Hunter shrugged off Miles' hand, annoyed. "Go away."

As Hunter drove to Diane Garrett's house, Miles' words echoed in his mind. He barely listened to Brenna as she gave him instructions for the evening. She continued to worry, although he'd tried to convince her not to. Everything would be fine. He'd met plenty of mothers in his lifetime and had impressed them all. He knew they were going to enjoy a very painless evening.

Brenna suddenly gasped.

Hunter turned to her alarmed. "What is it?"

Her voice held a note of panic. "Did I tell you I have five uncles, four aunts and four cousins?"

"No. Why?"

She stared at a house with cars spilling out of the drive way. "Because they're all here."

Chapter Six

"We have to go inside, Brenna," Hunter said as they circled the block for the fifth time.

"I know, but you need to know enough to prepare yourself."

"I am prepared. Besides I doubt that I will remember anything you have just said."

"Of course you will. You're a smart guy."

He sent her an amused glance. "Back handed compliments are not going to convince me to drive around again." He parked in front of a mid-size brick house and shut off the car. "Just follow my lead."

Brenna closed the door and stared at him as he headed up the drive. "Follow your lead? This is my family."

"That's why you're panicking."

"I'm not panicking. I just know we're headed for disaster." She stopped and turned. "Perhaps we could call from the car and say we're stuck in traffic."

He grabbed her arm. "No, they already saw us."

Before he could explain how he knew that, the front door swung open. Diane greeted them with a big smile.

Brenna sat paralyzed next to Hunter in the dining room as various family members introduced themselves to him and commented on how long it had been since they'd seen her. Brenna felt the same stage fright that had ripped through her at age nine. She'd been forced to do a speech in front of her class about her favorite animal--her mouth hadn't worked then either.

Hunter on the other hand seemed completely at ease. She still couldn't understand how a man who never smiled could look so cordial. She was grateful for his talent because she knew he was being studied. Especially by her Aunt Vanessa, whose sharp gaze could make an eagle blush. She was a woman Brenna held in abject awe. A woman who would never let anyone forget what a beauty she had been in her youth and all the lovers she had in the past. She spoke of Uncle Henry as 'my husband' as though he had no other existence outside that post.

Then there was Aunt Gwen who tried to make her small eyes bigger by drawing in her eyebrows a shade too dark and with a high arch. She only succeeded in always looking surprised. Aunt Patience, Aunt Carol and Uncle Walter--always referred to in that order since they regularly appeared as a three-some--offered bright smiles. Two of the three were married, though no one was quite sure which pair. The ladies peppered Hunter with questions while Uncles Jerome, Evan and Bruce stayed quiet trying to give the appearance of distrust although it was obvious they were impressed. Brenna's stomach twisted when one uncle smiled at her. She fought back a wave of nausea.

Her cousins Susanna and Judy, both only a few years older and conveniently married, came without their husbands. They didn't want to be distracted as they assessed Brenna's new man. Susanna, the less subtle of the two, openly studied Hunter's every move. The only one with eyes completely wistful was sixteen year old, Lauren, who wore two braids, held together with a butterfly clip, and a retainer on her teeth.

"I'm so glad you'll have someone to take to Trina's wedding," Aunt Patience said, offering a wide gummy grin.

"Shame Trina isn't here," Susanna said. "She would have loved to meet you. Perhaps at the wedding—"

Brenda quickly said, "Hunter can't attend the wedding."

Aunt Vanessa narrowed her eyes. "I'm sure he'll find a way. A smart man never leaves a woman alone long."

"Yes, well—"

"So how did you meet?" Uncle Jerome asked. "You seemed to have found this fellow out of nowhere."

"No, not nowhere," Brenna said carefully. "As I told Mom, we have both been busy."

"Too busy to mention his name? You were quick to introduce—"

"I thought you wanted to know how we met," Brenna said quickly before her uncle mentioned Byron's name.

Aunt Gwen raised her brows with interest. They nearly disappeared into her hairline. "Oh, yes please tell us how."

Hunter rested an arm around her shoulders. "I saw Brenna in a store and liked what I saw. So I asked her out."

Brenna stiffened. That was not the story they had practiced.

Uncle Bruce asked, "You just go after what you want?"

"I'd thought that was obvious," Hunter said.

Lauren sighed. "Oh, isn't that romantic?"

Brenna clenched her teeth. "Yes, romantic. Hunter, I need to get something from the car."

He began to hand her the keys; her pointed looked stopped him. "Okay." He stood and nodded his apology. "Excuse us."

He opened the car door. "What do you need?"

"To strangle you."

He spun around and stared at her shocked. "What?"

"How dare you change the story. You're not going by the plan. I thought you liked plans."

"Yes, but I also like logic." He closed the door and leaned against the car. "After considering your story I came to the conclusion that it lacked sense." He held up a hand. "Hear me out before you let loose any scathing remarks. Now be honest. Do I look like the type of man who would ask a woman's opinion in a greeting card shop?"

Brenna hesitated then shook her head.

"Do I look like the kind of man you would find in a card shop?"

She shook her head again reluctantly seeing his point.

"Exactly. I needed to come up with a more plausible meeting."

Brenna looked unconvinced. "So you say you saw me in a store and asked me out. Instant attraction."

"Correct."

She groaned. "And you think your explanation is any more plausible than mine."

"Yes."

"Do I look like the kind of woman you can pick up in a store?"

His eyes trailed the length of her. "Yes." He held up a hand before she could reply. "Because I look like the kind of man who can do it."

"Why you arrogant--"

"Now, now children," an amused voice said. "I don't think name calling is nice."

They turned and saw Stephen strolling towards them with his hands in his pockets. She looked at Hunter. "Another family member. My brother, Stephen. Stephen, meet my lack of judgment."

"I'm Hunter Randolph," he said holding out his hand. "Brenna's just in a bad mood."

Stephen nodded. "Have you eaten yet?"

"No."

He patted Brenna on the head. "That's your problem right there."

She slapped his hand away. "Did you know about this?"

"The ambush? Yes, I was going to tell you."

"Of course you were," she said doubtful. "So you knew they were all coming?"

His good humor died. "No, I didn't expect..." He took a deep breath. "Are you okay with it?"

She watched his face for any betraying emotion. "Do I have a choice?"

"No." Stephen shrugged as though trying to rid himself of an ugly coat. He forced a pleasant tone. "So what are you two doing out here? Has Mother driven him away already?"

"No, we're trying to decide how we met."

"You don't remember? I thought you told me he came barging into--ow!" Stephen said responding to Brenna's pinch on his arm.

"We want something a little more feasible," Brenna explained.

"I said I saw her in a store and asked her out," Hunter said.

"Works for me," Stephen said. "Come on."

Brenna rolled her eyes. "With a flimsy story like that we are not going to fool anyone."

THEY FOOLED THEM ALL. With coy glances and shy grins Brenna and Hunter created the perfect illusion that put her relatives under a spell. With the cleverness of shadow puppeteers they created images that were not there. At times their acting was so convincing, Brenna forgot it was a charade. The illusion masking dangerously as reality. She watched as Hunter chatted with her mother, complimented her aunts' dishes and settled an argument among them on who made the best bulla cake. He laughed with her uncles and charmed all of her cousins. Stephen, always the careful observer, wasn't completely taken in by the show, but wisely kept an impassive expression. By the time they served sweet biscuits and ginger tea, Hunter had been accepted into the family. Her cousins entertained him with tales from

Brenna's childhood. "And then there was the cane incident," Susanna said.

"The what?" Hunter asked.

Brenna sent Susanna a cold glare. "Forget it."

"No, I want to hear this," Hunter insisted.

Susanna held up her hands ready to set the stage. "Once in middle school, some kid stole Brenna's cane and replaced it with a rubber one from his father's magic shop. So when Brenna leaned on it, she fell flat on her face. It was awful, but she looked so funny you couldn't help laughing. She always dressed impeccably and there she was on the ground--crumbled and dirty. Every time she tried to get up the cane would bend at weird angles and she'd fall down again."

They were laughing so hard they didn't notice Hunter wasn't laughing with them. "And what did you do?"

She looked blank. "Do?"

"Yes, as she struggled to stand up with all her papers and books spread everywhere and the kids laughing. What did you do?"

"Well I--"

Stephen spoke up. "She didn't do anything. She laughed with the rest of them like always."

"Interesting," Hunter said. It was a small word and said with little inflection, but potent enough to cause an awkward silence.

"I got him back though," Brenna said to fill the air.

There was a hint of a smile. "You did? How?"

"I was his tutor for American History. He ended up having to repeat it."

Hunter nodded. "I put a kid in a locker once. He teased me about something that offended me. He didn't do it again. It's not fun being laughed at."

"No."

"Shame how some people don't seem to understand that," he said in a pointed tone.

Judy and Susanna finished their tea.

"Would you like more bulla cake?" Aunt Gwen asked Hunter.

"Yes, please."

The aunts stood to clear the table, shortening the awkward moment. Brenna helped in the kitchen.

"I like him," Diane said. She hugged her daughter. "I'm so proud of you."

Brenna placed some dishes in the dishwasher not knowing how to respond.

"Don't do that. You're the guest." She fixed Brenna's hair. "Take him out to the garden."

"Do it, Brenna," Aunt Vanessa said. "It's the perfect evening for it."

"And if you don't invite him to the garden," Aunt Gwen said. "One of your cousins will."

BRENNA PULLED at her skirt as she and Hunter sat alone in the gazebo.

It was still light. The sky a blue that reminded one of an ocean at rest. Moths landed on the nearby cotoneaster bushes whose tiny pink buds were opening into white flowers, while the buddleia bushes' dark purple flowers released a fruity fragrance. In the distance, she heard the cry of a blue jay. But even among the gentle night air and the blanket of sky that darkened into a navy blush, Brenna felt trapped. She felt as though the shadows had imprisoned her, the puppeteer becoming the puppet, performing for the joy and pleasure of others. She knew she wasn't far from wrong. Wasn't that what this whole evening was about?

Hunter sat quietly next to her, his sleeve brushing her bare arm in a soft caress, non-threatening in its innocence. She glanced at him wondering how much longer he could keep up the act. Dodging personal questions and poignant nudges of a more permanent future together. But as usual his expression gave nothing away. Instead she watched how the deepening sunlight touched his face, softening the planes and angles that should have been harsh and hardening a mouth too gentle for such a face.

She wondered if his face carried the secret to his true nature. A man of deep passions--a fact he denied--with a gentle heart. She brushed the thought aside annoyed with herself. In a few days it wouldn't matter. They would take their bow, close the curtain to thunderous applause then leave the stage of this illusion forever.

The wind carried the distant sound of laughter and the scent of lime. Though they were only a few feet from the house she felt miles away. Like most performers on stage they had their own world of secrets and deception.

"Should we wait until they come for us?" she asked.

"Probably not." Hunter's voice sounded uncommonly deep in the still air. Goosebumps formed on her arms in a delicious tingling sensation. "But I don't want to move in case that girl pops up again."

"Lauren is harmless. She thinks you're a romantic hero." Brenna grinned. "A prince charming."

"I'll have no trouble disillusioning her."

"I think you will."

He turned to her startled. "What?"

"Thanks for what you did in there." She put a hand over his mouth before he could speak. "That's the closest I'll come to 'You were right.'" She gestured vaguely to the house. "You really made them believe you're interested in me."

He stared at her a moment then said, "It wasn't hard to do."

Suddenly, he felt closer, larger, with the energy of a stirring storm ready to sweep her away. She sat still and waited. A part of her wanted to be caught up in the hurricane of power that always swirled around him, wondering if she could handle it once it was released. But she knew it was not wise to tangle with forces one did not understand and Brenna certainly didn't understand him. She stood. "Let's go inside."

He grabbed her wrist. "No. Let's enjoy the evening some more."

A sliver of panic seized her. "But I'm afraid." She said the words then regretted them.

Hunter looked puzzled, letting her wrist go. "You don't need to be afraid of me."

Brenna sat down annoyed with herself. "I'm not afraid of you." I'm afraid of what I feel for you. What you feel for me. She briefly shut her eyes. What was going on between them? It felt like a mutual need that had no voice. That could never have a voice. She didn't love him; he didn't love her. Then why did being with him feel so right, yet so threatening? Why did her instincts seem to be failing her? She thought of another subject. "My mother said she was proud of me." She laughed without humor, bitterness sharpening her words. "That's the first time she's ever said that. All the accomplishments in my life have been boiled down to one achievement--I got a man."

Hunter folded his arms and said in a smug tone, "Well, you have to admit I'm a big achievement."

Brenna rolled her eyes. "If I wanted hot air, you could fill a balloon."

He winced and covered his heart. "I surrender."

Brenna laughed at his expression, the tension she felt earlier beginning to ebb. They both fell into a companionable silence. For Brenna the sensation of being trapped soon transformed into something much more dangerous, but infinitely more fulfilling.

"Who's Byron?" Hunter asked suddenly.

The sound of his name chilled her, shattering her calm. She kept her tone light. "One of the major English Romantic poets who—"

"A more recent Byron," Hunter said with a knowing drawl. "Your mother said there hasn't been anyone since him."

"He's a man of my past."

"Did you love him?"

Brenna wanted to say no. To save her pride. To protect the memory of him that still beat in her heart. To sound more sophisticated and worldly, but she'd done enough lying this evening and was tired. "Yes. Very much."

"What happened?"

She smiled sweetly. "None of your business."

Hunter leaned forward, resting his elbows on his knees. "I was trying to make conversation."

"Then choose another topic."

He turned to her. "I don't think you understand your mother very well."

She looked at him stunned. "Do you always like to start conversations with explosive topics?"

He sat up. "I'm being honest."

"And you've made this assessment after only a few hours?"

He nodded. "Yes. It's hardly unusual. Most mother and daughter relationships are based on—"

"Don't lecture me."

He touched her arm in a soft, fleeting gesture. "She wants you to be happy."

Brenna shook her head. "No, she wants to show others that I'm happy. Unfortunately, that means having a man." Or a woman. The thought of Bette still made her groan.

"She loves you and I believe that if she didn't know deep down that you wanted to get married she wouldn't bother you."

Brenna clenched her hands. He was wrong. She was like every other mother who wanted to see her child wed so they could start nagging about grandkids. It was the natural order of things. But if he was wrong, why did his words upset her? Was there a hint of truth she couldn't ignore? No, it was his arrogance that upset her. He could think whatever he wanted to. She knew the truth. "You're very insightful for a man," she said casually, tucking her anger away.

His eyes twinkled. "No, not really. She told me."

"And you fell for the ploy." She patted his leg. "Poor boy. I don't blame you. She's very good. The truth is she feels guilty that I was ever born."

Hunter's voice hardened. "I don't believe that."

"You don't have to, it's the truth. She thinks that if I had the appearance of a normal settled life then everyone would forget how different I am. Do I blame her? No."

He watched a robin dart through the sky. "Marriage isn't so bad."

"That's an odd thing for a divorced man to say."

"No, it's not. I had a bad banana once that didn't put me off the whole bunch." He met her eyes, the expression dark, pulling her to him. "You have to stop being afraid."

Of what? She stared at him unaware that her question was a silent one.

He heard it anyway, his reply soft, "Whatever you're afraid of." He stood before she could reply, effectively ending the conversation and the sensuous connection between them. He held out his hand. "Come on. We have to end this evening and have them begging for an encore."

HIS WORDS PROVED PROPHETIC. Diane approached them as they stepped into the house. Lauren stood behind her with a dreamy expression directed at Hunter. Stephen looked suspiciously pleased with himself. In the distance, the rest of the family waited with expectant looks.

"Ah, there you are!" Diane said as though they had returned from a long journey. "We've decided that you must join us at the craft festival."

"We have a booth every year," Lauren explained looking eagerly at Hunter. "It's really a fair with rides and games, but they also have artisans. Aunty Gwen and I sell placemats and dolls."

Brenna held up her hands. "Mom, wait—"

Diane ignored her, focusing her attention on Hunter. "It's tomorrow and we'd love to see you there. I'm sure you can make it." She smiled. An expression as deceptively sweet as a sleeping lion. Brenna knew they would have to extend the show.

"How LONG IS this torture supposed to last?" Brenna asked as she and Hunter made their way through the festive crowd.

He squeezed her shoulder. "Relax and enjoy yourself."

That was the problem. She was. The wind toyed with her skirt and the scent of cotton candy clung to her blouse. She hadn't felt so carefree in years. Free of the gazes and stares, or her cane brushing through the grass. Free of being with a man she'd only known a few days feeling she'd known him for years. She wasn't sure she wanted to.

Hunter had arrived at her apartment early, coming before the sun settled fully in the sky. He wore jeans, a red polo shirt, and sunglasses that he didn't take off even inside. She was about to comment on them when she noticed that Tima had popped her head out of her apartment. She'd looked at Brenna and mouthed. 'Is that him?' She'd nodded and Tima had mouthed 'Yum' and licked her lips. She disappeared back into her apartment before Hunter turned.

"What are you looking at?" he asked.

"Nothing." Brenna looked down at the empty bag he carried. "What is that for?"

"My prizes."

She locked her apartment. "You expect to win enough to fill a bag?"

"Sure." He held up a hand. "No insults please."

"I wasn't going to insult your gigantic ego, although it is tempting." She grinned. "However, I would like to make a wager."

He held the front door of the building open for her. "No. I have an advantage. It would be unfair."

She stopped and stared up at him with a narrow gaze. "What advantage?"

He gently pushed her forward and closed the door. "I know you will lose."

He was right. She would have lost, badly. At every booth he

approached he won anything she pointed to. After a few games, the bag nearly burst with winnings--a gigantic stuffed snake the color of a lemon, a giraffe, a plush basketball and a purple teddy bear they named Amanda. The fair stretched the length of the park and after a couple of hours, Brenna's leg and hip began to ache. She ignored the discomfort, she was having so much fun.

The band organ music of a carousel floated towards her above the sound of the crowd and the inviting shouts of game attendants. Brenna looked at the spinning row of horses; the browns, the gray jumpers and palominos. Her eyes landed on a black horse with a silver mane and tail.

Hunter caught her gaze, reading the longing in her expression. "Okay," he said indulgent. "Let's go."

She didn't argue. She waited, clutching her ticket, with banked anticipation as she stood in line among the squirming children and their parents. She watched the carousel spin and weave its magic, its fantastic ornate center displayed paintings of forests and grasslands. Years ago her father had taken her on the same carousel, riding beside her and laughing at the funny faces she made at him. She loved to make him laugh, it was rare when he did. When Hunter lifted her on the horse, instead of feeling annoyed she felt grateful that he offered help so casually.

Brenna glanced up at the canopy with its rows of bright lights. A carousel was a lovely place to dream. She let her hand roam over the black head of the wooden horse and felt the cool of the brass pole.

"Hold on," Hunter said as the organ began to play.

Brenna gathered its reins and closed her eyes as the horse slowly moved up and down. Soon she felt it come alive, feeling the wind against her face, as its hooves swept across the ground and the world around disappeared. All too soon the horse slowed and she knew the ride would soon end. Brenna opened her eyes and caught Hunter staring. She felt a faint blush, but he just raised a brow, more out of mischief than mockery, and all embarrassment disappeared.

Hunter helped her down at the end of the ride. Without warning he pulled her into his arms and kissed her, his lips soft and sweet, turning her insides into mush.

"Have you awakened from your dream?" he whispered.

A slow smile spread on her face. "No." She tweaked his nose. "Only Prince Charming can awaken me from this dream."

He shook his head and grabbed her hand, it felt natural so she didn't protest. At one of the many food stands, Hunter bought a funnel cake with powdered sugar, which they ate under a white tent, while sitting on hard wooden benches, watching the crowd go by.

After finishing the cake, they headed towards a stage where a juggling act was getting ready to perform. Brenna stood entranced, watching swords and torches fly through the air.

Suddenly, a cramp slithered up her leg and clenched its teeth into her thigh, gripping her in a pain that brought a wave of nausea. She quickly ducked behind the stage before collapsing on her knees while the pain seized a stronger hold. She bit her lip to keep from crying out, vigorously rubbing the hardened muscle hoping for it to ease. Brenna shut her eyes against tears, wishing herself some place else, somebody else. She gulped the air determined not to succumb and be sick. Suddenly, a large hand dug deep into her muscle, forcing her to cry out.

She opened her eyes and stared at Hunter. At first she didn't recognize him. The pain seemed to alter his features, reminding her that she didn't really know him.

"Go ahead and scream," he said quietly.

She wanted to. She wanted to rage, stomp, cry, pound her fists against the ground, but she didn't. The world began to spin while a darkness came towards her and she welcomed it.

Chapter Seven

Brenna awoke to the smell of sugar and buttered popcorn, and felt the soft fibers of a cotton shirt against her cheek. That's when she noticed the arms wrapped around her. Brown arms strong and warm as if the very earth had risen up to embrace her. All pain was gone, but shame quickly replaced it. She straightened and noticed a wet patch on his shirt.

She touched her cheek and felt tears. She didn't even remember crying. She quickly brushed them away, heat burning her face. "Thank you. I'm better now."

His expression didn't change, the stranger quality lingered. She couldn't understand why. His eyes were no less intense, his jaw no less haughty, but something was different. "You're okay now." It was a statement meant as a question.

"Yes." She made a motion to move away from the comforting warmth of his body.

He stopped her and drew her close. "Rest awhile."

"I'm--"

"I know."

She struggled against the temptation to bury herself in his arms. "I'm fine, really."

His jaw twitched. "Then stay still for my sake."

Brenna glanced up at him then noticed his winnings scattered on the ground. Suddenly, as if a film had been lifted from her eyes, she understood his expression--fear.

Yet that didn't make sense. She couldn't picture Hunter afraid of anything. What had raced through his mind when he had seen her on the ground with tears spilling down her face? Was he thinking about the banquet? Wondering if he'd made a mistake in asking her. Was he concerned that he didn't know what to do? She brushed the grass from her skirt when a thought entered her mind that nearly choked her. He had seen her leg. Seen its deformity. Had he been horrified? Disgusted? Saddened?

She pushed such thoughts aside; it didn't matter now. She tried to pull away. "You can let go. I'm okay."

"Keep still."

"But--"

"You don't like being held. You think that's admitting weakness. It's not. You're very, very strong and you need to give your body a rest. And I'm going to hold you until you do."

Brenna tried to fight his words as she did his embrace. She moved her shoulders, his arms tightened. She gave up and looked up at him. "I promise I won't move, if you let me go."

He looked amused. "You hate the fact that I'm stronger than you. I am, so get used to it."

She turned away.

"Pretend you're in a chair and relax."

She couldn't relax. She'd never sat in a chair that felt like this or that brought forth such foreign emotions and thoughts. "Listen--"

"Shut up."

She balled her hands into fists. "You make me so angry."

"Anger is a nice shield."

She turned to glare up at him, but he met her with such an

amused, gentle gaze she just stared. The expression in his eyes didn't fit the man she had imagined him to be. For a moment she wanted to ask: Who are you? Instead she turned away, gathering jumbled emotions, wondering who was holding her in his arms--a man full of arrogance or someone else. She pointed to the discarded prizes. "Amanda is getting ruined."

He picked up her cane, his other arm dipped to her waist. "This is useless."

Her eyes widened at the disgust in his tone. "It's one of yours. A Randolph brand."

"I know. It's standard and it sells well, but it doesn't offer you the support you need."

"The cramp was my fault. I haven't exercised my leg as I should and my leg was beginning to ache, but I ignored it."

"You could have told me."

"I know, but I was getting greedy." Brenna managed a small smile. "I wanted you to win lots of prizes for me."

"You could have asked." He shook his head annoyed. "How like a woman."

"What do you mean?"

"I thought you were more forthcoming."

"I am."

"Then don't do this again." He dusted off the prizes and placed them back in the bag.

Brenna gathered her temper, annoyed by his scolding. "I don't plan to."

"You have to take care of yourself."

She adjusted her blouse. "I won't do this at the banquet so you don't have to worry."

He sent her an odd glance. "I wasn't worried about that."

"Well, just so you know you don't have to be."

He folded his arms and stared at her intrigued. "Wow. I didn't realize that."

"What?"

"You're an idiot."

She opened her mouth; no words came out.

He pulled her lips together. "You'll invite flies."

She pushed his hand away. "What do you mean, I'm an idiot?"

"It surprises me just as much as you. I think you're smart then you say something stupid."

"I do not."

"Do you think I'm worried about your leg?"

"You could be."

"Answer the question. Do you think I'm worried about your leg?"

"No."

He nodded pleased. "Good. Now you won't have to explain how your cane won't make too much noise in the banquet hall or how you may be awkward dancing or that you won't limp too much coming down the stairs."

Her lips thinned. "You are the most--"

He held out his hand. "Do you need help up?"

"Go to--"

Hunter pulled her to her feet. "That's better."

Brenna pushed him away, but it was like pushing against a tree. He didn't move. She lost her balance and fell backwards.

The corner of his lips twitched. "Shall we try this again?"

She dusted her hands off. "No."

He held out his hand. "Come on."

"No."

He gave a low whistle. "You are one stubborn woman."

"I can get up myself, just give me my cane."

"You have to be nice to me if you want something. Ask nicely."

She grabbed his ankle and jerked. She coughed delicately at the cloud of dust. "Will you please get my cane?"

Hunter didn't move, he just lay there staring up at the sky. "Now I know how Annie Sullivan felt." He rolled away before she could catch him. "You've been spoiled." He jumped to his feet and handed her the cane. "I suggest you use that cane to stand up if you don't want to end today sore and limp."

"You'd hurt me?"

His eyes twinkled. "There are other ways to make a woman limp."

STEPHEN GLANCED around the fairgrounds hoping to catch sight of Brenna and Hunter again. He'd seen them under one of the tents and couldn't help smiling. Hunter seemed the perfect match for Brenna. He hoped they would both eventually see they weren't acting as much as they thought.

"You look lost," a smooth feminine voice said behind him.

He felt the hairs rise on his arms. He glanced at a concession stand. "I'm not."

Tima stood beside him and pulled a piece of her blue cotton candy. "I may be able to help you find whoever you're looking for." She popped the candy in her mouth. "Is it Brenna?"

He turned and stared at the orange peasant blouse and denim skirt falling to a pair of red sneakers. Did she dress in the dark? "You saw her?"

"Yes, she ducked behind the juggling stage. Hunter followed." Tima winked. "I hope they're having fun."

He nodded and looked away.

"Have you seen the fun house exhibit? The lighting illusions are incredible."

"No."

"I could show you and Fiona--"

"No, thanks."

She held out her cotton candy. "Want some?"

He rested his hands on his hips wishing Fiona would return from the bathroom. Why wouldn't this woman just go away and leave him alone?

"I see her. She looks like your type."

He spun around. "What is that suppose to mean?"

Tima made a tut tut noise then put another piece of candy in her mouth. "A little touchy, aren't you?"

"Do you have something to say about her? That she's too sweet, too fragile, too cute? I know women like you--" He stopped.

She began to grin. "Women like me what?"

"Don't like women like Fiona."

"Come on." Tima playfully nudged him with her elbow. "Don't back down now. Say what you mean. You obviously have a theory about women like me. Exactly what kind of woman am I?"

"I'm not interested in this conversation."

She ignored him. "Women like me are bossy, controlling and demanding among other things. We're the unfortunate result of the women's movement. We set men on edge. And since I am likely all these things to you and I'm not really interested in changing your mind let me say one thing. What anyone else thinks about you doesn't matter as long as you're happy."

"I am happy."

Tima patted him on the back as though he were a good little boy. "I'm glad." She walked away leaving him feeling restless. A restlessness he'd promised himself never to feel again. His mind filled with questions he didn't want answers to.

"I hate that woman," he muttered.

Fiona took his hand and looked up at him. "That's not a nice thing to say."

No, it wasn't nice, but it was exactly how he felt.

AT HOME, Brenna stood by her window, but didn't see anything. Her mind still lingering at the fair, riding the carousel, enjoying the sweet taste of funnel cake and having Hunter hold her in his arms. His arms. She could still feel their strength, their tenderness. A melancholy descended as the night made its claim. She knew as the days passed they were getting closer to their final goodbye. It was a necessary conclusion, but it still saddened her a bit. Brenna turned from the window. That evening she soaked her aching side in a hot shower then made an appointment with her doctor for another set of injections, which she hated. After showering, she changed into a shirt and skirt.

The doorbell rang just as she began washing up her dinner dishes. She dried her hands on a dish towel, suppressing a sigh. No doubt her mother had stopped by for a full report on her new man.

She opened the door and stared.

"Have you eaten dinner?" Hunter asked, entering without an invitation.

"Yes," she stammered. She'd just relegated him to memory. It was a shock to see him live, real and very male with that magnetic, overwhelming energy in her apartment.

"Good, because I want to show you something." He held up a metal rod that bent like an old branch. It had an orange handle and flattened bottom like a duck's foot. "I've been thinking about your cane for hours."

Brenna closed the door, her mouth kicking up in a quick grin. "How romantic. Make sure to bring her back by eleven."

He blinked. "That's not funny."

She sighed with mock dismay. "This is why I never fulfilled my dream of being a comedienne." She turned. "Come into the living room." Brenna could feel his presence, as though he were a north wind. It was only in small spaces that she noticed he didn't just walk, he moved. He didn't just sit down he commanded the chair to seat him.

She sat on the loveseat, hoping he would take the couch in front of her. Instead, he sat beside her, crowding her into the corner.

Hunter placed the cane in front of them. "What I noticed with your cane was that it didn't give you effective support. The way your leg is angled--" He drew up her skirt.

She slapped his hand away appalled. "What are you doing?!"

"I need to demonstrate a point." He lifted her skirt again.

She snatched it away. "Then draw a picture."

He paused then slowly said, "It's easier to explain if I'm able to show you. The way your leg is--"

"I've seen my leg before. I know what it looks like."

"Yes, and I saw it at the fair."

She drummed her fingers on the arm of the seat unmoved.

"Brenna, it's just a leg."

"Is that the excuse you use to look up women's skirts?"

He raised a brow. "I just want to see your leg. Looking up your skirt would be a completely different--" He faltered.

"Goal?"

"Agenda. But goal works just as well." He shrugged. "Fine. Let me explain it this way. The way your leg is shaped creates a different walking pattern."

He dragged his finger along her knee down to her ankle, his touch causing heat to shimmer and shift like rippling waves. Somehow the way he touched her leg made it okay. Not strange or weird, just there. However, his gesture also felt oddly seductive, the slow trail of his finger, the way it lingered. He cupped her calf. "This leg's shorter. Did you stretch the bone?"

"Yes."

"Painful."

"Yes." Brenna remembered the braces and screws, the hospital visits and feeling as though she were made more of steel than flesh. It had been worth it. She looked down at the scar some parts still looked rubbery and disfigured like melted Play-Do instead of skin, but at least her leg functioned.

Hunter was quiet a moment then said, "Because your leg is structured this way it forces you to put pressure on the outside area of the foot. The cane is supposed to help you stabilize, but puts pressure on this muscle here." He gently squeezed.

She moved away uncertain she could tolerate the rest of his 'demonstration'. "Yes, yes," she said quickly. "I understand."

"My new design won't do that. Try it."

Brenna tentatively took the cane Hunter held out to her. She walked the length of the living room surprised that she instantly felt lighter. "Oh, it works well."

He nodded, pleased.

"But there's just one problem."

"What?"

She grimaced. "It's ugly."

Resignation replaced a look of hurt. "Yes, that's why it hasn't sold."

"It's bad enough having to use a cane," she explained, trying to soften her criticism. "You don't want to draw even more attention to it."

"You're right." He reached for the cane.

She moved it away. "Perhaps if you worked more on its aesthetics it would be more appealing. The color's all wrong. You realize that, don't you?"

"Yes, but the material--"

"I'm sure the material is very suitable for the structure, but it has to look attractive."

He sat forward. "My priority is function. I'm not good with aesthetics."

"Try another color and is this necessary?" She pointed to the large bolts.

"Yes, it--"

"Perhaps you could accomplish the same goal in a different way."

Hunter sighed. If only he had the time. He had reports to finish. "I'll see what I can do, but if I'm promoted I'll be moving to the Director of Research and Development and Marketing."

"Why?"

Her question gave him pause. "Because it's the next logical step in my Plan."

She sat. "Oh yes, your plan. I'd almost forgotten about that. So your Plan no longer allows you to develop new ideas?" She tilted her head to one side and studied him. "You don't seem the marketing type."

"I've created reports on our competitors and gathered and analyzed data, studied buyer demographics and--"

"I'm not suggesting you can't do your job, just that you could use your skills elsewhere."

"I won't be stuck in one area while others pass me by. I constantly strive to improve myself. As Director of these two divisions, I'll be expanding and refining myself."

"I can understand R&D, but why marketing?"

"Marketing is critical to moving up the ladder. My grandfather believes potential CEOs should understand every division if they plan to run the company."

She nodded. "Do you want to head the company?"

"Yes. I want to see Randolph Medical Supply Company become one of the most exemplary in the industry. I'd also like to segue into other markets. We've been a little closed in our thinking which has served us well in terms of stability, but may hurt us in the long run. There is a need for expansion. The company can handle a slow growth and is strong enough for some trial and error approaches to marketing and product development. It's falling a little behind the current technological advances available to companies like ours. I want to get it up to certain standards and beyond."

He spoke with such passionate conviction Brenna smiled. "I'm surprised you're not CEO yet."

"My Uncle holds the position. I have a while yet." He grabbed the cane and stood.

"Would you like anything to drink?" The question came without thought.

He hesitated. "Sure."

They went into the kitchen, but didn't know how to act cordial around each other without an audience. They weren't friends after all, just performers who were part of the same show.

But Hunter didn't want it that way anymore. Brenna was becoming dearer to him than he wanted to admit. He'd been intrigued by her at their first meeting, but now he could no longer deny his attraction. Hunter watched her, but not as a casual observer. He noticed her every movement his mind trying to capture every gesture so that when she was not with him he could conjure her up in his memory. He liked the way her hands worked. They weren't gentle, but swift and efficient. He liked the way she held her head--cocky almost defiant. He turned away annoyed. He was being irrational. Sure he was attracted to her, but watching her like this was not logical. He steeled himself against his emotions. He would not lose his heart again. "I've changed my mind."

He said the words so suddenly she nearly lost hold of the glass. She set it on the counter. "You can change your mind without shouting."

He lowered his voice. "I wasn't shouting. I have to go because...I..." His words trailed off.

She offered him an excuse. "Have errands to run?"

"Exactly."

She nodded. "Okay."

Their words were simple, innocuous. The look they shared was not. It steamed, heated with banked desire and longing. And the more it remained unspoken the stronger it seemed to grow.

Brenna broke the gaze and went to the door. "Thank you for thinking about me." She opened the door. "I mean the cane."

He passed by her and headed down the stairs. He suddenly stopped and turned. "You were right the first time." He started up the stairs.

Her body filled with anticipation as he approached her. "Was I?"

"Yes." His gaze dropped to her lips. "I'm going to kiss you."

"Why?"

His eyes met hers, startled. "Why?"

"Yes, why?"

Hunter rested his hand against the wall and leaned towards her. "Do I need a reason?"

"I thought this might be part two of your seduction agenda."

"No."

"Then what do you call this?"

"Experimentation."

"And what is your hypothesis?"

"I'll let you know." He kissed her, arousing a passion she'd thought she'd safely hidden away. Brenna faintly heard her cane drop. She rested her hands on his chest not to push him back, but she didn't want to claim him either. She only wanted to savor the moment, savor the emotions being lit within, savor him. She'd expected his mouth to become more demanding instead it became sweeter like the liquid taste of melted sugar. Brenna gripped the front of his shirt; his arms circled her waist. They stumbled into the wall.

At that moment Tima opened her door and stared at them. "Oh, sorry. I thought someone had knocked."

"No," Brenna said breathless. "Um. This is Hunter."

"Nice to meet you, Hunter. I saw you at the fair." She rested her hip against the doorframe and folded her arms. "Though I doubt you saw me."

He eyed her extravagant outfit. "I saw you. I just thought you were part of the fair." Brenna hit him.

Tima laughed. "Pauline was right."

"About what?"

"You."

Hunter wasn't curious enough to ask what her meaning was. He released Brenna. "I'd better go." He picked up her cane. "I'll give you my analysis in the morning."

She grabbed it. "Nothing handwritten and remember to double space."

He didn't release it. "I'll try to remember."

"Good."

Tima loudly cleared her throat.

Hunter let go and left. Tima pulled Brenna inside her apartment and shut the door. "Start from the beginning."

"It's not what you think."

"So you weren't enjoying yourself?"

"Lust was getting the best of us."

"Lust is a terrible thing to waste."

"The day after would be a nightmare. I couldn't imagine waking up next to him."

"Then let me paint a picture for you. First he's naked—"

Brenna laughed. "You're a bad influence on me."

"I just think you should have fun. And he'd be a lot of fun."

Brenna bit her lip. "I'm not sure. He's up to something."

"Of course he's up to something he wants to sleep with you." She shook her head in pity. "Has it been that long?"

"He has another agenda."

"His look spoke of only one. He's interested. If you two would allow yourself to drop the charade, you'd admit you were enjoying yourselves."

"Could a relationship based on deceit become real?"

"Sure. Why not?"

"We're too much alike."

"With one great difference. You're a woman and he's a man. Think about it."

MILES STEEPLED his fingers and looked at Hunter. "Sleep is an activity that allows our minds and bodies to rejuvenate. It is a necessary activity that allows us to restore ourselves."

Hunter glanced up from his desk. "Is there a reason for that mini lecture?"

"Yes, you look like you're not getting any."

He returned to his desk. Sleep wasn't the only thing he wasn't getting. "I'm not tired."

Miles stood, glancing at the calendar on his phone. The calendar on the wall was a month behind. He changed it. "That's not my point."

Hunter sounded bored. "What is it?"

"Forget it." He leaned on the desk. "What are you working on?"

Hunter held out the pad of paper. Miles studied it then set it down confused. "You're working on the Trandor cane? Why?"

He leaned back. "It needs some adjustments. Brenna gave me some ideas."

"She's into mechanical engineering?"

"No, she uses one of our canes, but it doesn't suit her so I gave her the Trandor."

Miles eyes widened. "You son of a bitch."

He fell forward. "What?"

"She uses a cane?"

"Yes, she uses a cane."

"Why?"

"She has a limp."

"She has a limp?"

Hunter clasped his hands together and said in a patient tone, "She uses a cane because she has a limp, what part of this cause and effect model don't you understand?"

"Was it from an accident?"

"She was born that way."

"She was born that way?"

"What is wrong with you?"

"You just happen to spot the right woman to introduce to your grandfather as your fiancée and she just happens--the magic word again--to have a limp and use a cane. A Randolph cane. I would imagine Doran doing this but not you."

Hunter pulled the pad of paper towards him. "I thought you agreed with my plan. I know using a fake fiancée isn't very ethical, but neither is presenting a man as your boyfriend who isn't one. We understand each other and I wouldn't have trouble lengthening our acquaintance."

"Which means you like her."

"I thought that was obvious."

"Yet, you don't see the angle to this relationship that is obvious to everyone else." Miles shook his head amazed. "Sometimes you're like a babe in the woods." He sighed. "It's more serious than I thought."

Hunter frowned. "I don't--"

"What did she say about the cane?"

"She thought it was ugly."

"She's being kind."

Hunter frowned. "At least it functions. Besides I can fix it."

Miles sat on the desk and picked up a pen. "Why are you working on it now? You've got reports to work on."

Hunter's voice tensed. "I'm fully aware of my duties."

He tapped the pen against his knee then a knowing smile spread on his face. "I get it. This is about the plan."

"She needs a new cane."

Miles pointed a pen at him. "You think if you present her with the perfect one she'll fall into your arms and want to sleep with you."

Hunter sketched a few lines.

"She only promised you one night as a fake fiancée."

The pencil tip broke. "I know that." Hunter shoved the pencil in the electrical sharpener.

Miles stood and patted him on the back. "Just try and get some sleep. It helps you think clearly."

Hunter sat back in his chair and tossed the pencil on the desk. He crumbled up the sketch. Miles was right. She wouldn't fall into his arms because of this. Besides he couldn't get it finished in time for the banquet and meet his other deadlines. He turned towards the trash bin then stopped.

Seeing her in pain continued to throb in his mind like a physical wound. If he didn't re-deliver the cane the image of her on the ground would continue to haunt him. He would have done anything that day to take the pain away. He smoothed out the sketch. He would finish it. Not for gratitude, but because it was logical to finish something he had started years ago. There was nothing more to it than that. He sighed because he knew there was more. He liked Brenna a lot more than he wanted to, but he only wanted to see her as a logical solution to his problem. He could only see marriage as a business transaction. He had to think and be this way to keep himself safe—to keep his heart safe. He wouldn't have his love rejected again. He'd always be strong and practical—he'd never be vulnerable to a woman again.

BRENNA TWISTED and turned in front of the dressing room mirror, watching how the gold silk dress floated around her. "I should not have to buy a new dress for this thing."

Tima raised a brow. "So make him pay for it as part of your expenses."

"No," Pauline said. "Then he may want more."

"This is part of a bargain," Brenna said. "He isn't paying me."

"He did offer you a dress, right?" Tima asked.

Brenna smiled. "Clever woman. Perhaps I'll get two."

Pauline sat back on the maroon couch and crossed her legs. "So he survived your family and your mother was convinced?"

"Completely. He can be very sociable."

"That's hard to imagine."

"He's a tad arrogant and overbearing, but he has his good points."

"Yes," Tima said. "I saw one when he was walking away."

Pauline sighed. "His only good point is his bank account."

Brenna turned to her stunned by the cynicism in her tone. "You don't like him."

She chewed her top lip then shrugged. "I don't know him and neither do you. None of us do. I don't like him using you."

"I used him." Brenna adjusted the straps on the dress. "It's one night of make-believe."

Pauline looked unconvinced. "Not in that dress."

Tima said, "It's gorgeous."

"It's dangerous."

Brenna grinned. "I know."

"Brenna--"

"There's nothing wrong with enjoying a man's attention even if it's not real. Especially, if it's not real. Then there won't be any awkward moments when it ends."

Pauline's green eyes met Brenna's brown ones in the mirror. "But you don't want to end it, do you?"

"It doesn't matter what I want," she said easily. She slipped out of the dress and tried on another one in turquoise.

"Just remember that he wants to get married so he can get a promotion that's all. It's important you don't forget that, just in case."

"In case what?"

"He asks you to marry him."

Brenna's heart raced at the possibility. From fear or joy she wasn't sure. She dismissed the thought. "He won't."

"He might. He's ambitious. He wants a wife. You're the most likely candidate," she said with an edge of regret.

"Why do you say it like that?"

"I don't want you to settle. He'll promise you the world, his type do. And what's worse he'll expect you to be grateful."

Brenna turned to her and folded her arms, preparing herself for the truth. "You don't think he likes me for me?"

Pauline chose her words carefully, in an effort to spare her friend's feelings. "Haven't you ever wondered why he chose you out of all the women he could have? He's a man of strategy." She shook her head. "You're a success. Good at what you do. You don't need him. I'm not saying you're not attractive to men, just that some men are more conniving than others." Her voice lowered. "He's not right for you, Brenna. If you took a moment and thought about it, you would know I'm right."

Pauline's honesty dampened her spirits. "I know I couldn't marry him. And I wouldn't want to," she quickly added in case she sounded disappointed. She began to change into her clothes. What woman would want to be the wife of such a man? One whose ambition was all consuming? One who was forceful, intimidating, kind, fun, tender? She shook her head. She wouldn't. She admired him because in many ways they were alike. When they wanted something they went after it. Fortunately, she was in control of whether or not he would get what he was after. She liked the position. "Don't worry, Pauline. Nothing's going to happen in one night."

Tima adjusted her earring. "I think—"

"We know what you think," Pauline said. "But you're older and wiser than Brenna. Brenna isn't you. She's not a live in the moment type of person. Hunter isn't really interested in her."

"He seemed pretty interested when I saw them in the hall."

"Just because he's interested in sex doesn't mean he's interested in her."

Tima frowned. "No, I—"

"He's a cunning manipulator." Pauline leaned forward and stared at Brenna. "He isn't right for you. Yes, he's good looking but so was Byron and he dumped you."

Brenna shook her head. "He didn't dump me, we grew apart."

"Right. He dates you for five years then you break up and within a week he's seeing another woman. That isn't fair."

"Byron wasn't the right one," Tima said. "He was a nice guy, but I thought he was a little flat."

"Byron was—"

"Enough!" Brenna said. "Let's forget about Byron and Hunter. They're not important. And as hard as it may be to believe I'm not under his spell. I like him and he may prove to be very useful."

"There's that word again. Useful. What does that mean?"

Tima began to smile. "It means I think you're warning the wrong person. Brenna's up to something."

"What are you up to?" Pauline asked.

"Nothing," Brenna replied. "Now what are you going to wear to the Single's Party?"

THE SPRING SINGLE'S Party was a success. The Mantron hotel party lounge sparkled with tea lights. They mingled with orchids floating in glass bowls on table cloths the colors of cream and red roses. Brenna proudly observed the singles and potential couples. Pauline was right. She was good at what she did. If her mother could look beyond her singleness she'd agree her daughter had chosen a suitable occupation for herself.

Brenna took a sip of her passion fruit aperitif, pleased she had chosen to wear a periwinkle satin shirt and navy slim trousers. The outfit gave her the right professional look with a hint of casual charm. She had to look approachable. She was on alert, expertly yet unobtrusively introducing people and separating others. Her intuition was in high gear tonight and she loved the feeling. Yet there was another feeling of excitement she'd never felt before as though something was about to happen.

A woman wearing a lime silk dress with wavy brunette hair cascading past her shoulders came up to her with a welcoming smile. It softened the jaded quality of her features that intimidated most men.

"Great party," Sara said her blue eyes filled with praise.

Brenna returned the smile. "Thank you. Have you made any connections yet?"

"Connections, yes. Whether they'll be matches, we shall see."

"As they say, 'The night is young'."

"Yes and..." She stopped and stared at something.

Brenna spun around and nearly dropped her glass.

Chapter Eight

Hunter stood in the doorway looking very large, very dangerous and completely out of place. He wore black jeans, a maroon T-shirt and sneakers. He looked as though he hadn't shaved in days. His sharp predatory eyes scanned the crowd, searching with the patience of an accomplished predator. Soon his eyes fell on her. Brenna swallowed as he made his way through the crush of people that seemed to part as he passed.

"Who is that?" Sara asked. With interest or horror, Brenna couldn't tell.

"No one you need to be concerned with," she said, trying to maintain an indifferent air. "Excuse me." She walked up to him, hoping to stop him from causing anymore of a disturbance. Whispers circled around him. "What are you doing here?" she demanded in a low voice.

"I fixed it."

She wanted to be furious with him, but he sounded so proud of himself, the emotion disappeared. "Fixed what?"

He stepped closer. Though he looked horrible, he smelled like cinnamon. "The cane."

She finally noticed what he held in his hand. "And you--?"

A man with a presumptuous air cut in before she could reply. He looked at Hunter, stroking his red handlebar mustache. "One of the sinks in the men's room needs fixing. You'd better look at it."

Hunter's dark eyes flashed with menace. "Certainly. I'll use your head as a plunger."

The man took a hasty step back.

Brenna spoke up. "He doesn't work here. He's a friend of mine."

"Oh, I see." He cleared his throat. "I've...uh..excuse me." He walked away trying to maintain a semblance of dignity, but it flopped around his ankles.

Hunter watched him leave. Brenna grabbed his arm and pulled him into the hallway. She pointed to the cane. "Couldn't this have waited?"

He ignored the question. "You're going to like this." He took her cane and handed her its replacement. "Look at it. Isn't it great?"

The bolts were smaller and the color a lighter silver, the handle was now a deep burgundy and the flat bottom less conspicuous. He patiently awaited her reply, but she could sense the tension in him. "It's beautiful."

The tension eased. "What I did was--"

She put a hand over his mouth. "You don't have to explain." She removed her hand. "I can tell you worked hard."

He rubbed his eyes. "Good. Now I'll leave you to your party."

She seized his arm before he turned. "When's the last time you slept?"

"Slept?" He repeated the word as though it were foreign.

"Got in bed and closed your eyes."

He paused then said, "About three days ago."

"Three days!" She shrieked. A clerk sent her a look of censure. Heat flooded her face. She lowered her voice. "Wait here."

Brenna went inside and made her apologies to a few guests, spoke with her event planner and hostess then went back into the hall. But Hunter was gone.

SHE FOUND him in the lobby looking at the aquarium. It covered the length of the wall with fish the size of footballs and the color of rainbows.

She wagged a finger at him. "I told you to wait."

He watched a fish swim behind a plant. "I am waiting."

She knew it was useless to argue with his logic. "Come on."

He followed her through the glass doors. "Where are we going?"

"I'm taking you home."

He stopped, confused. "You don't have to. I drove here."

She looped her arm through his and pulled him along. "Something that I find highly disturbing."

"I'm all right."

She unlocked her door. "Drunks say the same thing, that doesn't mean it's true."

He scowled. "I'm not drunk."

"You haven't slept in three days. I'm surprised your sentences are still coherent." She tossed her cane in the back seat. He sat in the car; his knees hit the glove compartment.

He felt around the chair for the lever. "How do you adjust this seat?"

"It's right at your side."

"I can't find it."

She reached over him and pulled the tab sending them both flying backwards, she sprawled across his lap. She scrambled off of him. "Don't say anything," she warned buckling her seatbelt.

His lips twitched. "I wasn't planning to."

She started the ignition then pulled onto the main road.

Hunter asked, "Do you want directions to my apartment or are you going to guess?"

"I'm taking you to my place. I want to make sure you go to bed."

"I could cross my heart."

"I wouldn't believe you."

He frowned. "You sure know how to flatter a guy."

Brenna stopped at a traffic light and looked at him. "Your design is brilliant."

To that he had nothing to say.

IN HER APARTMENT, Brenna went straight to the kitchen to put the kettle on for tea hoping it would help him drift off to sleep. She returned to the living room to ask what type he liked and found Hunter laying on the couch with his shoes and socks off.

"What are you doing?"

"I'm going to sleep." He clasped his hands behind his head. "Are you planning on giving me instructions? Might work just as well."

"No need to be nasty. I have a bedroom."

His eyes lit up.

"A guest bedroom."

He sat up and grabbed his socks and shoes. "You shouldn't raise a man's hopes like that. The disappointment could be fatal."

She turned off the kettle then led him into the guest bedroom. She instantly regretted it. The peach and pink decor had the sickening sweetness of an overstuffed cream puff. She hadn't gotten around to redecorating it after experimenting with a look she'd seen in a magazine. Lacy pillows and a pink crocheted blanket choked the bed while peach carpeting flooded the room. She nudged his paralyzed form. "Don't look so horrified," she said. "You're just going to sleep here."

"If I can." He took off his shirt and climbed into bed. One of the pink lacy pillows fell on his head. He tossed it on the ground where is squeaked. He looked at her amazed. "Your pillows squeak?"

"Just that one. I was trying for something different."

He squeezed the other pillows. "Congratulations, you succeeded."

His creamy brown shoulders looked oddly delectable in the

garish bed. Like the chocolate cake inside a petit four. He finally drew up the covers and laid back.

She looked away embarrassed for staring. She'd seen men's chest before lots of times. His shouldn't have a devastating effect on her. Too bad it did. She would see the sleek muscles of his chest and shoulders in her dreams tonight, not that she would complain. "Goodnight."

"'Night."

She turned off the lights and began to close the door.

"Wait!" He leapt out of the bed and came up to her. "I forgot something." He dug in his trouser pocket then slipped a ring on her finger. "Now we're engaged." It was an excellent imitation. The cubic zirconium looked like diamonds in the gold band. But she knew it wasn't just a ring. It was a symbol of how deep into this deception they had gone. She stared at the ring so long that by the time she could think of a reply he was asleep.

BRENNA DIDN'T FALL sleep right away. She lay in bed listening for every movement that came from the next room. He didn't snore and wasn't an active sleeper so there wasn't much to listen for, just the occasional shifting of sheets or a deep sigh. She liked to hear him sigh. He sounded like a child with a pleasant dream. She lifted her hand to stare at the ring. When he took it from her the show would end. Pauline was right, she didn't want it to. She wondered if that was the true reason she had invited him home. Was it so she could have him close, create more memories with him before he was out of her life? She pounded her pillow then fell into it face first. No, the truth was much more debase. She wanted him. Pure and simple.

That wasn't like her. What about compatibility? The meeting of the minds? Common interests? Yes, they were both committed to their careers, but that could be bad in a relationship. But she didn't want a relationship. She wanted him in bed with her and available to parade in front of her family every once in awhile. Nothing more.

She glanced at her new cane resting against the wall near the door. He'd fixed it for her. Why? Because he felt sorry for her? Because he cared about her? Or just because? She finally fell asleep with no answers.

Brenna woke up early the next morning ready to prepare breakfast. As she put on her navy cotton robe, she heard the shower turn on. She went straight to the kitchen determined not to picture him naked. She failed.

She opened the cupboards and stared at their contents. She wasn't going to do anything special and try to impress him. She intended to follow her regular routine of cereal and toast.

Nevertheless, she ended up making French toast and a fruit salad. She tried to convince herself that the breakfast was a treat for herself as much as for him, but didn't succeed. The door bell rang as she set the table.

Dread crawled over her skin like a series of centipedes when she glanced at the clock. Only one person would come to visit this early on a weekend. She took a deep breath then opened the door with a plastic smile.

"Mom, what are you doing here?"

Diane handed her a dish of casserole. "I had extra."

"Thank you. It was so kind of you to drop this off." She began to close the door, keeping her voice sweet so as not to appear rude. "I'll talk to you later and--"

Hunter's deep voice sliced through her words. "Something smells delicious," he said, coming out of the bathroom, steam from the shower spilling into the hallway.

Brenna slowly turned and saw him pouring a glass of orange juice, a sea-green towel wrapped around his waist. His bare chest just as magnificent as the night before. She spun around and stared at her mother. "It's not what you think."

Diane schooled her features to mask any shock then began to smile. "You are an adult, Brenna."

"Well, I wasn't being 'adult' with him. We're just dating this isn't a serious relationship." She furrowed her brows unsure how to interpret her mother's odd expression. "We came home and went straight to bed." She shook her head and waved her hands. "I mean to sleep in separate beds, in separate rooms." She drew out her words so there was no confusion. "Nothing happened."

Diane's smile widened. "That's okay, Brenna. I understand you wanted to keep it a secret."

Brenna narrowed her eyes. "Keep what a secret?"

"Your engagement of course." She hugged her and whispered, "Your ring is gorgeous."

Brenna glanced down at her hand. Dread turned into panic. "No, wait it's not--"

Diane stepped back ready to go. "I know I've spoiled your surprise, but don't worry we can talk about it later." She glanced at Hunter her eyes gleaming. "I can't believe I get to have him as a son-in-law." She blew her daughter a kiss then hurried down the stairs.

Brenna closed the door and rested her forehead against it. "I give her about an hour to keep it a secret."

Hunter came up behind her. "Keep what a secret?"

"Our engagement."

Hunter glanced at her hand then shrugged. "This is not a problem."

She spun around, held up her hand and wiggled her fingers. "You don't consider this a problem? What do you consider a problem? A volcanic eruption? A nuclear blast?"

His voice remained calm as hers rose. "I'm just saying there's a logical solution to this. Let her think we're engaged then later tell her we had an argument and broke up."

Brenna leaned her head back and shook her head defeated. "You want me to try to convince my mother that an argument stopped me from marrying a rich, eligible man?"

"You forgot handsome."

"Oh shut up."

He lifted the top of the casserole dish. "Hmm, looks good."

She took the top from him and set it back. "She'll never forgive me for losing you."

"There's another solution."

Brenna straightened. "What?"

"You could marry me."

Her mouth fell open.

"It's a possibility."

She gathered her thoughts. "Out of the question." She pushed herself from the door and walked past him. "Don't worry. I'll come up with something."

He let the matter drop and followed her into the kitchen.

"I borrowed your razor. I don't think you prefer beards."

"You're right," she teased, putting the casserole away. "That's why I leave it there for all my male guests."

He paused; she winked. "Jealous?"

"No. I'm starving."

Her eyes trailed the length of him. "I don't feed half-naked men."

He reached for his towel. "Should I take the towel off?"

"No."

"Why do I get the feeling you don't mean that?" He laughed. A few moments later she heard his bedroom door close.

"So what would a man have to do to convince you to marry him?" Hunter asked as he poured syrup over his stack of French toast. Brenna was pleased she'd made enough to satisfy his appetite although she'd have to buy a new loaf of bread.

"I've explained I don't want to get married." She sent him a warning glare. "However, if I did wish to marry, it wouldn't be to a man who wants to use me to secure a promotion. We had a bargain.

I'd be your fiancée for one night, nothing more." She bit into a melon cube. "You'll have to find a wife on your own."

"Fine." He cut his stack. "I could always use your services."

"Love by Design is for serious singles."

"I'm serious."

"I'd double your fee."

"I can afford it." He rested his arms on the table his tone becoming flippant. "I can afford a lot of things." He glanced up at the ceiling. "Nice house, car, clothes." His gaze fell to her face. "Trips to Paris for a shopping spree."

Brenna studied a raspberry she'd speared with her fork. "If you're trying to bore me to death, you're succeeding."

He resumed his meal. "I thought women liked men who could provide."

"They do, but money isn't enough."

"Money helps."

"Yes, but it doesn't keep a marriage together."

"If two people who are compatible get together, marriage can work. Especially if their essential needs are met."

She shook her head, firm. "That's not enough."

"What else is there?" He held up a hand. "Besides love."

She lowered her gaze and stabbed a grape. "There also has to be a mutual regard and a willingness to surrender."

"A willingness to surrender?"

"Married people call it compromise."

"So you're not willing to compromise?"

"Neither are you."

"Why would I need to? I'd be in charge."

"How long do you plan to be married? Three months, a year?"

"I'd like it to be forever."

He said the words with such sincerity Brenna could no longer be glib. She met his eyes. "Compromise is the ability to concede without feeling weak, to consider the needs and desires of the marriage above your own."

"But a marriage should reflect your needs not hinder them."

"A marriage is about two people not one."

"Yes, the head of the household and his partner."

She groaned. "As you speak, don't you ever feel the noose being fitted around your neck?"

"I am in no way lessening the role of a wife, but you cannot have two chiefs. There are marriages where the husband concedes to the wife, but that isn't me."

"And I won't concede to anyone."

He thought a moment. "Concede isn't the right word. Agree. I won't make unnecessary demands. I would take good care of you."

"I don't need to be taken care of."

"Yes, you do."

Brenna let out a breath, exasperated. "Sometimes I wonder if you see me or a hologram. The wife you're looking for is certainly not me."

"Yes, it is."

"You don't even know me."

"True, but you have all the qualifications I would want in a wife. It doesn't take months to be certain. If the right facts are available in a decision making situation you grab the opportunity. It's similar to finding the perfect employee and hiring on the spot."

Brenna gripped her fork, keeping her voice level. "You think of a wife as an employee?"

Hunter thought for a moment unaware of the hard edge in her tone. "Yes and no. There are similarities. Marriage is like a business. There's a contract and expectations from both parties. You create a product that happens to be children."

"Then the discussion is over."

"Why?"

"I don't want to have kids."

His eyes swept over her face trying to catch her in a lie. "But you'd make a wonderful mother."

"You don't know that. I might whack them with my cane when I'm in a bad mood."

He pushed his plate aside then rested his elbows on the table. His eyes watched her with intense speculation. She knew it was a dangerous look. She could almost feel him stripping her bare. "You're not telling me something."

Brenna was desperate to change the subject before he completely exposed her and she lost her temper. "Are you finished with your breakfast?" She reached for his plate.

He grabbed her hand. "I don't believe you don't want children."

She snatched her hand away, but knew she was trapped. She tried to break down the invisible snares with anger. She pushed herself from the table. "I don't care what you believe! I don't care that you and my mother and most of the world see me as a failure because I'm not married or have aspirations to be so. I don't care that you pity me or think I'm pathetic."

His voice was soft, although his eyes were hard. "I don't think that."

She gripped the table her voice low with venom. "You're missing the point. I don't care. I don't care about you. I don't care if you have a weird view of marriage because even if I did want to marry, I'd never marry you. Ever. Is that clear?"

He didn't answer right away, letting a few moments of silence chill the room. Eventually he said, "Very."

She stood. "So I wish you the best of luck on your search. I hope you find the best employee, I mean wife, you can buy. Someone who will settle for the salary you'll provide her in order to assure her loyalty to you. I'm sure there are plenty of women ready for that career. Becoming Mrs. Hunter Randolph will be quite an achievement."

Hunter leaned back in his chair, running his forefinger back and forth along the table. He sat with an unsettling calm that made her wary; he had the patience of a predator waiting to strike. "And just what will you do while I'm on my mercenary quest?" he asked in a neutral tone. "Hide in that beautiful office of yours and fix other people's lives so that you don't have to focus on your own?"

Brenna grasped the back of the chair. "I'm good at what I do and I help a lot of people."

He lowered his gaze his voice never changing. "No doubt. After all you're helping me." His eyes captured hers. "But you're scared of life."

"I'm not scared."

"Too scared to make this real."

"There is no this, no us, no relationship. There's nothing between us but a bargain."

"You think by denying it, it will go away?"

Her palms began to sweat. "You're trying to trap me, but it won't work. Your name suits you, but you will not be able to capture this prey. I know you, Hunter. I know that you're addicted to the chase. It's a high for you. An emotion so potent it could be mistaken for lust. Your passionate nature escapes, but you're too much in control to let it rule you. So you analyze it and make it suit your purpose. You can fool yourself into believing you want me, but you cannot fool me. You hate that I'm in control of this."

Hunter rose to his feet and came towards her. Inside she trembled, but she never moved. His voice grew cool as though a weapon to paralyze her in place. He didn't need to. The look in his eyes had the same affect. "Admit that you're afraid."

Brenna boldly met his gaze. "I'm not afraid of you. I'd no sooner fear my shadow."

"I didn't say you were afraid of me."

"I'm not afraid of anything."

He raised a mocking brow igniting her temper more.

"You have no idea what I had to survive. The rubber cane was only a fraction of the taunts and torture. The names are still in my head. The kids threw them at me like stones and they penetrated. They thought I was without feeling because I continued to hold my head high. I think it disgusted them that I--a freak--would have the gall to think something of myself. I can close my eyes and remember every humiliating moment. And the look on my brother's face when he'd try to get them to stop. He couldn't. But I was smart and got good grades. I joined clubs and made friends. Despite the surgeries, despite the part time job after school to pay for medical bills I survived. I'm not afraid of my past or my future. You're the one who is afraid. So afraid to disappoint your family that you're willing to marry a stranger to please them."

"I don't take marriage lightly. You should be flattered I asked you to marry me."

Brenna's voice cracked. "Flattered? You mean grateful. Don't worry, I am." She fluttered her lashes. "I'm very thankful kind, sir. It fills my desolate life."

He glanced away frustrated. "You're so quick to take offense. Why--" He stopped as something became clear. "I know what you're afraid of."

"What?"

"You're afraid to be loved."

Brenna stiffened. "And how would you know that when you don't love anything? Was that why your first marriage failed? She was so starved for love she left you? I know why Janice did."

His eyes flashed, he gripped her wrists until the heat of his palms threatened to scorch her. He was no longer a hunter, but a storm of emotions left too long shimmering beneath the surface. His voice carried the weight of his heart. "The marriage failed because I loved her and she didn't love me. I loved Angelina more than..." He bit back the words. "Anyway, she left me." He pulled her closer his breath warm against her face. "I loved her eyes, her voice." His lips brushed against Brenna's neck--wet, warm, wanting. The caress tender, yet painful since it was not meant for her.

"The color of her hair." He ran a hand through hers. His fingers gentle, yet every strand felt as though it was being ripped from her scalp. "Her lips, her hands were so light and small in mine." He brushed his lips against her knuckles. His hands slid to her waist, his lips capturing hers as the passionate love he'd felt for Angelina spilled out, shattering Brenna until she felt she would crumble into dust.

"I learned that women marry for other reasons than love. I didn't care as long as she was with me. As long as she was mine." His voice grew quiet, echoing with remembered pain. "But love wasn't enough to keep her so I let her go and the marriage ended." His eyes held hers. "And I vowed the next time would be different."

He released her, the storm dissipating as suddenly as it had come. Brenna gripped the chair to keep from falling. His tone turned neutral almost bored. "Do you see how suited we are together? You're afraid to be loved and I refuse to love ever again." His tone deepened. "I admire you." He watched her lips thin and sighed. "But not even that small compliment is something you can accept. So you're right. I do pity you."

She slapped him--hard. A thin line of blood trailed down the side of his mouth. She smiled coldly. "Do you pity me now?"

He gripped the side of her neck, his thumb grazing her jaw. "You expect me to hurt you because you believe men and women are equal. But I'm not your equal. I'm stronger." He brushed the back of his hand against her cheek. "I could knock you to the ground with one swipe of my hand." He brushed her other cheek. "And you know that. You know that I could hurt you very much. And a part of you wants me too because that's the language you understand. The language of pain. You understand taunts and torture not tenderness."

Brenna let her gaze fall no longer able to meet his. "I will not be pitied." She pointed to the door. "Get out."

Hunter dabbed at the blood on his chin. "No."

"Would you like me to slap you again?"

His tone was as cool as frost. "I'd like to see you try."

She turned away. "I'll call you a cab." She ignored her trembling fingers as she checked the phone directory and dialed. When she was through, she saw Hunter hadn't moved. He stood staring at the ground his lip swelling, a purple bruise forming. She grabbed a napkin and handed it to him. "Wipe your mouth." She clenched her teeth, hating herself for caring. "I'm sorry."

"An apology carries more weight when you mean it."

"I do mean it." She grabbed her purse and handed him several bills. "For damages."

He frowned at the money. "Twenty dollars? My face is worth at least a thousand."

She gave him a few more bills. "Here's fifty. Now shut up and finish your breakfast."

He sat quietly for awhile then said, "I wish I knew where Byron was."

"Why?"

"I feel like hurting him."

"I didn't realize you were violent."

He lifted a brow. "I could say the same."

She sighed. "I'm sorry."

He glanced up at her. "Now I believe you." He returned to his breakfast. "I think you were saving that slap for him."

"Because he pitied me too?"

"Yes, and because you loved him and he didn't love you."

Brenna sat down, clasping her hands together to keep them from shaking. "Do you know why people like me hate pity? Because pity means 'something to be regretted', something to be sorry for. As though we're a mistake in life and everyone can look at us and say 'Well I thought my life was bad, but look at you at least I'm not like that'. No matter how much I've succeeded. No one wants to be me." She grasped her leg. "People see this." She swallowed back tears; he'd never seen her cry. "So promise you'll never say you pity me again." She lowered her voice. "You can think it, but don't say it."

"I wanted to hurt you."

"I know."

Hunter rested his fork down. "I understand that I'm not your romantic ideal. Perhaps I'm no one's romantic ideal." He shrugged unconcerned. "That's okay because I don't believe the world can function on that. I'm a good man, I work hard and I'm decent to those around me. I don't like admitting any weaknesses, but I will admit that my previous marriage, although years in the past, was--is--a sore spot. I was good to her. " He sighed. "So I won't pity you if you don't mention her."

Brenna reached out and touched his hand, hoping the gesture would express her thanks. "Another bargain?"

"Yes."

She smiled gently. "Angelina lost a good man." They heard the horn of the taxi outside.

He picked up his fork, quickly finished his food then stood.

She followed him to the door. "You aren't really going to take my money, are you?"

"Of course I am." He stuffed the money in his wallet. "Serves you right. You can't go around slapping men because you feel like it. Besides it saves me from giving you a reason for really slapping me."

"Like what?"

He gently touched the side of his face. "Ravishing a woman on top of her kitchen table usually gets me into trouble."

"I don't believe you."

"You're right." His hand fell to his side all humor gone from his tone. "The last woman who slapped me did so because she saw in me something she didn't want to see." His voice dropped to a whisper. "A man who thinks she's wonderful."

Brenna took a step back. His words were too dangerous to believe. Yet she wanted to. "You think I'm wonderful?" She smirked. "You must be very lonely."

He pulled her to him, his voice insistent. "It's more than lust. No, listen to me. This coming weekend will be the last time I'll ever see you and a part of me is glad because I'm not your Prince Charming and I can't wake you from this dream you're in. This dream where you're just a woman with a bad leg and only successful in your career. A dream where you can't see that you're so much more than that. So much heart and compassion you're too afraid to see."

Tears built up in her eyes. Her voice was a whisper. "You're hurting me."

"Perhaps you're waking up to the fact that you should be flattered, even grateful, that I'm here with you right now. That all last night I thought about making love to you. That right now I could hold you in my arms and bury myself in your sweetness, your gentleness because it's there inside that armor, hiding behind that wit. That I think of caressing every part of you, kissing you. But I won't because it wouldn't be fair to either of us." He released her. "I don't love you. I doubt I ever will, but I admire you and if that's not a good basis for a marriage I don't know what is." He opened the door. "You're right, you're in control. The choice is yours."

Chapter Nine

Brenna shut the door determined to go on about her day, but she couldn't. The kitchen seemed to echo with the accusations they had hurled at each other. The foyer pulsated with emotions so heated they permeated the walls.

She was afraid to be loved? Who was he to say such a thing? A man who didn't even know her. Who didn't know how much she had loved Byron in hopes that his care and kindness would blossom into a deep love for her. She had studied every smile, every gesture hoping that his pity would change into something more. Something deep and beautiful that she could cling to. She'd wanted his love. And yet an insistent whisper of doubt plagued her.

Why had she felt comfortable with him for so long? Why had she let his crumbs of affection sustain her? If she were truly starving inside, why had she waited—hungered—for so long? She quickly dressed then went to speak to a man who could give her some answers.

HER FATHER, Crampton Garrett, lived alone in a three level apartment complex hidden deep in a wooded area. It gave the residence the feeling of a forest while providing the closeness of an urban town. Brenna stepped out of the car. The scent of newly cut grass hit her along with the harsh sounds of a leaf blower as workers pushed away grass cuttings, and a barking dog chased a squirrel up a tree. She walked to his first floor apartment. Though she hadn't called she knew he was home. He always was.

After knocking, she heard his grumbling reply, his uneven footsteps and the thud of a mahogany cane against the tile floor.

"Hello, Brenna," he said. There was no welcome or censure in his voice. Just a casual greeting that gave no indication of the months that had past since their last meeting.

Brenna stepped in and shut the door as her father headed for the cramped living room full of various newspapers and magazines. He was not meant to be a big man, but his large shoulders belied that fact, descending to a thick middle that was not quite fat, but far from trim. His gray hair had separated from his forehead years ago and kind brown eyes settled deeply in an ordinary face that rarely showed joy.

"It's nice to see you," she said.

He sat, resting his arms on the armrest of his favorite tan lounger. "You look well."

"Thank you."

He bent down, picked up a magazine and tossed it on another pile. "Your mother told me you're getting married."

She hesitated, wondering how much truth to share. "I'm not certain."

He shoved on his reading glasses and lifted a newspaper. "Why not? You'll probably do better than I did." He unfolded the paper, disappearing behind it. "It's different for a woman."

"What is?"

"Marriage." The paper fell to his lap. "How could I be a husband and father with this?" He gestured to his leg. "And then to lay the same burden on my off-spring." He lifted the paper again, shielding his face. "It was unbearable."

Brenna brightened her voice to combat his bitterness. "Stephen's doing great and--"

"Great?" he scoffed. "The kid hasn't progressed in years. Is that what he plans to do the rest of his life?"

"At least he's happy and I'm happy. You don't have to worry about me. I run an excellent business and you should see my apartment." She sat forward, wanting to rip the paper away so he'd be forced to look at her. "I wish you would come and visit me. I'd love to have you over."

The paper rustled as he turned the page. "Even after I abandoned you, your brother and your mother?"

"I told you all that is forgiven."

He sniffed. "Forgiven yes, but never forgotten..." His voice drifted away leaving a cloud of discontent that threatened to choke the air.

She refused to let the rain clouds form. She snatched the paper, startling them both. "Look at me, Dad." Brenna grabbed his chin when his eyes wandered to the window. "Look at me."

Slowly his eyes met hers glistening with tears.

"I'm a success." His eyes drifted to her leg. "No, look at me. Stop being ashamed."

"I'm not ashamed."

"Then why do you make it so hard for me to love you?" The words floated for a bit only to slap her in the face.

Why do you make it so hard for me to love you? Why can't you accept a compliment? Why does a man's interest make you skeptical? All the questions hid the true one--Why can't you trust anyone?

Would this be her future? Would kindness and care from others always be met with suspicion? Would her father's legacy be not just a deformity, but his fear that he wasn't meant to be loved? She realized how hard it must have been for her mother to have compliments discarded and affections ignored all because he couldn't accept that they were real.

He grabbed her hand. His words eager yet defeated. "I don't want to be this way, but I can't help it anymore."

She handed him the paper and stood. "You can, but it would hurt too much to try. It's a risk to trust someone."

"Bring your young man around..." he called as she opened the door. "If you want."

Brenna turned and stared at him surrounded by his papers and magazines, the sunlight desperately filtering through the closed blinds. Here was a man who fought all his life against pity, when that was the only thing he inspired. "Goodbye," she said, not just to him but also to her past.

Dr. Lopez gently touched her arm. An olive skinned man with intense brown eyes, he smiled at her with sympathy. "Are you ready?"

Brenna nodded. She bit her lip until she drew blood as the needle penetrated her muscle. There was inflammation in her hip joint. The flare ups occurred every few months and had become a part of her life, although she could never get use to the treatment. He sat after the injection and wrote something in her file then looked at her. "You had a cramp last weekend?"

"Yes," she said in a quiet voice. "It didn't last long."

"Have you been doing your exercises?"

She licked the salty taste of blood from her lip. "Yes."

He nodded. "Good. You can't afford to lose what little muscle you have there."

"I know. It still causes me pain."

"When?"

"Oh certain moments."

"Remember to regularly stretch or the muscles will lose elasticity. In several years we may have to replace your knee."

Too bad they couldn't replace the entire leg. "I know."

"You're doing an excellent job. I know the injections hurt."

"I'm used to them."

He tapped the folder hesitant. "Your insurance didn't accept the last one."

"I'm paying out of pocket."

"This is getting costly. I'll have to write something else down. Something they'll cover."

"Thank you."

Dr. Lopez was right. The injections were very costly as were the visits. The insurance company didn't cover either the visits or the injections because the treatments were considered 'alternative' and the drugs were considered 'experimental'. Her out of pocket expenses put a big dent in her savings. However, fighting with them was tiresome.

Back home, Brenna took out her files and went over her coverage. The phone rang.

"Hi," Stephen said. "I want to double date."

"Why?"

"The banquet is this weekend, right?"

"What does that have to do with anything?"

"This will give you another chance to be together."

Brenna clicked her tongue. "Won't work, little brother. I'm the matchmaker in the family."

"We'll go to the Steak House."

"No," she said firm.

"You have to say yes or I'll tell Mom you made this whole thing up."

She paused. "You wouldn't."

"I would."

"Beast. Pest. Rodent."

He laughed. "See you Friday."

"He could be busy."

"Make sure he isn't," Stephen said then hung up.

Brenna stared at the phone then set it down. After their last discussion Hunter may not want to spend more time with her. But she wanted to see him again.

***

"DID THE CANE WORK?" Miles asked.

Hunter glanced at him. The last thing he wanted to talk about was Brenna. She was already wrecking havoc in his thoughts. "No. I mean she liked it, but that was all." He shook his head annoyed he wasn't being more articulate. "I told her about Angelina. She said some things and I...I don't know how or why I let her get to me."

Miles rested a foot on his desk. "We all have buttons that can be pushed."

"Not me...at least not usually." He picked up a stapler then set it down. "I don't like anyone knowing them."

"I doubt she'll use it against you. You'll never see her again after Saturday anyway."

He wished that felt like good news. "Right."

"And she's not right for you anyway. I mean from what you've told me she has a bunch of insecurities."

"No, no she has confidence, she's very courageous. She's just scared. She needs someone who will be gentle and patient with her."

"And that's not you. You have a plan, a schedule you live by. You don't need her mucking that up."

Hunter shoved his hands in his pockets and sent his friend a level glare. "I know what you're trying to do and I want you to stop it."

Miles folded his arms. "I'm trying to give you a reason to forget about her."

"I know, but she's the best prospective wife I've come upon in years. You should have seen the party she put together. Excellent.

She'd be able to handle Randolph clientele with ease. I can't believe I haven't been able to convince her of the benefits of our match."

"Have you tried being romantic?"

"Yes. A picnic, a fair. I've kissed her. Nothing seems to work. I've even been honest. You'd think a woman like that would appreciate such efforts."

Miles grimaced. "How honest were you?"

"I told her that marriage was like a business and that she'd make a great employee."

He scratched his head. "Wow. A beautiful line like that and she didn't fall in your arms? I'm amazed."

Hunter ignored his sarcasm. "She has a weakness. I know what it is, I just have to find a way to use it."

"And there is of course, Plan B: Other women."

Hunter stared at his desk. "She's very clever so I have to alter my approach."

"Or just choose another woman."

"Perhaps being honest wasn't the best strategic move."

"Or you could save yourself the energy and find another woman. There are plenty out there."

He glanced up. "Plenty of what?"

"Women."

"Yes, I'm well aware of that but few meet my standards."

"And I'm sure of those few none can match Brenna."

Hunter twirled his pen.

"You know it's dangerous the lengths a man like you will go to sleep with a woman. It's not a good idea to marry someone just because you want to sleep with her."

Hunter set his pen down. "This is more than sex."

"You have a bad habit of fixing your mind on one thing and staying with it to the bitter end."

"People who are easily swayed lack conviction."

"So this is about conviction not an erection that won't go away?"

Hunter scowled. "More like an irritant that won't go away." The phone rang. Hunter answered.

"I need you," Brenna said.

He gripped the phone. His body responding to the urgency in her tone, giving credence to Miles' words. "What?"

"My brother is a jerk."

He regained control. "You want me to do something to him?"

"No, well. He's blackmailing me. He wants to double date or he'll tell Mom everything. Are you free Friday?"

"Sure."

"Thanks."

He hung up and stared at Miles. "Yes, this is about sex."

THE STEAK HOUSE was Stephen's favorite restaurant—loud and noisy with cheap food.

"I've invited another couple to join us," Brenna said once they were seated.

Stephen looked at her suspicious. "Who?"

"There they are." She waved to Tima and her date. A clean cut man in khaki trousers and Hawaiian top. A diamond stud glinted in one ear.

Stephen glared at her. "What are you up to?"

She smiled. "Revenge."

Tima sat and introduced her date, Ben Halton. He was helping with the set design at the theater.

Stephen and Fiona shared a menu. Fiona readily agreeing with everything he pointed to like an echo. Brenna finally lost her temper. "Wouldn't it be nice to try something different? Instead of the same thing? How about the grilled snapper?"

Stephen nodded. "That sounds good."

Fiona agreed. "Yes, that sounds good."

Brenna groaned. Hunter nudged her and whispered, "Leave them alone." She lifted her menu.

Once everyone had ordered, Brenna asked Ben, "So you're going to start production at the Anandale Theater?"

"Yes."

"What play?"

"The Glass Menagerie."

Brenna frowned. "Oh."

"You don't like the play?"

No. She delighted in the tales of bad little children, she was sick of the syrupy sweet Tiny Tims and Little Nells invalid children with angelic hearts. How she loved the spoiled cousin in Heidi. She knew as a child she wasn't angelic and that she dreamt of revenge. Of getting back at her tormentors in vicious ways. That she hated the teacher's encouraging smiles and patronizing pats on the back as they calmly sat behind the protective shields of their desks while she entered the school battlefields in the halls and cafeteria. She'd never succeed as the tender hearted cripple; she was too cocky and annoyed them. Tonight she wanted to be different. "It's a lovely play," she lied.

"Your sister told me you're a lighting genius, Stephen," Tima said. "How would you like to see what we're doing?"

He glanced at Fiona. "I don't know. I'm pretty busy."

"But I've seen you at the theater before."

He shot her a look, his voice cool. "You must have me confused with someone else."

"Oh, sorry."

"Stephen's not into the theater stuff much," Fiona said.

Tima only nodded, unconvinced.

Dinner became rather stilted afterwards and soon ended with no one ordering dessert. A light drizzle had started and the drivers offered to bring the cars around to the front of the restaurant. Fiona, Brenna and Ben chatted under the canopy.

"I did see you at the theater," Tima said coming up behind him.

He continued walking.

"Why did you lie about it?"

"You didn't see me."

"You shouldn't stop yourself from doing things in fear that you'll out grow others."

He spun around. "Are you finished?"

"Maybe." She lifted her umbrella. "Here, you're getting wet."

He knocked it out of her hands. The wind set it flying down the parking lot then into a ditch. He swore. He'd never responded to a woman in anger. He stared at her, ashamed as the feather in her headband wilted. "I'm sorry."

"That's okay. I knew you didn't like me. I didn't realize you had something against umbrellas too." She pulled a plastic rain cap from her handbag and put it on. "There. All fixed."

He turned. "Let me go get--"

She grabbed his arm. "Don't worry about it. I needed to get a new one anyway." She tried to push away the lingering sadness in his gaze. He looked young and lost standing in the rain. "I'm sorry for over-stepping my bounds, but I do think you'd make a great lighting direc-tor. You get along with people and you're good at what you do." She shrugged and walked away.

He followed. "You don't know that."

"Brenna speaks highly of you." She stopped in front of her car. He stared. "This is yours?"

"Yes."

"A Mustang."

"1974."

He ran his hand lovingly over the hood.

"Do you want to sit inside?"

He glanced towards the restaurant. "Fiona's waiting."

"So is Ben."

"I'll get your seat wet."

"It'll survive. Any more excuses?"

He got inside and fawned over the interiors.

"Come by one day and I'll show you under the hood."

He ran his hand along the dashboard then stopped and sat back. "I just go to look. I don't want to get too involved."

"Or in other words, Fiona doesn't want you to."

He slanted her a harsh look. "I'm not pussy whipped if that's what you're thinking."

"I'm not."

He twisted the ring on his finger. "I love her that's all. I don't think that's wrong."

She took off her cap and tossed it in the backseat.

"Do you?"

She looked in the rearview mirror and reapplied her lipstick. "Doesn't matter what I think, remember?"

He glanced at her then looked away. "It's just sometimes it doesn't feel enough."

"I love this car. It gets me places, provides shelter from the weather, I can sleep in it, eat in it get a DVD and watch a movie, listen to music. But it's not a home. Sometimes you need that something extra. But only you know what it is. Now get out so I can get back to my date."

He got out. "Thanks."

She waved his thanks away and drove off.

"I can't believe how long it took you to get the truck," Fiona said as they walked to his apartment. "Did you forget where you parked it?"

"No, Tima was showing me her Mustang."

"In the rain?"

"Yes." He entered the apartment and headed to the bedroom to change. He returned and saw Fiona in front of the TV. He glanced out the window. "It's stopped raining," he said. "How about we go for a drive and see the Grand Yardley Hotel?"

"It's late and we just came back."

"I know it's late, but the night is the right time to see the sun set behind the towers, to see lights reflecting on the water. We could pack a snack."

"If you're hungry, I could go and make you something."

He sighed and sat down beside her. "No, never mind."

She touched the side of his face in a tender, fleeting gesture. "You're acting strange. Is something wrong?"

"No, nothing's wrong." He slid to the ground.

"Funny how Brenna likes to tell everyone you're some sort of a lighting genius. I hope it doesn't embarrass you."

"Do you think I should be embarrassed that my sister's proud of me?"

"No."

After a moment he asked, "Are you proud of me?"

"Of course I am."

"I'm thinking about the theater. Tima said--"

"She was just being nice. I wouldn't take anything she said too seriously. You know I visited a gallery once and saw one of her paintings on sale. Oh my god. You should have seen the prices. She makes a lot of money. She dresses tacky, but that blouse of hers was pure silk. I could tell. I bet you your sister set her up to say something to you."

"Probably." He wouldn't be surprised if she saw him as a kid. Brenna's little brother. It was a humiliating thought.

Fiona liked him as he was. He'd never make enough to treat her to fancy restaurants and stuff and that was fine. She didn't complain like other women would. It was okay that she sometimes didn't understand him, it wasn't her job to. It was his fault for being restless not hers. He rested against her leg and stared at the screen.

BRENNA PREPARED for the banquet with care. She wasn't nervous. She knew the gold dress with its plunging neckline and low back looked stunning against her skin. That her hair, which was pulled back and hung in ringlets about her face, complimented her subdued make-up and gold hoop earrings. Tonight she'd give her final performance and play the role well.

When Hunter knocked on the door a half hour later, she took a deep breath and answered. She greeted him with a bright smile. "Hi."

He stared at her. "Where's your dress?"

Her smiled dimmed. "You're supposed to be my fiancée not my father."

"So I'll repeat the question. Where's your dress?"

"You don't approve?"

"It doesn't look like you."

"I have hidden depths."

"Interesting since you've barely hidden anything else."

Her confidence began to falter. Perhaps this wasn't the appropriate dress for a director's wife. "You really don't like it?"

His eyes trailed the length of her. "You look sensational."

She swallowed trying not to choke on the compliment. "Thank you. Come in."

He couldn't take his eyes off her and promptly crashed into the side table. He softly swore and rubbed his knee.

Brenna went towards him. "Are you okay?"

Hunter held up a hand, fending her off. If she touched him, he may not be able to control himself. He was sure if he touched her dress, it would fall apart in his hands. The image made him groan. "I'm fine." He limped to the couch and sat, trying to determine exactly what 'fine' meant. Physically he was fine; mentally he was a mess. He couldn't think clearly. She was beautiful. Every bit the queen he'd met that afternoon weeks ago and he wanted her.

He wanted her to be his. He wanted the charade to end, to really claim her and present her as his future wife. He didn't want this to be their last night together. He scowled and turned away.

"Perhaps this was a bad idea," he said.

She sat next to him and frowned. "You can't back out now. Do you know how much this dress cost?"

He inched away. "I'll pay you. What is it--one, two thousand?"

She hesitated the cost was considerably less than that. "Uh...no, but that's not the point. We've come this far."

He rubbed his hands together, attempting to put everything into perspective. Okay, so he was attracted to her. Very attracted. He had been from the beginning. Tonight was different because of the dress. Yes, it was the dress's fault. It was form-fitting yet left enough mystery to keep a man interested. It coated her like liquid gold, transforming her into a goddess.

He drummed his fingers on his knee. The plan, he had to think about the plan. She was right. It was sound. Once he secured the director's position, he'd focus on persuading her. He'd have lots of fun trying to. He jumped to his feet. Focus. He had to focus. Tonight was important. "This is the plan." He looked at her. She gazed up at him offering her full attention. He couldn't think of anything sexier than a woman hanging on his every word. He dove into her eyes, losing all thought.

"What's the plan?" she asked.

He blinked. "Umm..."

"Do we go to the party and introduce ourselves?"

"Right."

"And basically follow the same routine that we did with my family?"

"Correct."

She flashed a wicked grin. "Your plan sounds perfect."

He missed her sarcasm and nodded pleased. "Thank you."

Brenna's grin turned to concern. "Are you sure you're okay?"

Hunter began to pace. He had to remember that this was Brenna. The woman he'd argued with days ago. The woman who'd slapped him. He touched his cheek, trying to conjure up the memory that was quickly fading. "So this is our last night."

She tilted her head to the side as she watched him, unsure of his strange mood. "Yes."

He clasped his hands behind his back. "I realize that you find my views of marriage archaic."

"While you find mine unrealistic."

He made a noncommittal sound not wanting to start another argument. "However, I feel that we do get on rather well."

She shrugged. "When we're not arguing."

He stopped. "We don't argue that much."

"Yes, we do."

"No--" He continued pacing.

She stood. "Are you trying to make a point or is this an odd attempt at small talk?"

"Yes, I have a point." Hunter opened the door feeling frustrated. "I'm trying to--"

Brenna grabbed her keys. "You're nervous. Don't be nervous."

"I'm not nervous."

"Tonight I'm going to do everything I can to show them how stable and family oriented you are."

He let his shoulders drop knowing the topic was hopeless. "Thank you." He followed her down the stairs. "I'd be a marriage bonus."

"Why?"

"I'm different than other men."

"How?"

"I'm me."

She laughed as she opened the front door to the spring air. "Hunter, I'd never mistake you for anyone else."

Chapter Ten

The banquet met with Hunter's prediction. There was a spiral staircase where Brenna stood to look out at the champagne waterfall, floor-to-ceiling windows and over three hundred guests.

She seized Hunter's arm. "You didn't tell me there would be so many people."

He raised a mocking brow. "I thought you weren't afraid of anything."

Her quaking nerves turned to steel. The next hour she played the role of his fiancée like a seasoned actress. Smiling not too wide, but enough to show interest, laughing at the jokes of inebriated managers, and chatting with corporate wives. Hunter never left her side. She wasn't sure why, but didn't question it, drawing strength from his presence.

"Hunter!" a voice called. They both turned and saw a tall man with wavy brown hair and dark-framed glasses. He patted Hunter on the back in greeting. "So you're still here."

Hunter nodded, used to the familiar phrase. "Yes. Daniel, I want you to meet my fiancée, Brenna Garrett."

Daniel smiled and shook her hand. "Nice to meet you." He

turned to Hunter. "So am I ever going to convince you to jump ship and work with me?"

"I'm making progress where I am."

Daniel turned his hazel gaze to Brenna. "Perhaps you can persuade him. The man's a genius. The ideas he comes up with could change people's lives, but they all end up in the Randolph warehouse. Tell him he's being wasted where he is." He leaned forward and lowered his voice. "I could make him a rich man."

"I'm already rich."

Daniel quirked a brow. "Do you have an aversion to making more?"

"I have an obligation to my family."

He sighed. "Your family doesn't know how to use you. Besides I'm family too. I could--"

Hunter held out his hand. "Let us end this conversation and remain friends."

Daniel nodded, recognizing defeat. "Here's my card." He handed one to Brenna. "Just in case he loses it--again." He clasped Hunter on the shoulder. "I admire your integrity, but don't let it cost you your life. Please think about it."

Hunter absently stuck the card in his pocket. "I'll try."

Daniel sent Brenna a grin. "Make sure he does." He turned and left.

Brenna watched him intrigued. "Who was that exactly?"

"A cousin. One of the Merediths."

"I see," Brenna said although she didn't understand the need for the distinction.

"For some reason he sees me as an inventor."

"But you are. You invented this cane."

"True, but I'm more than that. Inventors are the little people of this world. Big business is where a man gains status and prosperity."

She stared at him amazed. "You can't be serious. Think of the inventor of the light bulb or the traffic light or the computer."

"Brenna, there are those who invent things and those who get credit for it. Where do you think I want to be?"

"Not all inventors are swallowed up by corporations. There are successful inventors who are valued in their field."

"I want to be bigger than a field."

"But—"

He shook his head. "This discussion is useless. My family has invested in me. They paid for my education and I've always received what I wanted. I plan to repay them with my loyalty."

"At all costs?"

"If that's the price I have to pay—" He stopped and stared at an older man talking to a solemn group. He was slim, clean-shaven with a shark-like smile that reminded Brenna of someone.

Hunter took her arm and led her away.

"What are you doing?" she asked.

"I would introduce you to Uncle Walter, but then you'd be forced to talk to him and I'd like to avoid that."

"You don't like him?"

"Doran's his son."

"Then I suppose we should pity him."

"Why? He congratulates himself on that accomplishment. I know my own father would like me to be—" He bit his lip. "Anyway we're safe now."

"Is this the one?" a booming voice asked.

Brenna jumped; Hunter spun around. "Yes, Grandfather, this is the one. Brenna Garrett."

Orson's cutting dark brown eyes surveyed her. She felt a sense of unease by the scrutiny. She wasn't easily made anxious, but he came close. "Not quite what I expected."

"It's a pleasure to meet you," Brenna said.

"Don't make hasty comments, my dear. You don't know me yet." He glanced at her cane. "Were you in an accident?"

"Yes, it happened at conception."

"You were born this way? Shame."

"I only find poor manners a true shame."

Hunter stiffened; Orson smiled. "I'm old. I'm allowed to ask rude questions."

"But I didn't give you permission."

His smile wavered. "Quite a woman of opinions."

"Every woman has opinions I just tend to express mine."

"So why did you choose Hunter?"

"Aside from the obvious attributes, he created this cane for me. I've never met a man so clever."

Instead of looking pleased, Orson frowned. He slanted Hunter a glance. "Did he? And when did he find the time to do that?"

"After hours," Hunter said.

Brenna shifted awkward by the sudden tension between them. "I think—"

"What do you do?" Orson cut in impatient.

"I'm the owner of Love by Design, a matchmaking service."

All polite formality left, leaving a cold piercing gaze. "And made quite a clever match for yourself." Before Brenna could respond he turned. "You two better mingle."

Brenna watched him leave. She thought the sense of unease would disappear at his departure, but instead it grew. "I'm not sure I handled that right."

"You were fine." Hunter took her elbow and led her to the ice sculptures. "However, I would prefer that you not mention the cane again."

"I didn't mean—"

"You didn't know."

She furrowed her brows confused. "You'd think he'd be proud."

He shrugged. "Come. There are more people to meet."

ORSON STOOD by the window eyeing the crowd, pleased with the success of the event. However, his gaze involuntarily continued to wander back to Hunter and his fiancée. Audrey approached him. "What has you looking so grim?"

"Have you met Hunter's fiancée?"

"A very charming young lady."

He tapped his glass pensive. Of course she would say that, simple as she was. She didn't know the necessity of a good match. He didn't even know why he'd asked her. He saw his younger son Curtis. "Get that boy over here."

"That boy is over sixty."

He sent her a look of annoyance. "Which is younger than me. Get him." Audrey caught Curtis' attention.

Curtis came over cautious. "You wanted me?"

"Have you met Hunter's fiancée?" Orson asked.

He glanced at the couple in question. "I haven't had the pleasure yet."

Orson's lips thinned. "Well, what are you waiting for? A formal invitation? Your son is thinking of marrying the woman. Your duty is to make sure it's a prudent match."

"If Hunter chose her, then I'm sure she's a good choice. I think-"

"Thinking never came very easily to you son. I suggest you meet her before drawing a conclusion."

Curtis kept any hint of anger from his tone, used to the careless insults. "I know Hunter."

"Hunter's just a man and there's something a little too calculated about her. She doesn't have the look of absolute devotion."

Curtis sniffed. "Few women do nowadays. They're a success in their own right."

"You can still find a traditional woman. The question is why didn't he?"

"He likes a challenge."

"Or perhaps she trapped him."

"Hunter wouldn't allow himself to get trapped."

Orson took a sip of his drink. He made it a slow process so they would have to wait for him. He finally said, "I'm not sure we should let him marry her."

"We couldn't stop him."

He glanced at a passing waiter. "I've intervened before," he said in a soft tone.

Curtis looked uncomfortable. "Hunter isn't a boy. He won't like his life to be toyed with."

"His life belongs to me. He'll do what's best for the company."

"Father--"

"Quiet, I have an idea brewing in my brain. Where's your brother?"

"Right here," Walter said, looking faintly amused. "Couldn't miss such an intimate family gathering."

"Have you met--?"

"Brenna? No, but Doran has. A bit of a wild card."

Orson's frown increased. "Dangerous. I was afraid of that."

"Yes." Walter pinned her with a cold look. "Wives can be very influential."

"Why do you think he chose her?"

"The cane."

"Hmm. Yes, that could be a motive, but I have a feeling he wasn't thinking about that."

"I'm sure she's a sweet girl," Audrey said.

They ignored her.

"We may be able to rein this donkey in with a carrot," Orson said. "He'll owe us and that will keep him in line."

Walter turned to his father stunned. "But Doran--"

"Will get his turn," he assured him. "Haven't I taken care of your other two? I always take care of my own. Curtis you only have one son and tonight is going to be his night. You'll welcome his fiancée and then announce the good news."

Brenna was trying to hide a yawn when a lean man with keen dark eyes--a bit hard and slightly off-putting--and a pepper gray beard approached them. "Let me meet this gorgeous creature."

Hunter introduced her. "Father, this is Brenna. The woman I plan to marry."

Curtis Randolph bowed over Brenna's extended hand. "My son has excellent taste."

Brenna felt a tingling of embarrassment and apprehension, but she managed to offer a charming reply. "It is a pleasure to meet you, Mr. Randolph. My father and I have used Randolph products for years."

He glanced down at her cane. "You don't know how much that pleases me." He tucked her hand through his arm. "Come, my dear. It's time to introduce you."

Brenna shot Hunter a panicked look, he responded with a wink. Curtis led her to the stairs. "Tell me if I'm walking too fast for you."

"She's no wilting flower, Dad. You can drag her along if you like."

"Ignore him," Curtis said.

"I usually prefer killing bugs," Brenna replied. "But I'll make an exception."

Curtis laughed and threw his son a look of pride. "Excellent choice."

Once they reached the stairs, Curtis signaled the string quartet to stop and the lighting dimmed while a spotlight shined on them. Curtis welcomed his guests then said, "But enough about business. I have exciting news. My son, Hunter, is going to be married to this beautiful woman beside me, Brenna Garrett. A woman who has used the Randolph products since she was a child. Help me welcome her into the Randolph family."

Everyone applauded.

"And I was going to wait to reveal who would take over the director's position, but I am also pleased to announce that after much consideration it has been decided that Hunter will become the new Director of Marketing and R&D. Although his uncle and I were worried that he would languish in the R&D department cooped up with his many strange designs." He paused allowing an appropriate wave of laughter. "We were relieved that he proved he can do much more. I am now certain that he has the capability to handle the job."

Everyone applauded again. Once Curtis ended his speech, Hunter and Brenna were inundated with people wishing them well. Brenna maintained her smile although all the faces blended together. Soon a familiar face appeared. An attractive woman in a gray shift dress with short brown hair cut in a bob. Her dangling earrings nearly reached her shoulders.

"I don't believe it," Janice said. "Is this for real? You and Hunter?"

Michael came up behind her. His thin, serious face offering a welcoming smile. "Of course it's real. They wouldn't announce an engagement that wasn't."

Janice gave Hunter a knowing look. "You'd be surprised."

Hunter shrugged. "I admit that it appears to be a hasty decision, but it is no hastier than your own engagement."

Janice had the grace to look embarrassed. "Well, you must admit that it seems a little odd that you'd become engaged to my matchmaker."

He turned to Brenna sending her a look that made her heart tremble. She had to remind herself it wasn't real. "Why? I took one look at her and realized I'd had my eyes set on the wrong woman. Three days later I knew she had all the qualities I wanted in a wife."

Janice's mouth tightened. "While I didn't?"

He shot her a cool glance. "You were engaged."

Michael spoke up. "Well, my joy to the happy couple."

Janice slipped her hand around Brenna's arm. "Do you mind giving us a chance for some girl talk?"

The men agreed and left them.

Janice released her hold and looked at Brenna puzzled. "So did he show you his precious plan?"

"We've discussed it, but there's a lot more to him than that."

She glanced at Hunter who was pretending to listen to whatever Michael was saying. "Not much."

"Enough," Brenna said. "When we were at the fair--"

Janice turned to her amazed. "He took you to a fair?"

"Yes."

"And what did he do? Analyze every ride?"

"No, he won lots of prizes. One, a purple bear we named Amanda."

"Really?" Brenna couldn't help but notice the look of renewed interest that entered Janice's eyes. "Michael and I haven't been able to do much since he's taking night classes."

"He's improving himself."

"Yes," she said without enthusiasm.

A cultured feminine voice cut in. "Janice, I hope you're not trying to scare her away."

Janice moved back to include the other woman. "Not at all, Ruby."

The woman turned to Brenna. "I'm Hunter's stepmother. I'm sorry I wasn't able to introduce myself earlier."

Brenna shook her hand, glad that she hadn't. She looked at the older woman who had short gray hair, a polish rarely seen anymore and eyes that saw too much.

"So Hunter convinced you to marry him?" Ruby asked.

"Yes."

"Having second thoughts?"

"Not at all."

Janice said, "I'm offering Brenna some tips."

Ruby glanced at Hunter who still looked alone among the crowd. "I think Brenna knows how to handle Hunter." She began to smile. "The question is, does he know how to handle her?"

MILES GRINNED AT HUNTER. Michael had drifted away giving him the chance to tell Hunter his assessment of his fake fiancée. "She's wonderful."

Hunter stared at Brenna and her two companions. "Hmmm."

"She's smart, funny. You didn't tell me she was funny."

"Hmm."

"I may pop round to that agency of hers." Hunter turned to him suspicious. "To find a match for myself," Miles finished quickly.

He glanced away. "I wonder what Janice is saying to her."

"Afraid she's talking about you? Why worry? You two aren't really getting married so it doesn't matter what she thinks of you."

"Hmm." He watched the women part.

"But you do care."

Hunter sent him a look of annoyance. "No, I don't. She's a grown woman who can make up her own mind."

"Unless someone makes it up for her," Miles said as he watched Doran make his way towards Brenna. "I suggest we get to her before he does." He turned. Hunter was gone.

"SO WE MEET AGAIN," Doran said, flashing a smile that was too wide to be genuine.

"Yes," Brenna replied, discreetly wiping her hand from his handshake.

Hunter approached them. "Where's your wife?"

"At home with the baby." He glanced at Brenna's cane. "You chose well, Hunter. I wanted to extend my congratulations." Sharp, dark eyes studied them. "I hope you both can make it to the wedding day."

"If we do break up, I'll let you know," she said sweetly. "That way you'll be the first to tell your grandfather the good news."

His smile faltered. "I wasn't trying to imply that I didn't believe this was real."

"Of course you were. You take pleasure in other people's misfortunes. I bet you'd laugh in delight if an old woman tripped and broke her hip." She winked. "More sales."

Hunter nudged her. "Brenna--"

"I'm sorry," she said without apology. "I suppose I shouldn't be so honest. We're not family yet."

Doran stared at her, his smile completely gone. "No, and I doubt we ever will be."

"Doubt or hope?"

"How about wish?" He turned and left.

She watched him go, thoughtful.

Miles patted her on the back. "Congratulations, you've successfully become the enemy."

"What a horrible man. I'd marry Hunter just to spite him."

Miles nodded. "I'll be a witness."

Hunter frowned. "This wasn't how I planned it."

"Janice and Doran got on well," Miles explained.

Brenna sighed. "Possibly because she has better manners."

Miles grimly shook his head. "I don't know how you will end this without him suspecting."

Hunter shoved a hand in his pocket. "Don't worry--"

Brenna and Miles shared a look then said, "We know. You have a plan."

They watched Doran speak to Curtis then both men came towards them--Curtis grinning, Doran looking smug. The trio instantly knew that didn't bode well.

Chapter Eleven

"Uncle Curtis has a fabulous idea," Doran said.

"You two must come to the ranch for Doran and Angie's anniversary. I want to get to know my future daughter-in-law some more so come early." He sent his son a secret look, making his casual statement an order. "I'll be expecting you."

Doran grinned. "See you there."

Brenna turned to Hunter as the men left. "Your cousin is a bastard."

"Actually he isn't, his mother is around here somewhere."

"That's not what I meant."

Miles raised his brows. "Is it time to panic?"

They both turned to him. "No."

He sighed wistful. "It's so nice to see two people so calm during a disaster."

Hunter shrugged. "It's a minor problem--"

"With a solution," Brenna finished.

Miles shook his head. "I'm pleased you two think so." He looked at Hunter. "I'll just take her for a little stroll while you think of a solution."

Hunter nodded, wanting to say no, but realizing he needed time to think. He watched the pair head for the garden, a strange restiveness descending as the pair disappeared out the door.

Ten minutes later, Brenna stood alone in the garden. She had convinced Miles she needed time alone, although she had enjoyed the tidbits of information he'd given her about Hunter (he liked to chew cinnamon gum when he was anxious or trying to figure out a problem). Right now she needed space.

She was glad to escape the walls of the ballroom. Although the spring air was ripe with the coming summer, she just wanted the night to end. She wanted to step off the stage forever and return to her life, her work. But she knew every time she saw a carousel or a storm darkened the sky he would enter her thoughts.

A FEW FEET AWAY, high on a balcony, Hunter thought about her. He watched her walk in the garden. He'd expected the evening to feel victorious. He had been promoted. Doran had lost; he'd won. Yet, the triumph felt empty.

"Are you in love with her?"

Hunter didn't turn at the sound of Ruby's voice. "No."

"I didn't think so."

"I loved once," he said in a grim tone. "I want her, there's no question, but I don't love her."

"Does she love you?"

He gripped the railing. "No."

"Would you like her to?"

He paused. "It's not a qualification."

"A what?"

"Never mind."

She spoke quietly. "So she won't marry you, hmm?"

He turned to her shocked.

Ruby slowly smiled. "Come on, Hunter. I know you. I know how you operate."

"Does Dad--"

"Know that this is all a facade? No. But be careful of your grandfather."

He rested his arms on the railing. "Yes, I know." He looked out at the garden and his frustration returned. "I can't figure her out. Why won't she marry me? I would treat her kindly, shower her with gifts, and whatever she wanted. And she'd have me as a husband."

Ruby shook her head with sympathy. "Poor Hunter, you don't even realize how arrogant that sounds."

"How can that be arrogant when I'm being truthful?" He rested a hand on his chest. "I'm a catch."

She merely sighed unsure how to explain the complicated feelings of a woman to him.

"Doesn't matter anyway," he said. "I've succeeded in executing one plan that, if not carefully concluded, will blow up in my face." He paused then said, "Here are the facts. I have formerly asked her to marry me, she has refused and after further consideration I may have to admit that she wouldn't make a suitable wife after all."

Ruby rested a hand on his arm. "You're very good with words Hunter, but what do you feel?"

That was the problem, he wasn't sure. He glanced at his watch. "I feel that it is time to go inside."

"Fine. You go then. I want to stay out here a little bit longer."

He nodded, his eyes briefly landing on the silhouette in the garden an emotion not quite clear flashing in his gaze. He turned abruptly and went inside.

Ruby watched him go then stared out at the same lonely figure below.

Hunter and Brenna drove back in silence. Neither discussed the success of the evening or what would happen next. All too soon they were in front of her apartment building.

Brenna's steps felt labored, almost painful as they walked across the parking lot and up the stairs. Hunter's steps were steady and sure--almost too much so.

She didn't want to leave him. Not because of any feeling of attachment although she was certain it was there. Something else bothered her. Something about his grandfather and his cousin. Why did she feel that if they separated tonight he was headed down a dangerous path? What could be so dangerous about an ambitious family? Why did Hunter seem so different somehow? She glanced at his profile. He definitely had the Randolph arrogance carved in the arch of his chin and nose. It was his damn mouth that was her undoing. Something vulnerable about him she wanted to protect. It was a silly thought, but wouldn't leave her.

"Thank you for this evening," he said.

"You're welcome."

He began to turn.

She took a step forward, resting a hand on his arm. "What if I were to say yes?"

He didn't misunderstand her. "I'd wonder why."

Brenna waved a dismissive hand and opened the door. "It's a stupid idea."

Hunter caught her wrist. "It's not a stupid idea. Why do you hesitate?"

"Because I have this dreadful feeling I could ruin things for you, yet another feeling that you need me."

"Of course I need you. How could you ruin things? I was promoted."

"I know." She tapped her cane. "I wonder why they made the announcement so soon. Why did they do it there in front of everyone?"

He shrugged. "Who cares?"

"If I were to marry you," she said slowly. "I do have some medical bills--"

He nodded. "Consider them taken care of."

Brenna tilted her head to the side and studied him: A man whose will equaled hers. She liked him and she trusted him and knew he would be a perfect match for her. "Okay. I will marry you."

Hunter folded his arms. "Why you little brat."

Her mouth fell. "What?"

His eyes lit with amusement. "You've been planning on marrying me this entire evening. No wonder you were so cool about Dad's invitation to the ranch. Why didn't you tell me before?"

Because the thought had just come to her. "I wanted to make sure I played the role well enough to convince you."

"And you wanted to make sure I secured the director's position."

She frowned. "No, that's not--"

"Clever move. I kept wondering what would convince you. You wanted to be sure that I'd get the promotion. You wanted to make sure that I truly had the drive to succeed and not waste my energy creating things like the Trandor cane and such--"

Brenna shook her head. She didn't like the picture he painted of her. "No, you don't--"

"It makes perfect sense. See? I do understand you. I have no aversion to being married for my position or money. At least you're honest about it." He drew her to him and held her snugly. "I've finally met your standards of a suitable spouse. I'm glad I have. With that kind of beginning we are certain to make this union work."

She looked up at him helplessly, knowing that he didn't understand how she felt and that she didn't want him just for what he could give her. "Yes, but--"

He stopped her with a kiss and soon she didn't care that their bargain sounded so cold. And he didn't care that his promotion had changed her mind. He deepened the kiss as he carried her to the couch. His hands roamed over her, gathering the silk dress in his fingers. He removed one spaghetti strap and kissed her shoulder, the floral scent of lilacs greeted him.

"We probably should stop," he mumbled.

"Yes." She placed a stream of kisses along his jaw, knowing she didn't want to stop. She wanted him body and soul.

His voice grew husky as his body responded to her. "But I'm not going to."

"I know."

Her hand eagerly ran up the length of his chest. "So which pocket are they in?"

"What?"

"Your condoms."

He slowly removed the other strap, his voice barely a whisper as his gaze roamed over her body. "I don't have condoms."

"Neither do I."

He stared at her stunned. "You're not taking anything?"

"No."

He thought for a moment, staring at the lace of her bra, and then said, "We could start a family tonight."

"No."

Hunter raised a brow, hopeful. "How about your friend next door?"

Brenna looked at him outraged. "I couldn't ask her for condoms."

He stood. "I could."

"No. Don't!"

He was out the door before she could stop him. He knocked on the door.

"Shh!" Brenna said behind him. "Do you want to wake everybody up?"

"No, just her." He knocked again. Brenna grabbed his hand; he raised his other one determined.

Fortunately, Tima opened the door before he knocked once more. To Brenna's relief she looked wide awake. "Yes?"

Brenna stepped in front of Hunter. "Sorry to ask you this, and I realize this is very inconsiderate of us to ask such a favor, especially at this time of night when you were probably very relaxed doing something else and here we are barging in on your privacy. However we were wondering --"

Hunter covered Brenna's mouth. "Do you have any condoms?"

Tima opened the door wider and smiled. "I have a selection."

"We aren't picky."

She turned. "I'll be right back."

Brenna removed Hunter's hand. "Let me chose."

"Why? I'll have to wear it."

She playfully nudged him. "Don't be difficult."

He nudged her back. "I'm never difficult."

Tima came out with a box. "I have flavored, glow in the dark, massage."

Brenna picked up one. "This looks interesting."

Hunter shook his head. "I'm not wearing a pink condom with things on the end. Looks like I have an infectious disease." He grabbed one. "This will do."

Tima raised a mocking brow. "Only one?"

"You're right." He took the box. "Don't worry I'll reimburse you. Come on Brenna."

Brenna followed unable to look at her friend.

She met him a few moments later in the bedroom, suddenly conscious of his magnetic, commanding appeal. There was no turning back from this moment and she had no plans to. Brenna wanted to be in the circle of his arms, feel him inside her. She licked her lips, trying to tame the tingling in the pit of her stomach. "Did you have to take the entire box?"

He tossed his shirt. "No."

Brenna swallowed soaking in his muscular, towering strength. Be gentle with me she wanted to say, but instead said, "Should we consider this sealing the bargain?" faking a nonchalance she didn't feel.

He unzipped his trousers. "Can't you talk and undress at the same time?"

"Of course."

"Then why aren't you?" He lifted a sly brow. "Nervous?"

Brenna pulled off her dress with trembling fingers and sat with her back to him. "I'm not nervous."

"How long has it been?" he asked softly, with a tenderness she hadn't expected.

"None of your business."

Hunter clicked his tongue in teasing pity. "That long?" He unlatched her bra, his knuckles brushing against her skin in a slow caress.

Her hands flew to her chest. "Hey!"

"You're taking too long," he said in a deep, coaxing voice.

She turned to him. He was naked and properly fitted. "Oh I see."

"Yes, and I'm waiting." He removed her hands and took off her bra. When his hands dropped to her panties she stopped him.

"I can do that myself."

"Fine, but let's get one thing clear."

"What?"

"I'll marry you anyway."

Her mouth fell open. "Anyway?"

"In case it's not any good."

"And why would you think it wouldn't be any good?" Brenna asked in clipped tones.

"I just know you're nervous."

"I'm not nervous."

Hunter rubbed the bare skin of her back, sending a warming shiver through her. "It's okay. I think it's sweet."

"I'm not nervous," she repeated with more force, hoping to convince him and herself.

"So far you're all talk."

Brenna swallowed hard then took a deep breath gathering her courage, afraid she would disappoint him and embarrass herself.

"Then let's stop talking," she said boldly. She pulled him towards her, but he kissed her first. With lips that could be classified as a dangerous weapon. They were as soft as they looked and drained her of any inhibitions as they left a moist trail up her cheek to her ear. "Not the ear."

"But I like your ears." He caught a lobe lightly between his teeth.

"I don't care."

He grumbled something she couldn't understand then kissed a path down her chest. He stopped between her breasts and rested his cheek against one then the other.

"What are you doing?"

"Surveying the landscape."

"And staking claim?"

"I will in a minute." He skimmed a hand over her stomach. "Stop holding your breath."

"I'm not holding my breath."

"Then stop sucking in...there that's better."

She felt heat rise, not from passion but embarrassment.

He suddenly stopped. "You're not enjoying this."

"Yes, I am."

"You're not even touching me. You're lying like a board. I know we're going to be married, but you don't have to treat this like a civic duty."

She circled one of his nipples with her forefinger. "Okay, I admit I'm a little nervous."

"Why?"

Brenna traced the other nipple a grin tugging on her lips. "Because I'm afraid you won't be able to keep up with me," she said ready to be reckless. She arched into him, surrendering to her decision that there would be no other man after this. "I'm not sure that you can satisfy all my needs."

His tone became a husky whisper. "I will satisfy needs you didn't even know you had."

Hunter covered her body and she relinquished herself to his

passionate assault, letting go of her dream of finding the perfect match and once she did something within her began to grow, soon she enjoyed the scents and textures of his skin. His fingers stirring her emotions making her bare skin feel as fragile as papyrus. She moved against the sleek caress of his body as heat spread through her. When she welcomed him inside her, something that was dying burst forth, spreading its arms wide and declaring itself. She was still a woman although she'd let Byron's hurtful words convince her that she didn't have a right to be.

Hunter knew she was all woman. She felt better than he'd thought. Tasted better. He remembered his first taste of rum. How it burned going down. Brenna had the same effect. His body burned and wanted more. He soon rolled off her and fell on his back.

She turned to him. "What did you think?"

"I enjoyed myself."

"Nothing earth-shattering."

"Who needs the earth to shatter?"

"I don't."

"Neither do I."

She bit her lip and grinned. "Want to try again?"

The second time had them breathless, by the third time Brenna nearly collapsed under the raw warmth of his body and the primitive energy that electrified the air between them. In his arms she could be any woman—she wasn't different. She was whole and unscarred. But he was far from being just any man. His name suited him and he had hunted until he'd tapped into her pleasure spot and aroused desires and sensations she didn't know existed. When they finally broke away the only sound in the room was their labored breathing. Brenna looked at him then down. She reached out and touched his erection. "We can't keep your little friend down, can we?"

Hunter shot her a glance. "He takes offense to the word 'little'."

"Oh." She rolled off his condom then touched the tip of her tongue to his penis. "I'm sorry."

"And you're not going to get him down by doing that."

"Who says I want him to go down?"

For the next hour Brenna made herself well acquainted with his friend and then Hunter made himself acquainted with hers. After they were both satisfied with their introductions they lay back and stared at the ceiling.

"Would you like something to drink?" Brenna managed to ask although she wasn't sure she could move.

"I'd like some coffee," Hunter grumbled.

She sat up and grabbed a robe. "Coffee takes time."

He stretched his arms the length of the headboard. "That's fine. I'm not going anywhere."

She went into the kitchen and prepared the coffee. He came up behind her and kissed the curve of her neck.

She jabbed him with her elbow. "I thought you had enough."

"I changed my mind. Ow!" He rubbed where she'd hit him. "Then you'd better give me something else to do."

"Sit down and twiddle your thumbs."

He sat. "I don't know how to twiddle."

"Think about your promotion."

He clasped his hands behind his head and smiled. "What a great evening."

Brenna stared at him stunned. She covered her mouth to keep from laughing. She failed.

"What?"

"You have dimples."

Hunter's smile disappeared, he let his hands fall. "Damn."

She handed him his coffee and sat. "You have a wonderful smile. Though you're right. It doesn't quite fit your image."

"Like putting bows on a rotwelier," he said disgusted.

"I could just picture you as a little boy."

He took a sip of his coffee. "I got them from my mother. She loved to smile." He sat back in his chair. "That's one of the few things I remember about her."

"And you don't smile because you don't want to be like her?"

"No, I don't smile because I don't want to remind anyone of her. She was different, that's why she couldn't stay."

"And you're not different?"

He met her eyes. "No. I'm like the rest of the family. Ambitious and determined."

"But if you were different, would that be bad?"

He shrugged. "I'm not different so I don't worry about it."

She nodded although she didn't understand.

He took another sip of coffee then stared at the rim of the mug puzzled. "This is lipstick." He wiped his mouth and stared at the napkin. He sent her an accusing look. "Why didn't you tell me I was wearing lipstick?"

Brenna fluttered her lashes. "It was your shade."

"Hmm." Hunter finished his coffee then set it down. "I don't want a long engagement."

"I know."

"You won't regret your decision I promise you."

"No need for promises. We're in this together."

"You're going to marry him?"

Brenna sighed, watching her friend across the restaurant table. "Pauline, calm down."

Tima ate the pineapple slice from her pina colada. "Congratulations."

Pauline tapped the table agitated. "Didn't I warn you to be careful? How did he persuade you? Diamonds, a new car?"

"It's not--"

She narrowed her eyes. "I know. He promised you a new wardrobe and while that would certainly persuade me, it shouldn't have been a deciding factor for you."

"He needs me and I need him."

Pauline stared as though about to choke. "Why?"

"He needs a wife and I could use some help with medical costs."

"That isn't a reason to marry him."

Brenna peppered her broccoli soup. "It's reason enough for me."

"So you're marrying him for his money?"

She set the pepper down. "In a way. I was upfront about this."

"You realize this makes you a gold digger."

Tima popped a cheese fry in her mouth. "Dig deep, sister."

Pauline sent her a look. "Marriage is a big step." She pointed a finger at Brenna. "Once he has you, he'll forget about you."

"I'll make sure that he doesn't. You don't have to be happy for me, but I'd prefer you stop discouraging me. I've made up my mind."

Pauline sighed. "I think you're making a mistake."

"I would never have guessed."

"At least marry someone who cares about you."

"Hunter cares about me."

"He cares about his promotion." She reached over and grabbed her hands. "Oh, Brenna, don't be desperate. You deserve better."

"I'm not desperate. I know what I want, and I'm taking the steps to get there. Plus think of how it will look for business. I would be married to a very eligible bachelor. A married matchmaker gets more business. You hinted at that once. I've thought this through."

Pauline sat back in her chair, folded her arms and flashed a skeptical look, but didn't reply.

To her amazement Stephen was just as unenthusiastic.

"I thought you liked him," Brenna said, switching the phone to her other ear.

"I do, but marrying a guy for his money? That's not like you."

"He's marrying me for a promotion. Isn't that the same thing?"

He was silent a moment then said, "Marriage is hard enough when you love each other, when you don't—"

"We understand each other."

"Divorce is hard you know."

"Why would you even think that way?"

"I don't want to see you get hurt."

Brenna slid into the couch. "That won't happen. I'll never let a man hurt me again."

VIRGINIA in the spring is very much like the Virgin Queen after which she was named--proud and prosperous. Especially on mornings when daylight arrives in hand with a soft mist swirling across tall grass that undulates like waves against the breeze. Brenna marveled at such a morning as she sat on a little mare Hunter had given her. It was their third ride and she was quickly becoming accustomed to being on a horse again. She had been an avid rider when she was young and occasionally took lessons when her doctor encouraged her to exercise. But to her it wasn't exercise, it was freedom.

She glanced at the Victorian house in the distance. On its white wraparound porch, she, Hunter and his parents had sipped raspberry lemonade for the past two evenings and talked about the wedding. She was glad she and Hunter had arrived early so that she could feel part of the family without his grandfather's watchful eyes.

The late spring air lifted the perfume from the rambling peony border around the house where white blooms burst with shots of yellow. She looked at Hunter on his stallion, a large brown horse with eyes just as intense and clever as its rider. Her mare took little notice of either of them. Brenna couldn't do the same. She was looking at her future husband.

It seemed appropriate that now surrounded by this open country where foxes and beavers ran wild that she would face the reality of her choice. She waited for unease, shock, doubt to hit, but none of those emotions claimed her, just a gentle peace, a firm knowing.

Suddenly, she felt wild, free, impulsive.

"Race you to those trees!" she called. Before he could reply she broke into a run. She was a shadow through the mist, becoming the wind; her horse the air. She could have ridden until time melted into nothingness, but she reined in at her destination. She threw Hunter a smug grin when he stopped beside her.

"Don't ever do that again," he said.

She raised a brow. "Did I worry you?"

He crossed his forearms over the pommel and glared at her. "Was that your goal?"

"You didn't need to worry. I know how to ride."

His eyes swept over the horse then her. "Obviously." He turned his stallion. "But don't ever do that again."

She followed. "What? Race you?"

"No." He shot her a glance. "Win."

She laughed and they trotted back to the stables.

THAT EVENING, Brenna changed for the reception with mounting dread. She did not look forward to meeting Doran or his grandfather again. So she was thrilled to see only Ruby and another woman holding a baby, sitting in the parlor room. They looked settled in the casual elegance of the room where hand stitched pillows lay on the sofa, and a dyed turquoise tapered vase welcomed conversation. She smiled at Ruby then introduced herself to the woman she assumed was Doran's wife, Angie.

She was not a beautiful woman. She didn't need to be. She had the confidence and grace that was devastatingly attractive to men and envied by most women. Dark eyes nearly swallowed up a heart shaped face. Her straight black hair curled up at the end.

"Hello, I'm Brenna." She glanced down at the baby's perfect, fine features. "He's beautiful."

"Thank you. His name is James." The woman smiled. There was no pretense in the expression so Brenna began to relax. "I'm glad we get to meet. My husband told me about you."

Brenna sat down beside her and grimaced. "That can't be good."

"I like to form my own opinions. I'm Angelina by the way."

Brenna started. "Angelina? Funny a couple weeks back Hunter was talking about a woman..." She stopped at the look on her face. "You mean..?" For some reason she couldn't finish the sentence.

She nodded. "Yes, I'm his ex-wife."

Chapter Twelve

Brenna didn't remember the rest of the evening, what was said or done. She moved as though in a dream. Faces and voices blended together. All that was clear was Angelina and Hunter. The woman Hunter had loved, could possibly still love, was only a few feet away from him, holding her perfect baby. A baby that could have been his. A perfect baby she may not be able to give him. She didn't love him so she didn't understand the wild surge of jealousy that gripped her.

She watched Angelina as Doran planted a kiss on her cheek, the love for her clear in his gaze. She hadn't thought him capable of such tenderness. She wondered if Angelina knew how lucky she was to have two men who'd married her for love. At dinner she could barely eat, her skin burning with anger and a sense of betrayal every time Hunter brushed against her. The tilapia, roasted potatoes and sautéed asparagus tasted like paper.

She could feel Orson's speculative stare as he sat at the head of the table. "I didn't picture you to be the quiet type," he said.

Brenna focused on her dinner, determined not to spar with him.

"Tonight I wish to enjoy a wonderful dinner and celebrate a long and successful marriage."

Audrey nodded. "Very beautifully said."

Angelina sent her a grateful smile. "Yes, thank you."

Orson grunted. "Hopefully, you'll give us a grandchild sooner than this pair."

Audrey touched his hand. "Let's not talk about it right now."

He pulled away. "I can talk about what I want to."

"Not when you're in the minority," Hunter said in a quiet tone. "And I can assure you that no one else wishes to discuss the topic."

"Oh, I'm not so sure," Doran said. "You plan everything else. Your family planning schedule may be of interest."

Hunter cut his tilapia in one swift movement. "Only if you would like to share why your family planning took so long."

Angelina touched Doran's sleeve before he replied.

Ruby turned towards the large window. "It's a lovely evening, don't you agree Brenna?"

"It's a lovely property," she said.

"You and Hunter are always welcome."

"We'll remember that." Hunter patted Brenna's hand. It took all her might not to pull away. His touch felt like needles sticking her flesh.

"Has he shown you the attic? When he was a little boy he used to be up there for hours."

Brenna feigned interest. "Doing what?"

"Creating things. We could never understand exactly what they were. His mother--" She stopped. A startled silence fell as though the chandelier had come crashing down from the ceiling.

Brenna glanced around the table amazed by the silence. "His mother what?"

"His mother liked to go there," Ruby said vaguely. "I believe it's time for dessert." She rang the bell, effectively stopping the topic.

After dessert they left the dining room and indulged in after dinner drinks and conversation but soon the air in the house felt too thin. Brenna escaped out to the porch and walked down the steps to the peonies. She bent down to inhale their scent. Suddenly, she felt an arm around her lifting her up. An anxious voice said, "Are you all right?"

She struggled against his hold. "I'm fine, Hunter. Let me go. I was just smelling the flowers."

"Oh." He released her and picked one up. "There."

"You didn't have to kill it." She brought the blossom to her nose and saw a sleeping ladybug inside. She gently set it back down then glanced up and took a hasty step back, surprised by the sight she saw. Hunter stood holding James, the baby asleep on his shoulder.

"What are you doing with him?"

He glanced at the baby with affection. "He was throwing one of his tantrums and I was able to calm him down. Everyone else just panics." He shoved his free hand in his pocket. "You've been strangely quiet."

"I thought it best to hold my tongue."

"Shame. I was looking forward to some sword play."

"Then let me start with you."

"By all means." He took his hand out of his pocket when she didn't continue. "Well?"

"I'm trying to think up the best way to insult you."

"Making me wait seems to be working."

"You forgot to tell me something."

"I did?"

"Yes." She tapped the head of her cane. "This afternoon I had the pleasure of meeting Doran's gracious wife, Angie; I also had the privilege of meeting your ex-wife, Angelina. Imagine my surprise when I realized they were the same woman."

He rubbed his forehead with regret. "I should have told you."

She tapped harder. "Is that an apology?"

"Things have happened so fast between us it didn't seem important. She's my past."

Brenna took a deep breath, trying to keep calm. "Your ex-wife, the woman whose very voice you loved, is married to your cousin and you didn't think it was important?"

"In all honesty, no." He shrugged nonchalant. "I don't have a good excuse."

"Let me be generous and give you one."

He bowed in challenge. "Proceed."

"She still means something to you. That's why you didn't tell me."

He shook his head. "No."

"Every time you look at her and James you think he could have been yours."

His eyes darkened dangerously. "No, he's not mine and I know that."

"Then why are you holding him right now as if it were the most natural thing in the world?"

"I told you why."

"Because you're the only one who can calm him?" she said doubtful.

"Yes."

"But I think it's because he's Angie's son."

"He's family. He's my blood and I love him for it. Nothing more. I don't look back. I never look back." He touched the curve of her neck, the warmth of his fingers only feeding the fire of anger within her. "Hopefully within a year I'll have a son of my own."

"Then we'd better start looking at adoption agencies."

His hand fell. "Adoption? I thought we'd have our own first then we can adopt if you like."

"I don't want to have children."

"But I do."

She nodded. "There are plenty of women who will carry a child for you."

He frowned. "I don't want that."

"Why not? It's an option. Just like getting a stranger to marry you."

"You're not a stranger and as my wife it's your duty to have my child."

"Yes, my duty as part of the plan," she said grimly realizing the weight of the bargain she'd made. "As much as I would like to fulfill my duty I recognize that it is impossible."

His voice became gentle. "You can't have children?"

"I can. But I don't like to lose."

"Neither do I."

"Then let's make sure the odds are in our favor." She patted her bad leg with sadness and regret, remembering how Byron had rejected her and her mother's fears that no man would want her. "This is genetic. It could be passed down."

"Could be is not a definitive term."

"But there's a risk. Doran and Angelina's children will be strong while yours could end up like me."

He glanced up at the sky exasperated. "What's the likelihood?"

"Too high to try."

His gaze met hers. "He could be healthy. Or he could be deaf or blind or anything! That won't make him any less my son."

"Yes, your son. There are many ways to achieve that without me. I'll raise him and --"

"No." He spun away.

She poked him with her cane. "Don't turn your back on me."

He slowly turned around. "Forgive me. I thought this discussion was finished."

Brenna set her cane down. She briefly shut her eyes. "I can bear many things, but I couldn't bear to marry a man whose children may be a disappointment to him. I know how it feels to have a father who doesn't..." She bit her lip. "I have no qualms knowing that you don't love me, but I will not stand by if you don't love our kids."

"Brenna--"

She blinked away tears as she glanced at James resting his little head on Hunter's broad shoulders with the beautiful innocence that comes with complete trust and security. "You have a good heart and I know you'll try to love the child whatever he or she may be, but this rivalry between you and Doran will affect that and our marriage. Our child would always be compared to theirs. We could lie and say I'm unable to have children and get a surrogate. It will be the same."

"No."

Her voice fell. "I will make an excellent wife, a great hostess, but this is one area I can't control. I know my limitations. I just can't compete. Not in this way."

"This isn't a competition."

"Of course it is. Your grandfather likes to fuel it too."

"It keeps us on our toes."

"But this isn't about business, this is personal. This is between you and Doran. You still love her."

"No, I don't," he said in a low voice. James shifted and his face scrunched up as though he wanted to cry, but Hunter gently stroked the baby's head until he settled and relaxed again.

His tenderness tore at Brenna's heart because all she could see was the love he'd had and could still have for Angie. "How do you know?"

Hunter hesitated, then clenched his teeth. "I just do."

"Because you've told yourself you don't love her?"

"Brenna, this has nothing to do with Angie."

"I know she's a soft spot, which means something."

He rubbed the back of his neck, as if he'd wished he hadn't shared that with her. "My marriage is a soft spot not Angie."

"Wasn't she part of it?"

"You don't understand. This is between us, no one else. As my wife you will have my children. Why are we arguing about something that isn't even a concern yet?"

"Because it will be. I know. I've lived it."

"This is different. As I agreed I will pay for your medical bills. If necessary, I will pay for any surgery or procedures our children may need if it came to that."

What if it did? Would it be fair to watch her child go through the series of surgeries she'd suffered in the effort to become normal? Had Byron been right to call her desires selfish? "I don't know."

"The bargain is to perform all the duties of a wife."

"So there's no compromise? No room for negotiations?"

He paused, for a moment looking uncertain, then shook his head.

Brenna fell quiet not sure if she was angry or disappointed then asked, "So, am I on probation now or am I fired?"

His gaze pierced hers. "It's up to you whether you wish to stay or quit."

She pulled off the ring with a steady hand.

He stared at her, ignoring the ring she held out to him. "You don't want to do this."

Brenna reached out and touched James' soft curls then let her hand fall. Here was something Hunter could freely love even he'd never admit that his heart belonged to someone else. "Yes, I do. I didn't realize how deep this game was. How much you needed to win it. I'm afraid I can't give you the winning advantage." She took his hand and placed the ring in his palm.

Hunter gripped it, his voice quiet. "I thought you weren't afraid of anything."

Brenna turned.

He jumped in front of her. "Was that a lie?" She tried to move around him. He blocked her path, his voice hardened. "Was it?"

She spoke in a raw, quiet voice. "Yes, it was a lie. Yes, I have fears. I'm afraid of being a failure. It terrifies me that it's possible that all that I do, all that I am will never be enough. Never. If I married you, how will I know that you aren't comparing me to her? That she doesn't still claim a part of you?"

His tone became amused. "You almost sound jealous."

"I am jealous. Jealous that everywhere I turn I seem to bump into my limitations."

"Because you put them in front of you."

She began to move around him.

He grabbed her arm. "Okay. I admit that I've handled this wrong.

But believe me when I say that this--us--has nothing to do with Angie or Doran or anyone else. This is about two people--"

"Following your plan. Don't you remember that the entire basis of this marriage was so you could get a promotion? I would have to say this marriage includes a lot of people. Do you think your grandfather would take kindly---"

"He'll learn to watch his tongue."

Brenna studied him a moment. He believed what he said, even if he was lying to himself. He honestly believed that their marriage could become something real: Something that wasn't about pressure, competition and dominance. She'd stop this charade for his sake as well as hers. She turned away. "I can't."

"So you're just going to walk away?" Hunter called after her.

She kept walking.

"You'll let fear rule your life?" he asked as a challenge.

She stopped then looked at him ready to offer him her own challenge. "Speaking of fear. Why don't you want to remind anyone of your mother? Why won't anyone mention her name or talk about her? What is the Randolph family afraid of?"

Chapter Thirteen

A pale sun splashed light over the parlor room early the next morning. It barely touched Hunter who sat in the corner, staring at the ring Brenna had left behind. It had only been a few hours since her departure. It seemed longer. In a casual tone he'd explained at breakfast that the wedding was off. His parents didn't take much notice, believing it was a simple lover's quarrel that would soon be settled. His grandfather nodded, sharing that he knew she had a temper. Hunter knew in time the truth would come to light.

Doran sauntered into the room and stood near the bay windows, looking out at the pristine lawn and white clouds. "You deserve a standing ovation, cousin. That was skillfully planned." He turned to Hunter. "You present a fiancée, secure the director's position, lose her and keep the director's position all within a week and no one suspects a thing." He stood by the chair where Hunter sat and patted him on the shoulder. "Impressive."

Hunter twirled the ring between his fingers.

"Answer one question for me." Doran bent over, resting his hands on the armrests. "Was she really crippled or was that part of the act?"

Hunter's hand shot out like lightning and grabbed Doran's collar.

His eyes slammed into his. "She has a limp. How would you like to walk with one?"

Doran grabbed Hunter's wrist even as he began to see stars. "You don't scare me," he wheezed.

"I'm not trying to scare you." He tightened his grip. "I'm trying to hurt you."

Angelina entered the room. "Hunter, let go of my husband," she said absently as though they were two children at play.

"You'll have to give me a good reason."

"Hunter," she warned.

He casually shoved him away.

Doran stumbled into a table then regained his balance. He rubbed his neck. "People lacking intellect always resort to violence."

"People lacking intellect also don't know when to stop," his wife countered with a significant look.

Doran straightened his collar.

"I want to speak to Hunter alone."

"You won't get far."

She gently pushed her husband towards the exit. "I'll get farther than you." Once Doran was gone she looked at Hunter. "So what happened?"

"He got on my nerves."

Angelina sat on the sofa and gestured for him to join her. He ignored it. "I'm not talking about Doran."

"I don't think there's anything else that is your business."

"Come on Hunter we used to be friends."

He pushed Brenna's ring into his pocket. "Yes, and I used to love you. Neither is true anymore."

Her voice was barely a whisper. "You could have asked me to stay. You didn't have to give me up so easily. If you'd fought for me--"

"Is that what you'd wanted? A fight? I didn't realize it was the husband's duty to fight for his wife's fidelity. Sorry to have disappointed you."

She frowned. "That's not what I meant."

"I loved you. I wanted you to be happy no matter how much that-
-" He drummed his fingers on the armrest. "Are you happy?"

"Very."

Hunter stood. "Then the story has a happy ending."

"But it's not the end. You--"

He picked up one of the pillows and studied its design. "You loved Doran, he loved you. You may have wanted me to be your rescuing knight for one day, but you would have grown to despise me. Don't blame me for our failed marriage. There were two people involved and only one heart."

Angelina's voice grew sad. "So you'll continue to hate me?"

Hunter threw the pillow on the couch. "Don't be dramatic. I'll never hate you." He went to the window. "I don't even dislike you."

She smiled. "That's something."

"Your husband; however, is an exception."

"You used to be friends."

He shook his head. "No, we were never friends. We just tolerated each other more."

"Then you should start again."

He turned, wary. "What do you mean?"

She bit her lower lip then said, "You and I both know Doran deserves the director's position."

He smiled coldly. "So that's what this is about." He nodded amazed. "Clever maneuver. For a fleeting moment I thought you cared about me." He clasped his hands behind his back. "I only intend to concede once in my life. I've already done that."

"You'll never be happy until this rivalry stops. Until Doran stops being the reason you go after things."

"That argument doesn't work. Try another one."

Angelina stood. "Why do you make it so tempting for women to walk out on you?"

He grabbed her arm as she passed him, his voice hard. "Is that your excuse for infidelity?"

Her eyes pierced his. "I was always true to you."

"But not to our vows." He let her arm go. "I made it easy for you to leave because I found no reason to make you stay."

Her bottom lip quivered. "You're being cruel."

"No, just honest. Think about how relieved you felt when I let you go." His voice deepened. "How you told me that my love scared you."

"It did. It was too much."

Her words hurt him as they had many years ago. Naturally, he gave no indication of that as he sat down and stared up at her with a bored expression. "Well then."

But Angelina knew him too well to let his expression deceive her. "You can continue to try, but you're not like the others. There's something different about you. Like your mother--"

"You never knew my mother."

She folded her arms. "Sometimes when I'm with you, I think I did."

Ruby entered the room before he could reply. Angelina turned. "I'll go check on James."

Hunter gathered his anger as Ruby sat. "Are you the next shift to look after me?"

Ruby took no offense to his tone. "You should have told Brenna about Angie," she said, quickly assessing the reason for Brenna's departure.

"I know. She thinks I still love her."

"Do you?"

He tugged on the cuffs of his shirt. "Do I act as though I still do?"

She crossed her ankles and adjusted her skirt. "When did your rivalry with Doran start?"

He sent her a sharp glance. "That was different. We've never got on."

"But once you knew he and Angelina were in love it turned to hate."

"Hate takes too much energy. He merely disgusts me."

"And when he married Angelina you were determined to beat him at everything."

"I have a plan for my life that's all. If he happens to be in the way…" He shrugged. "I have no qualms about crushing him on the way there."

Ruby grasped his hand. "He will always be in the way as long as you make him."

He pulled away. "Is my director's position still secure?"

"Your fiancée just left you."

"That wasn't my question."

"Perhaps it should be."

He stood, restless. "Have grandfather and Dad said anything about—"

"No, they think things will smooth over."

"Good." Hunter clasped his hands together and began to pace. "I can transition into the new position and perhaps put off the marriage agenda for a while. Or I could start another search."

"That wouldn't look good. First Janice. Now Brenna. That doesn't give the impression of a stable man. You can't introduce another fiancée."

"I'll explain Brenna away."

"You can't—"

His eyes flashed. "What do you expect me to do? Bow down and beg her forgiveness? She's putting everything that I've worked for in jeopardy."

"Maybe she's showing you there are other things in life."

"Like what?"

"Family."

"I know about family."

"No, you know about duty and loyalty and allegiance."

"The Randolph way."

Ruby sighed resigned. "Yes, I know."

Hunter folded his arms and pierced her with a cold stare. "Why did you mention my mother at dinner?"

She hesitated. "I wasn't thinking."

"Are you trying to sabotage me?"

"Of course not."

"Did Brenna put you up to it?"

"No."

He shoved one hand in his pocket. "It's not like you to make mistakes like that."

She stood and straightened the vase. "I met your mother once."

He took his hand out, curious despite himself. "What did you think?"

"She was full of spirit, but there's something you should know about her—"

"There's nothing he needs to know," Orson cut in, entering the room.

Ruby jumped and turned. "I was just—"

"There's no need to delve into the past when we have the rigorous future staring us in the face. His mother left him, that's painful enough."

"Yes."

He sat and stared up at Hunter. "You have a bad habit of women leaving you. Like your father."

Ruby sent him a look of such venom, he coughed chagrined. "I'm sure you'll do whatever it takes to get her back." He lowered his gaze. "However, if you find it necessary to find yourself another one we'll understand."

Hunter rested his hands on his hips. "You didn't like her."

"That's not true."

"You're too clever to look innocent."

Orson chuckled at Hunter's insight. "No, I didn't like her much. You want a wife who's well tamed. That one has a wild streak. Don't let that limp of hers fool you."

"I'm not easily fooled."

"A pretty face can fool any man."

"Not me."

"Women like that are better as mistresses; you want your wife to be more biddable if you get my meaning."

Ruby went to the window. "He isn't like you, Orson. Brenna is good for him." She turned to the two men. "And if he has any brains in his head he'll do whatever it takes to get her back."

"Randolph men don't beg. She doesn't come back to you, you get a replacement."

"Women aren't possessions. You don't just replace them."

"Honey, I think you're forgetting what you were."

Ruby gasped then raised her chin. Hunter watched her leave the room then shook his head. "That wasn't fair."

"I didn't get here by being fair. Too much leniency and people begin to walk all over you. Your father found a replacement. You can do the same." He paused. "I expect you to."

Chapter Fourteen

Hunter didn't return from Virginia until late evening. He stumbled exhausted into his place then paused when he saw a light on in the kitchen. A familiar scent drifted towards him.

He stormed into the kitchen where Janice sat finishing a fruit cocktail. "What are you doing here?" he demanded.

She jumped. "Oh, you startled me."

"I'm sorry," he said sarcastic. "Next time I'll knock when I come home."

"I expected a much warmer welcome than this."

He turned, opened the fridge and pulled out a soda. He took a long swallow then held out his hand. "Give me back the key."

"Listen to me first."

He wiggled his fingers impatient. "You can start talking as you hand back the key."

She reluctantly did so. "I guess your trip to Virginia wasn't as good as you'd hoped, but Doran always put you in a bad mood."

He put the key in his pocket and took another swallow. "Funny, you're not doing too bad yourself."

"I'm about to change that."

He set the can down suspicious. "How?"

"I want a second chance."

"To do what?"

"Be your wife."

He folded his arms and smiled. "Very funny."

"You're the only man I know whose dimples make him look both wicked and cute."

He stopped smiling. "If this is a joke, I'm waiting to laugh."

"Hunter, I'm serious. Michael and I ended our engagement. He's not right for me. He's still trying to establish himself and I'd much rather have a husband who already is."

He pulled out a chair and sat. "By established you mean wealthy, right?"

She pouted. "You're being mean."

He tweaked her chin. "Stop that. I want the facts. Nuances and euphemisms annoy me."

Janice straightened her face. "At the banquet I saw another side of you." She reached out and stroked his arm. "I found it very attractive. I know that you and Brenna were together for show so it's not as though I'm breaking you up." She grasped his hand and lowered her voice eager to please him. "I'm prepared to go with your plan. The marriage, the kids everything."

"I see."

She blinked. "That's it?"

He sat back in his chair and stared at her. "Yes."

"I think I love you."

He nearly burst into laughter. He managed to keep a straight face. "No, you don't. And you don't have to."

"I could learn."

He looked at her. He'd always liked doing so. She was very attractive. That was one of the first things he'd noticed about her when she became a woman instead of a teenager of all knees and elbows. She was well educated, shallow, but that made her easy to read. One thing a busy man didn't want was a complicated wife. All the reasons he had wanted to marry her before were still relevant and as suspected her engagement with Michael had been impulsive and rash. She'd come to her senses and realized what a good husband he would be. And he would be a good husband. Yes, the situation was perfect. Nevertheless he knew her and he knew that wasn't why she was here.

He undid the top button of his shirt. "You might as well undress."

Her eyes widened. "What?"

"That's why you came, didn't you? To have sex. You always come to me when you want to feel better."

"No, I came to say I'd marry you."

Hunter shook his head and rolled up his sleeves. "You don't want to marry me. You want the security of being married to me. I don't blame you, but you've made your choice. You're in love with him."

She stared at him unsure. "So you won't marry me?"

He rested his forearms on the table. "Oh, I'll marry you, but you'll have to do one little thing."

THE LAST PERSON Brenna expected to see in her office that Tuesday afternoon was Michael Peterson. She knew his presence was a bad sign, but decided not to take it as one. She offered him a bright smile. "This is a nice surprise. How may I help you?"

He didn't return her expression. "I need you to reopen my file."

Definitely a bad sign. "Why?"

"Janice and I broke up."

"You both need time away from each other that's all. Every relationship hits a rough spot."

His voice turned gloomy. "This is a big rough spot."

"What are you talking about?"

His brows furrowed confused. "I thought you'd know about it."

"About what?"

"She's marrying your ex-fiancée."

Her cool expression slipped. "What?"

"Yes," he said in a sour voice. "She told me she's convinced Hunter to take her back. She's going to get a new ring."

Brenna took a deep breath determined not to let the news shake her. So he thought he could marry Janice and ruin the lives of two people meant for each other for the sake of his 'plan'? No, she wouldn't let that happen. He'd have to find another suitable wife.

She folded her arms and stared at Michael without sympathy. "Hunter plans to marry Janice. Is that correct?"

Michael nodded. "Yes."

"Then what are you doing here?"

He looked blank. "What?"

"The woman you love is going to marry someone else who will probably make her miserable."

He shrugged. "He seems like a nice guy."

She leaned forward, resting her hands on the desk. "Michael, that's not the point. He doesn't love her. Doesn't she deserve someone who will care for and about her?"

"Yes."

"Then do something."

He looked wary. "Hunter is a big guy."

"I'm not suggesting a wrestling match, but sometimes a woman needs to know what a man feels. Let's be honest Janice is a little spoiled, but she needs to know that you're more than worthy of her. That your feelings for each other can sustain you, unlike riches."

Michael straightened, gaining courage from her words. "You're right."

"Are you going to live your life with regret wondering if you could have done more?"

"No."

"Are you going to let the woman you love make a big mistake?"

"No."

"Then I expect to be at your wedding."

His shoulders slumped. "I don't know."

Brenna groaned disgusted. She would have to fix things. "Get out of here. I'll call you later."

He stood watching her reach for the phone with gathering anxiety. "What are you going to do?"

"Nothing you need to worry about. Just be prepared when I call you."

"Okay." He ducked out of the room.

She called Hunter. "You can't marry Janice."

"Actually, I can. I want to thank you. It was your performance at the banquet that fixed everything. She realized that she'd wanted to marry a more established man. Seems everything came around full circle."

"She's marrying you for your money."

His voice grew bland. "I'm shocked."

"She loves Michael." Brenna could almost hear him shrug. "So you will take the risk of marrying a woman in love with another man again?"

"I was willing to marry you."

"I'm not in love with Byron anymore."

He paused then said, "I want a wife and unless you have another option for me..."

She gripped the phone. "Why you sneaky bastard. That's what you're up to."

"I'm merely making a suggestion. Either I marry you or Janice. The choice is yours."

"You will not blackmail me into marriage."

"I prefer the word persuade."

"Michael can win her back."

"Not when I'm in the picture," he said confident. "I don't plan on traveling any time soon."

She knew he was right.

"Are the medical bills still piling up?"

Brenna drummed her fingers. She'd just finished arguing with her insurance over the amount of one of the deductibles. She glanced at her cane and thought about Michael's face. "I have a proposition."

"Yes?"

"If you succeed in getting Janice and Michael back together, I will marry you."

"Baby included?"

She squeezed her eyes shut and took a deep breath. "Baby included."

"We'll be married in July."

She rolled her eyes annoyed. "You haven't succeeded yet."

"Yes, I have."

* * *

TRINA'S WEDDING progressed under softly misting skies. Brenna watched bridesmaids in pink taffeta dresses, with ruffles that threatened to consume them, walk down the aisle. Soon her cousin Trina appeared on a carpet of roses and walked to her future husband. He stood under a gazebo dressed with luscious flowers of different shades of red from maroon to coral pink. She wore a dress of turquoise stones and gold embroidery, her full skirt sweeping the ground. In her hand, she held a bouquet of cymbidium orchids and calla lilies bursting forth in yellow splendor amid hostas leaves. Her grandmother's earrings dangled against her neck.

Brenna glanced at her mother who pretended not to wipe tears. As a little girl she hadn't thought much about weddings or marriage. She'd just wanted a home life like the ones she saw on TV and in magazine ads. Families that had a mother, father and child that loved each other. She'd hoped to one day claim that dream for herself.

She looked down at her bare hand. Would Hunter be able to complete the challenge? Would she end up marrying him? Knowing him. Probably. And then she'd have to face the possibility of disappointing him. If she disappointed him, would he leave as her father had? Even though her parents tried to convince her otherwise there was always a feeling that she was the reason they'd split up. That if she had been normal or smarter or prettier he might have stayed. But what did she care if Hunter left as long as she got the money she needed? As long as she didn't invest in it.

Brenna glanced at her brother who looked distinguished and handsome in his tux. There was something different about him. A sadness she couldn't identify. They hadn't spoken in a while and she wondered how things were with Fiona. She wondered if he was remembering his own wedding day. Remembering the promises and hopes of that time that had yet to come true.

The ceremony soon ended and Brenna went to the reception canopy. She grabbed a flute of pink champagne and took a sip. She calmed her nerves and pushed aside any regret. Her mother's peach hat came into view.

"I can't believe you still ended up coming to Trina's wedding alone," she said.

"Wasn't it a beautiful wedding?" Brenna replied, trying to avoid the topic.

"I wonder what Hunter would have thought."

She shrugged. "Who knows? I never got his opinion on weddings."

"You can still have one of your own."

She took another sip. She probably would. "Perhaps someday."

"There's no someday about it. You have a bride, a groom, get yourself a preacher and get married."

"Why did you have me?"

Diane stared taken aback. "I'm sorry?"

"Why did you have me?"

"Because I wanted to have children."

"Did you know there was a possibility I would be this way?"

"We didn't think about it."

Brenna glanced around trying to make her question seem nonchalant. "When you saw me were you happy?"

"Yes, of course. You were beautiful. I loved you."

She met her mother's eyes. "Then why can't you do that now? Why can't you remember that moment when you held me and loved me just because I was there? Not because I did something to please you, or because I accomplished something to make you proud, but just because I was your daughter. I want you to remember when my leg didn't matter, when a man didn't matter. All that mattered was me."

Unshed tears made Diane's voice tremble. "I love you very much. I just... Your father had reasons for not doing a lot of things too—none of them good. It was as though, because he was lame, he thought he wasn't allowed to be happy."

Brenna took another sip of champagne. "I'm not my father and I am happy."

"If I could believe that, I wouldn't try so hard. I've tried to believe you. I want to believe you. I am proud of your accomplishments. I am proud of you. I am proud of the daughter I raised, but I worry about her because she locks so many things out. She shows so little feeling."

"I am not an emotional person."

"You never were. It was a shield I know that, but after Byron something inside you became paralyzed. A hope of some sort."

Her mother knew her too well. Brenna felt suppressed feelings rising to the surface ready to spill over into sorrow. She angrily brushed away a tear. "I'm fine."

"No use crying at a wedding," Aunt Vanessa said, coming towards them. Her large pinwheel hat sat at a jaunty angle. "There is no need for tears, especially at weddings. Unless you're a pretty crier, it does nothing for your complexion." She looped an arm through Diane's. "Come. Let's leave her alone. Perhaps she'll catch someone's eye and make Hunter incredibly jealous."

"Hunter doesn't get jealous," Brenna said.

Her aunt's eyes sparkled, but she didn't reply.

Brenna watched them walk away then went over to one of the tables and sat. She never considered that her mother could see through her. See inside her heart. For one who liked to hide her feelings the thought was embarrassing and painful. She closed her eyes.

"Do you have a headache?"

She opened her eyes and saw Lauren looking worried. "No, sweetie."

Her cousins Judy and Susanna came up behind her and sat. "We're sorry your fiancé couldn't come," Susanna said. "That must be hard for you." She touched Brenna's sleeve at the perfect angle to show off her ring.

"It's not that hard," she muttered.

"We were just wondering something."

Brenna nodded, wishing they would go away. "That's good."

"What?" Lauren asked interested.

Susanna lowered her voice. "Couldn't you have paid him to come with you?"

Lauren frowned. "Paid who?"

Judy looked at her with disdain. "You are so naive."

Brenna glared at them. "It's refreshing compared to your filthy minds."

Judy feigned surprise. "So you didn't pay Hunter to be your escort that night?"

Susanna said, "We thought since he came out of nowhere that it was all a hoax."

"You're right," Brenna admitted. "It was a hoax. He came out of nowhere. One day he walked into my office and asked me to pretend to be his fiancée. I agreed, if he would meet my family. So he did and I went to his banquet where I met his grandfather and he got a promotion. Then he asked me to marry him. I said yes until I met his ex-wife who is currently married to his cousin. He wanted me to have his baby, I said no, we broke up. End of story."

Susanna and Judy stared at her with wide eyes.

Brenna grinned pleased that she had shocked them. "It's amazing, I know. Unbelievable."

Susanna swallowed. "No, it's not unbelievable. Excuse us."

Lauren jumped to her feet and left. Brenna shrugged and grabbed her drink.

"I don't think that's the end of the story," a deep, familiar voice said.

Brenna nearly choked. She turned to the man sitting beside her. "What are you doing here?"

Hunter slanted her a glance. "Hello to you too."

Her eyes drank him up. It had only been a few weeks, but it felt like years. His presence filled the empty space in her heart.

"I never pictured you as a wedding crasher," she said, trying to maintain her composure though inside she trembled.

He rested his arm on the back of her chair. "Hmm."

She stiffened, determined not to weaken. "Where is your fiancée?"

He sent her an odd look. "Don't you mean ex-fiancée?"

"Ex-fiancée?" she repeated to make sure she understood him.

He nodded. "I did as instructed."

A grin spread on her face. "You mean Michael won her back?"

"Yes. I told you she wanted a Prince Charming to sweep her off her feet. Michael did just that in a very grand manner—just as instructed."

She narrowed her eyes. "Did he punch you?"

The corner of his mouth kicked up in a quick grin. "You sound hopeful."

"No, I'm just curious. I want to imagine how it happened."

Hunter thought for a moment then said, "Janice and I were having dinner at her place. She likes to show off her chef's cooking. Michael came in saying something to the affect of 'Janice I won't let you go' and a lot of other idealistic drivel I chose to ignore in order to keep my meal down."

Brenna shook her head. "You're such a romantic."

"Yes, well she tearfully fell into his arms begging his forgiveness, he then begged for her forgiveness. I quietly, or rather quickly, made my escape."

She couldn't ignore the rushed feelings of joy. Michael would marry Janice. All was well. "Amazing. I knew they were perfect. My record can be kept intact."

"Would you rather thank me on your knees or just curtsey?"

She scowled. "I don't know how your head holds your ego."

His hand brushed against her shoulder, his fingers lightly trailing back and forth. She pretended not to notice. "Strange. That doesn't sound like a thank you. Perhaps you should try again."

"Why didn't you take her back?"

His hand stopped. "Because she loved someone else."

"So love is important?"

Hunter hesitated. "In this particular situation it was clear—"

"Yes or no?"

He narrowed his eyes. "I will not let you trap me into a definitive statement I cannot qualify."

"Ever the businessman." Brenna leaned towards him. "Yes or no?"

"Loyalty is important. Janice's love for Michael made it clear that she could never be loyal to me."

"And you think I'll be loyal to you?"

His voice lowered. "Yes, I do." She turned away. He cupped her chin and forced her to look at him. "Am I right?"

"You'll find out."

"I want a promise."

"I promise." She turned as the crowd cheered and gathered into a group. "Oh, she's going to toss the bouquet."

"Too bad. They don't need to."

She looked at him confused. "Why not?"

He quirked a brow. "We already know who the next bride will be."

"Pauline, don't do this to me," Brenna begged, clasping her pearl choker. "Not on my wedding day."

Pauline glanced up from adjusting her shoe strap. "Do what?"

"Sulk."

"I'm not sulking."

"Then stop frowning."

She sighed. "I'm sorry, but—"

"I know you disapprove."

"Are you sure you know what you're doing?"

"Positive."

"You should marry for love."

Brenna sniffed. "Love? I've loved before thank you. I don't wish to repeat the experience."

Pauline ignored her. "And he should love you too."

She shrugged. "We're two adults going into this with our eyes open. That's enough."

Pauline looked at Brenna dressed in her ivory lace strapless gown, with her cane almost unseen covered in a garland of white roses. She hugged her friend silently wishing her happiness. It was a perfect July afternoon for a wedding at the Virginia ranch. Diane did cry with joy and even Aunt Vanessa felt tears touch her eyes, although she would never admit to them. Tima sketched the couple, Stephen looked at Fiona, and Fiona looked at the house. Susanna and Judy were still stunned, Doran even more so. Angelina watched remembering her own wedding to Hunter wondering if he would find happiness, Ruby felt certain he had while Lauren sighed as though she'd stepped into a dream. Crampton sat in the back feeling too self conscious to walk his daughter down the aisle, her Uncle Jerome proudly did the honors. Orson watched without expression and as the afternoon settled into evening, Brenna and Hunter were joined as husband and wife.

AFTER THE RECEPTION, Stephen watched the car drive away.

"You look worried," Tima said.

Stephen gritted his teeth. She still had the ability to irritate him. Fortunately, she looked semi-normal in a blue skirt and cream blouse although her boots appeared as though she'd stolen them from a Victorian era prostitute. "I'm not."

"You still haven't come by to see the car."

He shrugged. "Yea, I know."

"You don't have to schedule an appointment. Drop by any time." She smiled then headed for the reception canopy.

Fiona came up to him. "I see that woman got you cornered again. I don't know why she won't leave you alone." She wrapped a hand around his arm. "Brenna probably asked her to look after you."

"I don't need looking after."

"She is kinda weird, but she doesn't care. One woman was talking about her loudly and she just took another piece of cake and made a face at her. I mean she didn't even care. Isn't that amazing?"

Stephen stared at Tima laughing with a waiter, slowly beginning to see her in a new light. How nice it would be not to care what other people thought. "Yes, amazing."

***

STEPHEN TOOK a deep breath as he walked to Tima's apartment. He probably should have called first, but he didn't have the nerve. He wanted to sound casual. He'd say something like he'd come by to check on Brenna's apartment or something. So if she was busy it was no big deal.

He stared at her apartment door for a long moment. The watercolor picture had changed from spring to summer. After another deep breath, he knocked. When the door opened he said, "I just came to look under the hood."

Unfortunately, Tima wasn't the one in the doorway. It was a man in his early forties with a red towel around his waist. "What?"

Stephen took a hasty step back ready to leave. "Uh, I was just coming about the car."

"The car?" He raised his voice. "Hey Tima. There's something wrong with your car."

"No, there isn't," she said. "Stop making up stories and get naked."

Stephen took another step back and crashed into the wall. He cleared his throat. "I see you're busy."

The man frowned. "Do you want to come in and talk to her?"

He moved to the side. "No, that's okay."

"Do you want to leave a message?"

He fingered his goatee. "I was just in the area. Thought I'd see the car, but um forget it." He flashed an awkward grin then left.

Tima came out of the art room with her paints. "Well, who was it?"

The man closed the door and shrugged. "Some kid. One of your students, I think. He talked about your car. I guess he wanted to paint it or draw it or something."

She opened the door and looked down the hall. It was empty. "My car?"

"He was a little nervous. Nearly ran away when I opened the door."

"He didn't leave a name?"

"No."

She shrugged. "If it's important he'll come again. Now get rid of that towel and try to hold still this time."

STEPHEN SAT IN HIS TRUCK, feeling like an idiot. He shouldn't have come by in the first place. He didn't even like her very much. So why had he come? Because he was missing his sister? He nodded. That was it. Brenna had made her choice and he knew he had to make his. He stopped by the store and picked up some flowers. The only ones he could recognize were the baby's breath. Fiona liked their name. Since she stayed at his place more than at hers, he decided he might as well make it official.

As he jumped out of his truck ready to tell Fiona how he felt, he saw the stray cat crawl out from under a bush. "Nothing today. Sorry buddy. Wait, what's wrong?" He knelt down and saw the cat was limping.

"I'd stay away from that cat," a man wearing a sweat suit warned. "It may have rabies."

"It's hurt."

"Probably got in a fight." The man jogged past.

The cat rested his head against Stephen's knee. "He's not rabid just in pain." He gently picked it up and saw it was younger than he'd thought. He wrapped it in a windbreaker he kept in the truck and took it to the animal shelter.

"She's very sweet," the technician said.

"I'd uh...like to keep her if no one claims her."

"Okay. We'll give you a call when everything checks out. Now she may have some--"

"I'll pay for whatever she needs. I'd like to give her a chance."

"Okay."

Stephen left the shelter in high spirits, but groaned when he sat back in his truck. The sun had begun cooking the flowers. He hoped to get them to Fiona before they looked fried. At home, he found her in the living room reading a magazine. "Hi."

She didn't look up. "Hi."

"I got you these." He held out the flowers.

She smiled. "That's so nice." She took them and put them in water. She hugged him then pulled away. "You're covered in cat fur."

"I took that stray cat to the shelter."

"Did he bite you? That thing is filthy. Why didn't you just call animal control to get it?"

He glanced at the floor and sighed. "Please, let's not fight."

Fiona brushed some hairs from his shirt. "Okay."

He took a deep breath then met her eyes. Falling into the gentle soft brown ones facing him, realizing how much he loved her. How much he always would. "I want to give us another chance. I want to come home to you and wake up to you and start a family someday. I want to stay married."

She threw her arms around him. He smiled and he held her close for all the wrong reasons.

Part Two

There came a time when the risk to remain tight in the bud was more painful than the risk it took to blossom.
Anais Nim

Chapter Fifteen

January loomed like a monster. Giant snowflakes touched the large windows of the conference room and crystallized. The intricate design reminded Hunter of the crocheted sweater Ruby had given James. He wondered when she'd have to knit a pair of booties for them.

He toyed with his wedding band, which had been his constant companion for over the last six months as he stared out at the naked trees heavy with ice. A crow landed on a branch, shaking snow that shimmered as it fell.

He heard the door open. "What are you still doing in here?" Curtis asked.

"Just thinking."

Curtis sat. "The meeting wasn't to signal you out as the reason sales are stagnant."

"I'm aware of that; however that wasn't what I was thinking about."

"Perhaps it should be. Your revolutionary ideas are making people nervous."

Hunter shrugged. "New computer software will result in a more efficient inventory system, lower overhead and--"

"What about the cost?"

"I've already explained my plan."

"Perhaps you don't understand. You were hired to do this job the way it's always been done. The software we have works fine."

"Things are changing."

Curtis shook his head. "Not in this company. We want to see a change in the bottom line by spring. Doran can help you if that is necessary."

Hunter kept his voice level. "I can handle it."

"You've been dealing with a lot and--"

"I said--"

Curtis' voice hardened. "Did it sound like I'd finished speaking?"

Hunter felt heat rush to his ears. "Sorry, sir."

"You've been dealing with a lot of change. A new marriage, a new job. No matter how essential these events are they can also be a stress."

He glanced out the window. Two more crows landed on the tree. "I like stress."

Curtis grinned with knowing. "When you're a family man you'll have plenty of stress then. So you'll have to recognize which ones matter more."

"I know my priorities."

"I want to see you do more overtime."

Hunter clenched and unclenched his jaw. The company already threatened to consume his life. He didn't see a reason for that and wondered why they did. "I see."

"Randolph men have their wives, but Randolph is our mistress. You've been ignoring her and you can't afford to do that."

"Did he send you to talk to me?"

"This isn't about your grandfather. It's a little friendly advice."

Hunter's gaze slid to his notebook. "It's definitely advice."

"It is better to bow out than be pushed out."

He glanced up, his gaze sharpened. "You think I will fail?"

Curtis stood. "There are different ways to fail. Follow the rules, keep your wife in order and always remember what is important."

"Brenna understands that my work is important."

"Your mother understood too. She knew she couldn't compete."

Hunter shook his head. "She left because she wanted her own career."

Curtis tugged on his beard. His voice quiet. "Right."

"Why do you say it like that?"

"I want you to be careful. Your mother was different."

"Yes, I know."

He tossed some papers on the table. "Like you."

Hunter glanced down at the sketches of new products he had been toying with. He crumbled them up. "You know I doodle when I'm thinking."

Curtis rested his palms on the table, his gaze as hard as iron. "I want you to rid yourself of this compulsion. Break all your pencils if you have to. Keep things as they are. You have come too far to let your nature stand in your way. I have worked to mold you and groom you and guide you to become my successor. Nothing can stand in your way. Nothing. Not your wife, this or you." He tossed one of the crumpled designs in disgust. "Do you understand?"

Hunter stood and threw the sketches in the trash. "I won't let you down."

Curtis nodded. "No, you won't. I plan to make sure of that. Here is your schedule. I've assigned you to attend two conferences. You'll also host a cocktail party in a few weeks."

"Brenna hosted a Christmas party only a few weeks ago. She--"

"If Brenna wants to stay your wife, she will do exactly as you tell her. She's made a great hostess in the past and this will put you in contact with the right people. People you need to mollify. The guest list is on the next page. I've also sent you a soft copy. Your stepmother was kind enough to help. You will also need to make sure you never leave the office before Doran. Do you understand?"

"Yes."

"I'm waiting for a 'Yes, sir.'"

"Yes, sir."

"Your grandfather gave you this position. Don't think he won't take it away if he doesn't think you're up to the task."

Hunter shook his head. "But I have--"

"You will do exactly what I say if you don't want to lose everything we've worked for."

Hunter nodded; Curtis smiled. "Good." He left the room.

Hunter stood by the window. All his ideas for improving the company had met with resistance. Why? Was he so far off what Randolph wanted to achieve? After a few moments he finally left the conference room and marched down the hall silently swearing. He had to be more careful where he left his sketches.

"How did it go?" Miles asked.

He headed for the kitchen. "You know how it went."

"I can hazard a guess. People don't like change."

He poured himself some coffee. It was worse than that. He had a feeling they were hiding something. "They don't understand what I'm trying to do." Hunter took a sip from his cup and glanced at the clock. He swore.

Miles frowned in sympathy. "Did you burn your tongue?"

"No." He rested his cup down. "Brenna's coming by for lunch."

"To make up for the dinner you cancelled two nights in a row?"

"Yes." He scowled. "I won't be able to go."

"She'll understand. She always does."

He pulled out his wallet. "I'll give her my card. She can go buy something."

Miles pushed it away. "Bad idea. I'll go as your substitute."

"My what?"

"Someone should take her out. If not you, then why not me? Trust me. A happy home is a happy woman."

Hunter raised a brow skeptical. "This coming from a bachelor."

Miles folded his arms looking smug. "Who has learned from the folly of others."

Hunter finished his coffee then threw the cup away. Brenna's patience seemed endless. He knew it wasn't. "Hmm."

"Or you can forget about the work, take her to lunch and tell her the truth."

"Which is?"

"You hate the job. It's not working for you."

"It's working. I'm just facing a few obstacles. I plan to keep up my end of the bargain."

Miles let his arms fall. "Bargain? What bargain?"

"The promotion. She married a director and I intend to stay one."

"You were a success in R&D."

He turned and went to his office. Miles followed. Hunter glanced at a note on his desk calendar. "Take her to the Italian restaurant on Ridley. Don't worry I have a reservation. Make sure she has greens. She tends to skip her vegetables. Just give me the bill."

Miles sat, studying his friend. "I'd rather give you some advice."

Hunter stared at him his eyes dark and dangerous.

He quickly stood. "But that will be another time. I'll tell her you said hello."

Brenna stepped into the elevators of the Randolph building, rubbing her hands together. The cold had seeped through her gloves and boots, but the excitement of seeing Hunter was already warming her. She treasured the time they spent together although that time seemed to grow less and less.

She stuffed her gloves in her jacket and headed to his office. Doran's voice caught her attention as she passed a door.

"Hunter, won't last long."

She stopped by the doorway.

"Everyone knows it's his crippled wife that got him the job.

Unfortunately, he's too stupid to use her to the full advantage. Now if she were my wife, I'd have her in front of every camera limping around like a three legged dog and sporting one of our canes. He'll probably knock her up soon and if the kid ends up like her he might become CEO just for that. But eventually they'll pull him from the job because sales remain stagnant while he tries to overhaul the company. He doesn't seem to understand how this company works." He laughed. "Fortunately, I'll be right there to pick up the pieces."

Brenna rested against the wall fighting a wave of nausea as she faced the truth. It wasn't just because Hunter had a wife that he was promoted. He had a crippled wife. Could that have been the reason he'd chosen her in the first place? To give himself an advantage? Did she blame him? Hadn't she married him for her own less honorable reasons?

Miles stormed out of the room nearly crashing into her. He offered her a careless apology until he recognized her. His eyes widened. "Brenna. Oh, no."

She managed a smile. "Hi."

"Doran is a jerk," he said softly. "When Hunter finds out--"

She grabbed his sleeve. "Hunter doesn't need to know."

"What don't I need to know?" Hunter asked behind them.

They both turned. "How hungry I am." She grabbed his hand, drawing strength from his touch although she wanted to bury herself in his arms and cry. "Are you ready to go?" The look on his face told her the answer. Her heart fell. "You have work."

He held her hand not ready to let go. Wishing he had the words to rid the disappointment in her eyes. He saw a snowflake melt on her jacket. "Yes, but--"

"Forget it." She pulled her hand away. "I have most of your reasons filed alphabetically."

"Miles will take you."

"A babysitter, how nice."

"He's not a babysitter. I have a reservation and because I can't be there--"

"You thought of the next best thing."

He wasn't sure how to read her careless tone. "Yes," he said cautious. "You can order whatever you like." He reached for his wallet, ignoring Miles' grimace. "Here. You can go shopping afterward."

"I did not trudge through the snow and traffic just so that I could go shopping."

"I realize that--"

"Then you'd better put that card away." She turned.

He grabbed her arm, his voice low. "This is the reason why you married me, remember? My job is important."

"You don't need to remind me why I married you." She glanced pointedly at his hand. With a fierce sigh, he released her. She walked to the elevators.

He followed. "You're still angry."

"I'm not angry," she said pushing the down button.

She wasn't. That's what annoyed him, a part of him wanted her to be. An irrational part of him wanted her to show some annoyance that he couldn't be with her. Show some emotion that she cared.

The doors opened and she stepped in. "Bye."

Hunter stared as the doors closed.

"Go after her," Miles urged.

He briefly rested his palm on the elevator door then spun on his heel. "No, I have work to do."

BRENNA WELCOMED the cold as she walked to her car, the stinging wind invigorating her sinking spirits. She wasn't upset, she told herself, just disappointed. Yet she couldn't help remembering Pauline's words 'Once he has you, he'll forget you'. She hadn't required him to be a real husband, but she hadn't expected to feel this way. To feel like an extra appendage.

"You're back early," Pauline said when Brenna entered the office. "Lunch cancelled?'

"Yes."

"Again?" she said with emphasis.

"Yes."

"At least business is booming so it makes it all worth it."

Brenna hung up her jacket. Yes, that was true. Her business presently was booming. Word had spread of her advantageous marriage expanding her client list and income.

"Richard Denson called again," she said, handing her phone messages.

Brenna read the note then crumbled it up. "What a nuisance. He's a literary agent who wants me to write a book about how to marry a rich black man."

"You did it. Why not write about it?"

She tapped her other messages against her palm, her voice quiet. "Careful Pauline, you're about to make me angry."

Pauline turned to her computer. Brenna walked into her office. It was becoming more obvious how strained her relationship with Pauline had become. She knew Pauline didn't understand or approve of her marriage and she didn't blame her. It did seem like a cold union. But she and Hunter understood each other. She knew he had to prove himself at work and she wouldn't get in the way. She didn't have to worry about bills and being Hunter's wife wasn't as bad as it appeared. Nobody knew how they would come up with ideas for the company. Or the times he would lay on her side of the bed just to keep it warm or the extra bookshelves he'd had ordered for her books. It was a side nobody else saw. It wasn't love, but it was enough. Unfortunately, that Hunter seemed more of a memory than a reality.

At home, she wandered their large colonial house that sat on acres of land now blanketed with snow. She couldn't deny that there were advantages to being Mrs. Hunter Randolph. She had a chef, a housekeeper, a lovely home, a wardrobe any woman would envy and prestige. But she couldn't help comparing her marriage to the one he'd shared with Angelina. He'd probably rushed home to her. Laughed with her, smiled at her. Once, while going through his albums, she'd spotted his old wedding photo and noticed something different about him. Sure he was younger, but there was a special look in his eyes that wasn't just youthful optimism and joy. It was love, shining bright and proud. In her own wedding photo, Hunter looked like a man completing his duty. But she'd known why he'd married her. So why did his lack of affection hurt sometimes? He was always cordial, kind. She hadn't wanted him to love her and she didn't love him. Did she? She pushed the thought aside. She liked him a great deal, but it wasn't love. It was nothing like what she had felt for Byron.

Brenna glanced around the living room at the cream overstuffed sofa piled with pillows and a soft throw blanket. A mirror with a hand-painted frame sat on the mantle over the fireplace. Why couldn't this be enough? He'd given her all that he'd promised. She glanced out the window. Then why did the land sometimes call out to her to walk away and disappear? What did she want?

He arrived late for dinner. She wasn't surprised. He usually was. Brenna sat at the other end of the table as Mrs. Symnthon set his dinner before him. She had finished her own meal hours ago, but sat with him to keep him company. She didn't usually sit with him, but the tired look on his face persuaded her to. He looked exhausted-- worn. As though something was laying heavy on his mind.

"I came up with an idea to improve your scooter idea," Brenna said after a few moments.

"I'm not interested in that anymore."

"Why not?" she asked, trying to sound casual although the question was not.

"I have plenty of other things to focus on. My job is to help run a company, not waste my energy on ideas that will go nowhere."

She tried not to sigh. "You've been speaking to your father again."

"He is right."

"What is he right about this time?" she asked, noticing he wasn't meeting her eyes. "That a new computerized accounting system will be too costly to implement?"

"He just wants to make sure I head this company--"

"The way your grandfather wants you too. Have they approved any of your changes or do they continue to criticize all your efforts?"

"Sales aren't improving."

"At least they're not falling," she said annoyed. "I may not run a business as large as yours, but I know that a solid foundation is key. I don't understand why they keep blocking your ideas. They are fantastic." When he didn't reply she said, "You're not a disappointment."

Hunter met her gaze, startled. "They've never said that."

"They don't have to. Have they threatened to use Doran?"

He reached for his glass and took a sip.

"Of course they have." She sat back. "Hunter?"

He set his glass down. "Yes?"

"What's really going on?"

He looked at her then glanced away. He couldn't tell her until he was sure. But his father's behavior had made him curious. Curious enough to check the books. Curious enough to wonder why things in accounting didn't add up. Curious as to why inventory was disappearing and not being accounted for. "I just have a lot on my mind," he said in a tone that allowed no further discussion.

She ignored it. "Like what?"

"Like business."

"What you do in business effects me. I have a right to know."

"I'm frustrated by the lack of progress." His lie produced a smile of sympathy.

Brenna nodded. "Give them time. They'll come around."

Pleased with his deception he relaxed. "By the way, I want you to host a cocktail party."

"Okay."

He hesitated, surprised she didn't argue. "I have a list of guests."

"Okay."

He pulled the list from his jacket pocket and set it on the table. "If you have trouble, Ruby can help you."

She lifted the list and read it. "I think I can do very well on my own."

"Good."

They fell into silence, both not saying what they truly wanted to.

BRENNA SAT IN HER ROOM, staring at her vanity mirror. She was beginning not to like the Randolphs. They most likely didn't like her, although they were always polite. She was constantly aware of them watching her. Especially, his grandfather although she could never figure out why. Angelina had grown more distant in past months and Ruby more of an advisor than a mother-in-law. The sense of uneasiness still lingered though there had been little reason for it to. Until now. They threatened to destroy Hunter by forcing him to conform. He'd be nothing more than a puppet to them without his ideas and enthusiasm. She wouldn't let that happen. They wanted sales to improve and she would figure out a way to do it. She looked down at her cane then began to smile.

Chapter Sixteen

B renna stared at the door of the deli, sitting among the smell of pickles and pastrami. She saw Miles enter and raised her hand to greet him.

Miles took off his coat and sat. "So you've decided to use me as a substitute after all?"

"Something like that. How bad are sales?"

Miles grinned playfully staring at her uneaten sandwich. "Not so bad that you need to take up a hunger strike."

"But bad enough."

"It's not necessarily bad, but not great either. Randolph likes to see big numbers."

"I think I can help."

"You don't need to help. This is business." His face grew somber. "What Doran said was completely--"

"Doran is an insensitive jerk, but he gave me an idea. Who better to help with ideas than someone who has been a customer for years?"

Miles clasped his hands together. "Hunter wouldn't want that."

"Hunter wants to succeed. We both know that."

Miles sighed heavily. "He wouldn't want you involved with the company."

Brenna shook her head. "That's where you're wrong. Why do you think I'm here? Because he needed a wife because management should be composed of family men. And that's what he wants. To be in management so he can become CEO. I can help him with that." She halted at the expression of sadness on Miles' face. It was too close to pity. "I don't mind. Truly. I'm his partner."

"He cares about you."

"Yes," she said waving a dismissive hand. "Just as someone cares about their stock options. That's not the point. I can help. I'm good at this."

"No, you don't understand what--"

She picked up her sandwich ready to take charge. "When we come up with a plan, we'll go to Curtis first; Hunter won't be able to argue with him."

"I'm not sure--"

"We could do print ads maybe even a commercial one created for TV and one to go viral."

Miles frowned although her idea intrigued him. "We've never done a commercial. We don't know anything about that. And the cost—"

She began to smile. "Don't worry, I know someone who can help us."

"Sure I can make this work," Sara said. "But you'll have to trust me. I'll want information about the company, the clientele, goals etc..."

"Miles can get it for you." Brenna said.

He glanced up from taking lint off his trousers and shrugged. He hadn't said anything since they'd arrived.

"That means yes. The focus will be this cane. It has a spring and adjusts to one's weight, compensating for one's gait. It doesn't make a sound on hard surfaces which is a relief. It's a revolutionary design."

Sara glanced at the cane then Brenna. "I had an announcer in mind for this but I know someone else."

"Who?"

"You. You'll look good on camera; you're eloquent and know the product. And the fact that your husband created it will be a great angle."

Brenna inwardly rebelled. She'd spent her life behind a desk to hide that part of her and now they wanted to use it—use her—to sell products.

"It will be perfect."

"I don't know."

Miles stared. "You want Brenna to be the spokeswoman?"

"She's the best choice."

He groaned. "I can't allow this."

"Why not?"

"Hunter will kill me."

"When you're selling a warehouse load of canes and other products he won't mind."

Brenna nodded. "Okay. I'll do it."

He shook his head with all the enthusiasm of a condemned man, but remained silent. He stood and looked around the office at pictures of successful campaigns and awards.

Sara whispered. "I'm glad he at least has a pulse. I was afraid he was in a stupor."

Brenna leaned forward. "Interested?"

She glanced at him. "I never thought I'd go for an older man."

"He's in his mid-thirties, early gray."

Her eyes trailed the length of him. "Not bad looking."

"And smart, considerate. I can find out more."

She twirled her pen uncertain. "I may not be his type."

"You are," Brenna said.

"How do you know?"

"It's my job to know. Besides he kept trying to ignore you. You'll have to make that hard."

A masculine voice cut in. "She doesn't have to."

Both women turned to Miles who leaned against the desk. "I usually prefer pretty women, but I think you'll do."

Sara narrowed her eyes. "I don't like gray hair."

"So? I like red heads."

"I like brown eyes."

"I prefer gray." He grinned. "Free for dinner?"

"Yes."

"Here's my card." He straightened, winked at Brenna then returned to looking at the awards that lined her walls.

Sara frowned at his card. "What just happened?"

"I think you just met your match."

The two women shared a smile.

* * *

Two weeks later Brenna, Miles and Hunter sat in the conference room while Curtis beamed at them. He closed the marketing plan. "Hunter, it's an excellent idea. I'm very pleased."

Hunter gripped his hands under the conference table, but maintained an impassive expression. He didn't glance at Miles or Brenna.

"Using Brenna as our spokeswoman is inspired." He flashed her a smile. "Thank you, dear."

She returned the expression.

He shifted his gaze to the man next to her. "And Miles I didn't know you had some hidden marketing creativity in you."

Miles tried not to look ill, uneasy by the silence of his friend. "It's nothing."

"This is the kind of thing I like to see. You three understand that Randolph is about teamwork, helping each other, stretching boundaries. I am proud." He stood. "Feel free to leave early today. You deserve it."

He left; silence fell.

Hunter's quiet voice slipped through. "I ask you to take my wife out for lunch and the next thing I know I'm being congratulated for an idea I never had."

Miles cleared his throat. "Hunter, I--"

"It's a great idea," Brenna said, prepared to stand up for him.

Hunter took a deep breath, resting his arms on the table. "I didn't marry you so that you could sell our products."

"Don't worry. I know why you married me."

He shot her a glance, but said nothing.

"You don't have to agree," she continued, hoping to convince him of the plan. "This is all out of your hands now. You should be thanking us for caring enough about your job to save it."

"You think it needed saving?"

Miles spoke up. "We wanted to help."

"I was handling things."

"You were drowning and everyone knew it," Brenna said. "No amount of late nights in the office and meetings were going to fix it. Now you can sulk if you want to or be gracious and give us credit."

He picked up a pen and stared at it. "I was handling things," he repeated softly. "I had plans that I wanted to put into practice. Do you think I'm not qualified for the job?"

She tilted her head to the side. "Is this Hunter speaking or his ego?"

Their eyes locked in ready battle. "No, it's your husband," he was pleased with how cool he sounded although the voice didn't sound like this own. "I need you to trust me."

There was a flicker of surprise then weariness. The expression pleased him. "I do trust you."

He continued in the same cool tone. "That's why you asked me first?" he said sarcastic. "So that I wouldn't have to sit in front of my father like an imbecile. You respected me so much that my opinion was of utmost importance to you. Correct?"

"That's not--"

He held up a hand. "You don't need to defend yourself. Your plan is excellent. You both make a great team." He shot Miles a glance. "Congratulations." He stood and gave a mocking bow. "However, I had plans of my own and you two got in my way." He let his gaze fall, but the silence kept them still. "A fact that I find irritating."

"We didn't mean--"

His voice deepened. "This will never happen again."

Brenna spoke up. "Hunter--"

His gaze captured hers with such fury she nearly bit her tongue. "This will never happen again," he repeated.

"No," Miles said.

Brenna shook her head.

"Good." He left.

Miles groaned. "I think I would have preferred a fatal beating."

Brenna covered her eyes defeated. "He doesn't understand. He always comes from another angle I never think of." She let her hand fall. "We're helping him and he sees it as a lack of respect."

Miles paused then said, "Did we respect his opinion?"

"We didn't ask for it."

He nodded grimly. "Exactly."

Stephen stared at the row of drain cleaners with growing anxiety. He needed something fast or the bathroom would flood. He could still hear Fiona shrieking after the toilet had overflowed. He selected one then set it back down. Out of the corner of his eye he saw an old man wearing worn tan slacks and a tweed jacket, ask a young man where the crackers were. He rudely brushed him aside. Stephen pretended to look at a can of cleaner hoping the man would ignore him. He didn't.

"Excuse me," he said in a surprising baritone for man of slim build and many years. "Do you know where the crackers are?"

He sighed. Did he look like he worked there? He glanced up at a sign and pointed. "Crackers are in aisle six."

"Six?" He looked at him with blank gray eyes. Not blind just unsure.

"Yes. Six."

"Thank you."

He saw the man leave and head in the wrong direction.

Stephen groaned, grabbed what he needed then went after him. "Wait, it's this way. Come on."

Once in aisle 6, the man looked at the row of choices like a startled animal. Stephen picked up a box. "What brand are you looking for?"

"I'm not sure. I'm looking for something to go with this cheese." He lifted the block of Brie out of his basket.

"Oh. Well, my sister likes these. She puts ham and avocado and paste stuff on it." Yea paste stuff that sounds really clever.

But the man smiled. "That sounds good." He put the box in the basket then looked at his list.

Stephen tried to inch away. "Glad I could help. Enjoy your meal."

"Do you know where the wine is?"

He sighed. "Follow me." Once in the liquor section, the man stared at the row of bottles clueless.

"Do you know what kind of wine would go with this cheese?" he asked.

No, he didn't and the fact that this guy thought a black man in faded jeans and a T-shirt that said: Lighting Rod would know anything about wine and cheese amazed him. Beer and hot dogs? Sure. Wine? No way. "Give me a minute." He dialed Brenna. He saw a man frown at him and shrugged. Yea, now he was one of those idiots talking on the phone in a supermarket. Oh well. "Hi, Brenna. Do you know what kind of wine goes with um what was that...right...Brie cheese?"

"You're buying Brie? Have you forgotten where the cheese spray is?" She began to laugh.

He frowned. "No. Will you answer the question?"

"Brie cheese goes well with champagne. But it depends on where you got the cheese."

"At the store."

"The regular store?"

His tone turned surly. "No, that special store on the planet Neptune."

"I prefer Venus."

"Stop being a wise--" He glanced at the man and censored his words. "Guy. Just tell me what's wrong with the grocery store cheese."

"Unless you want cheese that tastes like wall paper paste go for Brick cheese in a regular grocery store. It's excellent with grapes and apples--"

"What kind of wine?"

"Chardonnay. I think you could--"

"Thanks."

"But you could--"

"Bye." He hung up and turned to the man. "I'd suggest you get Brick with--"

"Chardonnay. I heard." He gestured to the phone. "Girlfriend?"

"No, sister."

The man nodded and picked up a bottle. "I had a sister. She's gone now."

"I'm sorry."

He put the bottle back. "I'm not." His eyes twinkled. "She was a pain in the ass."

They selected the wine then picked some fruit. At the cashier, the man fumbled through his few bills. The cashier looked annoyed so Stephen offered to pay for everything. The man feebly protested, but Stephen knew he was grateful. Once outside they parted ways. Stephen jumped in his truck and glanced at the clock. Fiona was probably going crazy by now. The image made him both smile and groan as he started the engine. She was going to kill him for being so long. He glanced up and saw the old man running for the bus. The bus passed him, leaving him in a cloud of black smoke. Too bad, Stephen thought as he pulled out of his parking space. The next bus wouldn't arrive for a half hour. Probably even longer considering Murphy's Law about cold days. He gripped the steering wheel then swore. He couldn't leave him. Damn his bleeding heart. He drove up to the bus stop where people huddled in dark colored coats, while puffs of air escaped them as they breathed.

He rolled down the window. "How far do you live?"

"Few blocks."

"I could give you a lift."

The man smiled and opened the door. He climbed in as eager and trusting as a child. Stephen found it a bit unnerving, but was glad to help. "Thank you."

Stephen nodded then caught glimpse of a woman scowling and eyeing him as though she might have to identify him in a line up one day. He smiled and waved; her frown increased.

On the drive to his home, the man told Stephen his name was Percy Seaborn. He'd been a teacher for thirty years at a Vermont private school. He'd been married twice: divorced once and widowed once. A daughter had died in a car crash at thirty-six and he had a son who hadn't spoken to him in five years. He continued talking as they pulled up to a little gray and white house. One of the few original homes that hadn't been swallowed up by new development. Enormous half million dollar houses nearly swallowed up the neighborhood. Stephen helped the man take his bags inside and rested them on the kitchen table. It was a clean but dark house with furniture from the fifties with a well worn but functional green couch and orange carpeting. In the kitchen he saw light brown standing water in the sink. He looked around, his mind brimming with ideas of how to brighten the space. A nice lamp in the living room and recess lighting in the kitchen would help.

He watched Percy put his purchases away and wondered what he was celebrating. Did he live alone now? Was he going to invite a friend over or was it a treat for himself? He shrugged it was none of his business.

Percy handed him a few bills. Stephen waved them off. "It was no problem."

He shoved the money back in his wallet. "Aren't too many people like you around nowadays. What's your name?"

Stephen Garrett."

He shook his hand. "Thanks young man. I'll remember this day always."

Stephen shrugged then left.

At home, Fiona met him at the door with a loud shriek. "Where have you been?!"

Stephen slipped out of his jacket and tossed it on a chair. "There was this old man--"

She waved her hands. "I don't want to hear it. I've been waiting forever. Everything is soaked."

He fixed the toilet then cleaned up the mess. Once finished, he sat at the table as Fiona read a magazine and ate a bowl of chips.

"His name was Percy," he said.

She grabbed a chip. "Who?"

"The man I helped."

"Oh," she said without interest.

"He lives in this nice little house, but the plumbing is awful and the lighting terrible."

"Yea, a lot of old people live that way."

Stephen rested his forearms on the table. "Not out of choice."

"I'm sure he has family that looks out for him."

"I'm wondering if I could help."

Fiona glanced up suspicious. "How?"

"I could work on the place. Maybe even get one of the guys to help with the plumbing."

Her eyes lit up. "Do you think he'll pay you?"

"He probably couldn't afford to pay me."

She looked at him curious. "Then why do it? You'd have to pay for all the supplies and just think of all the hours wasted." She stood and kissed him on the head. "You're sweet, but impractical. You don't even know him."

"He seemed nice and--"

"Everyone seems nice to you." She wrapped her arms around him. He leaned against her, rubbing his cheek against her arms. She smelled good. "I'm glad you have me to keep you out of trouble. You'd give away half your time. It's not as though you're rich enough to do that. Now what do you want for dinner?"

He drew away. "I'm not hungry."

She straightened. "Are you sure?"

Stephen rested his palms on the table and looked up at her. "I think I could help him," he said more certain. "It wouldn't take long. I could --"

Fiona placed her hands on her hips. "Want to know what I think? I think it's a stupid idea to help some old man you hardly even know. I bet you he wouldn't even want your help. He has his pride. He's not a charity case. Someone to help you make yourself feel better."

His tone tightened. "I'm not suggesting this to make me feel better."

She rolled her eyes. "Oh sure. I know you. You always start coming up with strange projects when you're bored. Why can't you take up pool or something? You have ideas that never work. Remember that training course you took? A complete waste of time and money. I love you and I'm tired of seeing you get hurt. So please leave this alone." She patted him on the shoulder then headed for the kitchen. "Now I'm going to make your favorite soup okay? While I'm doing that give that cat a bath will you?"

The cat was named Lillian and she hated the flea dip, but endured it with cat dignity. To make up for the ordeal, Stephen took her for a ride. Lillian loved to travel, he'd discovered that when he first brought her home. She cried in the carrier so he let her out to see if she was hurt. Instead she crawled out and sat on the seat and began grooming herself. He began to drive and she jumped to the floor of the truck and fell asleep. He eventually created a harness for her because Lillian sometimes liked to climb on the door and look out the window. He didn't want her to get hurt.

"I think she's wrong," Stephen said to the cat. "I think I could help him. It will have to be a secret of course. Can you keep a secret?"

Lillian looked at him, blinked then turned back to the window.

A smile tugged at his mouth. "Yea, I agree."

THE NEXT WEEKEND, he knocked on Percy's door, listening to the sound of the melting snow, dripping from the rafters. He caught a glance of the neighbor a neat looking man who hurried into his house after sending Stephen a suspicious look. Stephen knocked on the door again. As he stood on the porch, he rehearsed what he would say. He'd offer to help him install a fixture or two nothing fancy. It was up to Percy to say no.

Percy peered out the door suspicious. "Hello?"

Stephen shoved his hands in his back jeans pockets. "Hi, um I'm Stephen Garrett. I've been thinking about your house and--"

He frowned. "It's not for sale."

"No, I'm an electrician and I see your house is kinda dark. I could help with some--"

"I'm fine." He began to close the door.

"It wouldn't cost you anything," he said quickly. "Actually, if you give me some time I bet I could at least fix your sink in the kitchen. You shouldn't have standing water like that."

Percy hesitated then opened the door wider. "Why would you want to help me?"

Stephen shrugged. "Nothing better to do." He took out his wallet and handed him his card. He remembered Brenna insisting he get one and now was glad. "Here's my card. As I said it won't cost you anything. You can check me out if you want. I encourage that you do."

Percy stared at the card then up at Stephen. He finally nodded. "I trust you. Come on in."

Stephen spent the rest of the day with him. They chatted as Stephen fixed the sink, then a rusty door. They ordered some sub sandwiches and talked about TV and sports then Percy's family. Midday he drove Percy to the site off of Riggs Road where his daughter was killed. Then they went to a bar later that evening where they watched a game of darts. Under a black sky they returned home. Stephen knew he could have dropped him off and returned home, but he didn't feel like going home just yet. He told Percy his ideas for his place. Percy listened impressed and asked him to check the lighting in another room. Stephen did and saw that it needed a lot of work. He returned to the living room to tell Percy his observation when he saw the older man sitting on the couch, hunched over a machine scanning a card.

"What are you doing?"

Percy jumped. "Oh, you're done looking already?"

His darting look made Stephen more suspicious. Stephen snatched the card from Percy's hand and read it. It was a credit card with his name on it. He then glanced at the machine. "Planning on robbing me?"

Percy looked sheepish. "I wouldn't have taken much."

"So this was your plan all along?"

He was quiet a moment, absently tugging on his right ear. "You're young. How old are you? Twenty? Twenty-one?"

"I'm twenty-five."

Percy nodded then leaned back to rest one arm the length of the couch. "This is all just a small misunderstanding."

"No, it's a crime."

"I didn't expect you to come back so quickly. I'm sorry. I couldn't help myself, but I'll pay you back for the things you bought." He reached for his wallet.

Stephen grabbed the machine off the side table and turned towards the door angry at himself for being duped. "Goodbye."

"I'm sorry."

He swung the door open. "I don't believe you."

"Will you still consider fixing my place?"

Stephen glanced at him. "Don't push it old man."

"Look I said I'd pay you back. I'm desperate. My Social Security doesn't cover everything and no one will hire me and I need the money, but I shouldn't have planned on taking from you. I made a mistake."

Stephen saw the sadness on his face and felt both disgusted and guilty at the same time. "So did I."

"Stephen I--"

"I've gotta go. My wife will wonder where I am." He raced into his truck and slammed the door. He swore as he pulled out of the drive and sped down the street. He'd been an idiot. Harmless old man my ass. Fiona was right. It'd been a stupid idea. He parked then took off his shirt knowing how much she hated him coming home sweaty. He changed into the shirt he'd brought to wear then took a deep breath before heading inside.

"Where were you?" she asked as he came through the door.

"Out," he said. He walked past her and headed straight to the shower.

Brenna glanced around the studio as the camera crew set up to see if Hunter was around. The make-up artist had almost given up on her for being so fidgety, but she couldn't help it. The success of this commercial depended completely on her. A part of her felt she was making a big mistake. Her entire reputation had been built on what she'd been able to do despite her leg and now...now she was making it a part of her. Admitting her limitations in front of thousands of people. How she needed a cane to walk, something other people did without thinking. Those kids who had taunted her at school, those patronizing teachers could now point and say 'See that's all she ended up doing.' Her spirit rebelled, but then surrendered. She had to succeed at this. It had to be done. The company was important to her and Hunter and she wasn't going to back out now.

She'd hoped he would have made the time to stop by, at least for some moral support, if not to see that everything went as planned. Unfortunately, he was nowhere in sight.

"Ready?" the director asked her.

She nodded and walked into position.

She smiled at the camera, ready for another performance although this time she entered the stage alone.

Miles came up to her once taping was over. "You're a natural at this."

She turned, pleased to see him. "It's my first time."

"I wouldn't have known. Nor will anyone else."

"I'm glad you came."

"Wouldn't miss it."

They both fell quiet as they thought of the man who did.

Brenna buttoned her coat. "I suppose when you spend your life pretending, you get good at it."

He looked at her curious. "Pretending what?"

She shrugged trying to make light of it. "Oh the usual. That you're strong, that things don't bother you, that you don't mind being different."

"Are you still pretending?"

All the time. "You know this is the first time that I've talked about my leg and struggles without defiance or worrying that someone will pity me." She paused thoughtful. "I hope to inspire others not to just use Randolph's products but to live with pride." The way she'd been unable to.

He rested a brotherly arm on her shoulders. "I hope you're ready."

"For what?"

"Once the commercial airs, everybody's going to want you."

He was right. The commercial was an instant success. As February slipped into March, sales skyrocketed. Soon news programs and radio shows (online and off) clamored for the attractive woman who had inspired her husband's latest creation. Fan letters started pouring in and Brenna was asked to speak at rehabilitation centers. She presented at colleges and nursing homes. Miles managed to attend every one.

She laughed when she saw him, flattered. "Miles, you can't keep this up."

"Why not? I like seeing you."

She glanced at Sara who was speaking to a photographer. She had expertly kept Brenna's image in the media without the threat of overexposure. "If you're not careful, you'll make Sara jealous."

"No, she understands." He watched Sara, his feelings for her clear in his gaze. "She's not bad."

"I know."

"You're not too bad yourself. Has Hunter said anything?"

Her eyes slid away. "What do you think?"

"I think he's an idiot."

She smiled. "That's okay. He's busy."

"As always. You have the right to demand more."

"And lose what I have? No thank you."

Hunter rewound the video of Brenna's commercial for the sixth time. He liked watching her, always had. Beside this was the only time he got to see her. Alone in his office at the end of the day. They were both so busy with work they may as well be passing strangers at home. He watched her, reminding himself she belonged to him although it didn't feel that way anymore.

He paused the image when someone knocked on the door. "Come in."

Ruby entered draped in a tan cashmere coat. "I was afraid I'd still find you here."

"I'm not the only one. Dad, Uncle and Daron are still here."

"They're different."

"From me?"

She took off her coat then sat. "Yes."

He hated how everyone thought he was different. He'd prove them wrong. "I will succeed. I have the drive, discipline--"

"Yes, but not the heart."

"Business doesn't take heart."

"Exactly." She glanced at the frozen image of Brenna on the TV. "And you have too much of it."

He shut the TV off and tossed the remote in the drawer. "Don't be

ridiculous."

"You don't want to be here. You don't want eighty hour work weeks. You want to be with your wife at home, and you'll want to be with your child when you have one. You'll want to attend soccer games, school plays and science fairs. All the things your father never did."

He shook his head.

"If you're not careful, you'll lose her."

Hunter punched in numbers on a calculator just to look busy. "Fortunately, I plan to be very careful."

"You know Miles has attended every one of Brenna's presentation."

He cracked his knuckles, keeping his voice level. "Yes, I know. Amazing how he finds the time."

"Your mother--"

Hunter steepled his fingers together. "My mother is not part of the equation."

"She was a wonderful woman."

"Was she?" he asked bored. "That's nice to know."

"Hunter this isn't like you. Your mother--"

He held up his hand. His eyes dark with warning.

Ruby crossed her legs at the ankles and started again. "I want to help you."

His jaw twitched with banked anger. "By suggesting I give the job to Doran? Come in second again? Is that how you want to help me?"

"Your father is worried about some of the things you're doing."

His voice became quiet. "He has a right to be."

Her tone sharpened. "What does that mean?"

It meant that he'd spoken to accounting and his suspicions had only grown. "I was afraid you'd see me."

"Then you could have saved me the trip." She sighed resigned. "I know there's money missing. You can't do anything."

"Why not?"

"That's the way it works here."

"What do you mean?"

"I mean a company can't steal from itself. Whatever is going on is perfectly legal just immoral. Leave it alone."

"Ask him."

"We're a family. We should be there for each other."

"So you admit something is wrong?"

"I admit that I have never seen your father or grandfather so anxious."

He raised a mocking brow. "And you're here to make sure I soothe their anxiety?"

"I want you to succeed. I want everyone to get what they want."

"They will. They just have to trust me."

She let her voice fall. "You used to confide in me."

He stood. "I don't need anyone to confide in. I'm here to do a job and I will do it." He lifted her coat and held it out. "Will I see you Saturday?"

She slid into the coat then grabbed her handbag. "Of course."

"Good."

Ruby opened her mouth to say more then stopped herself. They exchanged stilted good-byes then she left the office, feeling defeated. Curtis met her in the lobby. "Well?"

"He's being secretive, but he says he won't cause trouble." Though not in so many words.

Curtis sighed relieved. "That's something."

"At least he's willing to do the party. His wife will soothe things over."

"His wife may be part of the trouble," he said in a grim tone. "I wonder what he knows."

"Do you think he's told her?"

"We'll have to find out."

Saturday evening brought a cool March breeze. Brenna listened to the low murmur of voices, the tinkling of glasses. She watched the room filled with well dressed guests and trays of canapés carried by wait staff that effortlessly blended into the background. Brenna smiled pleased. The event was a success.

"Excellent job," Hunter said.

His praise made her smile, seeming to melt away the tense weeks between them. "So the family is adequately appeased?"

"Appears so. You look beautiful."

"Thank you, but you should be mingling with guests not complimenting me."

He glanced around unenthused. "I know."

"Boring people, aren't they?"

He grinned, a dimple winking at her. "Yes."

"We have another hour before we can get rid of them."

He set his glass down on a passing tray. "That long? If you need to leave early--"

"I'm fine."

Curtis came up behind him and grasped his shoulder. "There's someone I want you to meet." He nodded at Brenna. "Excuse us." He led Hunter away.

Brenna checked the kitchen and then the bar. Satisfied that everything was running smoothly she returned to the main room. Angie walked up to her with a gait that was a little too relaxed. "Nice turn out," she said, a snide coldness in her tone.

"Yes."

"I suppose you got the list?"

"Yes."

"Of course you would. You're a Randolph now. You must do things the Randolph way."

Brenna glanced at a passing waiter. "Would you like--"

"I remember my first party. I was so nervous."

"I'm not nervous."

"Of course. You are older than I was and Hunter was just starting out at the time. What does he plan to do next at Randolph?"

"I don't know."

"Doran and I talk about everything. When he finally comes home," she said with a bitter laugh. "Does Hunter? He used to talk to me all the time."

Brenna leaned against her cane. "I'm sure he did, but I can wager it wasn't about work."

"No." She measured her up and down. "I wonder if people came to see Hunter or the Randolph spokeswoman. Amazing the things a woman will do for her husband."

The words hit their mark, but she didn't flinch. "You can thank your husband for the suggestion."

Her eyes hardened. "Don't be so smug. You have no idea why Hunter's risen so fast."

"He worked hard."

"Doran deserves this." She looked around. "The house, the job." She spread her arm wide. "All of this." She returned her gaze to Brenna. "You don't know what this is doing to him." Her voice fell. "To us."

Hunter came up behind Angie and took her martini glass. "Still can't hold your drinks."

She turned to him. "Maybe not, but I can hold a few secrets." She wagged a finger at him. "And I have a big one about your mother."

"So?"

Angie faltered surprised by his disinterest. "She didn't leave you, you know."

He paused. "What do you mean?"

"She was taken away."

He frowned. "Taken away?"

Her mouth widened into a cool smile. "Yes, in a nice white jacket."

Brenna narrowed her eyes. "What are you talking about?"

Angie grabbed another glass and took a sip her eyes shining with malicious glee. "His mother was mad."

Chapter Seventeen

"Perhaps it's time for you to go home," Brenna said gently, taking her arm.

Angie snatched her arm away. "I'm not drunk. I'm nursing a very nice buzz right now, but I know exactly what I'm saying." She turned her gaze to Hunter. "The whole family watches you trying to see if there are traces of the madness in you. But I saw it once, didn't I? When you touched me

and--"

"Don't," he said in a harsh tone that was almost a plea.

"Told me how much you needed me," she continued in a taunting voice. "I could swear there were tears in your eyes. The strong man I'd married dissolving into tears like a baby. Holding me so tight I thought you'd never let me breathe again." She looked at Brenna. "He needs help. He's full of repressed memories." She touched the side of his face. "Why do you think he's so cold? If I didn't feel your skin, I'd think you were dead."

Hunter removed her hand.

She looked at Brenna. "How many lonely nights have there been?" She shook her head. "You don't need to tell me. When he wasn't begging me to be with him, he was shutting me out. He does that well." She grabbed his sleeve, pushing her face up to his. "They told me you were the one who found her. You were holding her in your arms as though you were a man strong enough to lift her. I'm sure scenes like that must affect a little child. And they're still buried there. And the whole family has conspired to make sure you keep them buried. And they'll continue to humor you and applaud you, even when you don't deserve it." She turned to Brenna. "I'd be careful. You never know when he might snap." She sauntered away.

Brenna opened her mouth, but Hunter shook his head. She knew he didn't want to talk about it but couldn't help herself. "Do you believe her?"

He shoved a hand in his pocket.

"I guess you're going to shut me out too."

He spun around and pinned her with a dark stare. "Have I ever been dishonest? Haven't I given you all that you wanted? Any question, don't I answer it?"

"Yes."

"Then never use her words against me."

She swallowed the gleam in his eyes worrying her. Pain, hurt, rage mingled too closely to the surface. "I'm sorry."

He stared past her. "I see Ruby. I'm going to ask her a few questions." He left before Brenna could reply. "I need to have a word," he said once he'd reached her.

She turned to him. "Yes?"

"Was my mother crazy?"

She took a step back startled. "I don't know what you're talking about."

He folded his arms. "You're a poor liar."

She looked uncomfortable. She glanced around and kept her voice low. "This isn't the place."

"Yes or no?"

She hesitated then said, "She had problems."

"Problems?"

"Yes, she came from a very difficult background and was haunted by things. Your father cared for her, but he couldn't care for her enough. It was decided she needed to be protected."

"From herself or from others?"

"It's not what you think." She rubbed her hands together. "Who told you about this?"

"The real question is: Why didn't you?"

"It was for the best," Curtis said behind him. "We didn't want to upset you. And now that you know it doesn't change anything. Your mother had become almost a myth in your eyes and now you see she was just an ordinary woman."

Hunter nodded his tone sarcastic. "Yes, a woman who was crazy and locked in an insane asylum. She sounds very ordinary."

"Facts," he said tersely. "Deal in facts. She was a woman with a mental illness, put in a facility able to deal with her special needs."

"If it was such a simple fact, why did you tell me she left to have a career?"

Curtis glanced at Ruby. She said, "You were young. It was a painful truth we wanted to keep from you."

"So you lied to me."

Ruby gripped her hands together. "This is not the place," she said lowering her voice to an anxious whisper. "Please. People could overhear us."

"Then that's your mistake for not telling me sooner."

"We didn't want her state of mind to influence your behavior," Curtis said. "Knowing your mother was mad may have affected your own behavior."

"You think I may have thought I was crazy too?"

"Perhaps."

"But he had a right to know," Brenna said.

Curtis turned to her, a biting anger sharpening his tone. "You, young woman, are imposing on a private conversation."

Hunter smoothed out an eyebrow. "Careful father. You're talking to my wife."

"I am very aware with whom I am speaking. I'm speaking to someone not part of your past. She will pass judgment on things she doesn't understand. We may have made an error, but the past cannot be changed. We said and did what we thought was best for you. So I suggest you leave it there--in the past. For your own good. It was bad enough dealing with your mother, she almost brought this company down. Promise me you won't do the same." He accepted Hunter's silence as acquiescence. "Good now why don't you two go and mingle with your guests?"

HUNTER SAT on the edge of the bed, staring at the dusk particles as they fell in front of the lamp light. Evening had settled in a warm darkness. The outside encased in stillness; inside he heard Brenna move about in the closet. He should be preparing for bed as she was, but he couldn't seem to move. All that he had known about himself-- his past--had been destroyed. Like a raging fire, Angie's words had turned everything it touched into ash. He felt as though his mother had left him again. The same desolate numbness entered his heart as it had years ago.

Odd how he never remembered seeing her leave. He remembered her coat being left by the door and wondering why she hadn't taken it. He had always expected her to come back. If not for him then at least for it. His father said she'd gone away. There was no sit down talk or chance for tears. It was a matter of fact report. He'd nodded and gone back to his room--numb. Left with the only truth he could grasp--one moment she was there then she was gone. He didn't remember much else. What did Angie mean by him finding her? What had he found? What did his family not want him to remember?

There had to be something. That night years ago when he'd gone to Angie in need (for what, he wasn't sure, he just wanted to hold her) still brought shame. There was something pushing its way through his mind. He'd just wanted to be with her, love her.

He was careful never to show that need now. Brenna would not see what Angie had. Although at times it welled up in him so strong he had to leave the room. There were times when he would bury his face in her pillow craving her warmth, craving to be inside her. He could feel that need now. Angie's words had left him without his shield, exposed like the soft flesh of a crab. He hated the feeling and fought to control it. He would control it. He was always in control.

He heard Brenna come into the room and felt his entire body tense. He couldn't look at her. Instead he continued to watch the dust particles fall. He closed his eyes when she sat beside him the scent of her lilac soap circling him. He felt her press her lips against the back of his neck.

He moved away then wished he hadn't. He moved to touch her, but Brenna had already put distance between them. He stood and paced.

"Your family doesn't like me," she said. "But they like you even less."

He stopped. "Don't be ridiculous."

"Then why the warning? Why can't you ask about your mother? You have a right to know."

"I don't care."

"You don't care that your mother was crazy?"

"It's the past."

"Your past."

His tone hardened. "A past I don't want to remember."

"This is what they wanted. They wanted you to feel ashamed so they can keep you in line. What if they're lying?"

He shook his head. "They're not."

"How do you know?"

"They wouldn't lie to me."

She bit her lip. "Why not?"

"They're my family."

"And they've never lied to you before?"

"They have no reason to lie."

She folded her arms then softly asked, "What have you been doing at work?"

He went to the bathroom.

She followed. "What have you been doing at work?"

"Regular--"

She held up a hand. "I want the truth."

He sighed exasperated. "I've been asking some questions."

"Such as?"

"Things in accounting don't add up. I wanted to know why."

"Did you find out?"

"In a way."

She nodded glad the pieces were coming together. "Then you have your reason. Someone wants to stop you."

"They won't be able to." He turned on the faucet and washed his hands although he didn't need to. "Someone probably made a mistake and is in deeper than they thought. I can clear things up then go along with my plan."

"If they let you," Brenna said in a voice so low, he didn't hear her.

BRENNA WAS NOT surprised by the invitation to visit the Virginia ranch that showed up two days later. She arrived as a chill wind blew, knocking against the bare branches of the trees that stood silhouette in the distance. Patches of snow was scattered about on the gravel drive. Ruby invited her to have tea in the kitchen nook where they could enjoy cucumber sandwiches and pastries.

"I'm glad you could make it," Ruby said. "I wanted to apologize for how poorly things were handled Saturday."

Brenna nodded. "It was an awkward situation."

"Has Hunter spoken about it since then?"

"No, he's following your advice and leaving it in the past. He's too focused on work to let it bother him."

"Of course. His work is a big part of his life. Most of us wives get used to it. Curtis and I used to talk about the company for hours."

Brenna smiled faintly as she put sugar in her tea.

After a delicate pause she asked, "Do you and Hunter talk about things?"

"Not about work."

"I see."

Brenna sipped her tea then set it down. She sent Ruby a direct look. "So if there's anything you want to know, you'll have to ask him."

She looked chagrined. "Not very subtle, was I?"

"I realize Hunter's proposed changes can be unsettling, but he has the company's best interest in mind."

"Yes, I know." She stirred her tea then set the spoon aside. "He just doesn't know how powerful Orson is."

"Orson should be proud of what Hunter is doing or trying to do."

Ruby's tone turned bitter. "Orson is only proud when things reflect well on him. Hunter must realize the company is not his to run."

"He knows that. He--" Brenna stopped before she mentioned the accounting errors. "He loves his family."

"In the strange way they are able to love I suppose. He was different not just because of his mother but because he was him. He was a very self-contained child. It was odd to see a four and five year old able to occupy himself for hours. He accepted me almost immediately when I came. Perhaps he was desperate for a mother figure, I was never quite sure. He was easy to handle, a good child except." She picked up a pastry and stared outside.

"Except what?"

She turned to Brenna with regret. "Except he had these moments of temper. We couldn't understand them. Moments when he would just tremble, his eyes turning black without any reason. It was quick, unpredictable then gone. His mother said they scared her."

"So you knew her?"

"I didn't know her well."

"How did you meet her?"

"I visited her once to tell her about Hunter."

Brenna leaned forward eager. "I want to know more about his mother."

Ruby's smooth tone dipped. "No, you don't."

"Since the beginning of our acquaintance I've sensed you wanted to tell me something."

"There's nothing more to tell."

"Could I at least know her name?"

Ruby let her gaze fall then reluctantly said, "Marlene."

"What did she do? Did she work? Is she still alive?"

"There is a trunk in the attic that may answer some of your questions. I think--"

"So glad you could join us," Curtis said, entering the kitchen.

"Thank you," Brenna said frustrated by his appearance.

"Must have been quite a drive for you."

"It was fine."

He squinted out the window. "You should have had Hunter drive you."

"I can drive myself."

He turned to her with faint praise. "An independent woman."

Ruby spoke up. "I sent the invitation directly to her. Hunter didn't need to come."

He nodded then left. Just when Brenna was about to ask about the trunk, the chef required Ruby's assistance with the dinner menu.

Brenna excused herself, asked for directions from one of the housekeeping staff and went to the attic. It was better kept than she'd expected. It had a little desk and chair, old clothes and toys and strangely no dust. She spotted the trunk Ruby had been referring to and opened it. There wasn't much inside. A journal of household expenses, childish drawings and reports, then she saw loose papers written in a woman's hand. One started 'Dear Ruby' and ended 'Marlene'. She grabbed the letters and began to read them. Unfortunately, they didn't make sense. Marlene spoke of a crying child and sadness then strange flights of fancy.

Suddenly, she heard footsteps as someone climbed the attic stairway. She heard the door open then a bolt lock.

Curtis came into the room. He tried to smile, but the expression didn't warm his eyes. "Now how did you find your way up here?"

"I was looking to see where Hunter spent his time as a child. Ruby told me he spent a lot of time here."

He held out his hand. "Whatever you found I suggest you give it to me."

"Why would I find anything?" she challenged.

He smoothed out his beard. "Because you have an active imagination."

"I don't have anything that would concern you."

"How would you know what would concern me?" He stood in front of her. "My first wife was ill. There's no hidden story to unearth. It's a painful chapter in my life. I'm trying to protect my son from it. This is how I like to remember her." He held out a picture.

Brenna took it and stared at the faded photo. She noticed the dimples, the easy smile.

"There was no sign of madness when I married her. Perhaps I ignored it. I was busy with work, I admit to not seeing any signs until too late. She stayed home with Hunter and his nanny. Things were fine until she began to hear voices. I'd come home and find Hunter under the bed or in the closet where she'd put him to be safe. I knew then that something had to be done. The Mitchell Home took her."

"Is she still there?"

"No, a sister of hers took her out after a few years and I haven't heard from her since."

Brenna handed him back the picture. "And you've made no attempts to find her?"

"There's no point. I doubt she'd even remember me."

"What was she diagnosed with?"

He hesitated. "Diagnosed?"

"Yes, the mysterious illness must have had a name. Psychologist love naming things."

"Schizophrenia I believe. They used a lot of technical terms."

"So that's all?"

"Yes."

"Then why did you lock the door when you just came in?"

He blinked. "I didn't lock the door."

Her brows furrowed. "But I heard--"

"You can check for yourself."

She did the doorknob turned easily.

"Active imagination," he said behind her, mocking. "I'll go get your coat."

Brenna didn't believe him. She drove home a decision seizing her: She would find out about the institution and Marlene Randolph.

STEPHEN SAT in front of the couch and turned on the TV. He was half asleep when someone knocked on the door. He rubbed his eyes and opened it. To two uniformed police officers stood there.

"Yes?" he said.

"Stephen Garrett?"

"Yes?"

"We have a warrant for your arrest in connection with the death of

Percy Seaborn..."

Chapter Eighteen

Stephen sat in the interview room trying not to stare at the acne pockmarks of the interrogating officer Ramos. He had a round face and easy manner unlike the other officer who stood in the corner. A lean man with a face like a boxer and small dark eyes which made his expression hard to read. Stephen let his gaze drift away still shocked that Percy had been bludgeoned to death.

"When I left him he was fine," he said, answering a question neither officer had asked.

Ramos rested a hand on the table. "We found your fingerprints on the murder weapon. Why don't you make this easy on yourself? I know he stole from you. He's done it to others. You got upset and things go out of control. Trust me, you weren't the first one this guy made angry. Identity theft is a personal crime."

Stephen leaned back in his chair, shaking his head. "I wasn't that angry." He lowered his head, scraping his shoe against the floor. "Actually, I felt a little sorry for him."

"So he did steal from you?"

He glanced up. "Yes, but I didn't kill him."

"We have witnesses that saw you leaving the residence in a hurry. An autopsy proved that he was dead around the time you left."

"I didn't kill him." He glanced at the guy in the corner then back at Ramos. "I'm not saying anymore until I get a lawyer." The man's eyes narrowed; Ramos sighed. That obviously wasn't the statement they wanted to hear.

THE NEXT DAY, Brenna stared at her brother through the glass barricade as he sat in his prison jumpsuit trying to look brave. She absently hooked her cane on the edge of her chair, hoping this was all a bad dream. Her mother's voice mail message still echoed: 'They're trying to hang your brother'. She remembered listening to the message three times certain that she'd misheard. She'd wished that Hunter had been home so that he could have heard it to. But he was away on business. So she stood by the phone in the large house feeling as though her world was collapsing.

Stephen didn't meet her eyes; he stared at the high window behind her. "You shouldn't have come here."

"Nothing could keep me away." When he didn't reply she said, "Are you okay?" She wished that she had something more substantial to say. He didn't look okay. He looked tired, anxious. She couldn't blame him.

"I'm fine." He let his gaze fall to the table. "The arraignment is to be held tomorrow."

"You should get off on bail. You're not a flight risk."

"Hmm."

"Scared?"

"Yea."

"Me too."

He rested his chin in his hand and sighed then lifted his gaze to her face. "Look after Fiona for me will you?"

Brenna inwardly cringed, but nodded. "Has she come by yet?"

"No. I don't want her to see me here anyway," he added in defense.

Brenna looked down at the table letting the subject drop. "It's all a mistake. I'm sure everything will get cleared up soon."

He tugged on his goatee. "Yes, have you told Hunter about this?"

She hesitated. "No, he's busy. This is a family issue."

"You're ashamed of me?"

She widened her eyes in surprise. "Of course not. This is a big mistake. You're innocent. Why would I be ashamed?"

"I was once ashamed of you for something you couldn't control."

Brenna managed a smile. "Fortunately, that's no longer true."

He glanced at the metal bars over the windows. "Brings back memories, doesn't it?"

"This is different. Don't think about last time." She glanced at her watch. "I'd better go."

"Yea."

"Take care of yourself."

"You too."

She stood hating to leave him there. "I love you."

He smiled and she saw a bit of her devilish brother shine through. "How much?"

"Very much."

"Then how about switching places?"

"I'm going to do much better than that. I'm going to get you out of here."

Over a week later, Brenna walked into the courthouse prepared to see her brother released. She'd made reservations at a restaurant to celebrate that victory. She knew that her mother had chosen a top attorney to defend Stephen although she wouldn't tell her any details. She hurried down the corridor her heels making a clicking noise against the tile floors.

"Where's the fire?" an amused male voice said.

She ignored him and dashed into an elevator. He followed

behind her, noticed the floor number she pushed and said, "We might be going to the same place."

"I doubt it."

"You shouldn't be so certain, Brenna."

She froze. Her stomach twisted as an icy fear wrapped around her heart. She didn't turn around and she didn't ask him how he knew her name. She already knew the answer. When the doors opened she stood paralyzed as people exited and entered the elevator and rushed past.

Byron gently took her elbow and led her out. "The court is this way."

His voice broke through her paralysis. She yanked her arm free and stared up at him. For a moment she wished she hadn't. He hadn't changed. Time hadn't seemed to touch him. He possessed a nonchalant grace that age should have tempered but instead seemed more defined. He flashed a quick confident smile that should have been off-putting, but offered a teasing invitation. Eyes brown like hazel nut coffee gazed down at her. She fought against the tug in her heart and kept her tone level. "What are you doing here?"

"I'm representing your brother."

"Since when?"

"Since your mother hired me."

"My mother," she said as though it was a curse word.

He glanced at his watch. "We'll discuss this later."

"We won't discuss this at all."

He smiled then jogged down the hall. Brenna slowly followed behind. When she reached the court room she watched Byron talking to Stephen. When he saw her, he winked. She gripped her cane and left the room. She couldn't watch him. She stood outside the room staring blankly at the wall trying not to analyze her feelings. Trying to force herself not to care. When the doors finally opened she spotted her mother and rushed up to her. "Mom."

Diane gripped her hands and smiled. "Byron got Stephen off on bail. He's wonderful, you should have seen him."

"Why him?"

"I had no choice."

"Of course you had a choice," she said, struggling not to scream. "You could have used the public defender."

"She didn't care. She was ready to enter into a plea. Brenna, he was the only one I could think of. Are you upset about this?"

Yes! "Does it matter? I doubt if I said I was you'd find someone else. So let's just say I'm fine. I'm perfectly fine that you hired my ex to defend my brother. Everything is just perfect."

"What happened between you two?"

"Silly dreams crushed by reality that's all."

"I know that Hunter's not there. You're in that big house all alone. Perhaps I should come over and--"

Before she could reply, Stephen came up and hugged her, lifting his sister off her feet. "She meant well," he whispered in her ear.

"That doesn't fix things," she whispered back.

When Stephen set her down she saw Fiona wiping tears then Byron standing behind him. "How would you like to finish our discussion?"

"I have work to do." She turned and left.

At home, Brenna sat in the living room, staring at the phone. She picked up a pen and chewed on the end then put it down. She should call Hunter.

She picked up the phone then set it down. No need to get Hunter involved in this until he got back. There was nothing he could do. He'd be a nice shield though. A husband made a nice statement. A statement of: See you may not have wanted me, but someone else did. Not that Byron would care. Was he married too? Did he have kids? Perhaps she could orchestrate a way to never meet him except in the courtroom where they would be surrounded by lots of people. Yes, that would be perfect.

A few days later, that hope died.

Pauline came into her office with a knowing look. "You have a visitor."

"Who?"

"You'll see."

Brenna turned to the computer then spun around in her chair. "It's

not--"

Pauline nodded. "Yes, it is."

She briefly shut her eyes. "What is he doing here?"

"I didn't see a ring on his finger. Perhaps he needs a date."

"Tell him I'm busy."

"No. It's for your own good."

"Fine," she said resigned. "Send him in." She picked up a pen then tossed it aside. She was fine. He couldn't hurt her. She wouldn't let him. When he walked into the room, Brenna steeled herself for the impact.

It didn't help. He still made her insides tremble. "Hello Brenna," he said in a sweet baritone.

She struggled to keep her voice professional. "How may I help you?"

He sat. "You know why I'm here."

"Either you're looking for a woman or a reason to waste my time. I'm not sure yet."

He raised a brow surprised at the tone. "I thought we'd parted as friends."

"Are you seeking a discount?"

A flash of temper crossed his gaze, the emotion quickly disappeared. He smiled and glanced at her hand. "I see you're married now."

"I see that you're not."

Byron leaned back with a casual air as though he had all the time in the world. "I decided to focus on my career." He folded his arms. "So you're Mrs. Hunter Randolph now."

"Is that a statement or a question?"

"Brenna, please." He shook his head with regret. "Did I really hurt you that much?"

Yes. But she wouldn't give him the satisfaction or advantage of thinking so. She was married now; he was no longer a threat. She wouldn't let him be. "What are you up to?"

"You're looking well, Brenna."

She leaned back in her chair. "You're looking surprisingly well yourself."

He raised his brows. "Why surprisingly?"

"You dress well for a man who's lost his last three cases."

He paused then sighed. "How did you know?"

"Research. I looked you up."

"I didn't know you cared."

"I care about my brother."

"So do I."

"If you lose this case—"

He folded his arms. "I don't plan to lose."

"Did you plan to lose your other cases?"

His arms fell. "Don't push me Brenna."

"I suggest you leave." She sat forward ready to dismiss him. "If there is any way I can assist you with Stephen's case--"

"You can let me take you out for coffee."

She frowned. "How will that help Stephen?"

He smiled. "I like coffee." His smile grew. "Are you scared to have coffee with me?"

She tilted her head to the side. "I don't remember you being arrogant."

He leaned forward. "I don't remember you being timid."

It was a challenge she couldn't resist. "Coffee's fine."

Byron chose an upscale cafe off a main street that boasted design boutiques and expensive furniture stores. The quiet cafe held the scent of cream, coffee beans and vanilla. Brenna didn't like fussy coffees so she ordered hers black. Byron ordered a Colombian mix.

He rested back in his chair, his brown blazer intensifying the color of his eyes. "Did you tell your husband about this?"

"My husband is out of town."

He raised a brow, from surprise or censure she wasn't sure. She told herself she didn't care. "You didn't tell him about the indictment?"

"No."

"So you're dealing with this all alone?"

"I have my family."

Byron nodded, a smile quirking his lips. "Your mother hasn't changed."

Brenna couldn't help but smile too. "No."

He lifted his cup. "Tell me about Stephen."

She sipped her coffee wondering what she could say. "He's a wonderful hardworking man."

"What about his personal life?"

"He's married."

"Yes, I've met her."

It was his tone rather than his words that caught her attention. She narrowed her eyes. "What did you think?"

"Do I have to tell you?"

They shared a look then began to grin. Brenna said, "No."

He exaggerated a look of relief. "Thank you."

"He loves her though."

"Is he happy?"

She turned the mug handle away, trying to choose the right words. Was Stephen happy? She couldn't tell. "I don't know. Why would that matter?"

"Law is as much about psychology as it is about evidence. The DA is going to paint a picture of him as a calm decent citizen who snapped under the pressure of his life. I need background."

She paused. "Stephen would never snap. He's always easygoing."

"Everyone has a breaking point."

Brenna's eyes met his, her tone firm. "Stephen would never break to the point of murdering someone. Especially an old man. And if you think--"

Byron held up his hands in surrender. "I'm on his side, remember?" He rested his arms on the table his tone teasing. "Still have that defiant spirit." His voice filled with regret. "Shame I could never get you to follow me into law."

" Even though you could get me to follow you everywhere else?"

His gaze dropped to his cup. "Yea." He glanced up at a man trying to balance three drinks and a muffin then he looked at her. "So how did you meet him?"

"Well when Mom brought him home from the hospital, I didn't really have a choice."

"I meant your husband," Byron said in a dry tone.

"Planning on putting him on the stand?"

"No, just curious."

"You'll have to ask my mother how I met him." She couldn't remember the story they'd constructed. "It's nothing riveting." He just barged into my office one day and asked me to stand in as his fiancée.

"What's he like?"

Brenna tried not to smile. Hunter seemed to defy description. "He's ambitious."

"Is that why he's not here with you?"

She narrowed her gaze. "Objection. Relevancy."

He folded his arms. "Overruled."

"You can't be both the judge and the prosecution."

"I can in this court. Answer the question."

Brenna lifted her mug, glad her grip remained steady. She felt alive and suddenly as hot as the beverage in her hand. She was surprised and dismayed that he could still make her feel this way. "When it becomes your business I'll tell you."

"Are you happy?"

"Are you?"

Byron looked at her for a long moment then glanced away. "The prosecution rests."

"Good."

He shook his head amazed. "I wish—"

"Don't."

He turned to her, his eyes sweeping her face. "You're right. No good comes from looking back." His expression suddenly became grim and a little ruthless. It was a side of him she'd suspected but had never seen. "This case is going to be a difficult one. The DA is confident. That is never a good sign, but I promise you I'll do everything I can."

Brenna met his eyes and for a moment her heart stopped and she feared that once again it would begin to beat in time to his. She twisted the ring on her finger, remembering the silent promise it made. "I know."

Two DAYS LATER, Brenna sat in a restaurant with Miles.

"You're quiet today," he said. He'd been kind enough to invite her to lunch and she welcomed the distraction.

"I'm sorry I'm such bad company."

"You could never be that."

"How are you and Sara?"

He waved a fork. "Don't evade the issue."

"Which is?"

"You're worried about something."

"I'm worried about a lot of things. My brother, my marriage." She glanced up guilty.

"Go on."

"Sometimes I forget you're Hunter's friend."

"Yes, sometimes he forgets that too. I like you both, so you can consider me a neutral party." He raised a hand as though ready to make a pledge. "Anything you say to me won't reach him okay?"

Brenna chewed on her lower lip then said, "A few days ago I had coffee with my ex-boyfriend who happens to be my brother's attorney."

Miles blinked. "I take back what I said."

"You'll tell Hunter?"

He thought for a moment then shook his head. "No, but you'll have to. Have you called him?"

"He can't help me right now."

"So you didn't call him?"

"No."

"But--"

"Trust me. I know him."

"I know him too. He'll--"

Brenna pushed her salad around on her plate. "You don't have to worry about me being faithful to him."

"I'm not, but don't shut him out even though it's easy to do."

She glanced up ready to change the subject. "How are things at work?"

"Fine since Hunter's been away. Nobody is getting nervous."

"Do you know what he's up to?"

"No."

"Are you lying?"

"Maybe." Miles held up a hand before she could speak. "This time we won't get involved."

She reluctantly agreed.

An hour later she sat in her office. Pauline entered a few minutes later. "If you're hungry, get something to eat."

Brenna looked down at the pen she'd been chewing. "I'm just thinking." She glanced at her watch. "In about forty minutes I have to give Carlotta some tips about her date. She's nervous. Then I have a quick speech at the Abby House for seniors, I'll get back here for my appointment with a possible new client, meet with Sara for a new commercial idea and print ads. Then I'll call Stephen."

"What about your doctor's appointment?"

She waved that away. "Oh, I'll have to reschedule."

Pauline sat, her voice concerned. "Brenna, you can't keep this up. You can't run Love by Design and be the spokeswoman for Randolph and worry about your brother. You have to take care of yourself."

No. She had to keep busy to keep her mind from going crazy. "I do take care of myself."

"What about Hunter? What does he think?"

Hunter?! Why did everyone care about what he thought? She was married, but she was still an individual who could take care of herself. "He agrees." She read Pauline's face and shook her head. "You may not like him. I respect that, but remember he is my husband."

"No, he's not. He's your business partner. A husband would be there for you no matter what. There are no conditions. It's not dependent on his career success."

Brenna's voice became neutral. "I like helping the company and I have the energy to do it."

"You mean to run away from the truth. You're doing all this because you're afraid," she said impatient. "You're afraid he'll leave you if he loses his job. So you think if his career is strong he'll stay no matter what. Right?" She shook her head. "You don't have to prove yourself to him or anyone."

Brenna took a deep breath then said quietly, "You don't understand and I don't expect you to."

"If he loved you he would--"

"But he doesn't," she snapped. "And I accept that."

Pauline threw up her hands. "Why do I feel as though I don't know you anymore? How can this be the Brenna who believed in the importance of good matches? Matches based on compatibility and some affection? Maybe even true love? Where's the Brenna who used to talk to me? Who are you? Your brother's suspected of murder and I don't even know how you feel. Your ex-boyfriend comes back into your life. Do you even care?

"You come to work and pretend that everything is fine. If your husband is so good at his job why does he need you to help him?" She crossed her legs and swung her foot. "You sure are working for the money you married. Fortunately, that doesn't bother you, nothing does."

Brenna tapped her pen against her palm, then set the pen down. "All I have to keep me sane is my work. Tell me what good tears will do? They've never helped me through anything before. They've never fed me, clothed me or comforted me. All they seem to do is make other people feel better." She let her gaze fall. "I'm sorry I can't perform that ritual for you." She looked up. "I will never perform it. I will never come into this office less than a professional. My personal life is just that--personal. I will continue to help my husband climb the ladder at his company and I will run my life the way I see fit. Now if the way I do business is contrary to your standards perhaps we could come to an arrangement--"

Pauline stood. "It's been made. I'm giving you my two weeks' notice."

Her words fell like a hammer on Brenna's heart. She'd considered Pauline a friend. She hadn't realized how far their friendship had disintegrated. She picked up a pen then set it back down. "I'd like you to reconsider that option. You are an asset to the company. I enjoy you and..." She stopped. She would not beg or crumble although she felt her insides doing so. "I was hoping to take time to be with my brother during the trial. I'd appreciate it if you'd stay. With me out of the picture, you could take time to--"

"I can't," Pauline said both her tone and eyes flat.

Please don't leave me now. She swallowed. "I understand."

"I'm sure you'll find someone else," she said with a level of disdain Brenna had never heard before. "Now I'd better return to my desk."

AT HOME, Brenna went to the library and stood in front of the shelves. She ran her hands over the spine of the books. She picked a few up and flipped through, reading old passages that had given her joy. Her old friends. Books could never betray her. She remembered burying herself in their pages, disappearing from her own life. But now, not even her old friends could offer her comfort. And there was no one to talk to. She couldn't burden Miles. She'd already spoken to him today. Her mother certainly wasn't an option and she'd hate to discover if Tima shared Pauline's views. She had to be strong for Stephen. And Hunter...

She turned away from the bookshelf and sat, feeling the weight of resignation. Pauline was right. Hunter was just a partner not a friend. She wished she could imagine her calling him and he saying he'd come home right away to be with her. But he was more practical than that. He'd help her think things through. Come up with a plan. But she didn't want to think or plan or rationalize. She wanted to scream and tear things and make it all go away.

Suddenly the big house felt so empty; she so alone. And for once she didn't want to be alone. She picked up the phone and dialed without thinking. Having memorized his number from his business card. His voice came on the line before she could hang up. "Hello, Brenna," Byron said.

"How did you know it was me?"

He ignored the question. "Did you need something?"

"I just wanted to know how the case was shaping up."

He paused. "Is that really why you're calling?"

"Of course."

He was silent a moment then said, "I'm splitting a pizza between myself. Like to come over?"

An eager delight gripped her. "Yes."

He gave her the directions then said, "I'll see you soon."

Later Brenna stood inside his exclusive condo complex. When she rang the bell, he answered the door dressed in jeans with his worn green shirt sleeves rolled up to his elbows, displaying his powerful forearms.

She held up a bag of vanilla wafers. "I brought dessert."

He kicked the door wider. "A woman after my own heart."

They sat in the living room and shared a veggie pizza. His place was comfortable as always. Instead of a crowded dorm room there was a chrome kitchen and large entertainment center and furniture from an expensive catalog. Everything was exactly how she would have expected it to be.

Brenna rested her head on the couch. "So why didn't you get married?"

Byron picked up a third slice of pizza. "I don't think you want to know."

"Of course I do." She tapped a finger against her lips. "Let me guess. You found the perfect woman and she turned you down leaving you forever heartbroken."

He gave a world weary sigh. "No, I found the perfect woman and she asked me to marry her and I said no. I've regretted that day for years."

Brenna shook her head unmoved. "You could have called."

"I wanted to become a top lawyer first. If I was going to come back on my knees, I wanted some leverage."

"I don't see you on your knees."

"I'm waiting for the right moment."

"That moment will never come." She pulled out a card and placed it on his lap. "However, if you ever want to use my services."

"I'll keep that in mind." He studied the card then tucked it in his back pocket. "So have you spoken to him?"

"Stephen--"

"No, your husband."

She became irritated. "Why are you so interested in him? What does it matter?"

"You and I both know that it matters. Or do you want to pretend that it doesn't?"

"If I told you I was unhappy would you feel better?"

"Maybe. Are you unhappy?"

"No. Why do you ask?"

"Because I want to know what's going on."

Brenna stiffened. "Nothing."

Byron swore under his breath then leaned towards her with sharp, assessing eyes. "You wanted someone tonight. I know you, Brenna. You can fool others, but you can't fool me. You needed someone and I want to know why it was me. Why did you call me?"

She turned away. "I was lonely."

"And you couldn't reach him?"

She poured more cola in her glass then took a long swallow.

"You didn't call him, did you?"

"No."

"Doesn't he know about the case?"

Brenna shook her head frustrated. "I don't know."

"You didn't tell him?" Byron said surprised.

She tapped the side of her glass. "No."

"Why not?"

She stood. "I'd better go."

"Why not? Doesn't he care?"

"Yes, he cares."

He stood, blocking her path. "Are you afraid of him?"

She moved around him. "No."

"Then why don't you call him?"

"I can't." She grabbed her handbag and headed for the door.

"Why not? He's your husband."

Her patience snapped. She spun around. "In name only! There. I've said it. My marriage is a sham. So now you can gloat. Now you can feel relieved I'm not happier than you."

Byron searched her face confused. "But why? I don't understand."

Brenna took a deep breath, hoping to sound casual. "We have an agreement. He helps me with my medical bills and I play his wife.

He needed one and I happened to be available. It works for us." She smiled bitterly. "Poor Byron, now you have another reason to pity me." She opened the door. He extended a hand and closed it.

"No," he whispered, his breath warm against her neck. "I envy him."

She didn't turn although she could feel him close behind her. Every part of her aware of him. He extended his other hand effectively trapping her. He dropped his head and placed a kiss on her neck.

The touch of his lips made her skin tingle. "Don't," she said softly.

Byron kissed her again. "He won't have to know."

"I'll know."

"How do you know he isn't somewhere else doing the exact same thing? He's been gone for awhile, hasn't he?"

"That's not the point."

His hand slid to her waist, he pulled her against him and she felt the evidence of his desire. "I want you Brenna. And don't deny that you want me. You used to tremble like this so many times before. Do you remember?"

Desire warred with anger. He shouldn't do this to her and she shouldn't let him. "Let me go."

"No."

She hit him with her cane.

He released her and swore. "You're being stubborn."

"I'm a married woman."

"You just said--"

"I'm still married."

"And you plan to respect your vows," he said sarcastic. "You plan to love, honor and obey? We both know you failed the first one. Except if you count loving his money."

She opened the door; he grabbed her arm. "You're living a lie, Brenna."

"Let me go."

"I'm going to win you back."

"It will be nice to see you win something."

Byron gripped her shoulders. "Don't underestimate me. You don't know anything about those other cases. But I've won before and I've won big and when I want something I mean to get it. I admit that my life hasn't been what I had expected, but that's all going to change." His hands slid down and captured her wrists. "I'm not ashamed of how I feel and I don't want you ashamed of how you feel."

"You don't know how I feel."

He caught her eyes. "Yes, I do."

Her breathing grew shallow and she turned away. "No."

"I know you're good at lying to yourself."

"Yes, I'd convinced myself once that you truly wanted me, but not again."

"I did want you. I just couldn't take the risk--"

"Yes, I know." Her voice cracked. "I remember."

"You came to me, Brenna."

"I made a mistake."

"No, you took a risk. A risk I should have made years ago. Well look, I'm taking the risk now. I want you. I want to start again."

She walked into the hall.

"Take your time Brenna. Think things through and remember. If you need me I'm here."

Yes, he was here. Back in her life where she had always wanted him. That was the danger.

BYRON STOOD by the window and watched Brenna head to her car. He shouldn't have let her go. Tonight or those many years ago. He'd never expected regret to be such a bitter pill to swallow. He was seriously beginning to wonder about his judgment and he knew others were too. Wallace Roberson, the DA, stopped by his office just to share his opinion.

"I heard you took the Garrett case," he said, settling in a chair.

Byron nodded. "Yep."

Roberson stared at him a long moment, his keen blue gaze clear with disbelief as though he'd hoped he'd misunderstood. When Byron didn't say more, he sighed and smoothed down his long silver mustache. "Look if you want to start winning cases you don't saddle yourself with a dog."

"The kid is innocent."

"Evans thinks you have a howler and her heart bleeds for almost every case that comes before her. Now if a PD thinks your client's guilty, you know you've got an ugly case."

Byron shrugged.

"What do you think your uncle would say?"

Roberson cleverly hit a sore spot. Byron's uncle had raised him and led him into the law. They'd both considered themselves avenging angels using the power of the law. But his Uncle was gone and he hadn't recovered as quickly as he'd expected. He hadn't been able to focus, he'd made mistakes in his last cases, but he wouldn't make a mistake this time. He couldn't afford to.

"You're not going to get him off." Roberson leaned forward. "Make life easy for yourself. Convince him to enter a plea."

Byron continued to stare at him.

Roberson shrugged and stood. "I guess I'll see you in court."

Byron turned from the window and picked up the empty pizza box. He had two fights on his hands. One to get Stephen off and the second to get Brenna back. He knew she had no idea what kind of family she had married into, but he'd dealt with the Randolphs before and knew what damage they could do. She was alone and sad just as she'd been all those years ago when he'd seen her alone in the library. He'd rescued her then and he'd rescue her again. First he was going to find out all he could on Hunter Randolph.

Chapter Nineteen

Hunter left the airport parking lot glad the Detroit conference had been a success. At the office he was annoyed to discover that nothing had changed. Unfortunately, he doubted anything would change. But what should he do? Hide in the sand and ignore where the company was headed while he flew here and there to be kept out of trouble? Should he leave? Leave the one thing he'd been groomed to become? He pushed the thought aside as he sorted through the office mail.

He looked at the phone and wondered if he should call Brenna and tell her he was back. The conference had been the first time he'd been away from her. Over a dozen times he'd picked up the phone to call her only to put it back. He didn't know what to say. She wouldn't miss him. She'd lived on her own before. And if anything had happened she knew how to reach him. He sat back and read an office memo. There was another discrepancy with inventory. He swore. There was no reason for this. But there was no way they would let him change things.

He balled his hands into fists. He had to think, reason, rationalize. He pulled out Daniel's card from his desk drawer. He shouldn't have kept it, but this time he hadn't been able to throw it away. He placed it on the desk and sat back, glancing up at the ceiling. The reflection of light on his watch created a dot of light.

He suddenly had a flashback to when he was young and his mother had been his world. He remembered she used to wear earrings the size of silver dollars that dangled against her neck. Once, she'd taken him on a walk and suddenly started laughing. He looked at her confused and asked her why she was laughing.

"Because I want to," she said. "I don't have to have a reason." She bent down and met his eyes. "You must always have the courage to do what's right for you." She cupped his chin. "Promise me."

"I promise," he said, knowing he would have promised her anything.

She nodded satisfied and straightened. "Then you'll always be happy. Some people won't understand, but you'll be too happy to care."

Was that truth or her madness speaking? He wondered if she had been happy or delusional. Back then he'd never fully understood why she had left him behind. Career or not she could have written him a letter or sent him a postcard. One moment she had been there; the next she was gone. Leaving him with a father and uncle determined to make sure he had no traces of her in him. He had complied with their constant admonishments of his temper, wild ideas, and his ability to laugh easily. He didn't want to be like her. He never wanted to hurt anyone as she had him.

Although he now knew her disappearance hadn't been intentional the pain didn't ease. If she'd been mad, why hadn't he sensed anything? She was childlike at times, but she never scared him. But perhaps he was too young to know the difference. And at times when he was with her, he knew she wanted to be somewhere else. With Ruby he never felt that. She moved almost seamlessly into his life as though she'd always been there.

He loosened his fists. The past didn't matter. Only the future. He should only think of the future.

Doran stopped in front of his door. "Well, well, well," he drawled. He stepped inside and sat down. "Look who's back."

Hunter glanced up without interest. "Hello to you too."

"So what are you going to do about it?"

"About what?"

"That fact your wife's family is causing a mess."

He furrowed his brows. "What are you talking about?'

"I guess the case wasn't big enough to reach you. However it was big enough to reach the papers here. Grandfather was annoyed that they had made a connection with us. Fortunately, it was a distant one."

Hunter stilled. "What are you talking about?"

Doran smiled pleased to deliver the bad news. "Seems your wife's brother decided to bash an old man in the head because he stole from him."

Hunter stared at his cousin suspicious of his smug tone. "This is a joke right?"

"We weren't laughing."

"Brenna would have called me if there was trouble."

Doran's mouth spread into a polite sneer. "Don't worry. She's found another shoulder to cry on."

Hunter leaned back tapping a beat on the desk. "Go on."

"Miles has been, shall we say, very solicitous? It's always nice to see a friend so available to look after our interests. But I'm sure you know from previous experience. You know how comforting it is to have someone else look after your wife." He shrugged. "But as they say, when the cat's away the mice will play." He stood flashing a cruel grin then left.

Hunter gently closed the door then sat behind his desk. If he were a jealous man, he'd be upset. Fortunately, he wasn't a jealous man. He never got jealous. Even when he had returned from a trip and discovered that Angie was in love with Doran, or that Janice had decided to marry Michael he hadn't been jealous. No, he wasn't jealous now.

He wasn't jealous that Brenna had gone to Miles instead of him. He didn't care that everyone knew about it. He wasn't jealous that she had shared her fears with another man. That she made him look foolish as she had once done before. No, he wasn't jealous. He was mad...almost as though the madness his family whispered about had seeped through the cracks of his mind ready to claim him. Ready to turn his thoughts into chaos. Ready to program his brain so that all he could see was Brenna and Miles plotting and planning behind his back. Whispering and laughing and...

He shut his eyes against the image only making it clearer. He pressed his palm against his eyes. It was a betrayal of loyalty, not jealousy, that made his blood feel like acid shooting to his skull.

He took a deep breath and let his hands fall to the desk. He had to remember the messenger. Doran was no friend of his. It could be harmless. It could be nothing. But he knew it wasn't. If Stephen was in trouble, Brenna should have called him. Him and nobody else. He took another deep breath gathering his control. No he wasn't jealous and now he was no longer angry. He was a practical man. He'd let Brenna explain herself.

Exhaustion sat like a heavy blanket on her shoulders by the time Brenna reached home. Fortunately, she'd convinced her dating consultant Margaret to help in the office, but it didn't lessen the load. Her heart lifted at the sight of Hunter's car in the driveway and a bit of her exhaustion fell away as she walked to his study. She was surprised not to find him behind his desk. Instead he sat in the corner his body encased in darkness while the lamplight shone on the thick book resting on his lap.

She walked towards him, her voice filled with warmth and greeting. "You're home."

"Yes." He snapped the book closed and set it aside. "Disappointed?"

She hesitated confused by the statement. "Should I be?"

"I'm not sure. Would you like to take a seat?"

"No."

"I want to talk to you so I thought you'd like to be comfortable."

"I am comfortable."

"Good." He stood. "Why didn't you tell me about Stephen?"

Brenna sat down heavily and stared up at him. "I didn't want to concern you."

"Why not? It's my duty to be concerned. I'm your husband."

"I know. You don't need to tell me." She glanced at her hand. "This ring is a suitable reminder."

"Shame that you would need a reminder."

A shiver of guilt coursed through her. "What does that mean?"

Hunter clasped his hands behind him and began to pace. "I realize that this was the first time we've been apart and I recognize the possibility that my absence may be misinterpreted as negligence." He stopped in front of her, his eyes measuring her as though taking inventory. "But I can assure you that every day..." He stopped and cleared his throat. "That your well being was of utmost importance to me."

Brenna stared at him confused then suddenly smiled relieved. "Oh, I get it." She stood. "You wanted a more enthusiastic welcome home."

She meant to kiss him on the cheek, but he turned his face so her kiss fell on his lips. His lips were softer than she remembered. Had it been that long? So long that she'd forgotten how delicious he tasted. How his slow, drugging kisses could make her forget everything. How unhappy she was. How nearly every day she questioned her decision to marry him. How in his arms she didn't care that he remained elusive and that her feelings for him were so unsure.

Hunter brought her body close, knowing she could never be close enough. He inhaled her sweet scent as he kissed her face, her shoulders, her throat, wanting to remind her that she belonged to him just in case she forgot. Instead he learned how much he belonged to her as her husband. That acknowledgment felt like fire racing through his veins melting any icicles of fear that she would leave him. This was right, she knew it was right.

Brenna stepped back breathless, holding onto his shoulders to steady herself. "Well, it's nice to have you home."

A dimple winked. "I'm glad you think so."

"Did you kiss me to make sure I didn't have the taste of any lovers on my lips?"

His gaze darkened at her accuracy. "Would I have to worry?"

"No. No current lovers." An ex-lover perhaps, but she'd leave that for later.

He kissed her again, surprised by how much he enjoyed it. Did other men enjoy coming home to their wives this much? He lifted her chin. "You look tired."

"I've been busy."

"I don't want you doing any more commercials."

"But--"

"This isn't a discussion."

Brenna made a face. "If you're going to be autocratic, perhaps I should send you away again."

Hunter smiled. "No, I don't plan on leaving anytime soon. How is Stephen?"

"Out on bail. He's got an attorney."

"Good. What's his name?"

She tugged on her earring. "It's going to be a tough case to defend."

"I'm sure. What's his name?"

"Mom's really worried, naturally. We're doing our best to keep it together. We've never gone through anything like this before."

Hunter's tone grew sharp. "What's his name?"

"Byron Suncliff," she said in a rush. "Mother hired him. I probably would have strangled him if Miles hadn't convinced me otherwise."

"Miles? Did he come by while I was away?"

"A few times. He's wonderful, I couldn't have..." She trailed off as his expression grew more impassive. "Anyway I'm meeting with him tomorrow for lunch."

"I see," he said quietly. Too quiet for her to read his tone.

"He's been so kind attending my speeches and encouraging me. He's a good man."

Hunter drew away and stood by the window. He pulled back the drapery and stared out at the evening sky. "I'm glad."

Brenna bit her lip, watching him. Something was wrong. She wished she could figure out what. "Hunter?"

He heard the sound of worry in her voice and turned. He'd heard that note of worry in Angie's voice too. He had to remember not to scare her. He smiled, trying to allay her fears. "Everything's fine, Brenna." He rubbed his knuckles. "Do you trust me?"

"Of course."

"Do you trust me more than anyone else?"

She felt he was asking her another question if only she knew what. "Yes."

"Good." He nodded then said almost absently, "So you're having lunch with Miles tomorrow?"

"Yes."

"Hmm." He headed for the door. "I hope you enjoy yourself."

For some reason she didn't believe him.

Chapter Twenty

Miles had no warning. One moment he was in his seat. The next he was up in the air hanging by his collar.

Dark brown eyes pierced his own. "What do you think you're doing?" Hunter asked.

He gasped. "Release me and I'll tell you."

Hunter considered the request then dropped him.

Miles fell to the ground. He held up his hands in surrender. "I don't want to fight."

"Shame," Hunter said softly. "because I do."

Miles scrambled to his feet. "Is this about Brenna?"

"No, this is about secrets. This is about lunch dates you've had with my wife."

"They weren't a secret."

His tone hardened. "They were a secret to me." He leaned against the desk. "Why didn't you encourage her to call me?"

"Why didn't you call her?"

"I didn't know anything was wrong," he said annoyed. "She was supposed to call me."

"How was she to know that?"

"Because I'm her husband."

Miles straightened his collar. "Perhaps if you say it enough you'll start acting like one." He folded his arms. "Why are you here anyway?"

"I wanted to get a few things clear."

"Or maybe you're jealous?"

Hunter sat on the desk and toyed with a ruler, his tone laced with steel. "You know I don't like people who play games with me."

"I didn't realize losing your wife was considered a game."

Hunter tapped the ruler against his knee. "That was a very bad move."

A smile tugged on Mile's mouth. "I think it was very clever actually. You need to be aware of what you might lose. I've done you a great service by standing in the way of a more worthy opponent."

"Byron."

Miles raised a brow surprised. "So she told you. That's a good sign."

He put the ruler down and swore with feeling. "I know."

"Still ready to snap my head off or can I come off the defensive?"

Hunter began to pace, irritated that Doran's words had gotten to him. He had always prided himself on acting reasonable. "I apologize."

Miles studied his friend then rested a hand on his shoulder to stop him. "Byron's a problem."

"You mean a threat?"

"Could be."

"Did she say anything?"

"No, it's more the situation than the people involved that pose the trouble."

He scowled. "The situation? What is this? A play?"

Miles snapped his fingers. "That's an excellent way to see it." He held up his hands. "Now try to follow me. You're the husband away in battle leaving the wife home alone in the castle. Her brother is charged with treason. She doesn't know what to do then a knight comes to her rescue. A knight she's loved before. Now it's up to you how the story will end."

"What if the husband returns home and kills the knight?"

Miles tried not to laugh, knowing his friend was serious. "Try for a less blood thirsty ending."

Hunter rubbed his hands together. "Don't worry. I'll think of something."

BRENNA SCANNED the contents of a new file, still confused by her lunch with Miles. He must have read a book on medieval life because he kept referring to castles and knights. She'd smiled with interest although none of it made sense to her. She would give him a book on the time period for his birthday.

"You have a visitor," Margaret said.

"Send them in," Brenna said absently. She glanced up when the door opened. Her eyes widened. "Dad!"

Crampton shuffled into the office. "Hello, Brenna."

She came from behind the desk, smiling. "Come in. Sit down. It's so nice to see you."

He hung his cane on the back of the chair then sat. He stared up at her.

"So?" she asked.

He glanced around. "Nice office."

"Thank you." She sat behind her desk and waited.

"I saw your commercial," he said.

Her heart began to race. Did he like it? Was he proud of her? "Oh

really?"

"It made things clear for me."

"What things?"

"Why Randolph married you."

Her heart fell, dashing all hopes. She kept her voice light. "What are you suggesting?" she asked, although she already knew the answer.

He folded his arms, his face pensive. "I couldn't figure it out at first. I wanted to believe it was love, but something in me knew otherwise. Now I know the truth. I don't blame you. I know you wanted to get married and you certainly found a way." He pointed a finger at her. "However, I didn't raise a daughter who exhibits herself for profit."

Her lips thinned. "No, you didn't. You didn't raise me at all."

"I'm your—"

"I know who you are. However, I cannot believe you have the audacity to come in here and scold me."

His eyebrows shot up. "Scold you? I'm here to warn you. You think it will stop with a commercial? No way. Soon they'll want you to write a book and then go around the country parading your leg like a side show."

"The commercial was my idea, and I'm proud of my involvement. The Trandor cane is an excellent product and I recognized that I was the perfect candidate to market it. I'm not ashamed of who I am."

"Well, you should be! Heaven knows I am."

Brenna replied with silence. A cold silence that made Crampton shift awkwardly in his seat.

"So that's why you came?" she asked softly. "To make sure that I stayed as unhappy as you are? Everything was okay as long as I stayed behind my desk and kept quietly single. That's all you expected of me. But my success is showing you all the things you didn't do with your life."

His gaze fell.

"Dad, can't we get past this, please? Can't you just accept me and be happy for me?"

He met her eyes. "Does he love you?"

"We're not talking about my marriage we're talking about us."

He sniffed scornful. "He doesn't. I can tell by your voice. I agree that I compromised my life. I'm not proud of that. And your success does make me ashamed of the choices I've made." He leaned forward smug. "But think of your own choices. Aren't you doing the same? You're settling because you don't think you can get better."

"What I have is good enough for me," she said in clipped tones. "And that's all we'll say on the topic."

"What about your brother?"

There wasn't a moment that went by that she didn't think of him. Worry about him. "Things will work out."

"You're optimistic."

"I don't have the privilege to be otherwise."

"He's got himself in quite a mess."

"Have you talked to him?"

He shrugged. "I have nothing to say."

Her lip curled. "Not even 'Hello son'?"

"I'm not good with words."

"You had plenty a few moments ago."

He fiddled with his cane. "I want you to be happy, just not this way."

She turned to her computer. "The door is behind you."

"It was just—"

"I said the door is behind you," she repeated firmly. "You can come back when you learn to be a father."

His voice shook with an anger she'd never heard before. "How can I be a father when you won't treat me like one? You say you forgive me, but when I offer advice you keep reminding me that I was never around. You want me to be proud of you, but you're ashamed of me. I am not perfect but by God I love my children to my bones. I left because I couldn't be what I wanted to be for you. I don't understand you Brenna and I don't understand your brother but that doesn't stop me from caring about you. I'm here because I don't want to see you mistreated by anyone. I don't care how much money he's got, how much power they have. You deserve to be loved Brenna." Tears fell down his face. "You're my little girl and that's the one lesson I want to teach you. So listen good. You deserve to be loved."

Brenna watched her father leave as she swallowed back tears.

———————

Stephen stared at Byron as he went over his notes. He hadn't changed from the man who everyone had touted as Brenna's savior. The family had been shocked when Byron had asked her out. But Stephen had never quite trusted his reasons for dating Brenna. Not that he was surprised anyone would be interested in his sister. Byron just didn't seem the type. He appeared open and carefree, but Stephen always wondered if it was genuine. Even now he wondered about Byron's reasons for taking the case.

"Are you here because of Brenna?"

Byron glanced up and flashed a grin. "That's immaterial."

Stephen sent him a cool look. "Is that lawyer-speak for none of your business?"

His smile fell. "Do you want to talk about something?"

"Yea, why you're here. You read about my case I know. Did you want to help me or impress Brenna?"

"Both."

"Why? I'm sure before you came here you knew she was married."

"Yes. I was surprised."

"Why? Because you didn't want to marry her?"

He hesitated. "No."

"She told me she'd proposed."

"Oh."

"Why did you say no?"

He shrugged. "I was young. I thought it was a risk."

"Thought what was a risk?"

"A family."

Stephen's face cleared in understanding. "You—"

"I was being honest."

"Fortunately, Hunter's a bigger man than that."

"Maybe or maybe he just knows how to use her to his advantage."

"He's not using her."

Byron stroked his chin. "I've seen her commercials."

"That's not why he married her."

Byron only smiled.

***

HUNTER HAD DREADED this moment for weeks. But he could no longer deny the facts in front of him. He shut off his computer and went to his father's office.

"Come in." Curtis glanced up at him then back at his desk. "Yes?"

He sat down. "I know what you're doing with the inventory."

Curtis didn't ask what, why or how he knew. He just stared at his son across the desk with a bored expression. "And why should that be a concern to me?"

"Your little set up won't be safe for long. This isn't a threat, just a warning. I'll give you a month to get things in order."

A cold smile spread over his face. "The fact that you're here tells me that you don't know anything. You disappoint me. I thought you were smarter than that."

Hunter frowned confused by the anger under his tone. "I'm trying to save you."

"I don't need you to save me. Who are you going to tell? People already know. Even your beloved grandfather. So why don't you do us all a favor and go back to your room and behave like the good little boy we're paying you to be."

"But this is wrong."

"A matter of judgment. I consider what you're doing wrong. You've forgotten your duty."

"I know my duty."

"And your duty is to protect the family."

"It's my duty to make sure this company—"

"Runs the way it's always run. You're not a company spy so go back and do your job. I'd hate to see you lose it."

"Would you?"

Curtis merely blinked. Hunter nodded then left. Once he was gone, Curtis picked up the phone. "He came and made a threat."

"What will he do?" Orson said.

"He didn't say. I don't need him breathing down my neck. Make him back off."

Orson laughed at his son's uneasiness. "Don't worry. I will."

Chapter Twenty-One

Somehow Brenna always knew he would come. She never knew when just that he would. So Brenna was not surprised when Mrs. Symnthon found her in the library one Saturday morning to tell her she had a visitor. She doubted it was a coincidence that Hunter was at work that day and she was alone. She composed herself and entered the sitting room where Orson stood by the window. It was a large arc structure that framed the landscape. It now framed him like a portrait of a man of power. He was still a big man, despite the years, with the physical build of a much younger one.

"This is a surprise," Brenna said, taking a seat.

He didn't turn when she entered. He watched a passing robin.

"Would you like anything to drink?"

He lifted his glass. "I've been sufficiently refreshed thank you." He fell quiet again. He was a man who knew the power of silence and used it well. After a few more moments she stood, determined not to play his game.

"Hunter is at work," he said when she reached the door.

"I know."

"He will make an excellent company President one day."

She sat and smoothed out her skirt, knowing his statement didn't require a reply.

He abruptly turned. "Do you love him?"

His question did not startle her as it was meant to. She merely stared back.

"He doesn't love you."

"I am fully aware of his feelings towards me."

He sniffed. "Or his lack of."

She met his piercing gaze straight on. "The truth doesn't wound me so you may as well try another tactic."

Orson flashed a cool grin. "Full of iron, aren't you? Like your cane?" His eyes trailed the length of her. "There's no softness in you. You've spent too many years protecting yourself."

"Don't waste my time with your analysis. Get to the point."

"I'm offering you a kindly warning. You've been asking about his mother. I want you to stop."

"You want me to stop. Is that your warning?" Brenna sighed with feigned disappointment. "I'd expected more."

"I'm a very powerful man."

"Yes," she agreed with an unwavering stare. "And you wield your power well, but not over me."

"You don't know that yet."

"You use his past against him. Why? What are you trying to protect?"

"His past is best forgotten."

She drummed her fingers on the head of her cane. "Let's try to come to an understanding. We're two intelligent people I'm sure we can find some common ground."

"Then let's understand that the common ground you stand on belongs to me."

Brenna let her gaze roam to the window. She knew it was best not to antagonize one's enemy. Like staring a bear in the eye, it only invited more violence. "In a way I admire you. You're a man who struggled. A Southern boy, whose father had been a man who'd come back from the war more as a commander than a family man. Your mother was little more than a shadow. You lived in a time when your limitations where sanctioned by a government. By the complacency of an entire nation." She moved her gaze to a light in the corner and kept her voice free of pity. "You saw your father fight for a country that'd still shoot him in the street if they had the opportunity."

She returned her gaze to him. "How it must gall you to see the freedom of thought Hunter has. He has no chains gripped to his mind to keep him under your control—so you created those chains, those handcuffs. You call them honor and loyalty so he will heed to your beliefs. However, I won't succumb to your chains."

Orson walked to a picture. A simple charcoal sketch of a man's face. He studied it giving no indication of how her words affected him. "He once had a younger brother. We named him Lionel. He was found dead in his crib one day with a towel wrapped around his neck. Hunter held him in his arms. Hunter had always been jealous of his mother's affection. Marlene came and saw what Hunter had done and lost it."

"I don't believe you."

Orson turned to her. "You've never seen him jealous. He doesn't care enough about you enough to reveal that side, but we've seen it. Angie's seen it."

His words made her inwardly tremble. "You're telling lies so that you can control me too, but this..." She shook her head. "No, I won't believe a word."

"Exactly and if you can't handle this truth how do you think Hunter would feel?"

"Were you there when it happened?"

"No."

"Who was there?"

"I could show you his grave."

Brenna smiled with condescension. "You could show me a grave. It may not be his."

"Why would I lie about a five year old boy?"

"Knowing you, I'm sure there would be a reason. You could make this easy and tell me why."

Orson made an impatient movement with his shoulders. "Don't try to change the topic."

"The subject is Hunter. Why did you really give him the job? Especially if you'll continue to run it."

"Because it's my company."

She nodded. "As long as you're alive. But the years are catching up to you. You're powerless against time. But you know about feeling powerless. You lived with it. When society had tried to take away your right to be a man. A fully grown man not just a Southern black boy. Weakness in any form is abhorrent to you from what you've seen. How many times did some shopkeeper call you boy? A grown man with a wife? How many times did you actually feel the color of your skin as though it were a disease that you wished you could peel off?"

"I've never been ashamed—"

"How many times did your worth feel less than the mud clinging to your shoes? How often and how long were you a Boy?"

He tossed his drink in her face. "Now that there was just a nice cool whiskey," he said with a hint of a smile as sweet as venom. "Don't force me to throw my fist."

She wiped her cheek unafraid although she could feel her anger build. "I thought a gentleman like you would be against hitting a woman."

"I don't see one standing in front of me."

Brenna lifted a brow and grinned. "I will decline sharing what I see in front of me."

"People need to know their place whether they be man or woman."

"Hunter's dangerous to you, isn't he? In Hunter's eyes you see a rebelliousness, a spirit on fire just barely tamed and you watch and study it not because it reminds you of the young man you used to be. No, Hunter is something far worse. In your sons you can see your face reflected. Even in Doran and his siblings, but in Hunter it's something new. Something that threatens the castle walls you've erected. You see a man in a different form. A man who can be gentle and strong. A man who can love freely, passionately."

Brenna raised her voice before he could speak. "I know he doesn't love me. But I know he loves by the way he cares for his family. Call it loyalty if you must. In him you see another way to live in this world. A way of being that is the antithesis of your truth. Eighty is a long time to be alive. You've seen a lot, but allowed yourself to only experience a small amount. In order for survival, for your spirit to be intact you had to forge your own rules. But those rules don't apply to everyone. And they don't apply to him."

Orson set his glass down. "Fine words, young woman, but what do you know about experience?"

She tilted her head to the side. "You have me there, sir. But see I'm too clever to get into a competition with you. You only compete when you know you'll win. Your ego couldn't stand it otherwise."

Orson rocked on his heels. "And what do you know of my ego?"

"Hunter is stronger than you. That's why you won't let him create. You won't let his ideas ever succeed. They'll stay in your warehouse or on your desk until they turn to dust. You need to keep him down. You need him to fail. My question is why?"

"He's free to do what he wants."

Brenna stood, anger making her tone falter. She took a deep breath knowing anger was her enemy. "You know he's trapped by his loyalty to you."

"Yes, and I'm proud of that. It's for his own good. A man needs a code to live by. His mother was crazy and he'll end up the same way too without rules to keep him in line. I've seen men drown in their despair, because of their compulsions. You think I'd let any blood relation of mine do that?"

"But there is no compulsion in him."

"Angie told me—"

"How quick you are to believe the worst of him. You are labeling something you don't understand."

"I'm a man. I understand him far better than you. He may be safe at home in your loving arms." His mouth twisted in sarcasm. "Though I expect your arms are pretty cold. I won't be surprised if he finds those loving arms elsewhere. A man knows there are wolves out there."

Brenna sent him a significant look. "I'm well aware of the wolves out there."

Orson chuckled in amusement. "Yea, I'm one of them, no shame in that. And I have no shame saying his life belongs to me."

Her tone hardened. "No, it does not."

"You like living well." He gestured to the surroundings. "But this can change. I own this house and all that's in it."

"No not all. But what you do own, you could take it all away and it wouldn't matter to me."

"Yes, I know it wouldn't bother you, but it would make Hunter topple like a rotten barn." Orson sat, his tone becoming slow and nonchalant creating the enticing web of the southern storytelling tradition. "You don't know what being a man is so I'll explain it to you. It's the ability to provide. It's the ability to stand head to shoulders with other men. It's status. It's pride in your work, knowing your place in the hierarchy of things." He stood and walked towards her. He waved a dismissive hand. "We know you women like equality, circle type systems with lots of hand holding and God knows what else. It has its place for women. But take away a man's work, his dignity, his purpose. You could love him all you want and what you'll be loving is a dead man. I suggest you think about it." He looked so pleased with himself she knew all he needed was a brandy and cigar.

She stood and stared up at him. "You're afraid he's better than you."

"I'm better than both of you." He grabbed her cane with such swiftness she lost her balance and pitched forward onto her knees. A sharp pain shot up her thigh. She adjusted her position before her knee locked. She swallowed back tears.

Orson casually tossed the cane up in the air then caught it. He gazed down at her. "Not so tough without this."

Brenna held out her hand. "Give it back."

He watched her in a detached way, as though she were a beetle in his path he had the choice to step over or crush. He sat down. "Come and get it. I'd like to see you crawl. Might teach you some humility."

"How do you live without a heart?"

"Oh, I've got a heart and it will stop one day. Unfortunately, for you that day's not today."

"Too bad I can't rip it out for you."

"Pretty hard to do when you can't reach me. So full of words, but useless. Like a bucket full of air. Pity."

His words pierced her heart. Instead of rage—her shield, her protector—she felt sorrow. A sorrow beyond tears, beyond any type of healing. He'd left her naked and now taunted her because he knew his power and knew he could win.

Orson rested a hand on the armrest. "I wasn't sure I should let you marry my grandson. You're stubborn. But you're teachable and today I'm going to teach you." He leaned forward as if to pat her on the head. "See you might be surprised, but I know a few things about being a woman having had so many in my life. I know that looks are important. We say that they aren't, but we know that they are. You have looks, you're a pretty woman, but you were cursed. They don't use terms like that nowadays, but it comes down to the same thing— like a black mark on your soul you could never be like the others. Women like Angelina will always be above you."

Hot tears burned behind Brenna's eyes, but she refused to let them fall. "No one is above me."

He tossed the cane to his other hand. "Love is important too. Women like to be loved. Hunter doesn't love you, but you're a practical woman so you know that and you think you can live without it, but you can't. As the years drag on it will gnaw at you. Don't think

he'll be faithful because he won't. As the other women take prece-
dence in his thoughts it will make you bitter. But you'll have your job
and maybe a kid or two so you'll focus your love on them. But you'll
never have him." Orson pointed the cane at her. "I saw him with
Angelina and I see him with you and you don't even come close.
Hurts doesn't it? Yes, you can stiffen that chin of yours, but you're not
that strong." He stood and grabbed her arm, pulling her to her feet.
He stared into her face then smiled cruelly. "You poor little bitch."
He laughed, the sound raking her ears. "You do love him. You nearly
had me fooled. Bet you even fooled yourself." His grip on her arm
became a vice, his tone like poison as his brown eyes met hers. "I
want you to learn to fear me. I suggest you start now."

"I'm not afraid of you."

He tightened his grip causing tears of pain, but she refused to cry
out. "Only fools speak without thinking. Are you afraid of seeing
your brother go to prison?"

She clenched her teeth. "He's not going to prison. He's innocent."

"He's a blue collar worker—"

"With no record."

"And evidence stacking against him."

"He's innocent."

"It would be a shame if any more evidence started to appear."

"What do you mean?"

"Control your husband, stop your investigation about his mother
and you won't have to find out."

"No."

He stroked her head and said in a soft tone, "You disappoint me.
When I'm disappointed I do unfortunate things." He handed her the
cane. "One day you're going to beg—"

The only thing I'd ever beg for is the day I can smell your flesh
roasting in hell."

He abruptly released her. "So you've made your choice." He
began to grin. "You're going to regret this day for the rest of your life.
I'll make sure."

Chapter Twenty-Two

The elevator smelled like stale potato chips. Stephen barely noticed as he hit the button for the right floor. At least he wasn't home. He was tired of hearing Fiona remind him that he shouldn't have gone back. Crying about how alone she'd be without him. He still couldn't believe he was out on bail. In a few weeks he'd face a judge and jury that might convict him of a crime he hadn't committed. He could go to prison. He smiled bitterly. All his life he'd been a decent, law-abiding citizen and that seemed to mean nothing.

When the elevator stopped, he shook himself of his melancholy thoughts. He just wanted to see Tima's Mustang. He might as well do what he could before it was too late. He knocked on the door.

A man answered, not the same man as before. This was a young man a few years older than himself with paint splattered on his gray T-shirt and sneakers. Stephen hesitated then said, "I'd like to speak to Tima."

"Okay."

Tima came to the door and stared at him, surprised.

Stephen rested a hand on the doorframe. "I'm not here to kill you if that's what you're afraid of." It was a poor attempt at humor. She didn't laugh.

Instead she hugged him. He hadn't expected that and for a moment rejected it. Rejected the soft feel of her—the support, the comfort. He felt his throat close and shut his eyes. He didn't need her kindness he didn't want her pity, but somehow he couldn't let go. She smelled like turpentine and strawberries. When she drew away he opened his eyes and saw tears streaming down her face. Her eyes were red and her nose was too. But she stared at him unashamed.

He looked around for a tissue. "Don't do that. I—"

She covered his mouth and shook her head then motioned him to wait. She grabbed her coat, key and handbag then took his hand.

He pointed to the other man. "What about--?"

"He's fine."

The sun shone brightly outside, Stephen squinted against the glare. For the first time in weeks he allowed himself to experience spring crawling through the air. He reminded himself of the season and inhaled the fresh earthy scent of new leaves and grass emerging from the stubborn lasting patches of snow. A balmy breeze touched his skin. Tima stood by her car then opened the hood. They didn't speak as though they were two people in a museum admiring a sculpture. The engine was beautiful.

After a while she handed him the keys. Without a word they got inside. They drove with the windows down and music blaring, not knowing where they were headed and not caring. She began to sing off-key; he followed. They looked at each other and laughed. At a small highway restaurant, they ordered fried clams and ate with their fingers; made bad jokes and funny faces. People stared, they didn't care. In the car, she sketched him and he tried to sketch her. He hated the outcome but she stopped him from tearing it up. They finally drove to the Grand Yardley Hotel as the sun was beginning to set. It was his favorite place, a place that brought him calm. But he knew he didn't need to tell her that.

Tima rested her head back. "When this is all over I want you and Fiona to rent a room and watch the sunset from the towers."

Stephen rested an arm on the doorframe. "Fiona's busy."

"She can make time."

"It's expensive."

"I'll pay for it." She turned to him and smiled. "Any more excuses?"

He smiled back. "No." The smile soon fell and he hung his head. "I shouldn't have gone back."

"Why did you?"

"I don't know. He was just on my mind." He stared ahead. "I thought I could help him. I was stupid."

"Why? Because you're a good person who saw a lonely old man in need of a friend?"

"Lonely old man," he said with contempt. "He just saw me as a mark. I should have known."

"You couldn't have known."

"I can't believe I'm putting my family through this and Fiona." When he said her name, the discord between them came to his mind threatening to overshadow the joy of the day. "Fiona will never forgive me for this."

Tima scratched her head. "Why do you need her to forgive you? You didn't do anything wrong and your lawyer will prove it."

"She told me not to go back."

"And you did. So what? You were living your life. You're allowed to. Despite what happened you made his last day happy. That's important. What I don't understand is why you feel guilty. Tell her to go—"

He shook his head. "She cares about me. She nags when she's concerned."

"Fine." Tima opened her purse and pulled out a candy. She offered him one. He shook his head. She shrugged and popped one in her mouth.

Stephen draped his arm over the steering wheel and stared at the building. He saw one of the tower lights turn on as a couple entered the side entrance. "He had this bottle of chardonnay I helped him buy. He never got to drink it. I saw it on one of the shelves. The sight of it appears in my dreams."

"Because your life has been like that bottle? You've been waiting so long for the right moment you may never get to taste it?"

He shot her a glance. "You annoy me."

She laughed. "I know."

The setting sun dyed the towers a red and yellow, igniting a purple hue across the water of the pond. The green on the trees became an almost iridescent color as they gently swayed. "How old are you?" he asked.

"At times like this I forget. I feel as ageless as the sky. And then there are days—"

"You feel older than stones. Me too." He rested his chin on his arm, pretending to look at the building although he stole glances at her. Almost as though he was seeing her for the first time. He didn't understand her, yet everything about being with her at this moment felt right. He didn't care that her sandals didn't match her clothes, that her sweater had a hanging thread and was the strangest color purple he'd ever seen. He didn't care that she wasn't thin or dainty or tactful. He didn't even care that in her strange career she'd probably make more money than he'd ever see.

"Why doesn't it matter to you?" he asked.

She turned to him. "What?"

"Me. Brenna thinks I'm not motivated enough. Fiona thinks I'm too motivated, but you...you don't care."

"It's not that I don't care. I just keep opinions to myself." She winked. "Sometimes."

He sat back. "What's your opinion of me?"

"What's your opinion of yourself?" She sent him a direct gaze that made him uncomfortable.

He shrugged. "I think I'm a good guy."

"What does that mean?"

"I do my job; live my life."

"Do you think you're good looking?"

He touched his chin with regret. "They made me shave off my goatee."

"Yes, which makes you look about seventeen and will hopefully gain you sympathy, but that wasn't my question."

"Doesn't matter."

"If you were ugly it would." She tweaked his chin. "You're too humble for your own good." She raised a sly brow. "When I first saw you I thought, "What a gorgeous guy", "what a great body."

"What about this?" He tapped the side of his forehead.

"At the moment you could have had a brain full of mush. But don't worry I'm not coming onto you. I'm just being honest. Fortunately, you're not my type."

"What do you mean by fortunately?"

"I mean fortunately." She sent him a significant look.

He nodded. Yea, fortunately. Fortunately, she wasn't his type either. "So do you have a type?"

"Yes."

"What?"

"Someone who adores me."

Stephen shook his head amazed. "You don't ask for much."

"No, just the bare minimum." She popped another candy in her mouth.

"Have you ever been married?"

Tima's face dimmed. "Yes."

"What happened?"

She took a deep breath as though about to dive into something painful. "He died."

"I'm sorry."

"I loved that man so much sometimes I wonder if I'd killed him. That he was taken away because I was so lucky."

"What was he like?"

"He was an older man, fifteen years older. A man in every sense of the word. I knew he'd likely go before me, but... He thought I was beautiful, talented and clever."

Stephen saw her eyes bright with tears. "I didn't mean to make you sad."

She brushed away tears. "Sad? No, I'm not sad. How can I be sad remembering being so loved?"

He suddenly envied her. Wishing someone could make him feel the way she looked. Knowing that Fiona never did. She loved him, he knew that, but would she ever speak about him like that? Did her face ever light up at the memory of him? Perhaps he asked too much. It was an unfair comparison. Fiona was more reserved as he was. He'd be exhausted with such a show of passionate emotions. Perhaps Tima had exhausted her husband to death, though a part of him was curious why she hadn't shared how he died.

She sniffed. "We've gone off the subject."

"Which is?"

"What I think of you."

"And?"

"I think you've made yourself a shadow so Brenna could shine. It's hard being the 'normal one'. Especially with a father in competition with you. Since you are everything he couldn't be. I think you're ambitious in a different way, but didn't want your parents to focus on you. You thought, or perhaps knew, Brenna needed their attention more. I think you keep a lot inside. Actually you make me nervous."

He stared at her surprised. "I make you nervous?"

"I wonder what's going on in your mind. I wonder who you are. Even as I talk, what I say about you seems true, yet I feel there's so much more to you. You're very reserved. In a way I envy that about you. There's a benefit to keeping certain feelings hidden."

He turned away and stared up at the sky. "Yea, sometimes."

Miles approached Hunter as he walked down the hall. Hunter stopped. "What's wrong?"

"Your father and grandfather are in your office."

He was grateful for the warning. The two men made a formidable sight. His grandfather sitting at his desk; his father standing at his side like second in command. Orson pushed a paper toward him and held out a pen. "Here is your resignation. Put your signature on it."

Hunter stared at the paper frozen; something ugly gripped his heart. "You're making a mistake."

"I don't make mistakes."

He glanced up. "But why?"

"You didn't follow the rules."

He looked at his father then his grandfather. "What's going on?"

"Sign the paper."

"There are significant discrepancies in orders versus shipping. My computer system would help control inventory irregularities."

"That's not your concern anymore. Take the pen and sign. You have an hour to gather your belongings then these two gentlemen will show you the door."

Hunter spun around and stared at the two guards who seemed to have appeared from nowhere. He turned back to his grandfather. "Listen--"

Curtis sent him a look of disgust. "Are you ready to shame us more by begging?"

Hunter shifted his gaze to his father. For the first time Hunter saw hate in his eyes. Why? He knew his father never had tender feelings for him, but why this? Did his mother's madness make him bitter towards whatever ignited her memory?

Orson smiled. "Some pleading might prove entertaining but it won't change anything."

Hunter took the pen and signed.

"You have two weeks to move out of my house."

His cool faltered. "Two weeks? Couldn't you wait until after the trial? Brenna's under enough stress and--"

Orson flashed a shark-like grin. "She'll understand."

Curtis took the resignation. "Hopefully you do too." He gave him an insincere pat on the shoulder then left. Orson slowly rose to his feet. "You lost your chance, boy. You had everything in your grasp and you failed." He walked to the door then turned. "Remember to leave all your little scribbles behind. They belong to me. I wouldn't want you trying to make a fortune off of what's mine."

Hunter didn't move as his stomach knotted like a ball of twine scratching his insides. All that he had worked for: his name, his reputation gone. In an instant. How could his life come down to this? How could all his training, all his work, come down to this moment? His entire life had been in service to them--to the Randolph name. This was all he knew; all that he was. He'd lost his job, his house, his respect. He bent over a trash bin and promptly lost his breakfast.

Chapter Twenty-Three

Brenna sat in the living room, absently rubbing the pain in her leg that had been there since her fall. She tried to focus on a story that failed to hold her interest. She jumped when she heard the front door close. She glanced at her watch surprised. Hunter must have left work early. That wasn't like him. She hurried out of the living room and found him in the foyer hanging up his coat. Words caught in her throat when she saw the look on his face. She'd never seen such a look of devastation before. He walked past her, went into his office and shut the door.

She broke through her paralysis and followed him. She turned the doorknob. It didn't move. He'd never locked the door before. She pounded on the door, panic rising in her throat. "Hunter open the door. Hunter? Hunter! I know you can hear me. Open the door. Whatever it is we can figure it out. We always do, don't we? Hunter? Hunter! Open this door or I swear I'll go outside and break the window."

He abruptly opened the door. He caught her as she stumbled into the room. "That won't be necessary." He returned to his desk.

"What happened?"

He clasped his hands together and stared down at his papers.

She stood in front of him and pounded her fist on the desk. "Tell me what happened."

He didn't look up. "I was forced to resign. We have to leave this house in two weeks."

So Orson had made good on his threat, but Brenna wouldn't see this as a defeat. "At least you're free."

He captured her eyes with his. He stared at her as though he didn't know her. "Free? Free with no job, no reputation, no family, no right to my ideas? Freedom comes with prestige, status. Otherwise you're a nobody. A slave to the system, dependent on its mercy, its prisoner."

"He can't steal your ideas."

"It's company property. I'm an employee."

"We could prove--"

"He's not a man you want to battle in court."

Then she saw the truth. The danger. Orson could destroy Hunter. He could use her love--if it was truly that, she still wasn't sure--against her and make her regret the day she'd defied him. It was her pride that had brought this. Her stupid pride. She fell into a chair. "This is all my fault." She whispered the words not meaning for him to hear, but he did.

Hunter narrowed his eyes. "How?"

Brenna knew he would take his anger out on her. He had every right. She was the reason for his downfall. The reason he had lost everything that meant something to him. All because of her pride. She closed her eyes ready for his anger. Ready to lose him as she may also lose her brother. She opened her eyes and said, "Orson came by and he wanted me to stop you from looking into the company accounting and me from trying to find out about your mother. I defied him. I said you would not be chained to him by false loyalty. He promised to make me sorry."

Hunter spoke with a quiet patience that chilled her. "When did he come by?"

"Does it matter?"

"That depends. I noticed you limping one evening. I was wondering if there was any connection between that and his visit."

"I don't understand."

He traced a pattern on the desk. "I'm not in a good mood, Brenna. Don't be coy."

"I fell on my knee."

"How?"

"He was angry."

"And?"

She hesitated. "He took my cane and I fell."

"And why did he take your cane?"

"I told you he was angry. I said a few things." She shook her head exasperated. "It's complicated."

"And why didn't you tell me about this?"

"I--"

"You could have warned me so I could have been prepared," he said in a harsh, raw voice. "I come home and discover your brother's been indicted for murder. I go to work and discover I'm fired. In two weeks I'm going to be out of a house and you knew something like this was coming and you didn't say anything."

"Hunter--"

"Did you tell Miles?"

She lowered her gaze, her voice quiet. "No."

"Byron?"

"No. I didn't tell anyone."

"Look at me."

She didn't move.

"Brenna, I've made a simple request."

"It's not simple," she whispered. "You want me to face the disgust in your eyes."

Hunter rubbed his knuckles angered by her quiet defiance. "When are you going to learn to trust me?"

"I was trying to protect you. Your family is not good for you."

"Can't I be the judge of that?"

Brenna met his gaze. "No, because you can't see it."

"He warned me about you. Warned me that you wouldn't understand. Carrying the Randolph name is a responsibility that you don't seem to grasp. I almost regret the day I gave you the privilege of my name."

"You can have it back any time."

The corner of his mouth twisted in a cynical grin. "So you can run off to be with your precious Byron?" He snorted. "Wait, I forgot. You can't--" He stopped before he said 'run', but it was too late. The damage was done.

Brenna gasped and stared at him as though he'd stabbed her. He swore fiercely. He said something but she didn't hear him. She just continued to stare at him overwhelmed by a primitive despair. She held out a hand when he moved toward her. "No." She laughed bitterly. "You're right. I can't run. I also can't skip, I can't dance and I can't help you."

Hunter grabbed her shoulders; Brenna shoved him away. "You promised not to pity me, but you do."

"I didn't mean it." His words echoed his regret.

"Leave me alone."

He stared at her for a long moment then did.

Brenna wrapped her arms around herself and rocked, hoping the pain would ease with the movement. She'd angered so many people. Pauline, Byron, Orson, him. She briefly shut her eyes, rocking harder. She could move in with her mother until she found a place. Probably wouldn't start divorce proceedings until after Stephen's trial. She could go to the Randolphs and beg Orson for mercy on Hunter's behalf. She knew he was right. She didn't have what Hunter needed. She couldn't offer him the status or the prestige he craved. Without the Randolph name she was just his crippled wife.

Oh her pride. What the hell did she have to be proud of? Her father saw her as no more than a successful carnival act, Hunter a conniving spouse, Pauline a romantic fraud and Byron a pathetic con artist. Perhaps she was all those things. She didn't know anymore.

She rigidly held back tears. She would not cry. She couldn't afford to. She couldn't afford to feel sorry for herself. She was strong. She had made choices and she would live with the consequences.

"Brenna."

She turned away when Hunter sat beside her.

"I don't think you could hate me more than I hate myself at this moment."

"I'm not so sure of that."

He fell quiet but she could feel him staring at her. She spun around. "Stop staring."

"I can't help it."

"What do you want?"

He looked at her bewildered. "I don't know. For the first time in my life I don't know. I don't know what to say or do next."

She turned away.

"Will you let me apologize?"

"No."

"Okay." He fell silent again then swept her up in his arms.

"What are you doing?" she demanded as he carried her out of the room.

"I prepared a bath. I'm thinking of dropping you in."

"Let me go."

He climbed the stairs. "Will you let me apologize?"

"No. This is not funny," she said as he entered the bedroom.

"Do you want your clothes on or off?"

She shot him a glance.

"Okay on." He pushed opened the bathroom door. "Will you let me apologize now?"

"No."

He released her. She fell into the whirlpool tub with a splash. She came to the surface sputtering ready to shout at him when she suddenly found him beside her.

"What are you doing?"

He scooped up a handful of water and splashed his face. "I wish you'd stop asking me that."

You didn't even get out of your clothes."

"Neither did you."

"Are you having a nervous breakdown?"

He leaned back and looked at her through lowered lids. "Perhaps."

She pulled herself out of the water and sat on the rim. "Great."

"I'm sorry," he said. "I'm angry at myself. I shouldn't have taken it out on you."

His sincerity helped although she knew she would need time to forgive him. "You left my cane downstairs."

"I'll carry you to bed."

"I'd rather crawl."

He sat up amused. "I'd like to see you crawl."

She stiffened, remembering another man who'd said those same words.

His tone grew serious when he saw the expression on her face. "I was only teasing."

"I know."

"I'll get someone to bring it up." He reached for the buzzer.

She stopped him. "I don't want anyone to see us in here like this. Nervous breakdowns are usually private affairs."

"Oh." Hunter sank back into the tub and closed his eyes. "I've lost

everything."

Although it galled her to do so, Brenna sank back into the water beside him. "No, not everything," she said gently.

Hunter drew her to his side. "I know you were trying to protect me. You were trying to protect me from the look my father gave to me today. He hates me and I don't know why. I don't know if I want to." He shook his head then looked at her as though she could give him the answer. "What did I do that was so awful?"

Brenna rested her head against his shoulder. "I don't know," she said hoping that what Orson had said about his brother Lionel wasn't true.

He was going to turn him down. After ten interviews, Hunter was used to the expression. The expression of polite detachment and inevitable regret. The only difference was Aaron Rosenberg's bushy black brows came together over deep-set eyes as though he didn't want to give him bad news. The others seemed to delight in it. Rosenberg had been the last on his list of business contacts and the pattern had been the same. They invited him in for an interview only to say no. As if they wanted to see for themselves how desperate he was.

"You have an impressive resume," Aaron said.

"Which is pretty useless if it doesn't get me a job."

His bushy brows rose at his tone. "I'm sorry." He set his reading glasses aside.

Hunter nodded. He took the resume and put it in his briefcase.

Aaron clasped his hands together, his voice casual although his gaze grew sharp. "I received a call not too long ago. A call other people likely received. It advised me that any new hires would not be in the best interest of my company." He tucked his glasses in their case and opened a drawer. "And since I treasure the health of my company, I intend, as others are likely to, to heed that advice."

"I see."

"Let's be honest. The East Coast is his turf. You can find success elsewhere. I know the market's bad, but maybe go out of the country. Don't let your pride blind you to the fact that you're beaten." He shrugged. "Just a little advice."

Hunter stood.

"I know a man in Oregon--"

"Thank you. When I consider moving I'll let you know."

Hunter left the office wanting to tell Rosenberg where his friend in

Oregon could go. He threw his briefcase in the backseat and slammed the door. He sat inside and drummed his fingers on the steering wheel. Think Randolph. Think. He could move west, but Brenna had her company here. It was established and successful and unfortunately their sole income. The thought made him sick. He swallowed. Things wouldn't last this way forever. It was a temporary setback. Besides would she be willing to leave it and start over elsewhere? Plus her brother's trial was to be held here. They couldn't move until that was over. But how long would that last? No he couldn't move now. He didn't want to. He shouldn't need to. He would stay and fight.

He had investments that should last them awhile as he got things back in order. It would cover Brenna's medical and perhaps pay for some help. Yes, this was a great plan. He went to the bank his spirits lifted.

The female associate looked at the screen with concern. "I'm sorry there's nothing in the account."

He felt blood drain from his face. "What?"

"The last withdrawal was three weeks ago."

"That's impossible. Mr. Baladasso handled my account."

"Mr. Baladasso no longer works here. If you'd like to speak to a manager--"

"Forget it. Thank you." He left the bank impressed with his calm. Once outside he dialed Orson. "Where the hell is my money?"

His grandfather clicked his tongue in sympathy. "Poor Hunter. Money troubles already?"

"You know damn well that Baladasso worked for you. He oversaw all my investments."

"I know."

"He's gone with my savings."

"Shame."

"Where is he?"

"I don't know."

"Try to remember."

He paused. "I'm an old man. My memory is fading. Of course if you need a loan--"

"I want my money. Brenna's medical--"

"See now that isn't my problem, boy. I warned you about marrying her. If you buy a sick heifer, expect to pay the fees."

Hunter felt a cool anger that seemed to numb him. "You'll pay for this. You're an old man, Orson. I've got time on my side."

"Yes, and nothing else."

A SPRING WIND whipped through the darkness descending around the large colonial-style house. The distant call of an egret swept through the air. Audrey sat in her large oak poster bed adjusting the black silk scarf around her head as she waited for Orson to come into the room. She remembered the first apartment they'd shared. It could fit into her closet. How far they'd come. She didn't mind admitting that there had never been true love between them. She'd never expected that. She'd just wanted to fulfill her duty as wife and mother as God had ordained her role to be. She felt she had done her job well and God had blessed her, but tonight the blessing felt empty. She pulled up the bedclothes not glancing up when she heard the door open.

"You will not sleep here tonight," she said in a quiet voice.

Orson walked to his closet almost annoyed that she'd spoken to him. "What?"

"You will not sleep here tonight."

He unbuttoned his shirt. "What are you chattering on about woman?"

"I heard about what you did to Hunter."

"So?"

"Orson--"

He stepped out of the closet, his chest bare. He pointed his finger at her in warning. "I told you that boy was a dark horse, didn't I? He needed to be taught a lesson. I gave him everything and he thought he could walk into my company and change things."

"What's wrong with change?"

"Things change when I say so."

"What are you hiding?"

He waved a dismissive hand. "You don't know anything about business."

"No, but I know a lot of things about you."

He stepped back into the closet.

She raised her voice to make sure he heard her. "I've been with you over sixty years and I have been by your side. I've seen your triumphs and failures. Lord knows I've put up with a lot from you with your women." She sniffed. "But you're only a man so I forgave you. I've always done as you've said. I've been a good wife. So good you hardly notice me. Fortunately, I don't need you to notice me anymore as the gates of heaven call me closer each year. You were never a kind man Orson, but I knew that when I married you."

He closed the closet door and came towards the bed, his expression bland. "You have a point?"

She pulled out a gun and aimed it at his face. "You know my papa taught me how to use this thing in case I had unwanted visitors."

He halted startled then began to chuckle amused. "Put that thing away before you accidentally hurt someone."

"If I hurt someone it won't be an accident. Tonight I thought about what we've done to Hunter. We've lied to him his entire life and we continue to lie, and now you're punishing him because of your own guilt. I'm as much to blame as you are. If I'd spoken sooner, been stronger. But it's too late for wishing. Now we've shamed him. All of us. Just to keep the secret. I can hardly sleep with myself tonight so I'm certainly not going to sleep with you."

He pulled back the sheets. She fired. The bullet whizzed past his ear and shattered a statue. "I'm not foolin'."

Orson's temper peaked. "Audrey, that boy needed to be taught a lesson. Now--"

"Yes, through the years you've taught a lot of people a lesson. But for the first time in my life, you made me ashamed to love you." She motioned to the door. "Get out."

They stared at each other for a long time. Remembering, regretting then finally resigning themselves to the choices made. He went to the closet and grabbed his robe. "I'm going to be lenient this time because you're tired."

"You're right. I'm tired. Very, very tired." She took the gun and placed it back in the drawer.

HUNTER LOOKED up at his second floor apartment window with disgust. The two weeks in which he'd been forced to call the place home hadn't made him enjoy it anymore. He'd never lived in anything but a house. The neighborhood was decent, he supposed. Brenna was pleased with the view of the man-made lake and landscaped trees and their one bedroom. He walked into the apartment greeted by the smell of chicken and fried rice. Brenna had done her best to make the place feel like a home. Only he knew the paintings and most of the furniture were second hand. He hated the thought of using someone else's throwaways. He hated the thought that they'd had to leave everything behind and that it was Brenna's job that had afforded them this place. He hated the fact that every day he returned home after another unsuccessful job search.

"Hi," Brenna called from the kitchen.

He hated seeing her there even more. This wasn't the life he'd promised her. He opened his mouth to say something to the fact when he glanced at the table and noticed an extra plate setting.

He lifted the plate. "We're having company?"

"Yes."

He set it down. "Who's coming?"

"A cousin. Did your interview go well?"

He stopped her as she walked by holding a pitcher. "Which cousin? I thought you didn't like your cousins."

"I don't. It's one of yours."

Hunter took the pitcher from her and set it on the table. "Which one?"

"Daniel. How was the interview?"

"Bad." He rubbed the back of his neck. "I'm not in the mood for guests. Call and cancel."

The doorbell rang. Brenna smiled and patted him on the shoulder. "Too late."

Chapter Twenty-Four

Brenna and Daniel talked about various things while Hunter pushed his food around on his plate. As dinner came to an end Daniel said, "So Hunter, what do I have to do to convince you to work with me? With your ideas--"

Hunter started smashing peas with his fork. "I don't have any ideas."

"Yes, you do. Brenna told me what happened but you've always come up with new things."

"Not anymore." He couldn't remember the last time he'd sketched an idea or even doodled.

Brenna stood. "Why don't you two move into the living room while I clear the table?"

Hunter glanced at her. Was that a joke? The dining room was basically in the living room. He could walk the entire place in five minutes. Fortunately, Daniel didn't find any humor in her statement.

He pushed his chair back from the table. "It's a nice night. Why don't we go out on the balcony?"

"Good idea," Brenna said. "I'll put coffee on."

Hunter followed him to the balcony. It was a warm evening with fireflies dotting the sky. Daniel closed the glass door then said, "Give it to me straight. How bad is it?"

Hunter gripped the railing ready to lie. Ready to say everything was fine. That he had it all worked out. But Daniel waved a hand to stop him.

"I know you Hunter. You've sketched ideas since we were kids. Only something really bad could stop you. The last time was Angie. What is it this time? Brenna threatening to leave you?"

He shot him a glance. "Would you blame her?"

"She seems loyal."

"She is."

"So what's going on?"

"Besides losing my job, my house and living off of my wife's income? Baladasso ran off with all my savings. No doubt Grandfather helped him."

Daniel swore. "What the hell did you do to him?"

"I'm not sure. I thought—God I've been stupid. I didn't look into things. I trusted...I don't know what happened." He thought he was helping the company. What did he do that was so wrong? He shook his head it was no use trying to figure it out.

"How much do you have?"

"Enough to live like this."

"This isn't so bad."

Hunter rested his forearms on the railing. "I'm not telling Brenna. She has enough to worry about."

"Don't worry I won't say anything. I'll talk to Dad. We may have something for you." The Merediths owned a small company that distributed office supplies.

"It might not be such a good idea to work with me."

Daniel understood the warning and patted him on the back without concern. "He can't touch us. His sister would give him hell."

"Too bad she can't send him there."

"Careful. If you begin to hate him, he wins."

Hunter glanced at the sky. "Then he's won," he said softly.

Daniel patted his cousin on the back again. "Come by tomorrow. Let's see what we can do."

The next day, Daniel greeted Hunter as he entered the lobby. He showed him around the cramped offices then took him to his father's office.

Adrian Meredith looked at Hunter with smug disgust. The expression suited him. He was a bulky man built like a truck with cutting brown eyes. "So a Randolph needs a job. Tell me, what's the view like from down here?"

Daniel shifted awkward. "Look, Dad."

His father ignored him. "You Randolph's have snubbed your noses at us for decades. Why? Because you think you're smarter than us, richer than us--"

"He's different."

"And what makes him so different?" Adrian rested two forearms the size of cement blocks on the desk. "You were just like the rest of them. I don't remember you ever seeking out our company before. So now you need a job and you expect because we're family that I should give you one, but I'm not sentimental. So you'll have to come up with something more. Why should I help you?"

Daniel spoke up. "Because I asked you to."

"Let him speak for himself."

Hunter said, "I need work."

"I'm sorry, but we don't have any positions open right now."

Daniel began to speak; Adrian held up his finger in warning then spoke to Hunter. "Again I'm sorry, but it can't be helped."

Hunter swallowed back the bile in his throat. "I understand."

"Good." Adrian went back to work.

Daniel stared at his father stunned then followed Hunter out of the office. He shut the door then said, "I don't know what to say."

"Your father said plenty."

Daniel shook his head. "No, this is wrong." He turned. "I'm going to talk to him."

Hunter stopped him. "Why? He's right. I had the Randolph pride and arrogance. I've gotten what I deserve. I don't even know why you've believed in me all these years."

"Because you believed in me once."

"When?"

"Remember when my mom and I used to grow tomatoes and I tried to sell them? You bought the whole batch."

"So?"

"You were the only one who bought anything from me. It was the first time a Randolph had ever done anything for a Meredith. My mother said it and I knew it to be true. You were different and you still are. I don't care if Dad or Grand-Uncle don't see it. You're never going to be beat as long as I'm around." He paused. "Wait a minute." He disappeared into his father's office, raised voices soon followed then Daniel reappeared.

"What happened?" Hunter asked as Daniel dashed to the main exit.

"I just quit my job."

"Are you out of your mind?"

Daniel flashed him a grin. "No, just motivated. Now we have to come up with a brilliant idea fast."

* * *

Unfortunately, they didn't. And as two weeks slipped into four things began to look dire. Hunter roamed a mall hoping an idea would strike him. He didn't want to let Brenna and Daniel down, but he couldn't think of anything. He couldn't sketch, draw, or think. His mind was blank. He sat in front of a shoe store and stared sightlessly at the customers coming in and out.

"Those shoes look gorgeous," an older woman in a pink tam told her companion.

"I would buy them but my hose don't match. You know I can only wear diabetic hose."

Hunter straightened and listened.

"Couldn't you get a different color?"

"They only have black and white. I like this brand the best, but they have a poor selection and it's going to close soon because of bad business."

"That's a shame."

"I know. They're a local company not far from here. I remember when the paper did a story on them."

"What's their name?" Hunter said.

The two women looked at him surprised then scared.

He cleared his throat. "My sister could use another pair."

"They're called FreedomWear," the woman in the pink tam said. She then gave him the address.

Hunter jumped to his feet suddenly renewed. "Thank you." He grabbed their hands and kissed the back of them then ran out the door.

Three days later Daniel and Hunter stood in front of the dilapidated building that housed FreedomWear. The company they now owned after persuading the owner the benefit of selling to them.

Daniel scratched his forehead. "What does Brenna think?"

"She doesn't know," Hunter said.

"Why?"

"It's a risk I don't want her to worry about."

Daniel was quiet then said, "Are you having second thoughts?"

Hunter rested his hands on his hips and shook his head as he stared at the sun softening the crumbling sides of the building. "You made a big investment. I won't let you down. There's treasure in this trash. The system is here, they just didn't know how to use it."

Daniel grinned, knowing what his cousin was saying. "You think we're going to be rich."

Hunter nodded. "That's the plan."

THE TRIAL of the State of Maryland versus Stephen Garrett began on a rainy morning. Brenna sat in the crowded courtroom expecting to hate the DA--a clean cut man in his mid-fifties with a drooping mustache. But there was no doubt he considered himself a passionate advocate for the voiceless. She glanced at her brother looking handsome in a dark blue suit. When was the last time she'd seen him in a suit? Oh yes, at her wedding. It seemed ages ago. She then let her eyes drift to Byron. He looked easy-going, casual, and confident. The complete opposite of the man beside her. The one she'd married.

She was glad that Hunter's new job wouldn't allow him to attend the entire trial.

She listened to the opening statements. The DA started in a low voice. Not theatrical as one might expect from one so long in the field, but just as engaging. He talked to the jurors as a friend. He painted the picture of a man who had lived his life quietly, but had an inner anger. A man whose life pressures caused him to snap.

Byron countered that portrait with an easy grin as though his opposition had a tendency towards melodrama. He concluded that Stephen was a good citizen who had wanted to help an old man. He agreed someone killed Mr. Seaborn, but stressed that it wasn't the man sitting in the courtroom. Then the DA called his first witness the investigating officer on the scene and then a forensic expert. Brenna didn't pay much attention until he called Seaborn's son to the stand.

Nathan Seaborn was a tall plump man in his forties with long hair pulled back. The DA encouraged him to talk about his father and share what kind of man the victim was.

"You speak highly of you father," the DA said. " Yet you hadn't spoken in years. Why was that?"

"Dad engaged in a behavior that I didn't approve of."

"What was that behavior?"

Nathan cleared his throat. "He liked to con people."

"How do you know this?"

"My mom told me. And when I asked him he said it was true."

"Do you know why he did it?"

He shrugged. "Because he could and he was good at it. He and Mom had a good marriage until she died."

"What did you find most offensive about his behavior?"

"I thought it was cruel and dangerous. You can't go around making people trust you and then steal from them. One day you'll con the wrong person. Unfortunately, he found that out."

"Did your father have a certain type of person he would target as a mark?"

Nathan glanced at Stephen. "He liked them young, kind of quiet, easy to manipulate. As he got older he perfected his helpless old man act."

"No further questions." He turned to Byron. "Your witness."

"No questions," Byron said.

Next the DA called Seaborn's neighbor Mrs. Natalie Brighton. A woman with big eyes, wearing an outfit suited more for a fine restaurant than a courtroom.

"Did you know Mr. Seaborn well?" the DA asked.

She nodded vigorously. "Yes, we've been neighbors for a while now. A very kind and generous man."

"What were you doing when you saw the defendant leave the house?"

"I was letting my dog in the house."

"How did he look?"

"He looked like he was in a hurry."

"How so? As though he was escaping something?"

"Objection," Byron said. "Leading the witness."

"Sustained," the judge replied.

The DA changed his tactic. "When did you know something was wrong?"

"The next morning, when Mr. Seaborn didn't get his newspaper. Mr. Seaborn always picked up his newspaper at 7:30 am." She glanced at the jury. "Always."

"Thank you. No further questions." He returned to his chair.

"Are you sure you saw my client at the residence?" Byron asked.

"Yes."

"How?"

"He fit the description."

Byron grinned. "There are many men who could fit his description."

Mrs. Brighton bristled at the implication. "I saw that man sitting over there. I could even describe his truck. My husband knows a lot about trucks and so do I. I saw him under the street lamp and his truck has a unique indentation on the side."

"So the man you saw, you say was in a hurry? There are many reasons to be in a rush. Don't you agree?"

"He looked guilty."

"How do you know?"

"By the way he moved," she said certain.

"Perhaps he had to be somewhere. Home to his wife or maybe he forgot to pick up something before the store closed. It was a late night. You couldn't read his expression could you?"

"No, but--"

"So he was walking fast but you don't know why?"

"Yes, but--"

"Thank you. No further questions."

The DA called another neighbor, Ralph Parkov. A thin middle-aged man with cropped blonde hair and a shirt so pressed it looked fake.

"You also noticed Seaborn did not pick up his paper?"

"Yes. I was cleaning out my car that morning and was surprised to see his newspaper still in the box. I would have gone over to see what was wrong, but my eyes were watering so I had to go inside."

"Did you see the defendant the night of the murder?"

"Yes. Actually, I'd seen him before. He'd come by a couple of days before that night. He went into the house, but didn't stay long."

"Did you notice anything unusual in their behavior?"

"Objection," Byron said. "Relevance."

"I withdraw the question. Thank you. Nothing further."

Byron stood. "Would you say Mr. Seaborn was a popular man?"

"What do you mean?"

"Was it regular for him to have guests over?"

"Yes."

"So there's a possibility people could come and go and you wouldn't notice."

"Yes, but I noticed that night. I saw that man." He pointed to Stephen. "I didn't see anyone else."

"No further questions."

"You may step down," the judge said. "The court will reconvene next Thursday."

Hunter walked up to Byron and held out his hand. "I'd like to introduce myself."

Byron turned and shook his hand. "There's no need for introductions. Hello Brenna."

"Hello."

He clapped his hands together. "Anyone in the mood for coffee?"

A few moments later the three of them sat in a booth at a local restaurant.

"How do you think it's going?" Brenna asked.

Byron stirred his drink. "It's early."

"The police sound certain as does the forensic expert."

"Yes, they are supposed to. Besides the question isn't how he was killed, but by whom."

"And you're going to prove it wasn't Stephen?"

"I'm going to try."

"You're not worried?"

His eyes twinkled over the rim of the cup. "If I'm worried I never tell and never show it."

Hunter watched him, grim. He didn't like him. He didn't like how he looked at Brenna. Even more he didn't like how Brenna looked at him. "You take everything in stride?" he said.

"Pretty much. So, what exactly do you do?"

Brenna piped up. "He's an inventor."

"Does that mean you're unemployed?"

Hunter merely stared at him, a look full of warning.

Byron cleared his throat and finished his coffee.

ON THE DRIVE HOME, Hunter said to Brenna, "I noticed he isn't married."

"Yes."

"Are you glad?"

She turned to him startled. "What kind of question is that?"

"I see the way he looks at you."

She glanced out the window. "I can't help the way he looks at me."

"How about the way you look at him?"

"And how is that?" she challenged. "With admiration? With respect? He's defending my brother for half his fee. How do you want me to look at him? With contempt because he didn't love me when I wanted him to? If I had contempt for every man that didn't love me we'd—" She stopped and tugged on her seatbelt.

"We'd what?"

"Forget it." She shifted in her seat irritated. "I know you didn't like him."

"He didn't like me."

"You didn't give him a chance to."

"No, I have the feeling he made up his mind before he met me."

"You're being paranoid."

"You're being defensive."

They fell into a tense silence. After a moment, Hunter reached over and squeezed her hand in a tender gesture of support. "I think he's an asshole, but I hope he gets your brother off."

"I think you're obnoxious." She squeezed his hand, gaining strength from his support and smiled. "But thank you."

MILES MANAGED NOT to smile when he saw Curtis standing outside his office door. "Now why is this not a surprise?" he said.

"Perhaps you know the sound of opportunity knocking."

He opened the door to his office and gestured to a seat. "How can I help you?"

Curtis glanced around. "I believe you and Hunter used to share this space."

"Yes."

"Kind of small."

"Kept the cost down. R&D isn't a big priority."

"But it's a valuable part of the company. A lot of good ideas have come out of this department."

Miles nodded noncommittal.

"You must have enjoyed the extra space when Hunter was promoted."

"Yes."

"Shame he thought it was best to resign."

"Yes."

"Did he tell you why?"

"No."

"I'm surprised. I thought he counted you as a close friend. Didn't you look after his wife while he was away?"

"Yes."

It was clear Curtis was getting annoyed with Miles' monosyllabic answers, but he maintained a calm expression. "Did she express any concern about Hunter? Did she think he might be unhappy with us? I hate to admit that Hunter and I aren't close as father and son should be so I have to find another way to convince him to return."

"I can't help you."

"I believe you have a sister you're supporting in college."

"Yes, I also have a lawyer on retainer so I suggest you don't make threats."

He held his hands out innocently. "Why would I threaten you? You've been a loyal employee for years. I consider you one of the family. I just wanted to assess your economic responsibilities before offering you a more elevated position."

"Thanks but no. I'm happy where I am."

Curtis studied him. "Ambition is not a dirty word."

"No, but I know the price of ambition with the Randolphs and it's just too high for me."

He stood. "If you change your mind, you know how to reach me."

It was the worst shift. Hunter lifted the last box on the truck then signaled for a break. He headed towards the candy machine then stopped when he saw Miles.

Hunter looked at Miles, startled. "How did you--"

"Daniel." He yawned. "This is too early to be out of bed. Couldn't you get a better shift?"

Hunter shoved his gloves in his back pocket. "Two guys called in sick and I need this shipment to go out."

"Things aren't picking up as fast as you thought?"

"They will."

"Do you think Orson—"

"He doesn't frighten me."

"Your father tried to frighten me. Don't worry," he said quickly when Hunter's expression changed. "I took care of it. I felt flattered he thought I was worthy of a bribe. He wanted to know if you had told me anything. Is there anything you need to tell me?"

"No, unless you also want to find yourself lifting boxes."

"Thanks, but that would not be the best career move for me."

"How long do you plan on keeping this a secret from Brenna?"

"Until things work."

"You need to tell her."

"I will when the time is right. She's under a lot of stress right now. She doesn't need more." Hunter hesitated then said. "But you could do something for me."

"What?"

"Find out more about these." He handed Miles an object.

Miles stared at them confused. "Pantyhose?"

"Diabetic hose. I plan to broaden the selection. I know that diabetics have special needs regarding foot care and the material used for hose or socks is critical. I'm curious as to why manufactures stick to these three colors—black, white and tan. Also look into ways to reduce varicose veins and other ailments."

"You think there might be something to this?"

"Yes."

Miles shook his head unsure. "What could two guys know about hose?"

"That women like to buy many pairs."

His interest peaked. "Hmm, I'll see what I can do."

"Thanks."

"In the meanwhile, be careful."

Hunter pulled his gloves on. "I will."

Miles held out an envelope. "Here."

Hunter stared down at it. "No."

Miles shoved it in his hand. "Don't be a damn martyr. I know you'll pay me back, with interest. Think of it as a business invest-ment." He picked up a box. "I plan to be head of R&D."

"What are you doing?" Hunter asked watching Miles load the truck.

"You've got a new employee."

"I can't pay you what you're worth yet, but online sales are growing and—"

"We'll come up with something."

"It's a risk."

"I don't see you shaking."

Hunter nodded and handed him another box. "Then welcome aboard."

BRENNA THOUGHT it was an odd choice for the DA to put the guard from the apartment complex on the stand. She couldn't rationalize what relevance the guard would be to the case. The guard was a large black woman with four earrings in each ear.

"Is it true that you consider yourself a friend of the defendant's wife?" the DA asked her.

"Yes."

"Did Mrs. Garrett share with you how her husband acted when he returned home that night?"

"Yes."

"How did she describe him?"

"Agitated."

"Did she say why?"

"No, she says he gets in his restless moods from time to time and doesn't say much."

"What was it that bothered you and convinced you to call the police? Was there something you noticed?"

She nodded. "Yes."

"And what was that?"

"He was wearing a different shirt."

"Thank you." The DA returned to his seat. "No further questions."

Byron stood and shrugged with nonchalance determined to make light of her observations. "So he changed his shirt? Is that unusual?"

"Objection," the DA said.

Byron rephrased his question. "Are you sure you saw him in a different shirt?"

"Positive. Yes, he was wearing a crew neck T-shirt when he left and he came back in a blue button-up one when he returned."

"Do you usually notice what people wear?"

"No, not always."

"So what made you remember the defendant?"

She looked embarrassed. "Well, he's the kind of guy you notice, you know."

Byron stroked his chin as though weighing her words. "Is it true that his job is of a physical nature?'

"Yes, Fiona told me it can be physical. She says she hates when he comes home sweaty."

"So it would make sense that he's in the habit of changing shirts, correct?"

"I guess."

"Therefore it would make sense that after working at Seaborn's all day he'd change his shirt?"

"Yes."

He tapped the stand. "Thank you. No further questions."

"Any cross?" the judge asked.

"No, Your Honor," the DA replied.

The judge looked at the guard. "You may step down."

***

LATER THAT DAY, Byron sat alone in his office as the rays of the sunset filled the room. Things didn't look good for Stephen. Unfortunately, he didn't have any tricks up his sleeve. He'd noticed some jurors had already made up their minds about him. He knew it was difficult to plant a seed of doubt in a slab of concrete, but he did believe in miracles. And he planned to get Stephen off. Bryon rubbed his eyes and sighed. He just wished he didn't feel so alone. He missed his uncle and hated the prospect of dealing with another failure. He let his hands fall to his desk. No, he wouldn't fail this time.

"The prosecution made quite a case," Brenna said, standing in the doorway.

Byron sat up surprised. He'd always hoped she would come by to see him, but never believed that she would. He nodded, not trusting himself to speak.

She sat, resting her cane on the ground. "Do you still think you can get him off?"

He nodded again.

"I probably should have come before to help you with the case."

"No other reason?"

Brenna ignored the undertone of his question. "There are some things you should know."

Byron glanced at her hands as they fiddled with the strap of her handbag, she wasn't as calm as she seemed. "I already know about your uncle."

"Do you think the DA knows?"

"Yes."

"But it doesn't need to come out in the trial."

"It will if it has to."

She yanked on the strap. "You can make sure it doesn't."

He flashed a smile of sympathy. "I can't make sure of anything. I can only try to use it to my advantage."

Both her gaze and her voice fell. "Oh."

Byron leaned forward eager to lift her spirits. "Do you remember—?"

"No," she said quickly, meeting his gaze. "Or rather I don't want to remember."

"I don't have a choice." He clasped his hands together and studied her for a moment. "Do you plan on having kids?"

Her gaze didn't waver. "What do you think?"

"So the Randolphs wouldn't mind if—"

"Hunter wouldn't mind," she said in a tight voice. "And that's what matters."

He rested back. "You don't know everything about your husband."

"Neither do you."

Byron shrugged then came from around the desk, closing some of the distance between them. "Why did you come here? You could have just called."

"I know. I wanted to offer support." She grabbed her cane and stood. "But if you don't need me for anything—"

He blocked her path. He stood close, but didn't touch her. He could hear her breathing quicken. His body came alert at the rush of red that came to her cheeks and how she moistened her lips. "I don't need you," he said. "But I want you real bad."

Her knuckles grew pale as she grasped the strap of her handbag. "I'm sorry to hear that."

"No, you're not. Brenna, don't do this to me."

She moved around him. "I'm not trying to do anything."

"Okay, forget about us," he called before she reached the door. "I could use your help."

She paused then turned. "I'm listening."

"Are you willing to work with me?"

She looked at him with interest. "I'm willing to do what's necessary to help my brother."

What's necessary. How very practical and like Brenna. There was no way he could convince her to sleep with him—at least not yet, but at least he was no longer alone.

Byron gestured to the seat and smiled. "I'm glad to hear that."

LATER THAT NIGHT Byron stared up at the ceiling. It wasn't like him to be unable to sleep, but no matter what he tried, sleep wouldn't come. He thought about the prosecutions' witnesses: the guard who'd seen Stephen change his shirt and Seaborn's son. But aside from that he thought about Brenna. He shouldn't be alone tonight. She should be beside him, beneath him and he wouldn't stop until she was. They belonged together. He'd been weak, but he'd always been weak and that weakness had cost him. But not again, never again. He wouldn't let her down. With his good looks and background he was used to things coming easily to him. Brenna's resolve amazed him. He had to admit that when she'd asked him to marry her he'd been scared. Scared that he couldn't be the husband she needed. He'd taken the coward's way out, but not this time. He'd fight. She didn't know the man she'd married or the family she'd married into.

Part Three

The true measure of life is not length, but honesty.
John Lyly

Chapter Twenty-Five

The Present

Brenna set her glass aside and looked at Byron. It was dangerous to be here with him. It was a simple invitation to a friend's party, but she knew they were headed to much more. She'd let him kiss her. And as he did she thought of how much Hunter had loved Angelina. She remembered his words while indulging in the sensuous feel of Bryon's lips on her skin. She shut her eyes. It could always be like this. She could be loved too.

"Come away with me," Bryon whispered.

She reluctantly drew away. "I can't. And this is wrong."

"What's wrong is how you continue to lie to yourself."

"I have to go home."

"To what? You have nothing and no one to go home to."

BYRON'S WORDS echoed in Brenna's mind as she stared at the large brick wall that slowly came to life under the artistic hands of twelve high school students. Tima had invited her to see the progress of a mentoring program she volunteered with.

"Feel the story," Tima instructed. She looked over at Brenna and waved. "Hi."

"Hi."

"Is your leg hurting you?"

"Just a little. I've been working with Byron the past few days and trying to keep everything at work running smoothly. It's just nerves." She glanced around. "This is impressive."

Tima folded her arms and shot her a knowing look. "Stay away from him, Brenna."

She didn't turn her eyes away from the mural. "Who?"

"You know who. You're thinking about him right now. Personally, I don't blame you." She wiggled her eyebrows. "I've seen him. But you're married."

"The marriage isn't real. Sometimes I wonder if I've made a mistake."

"You didn't make a mistake marrying the man you love."

Brenna continued to stare at the mural. "Everyone knows I married Hunter for his money."

"That's what you want everyone to believe and most people do."

Brenna turned to her. "But not you."

Tima shook her head. "Why don't you just admit that you loved this man the moment he walked into your office?"

"I can't admit that," she said in a tense voice.

"Why not?"

She gripped her cane and fought hard against tears. "Because I promised myself never to feel this way again. Never to love a man who didn't love me. How could I be so stupid? How can I love a man like Hunter? Do you know what I am to him? An employee. I have my duties and my place and nothing more. I should leave him..."

"Why don't you?" Tima said bluntly. "He doesn't have money any- more."

Brenna ignored the question. "Byron wants me. Do you know how good it feels to be wanted in that way?" Her gaze fell as she thought about the time she'd spent with him. The forbidden kiss that night on the balcony only days ago and the questions she refused to answer. "I've told him no, but..."

"You don't know what you want."

"What's better? To love or be loved?"

"It depends on what makes you happy."

"Byron's coming by tonight. Hunter's working late so there'll just be the two of us."

Tima studied her friend, uneasy. "Be careful, Brenna."

"Don't worry. I am."

HUNTER DID NOT APPRECIATE the sight of Brenna and Byron saying goodbye in the parking lot. But it wasn't the first time he'd seen them together. Brenna had explained that Byron needed her help in uncovering some information and he couldn't object. But there was no doubt he couldn't wait for the trial to end. He watched Byron walk to his car then followed.

Byron saw him and smiled. "Hello."

Hunter didn't return the expression. "You're heading in the right direction. I suggest you keep going."

Byron looked amused and shoved his hands in his pocket. "You can't stop me from seeing her. You've denied her enough things, don't you think?" He glanced at the building. "This little set up of yours isn't working anymore. The main thing is you can't make her happy." He rested a hand on his chest. "I can. I know she loves the scent of pumpkin pie and fall afternoons and the taste of blackberries in cream. What do you know about her?"

"Enough to know she belongs to me."

"The great thing about belongings is that you can always get a fair exchange," Byron said. "How would you like your old life back? A time when you could afford anything you wanted? Fortunately, people will pay a lot of money for the right kind of secrets. And I know of someone who could use a few."

"I'm not interested." Hunter began to walk away.

Byron shrugged. "The Randolphs have treated you badly," he called after him. "In a way we're on the same side."

Hunter slowly turned, his voice laced with ice. "And what side would that be?"

Byron flashed a ruthless grin. "We both wouldn't mind a little revenge."

Hunter folded his arms curious. "What do you have against the Randolphs?"

"Orson got my uncle disbarred. He had discovered Orson and a bank executive had hired a corrupt lawyer to throw a case against a bank manager indicted for embezzlement. The manager went to prison and they made a hefty profit from the 'missing funds' that were never recovered. When Orson discovered my uncle was investigating the case, he pulled some strings and made sure my uncle never worked in law again. I'd like to repay him for his kindness."

Hunter was silent a moment. "When you heard about this case, what caught your attention more? The name Randolph or Garrett?"

"I was swayed by both."

"Perhaps one more heavily than the other?"

"Perhaps."

Hunter shoved his hands in his pockets. "Which would you prefer? Company secrets or Brenna?"

Byron rocked on his heels. "I don't make choices when I have the advantage."

"And what would that be?"

"I have money and Brenna needs me. As I said earlier it's a friendly exchange." He grinned then turned. "Think about it."

***

Hunter sat at the table thinking about Byron's offer. He did want revenge. He did want money and prestige, but not at his price. He'd deal with his grandfather on his own terms and he would do whatever it took to make Brenna happy. He wanted to make her happy, but didn't know how. He glanced up when she put a fruit smoothie in front of him. "What's this?"

"Your dinner. Since you won't eat anything I cook. I thought this might help."

He felt heat stealing into his cheeks. Lately, he hadn't had much of an appetite. "It's not the food--"

"Just drink it. You need nutrients."

He lifted the glass and studied it before setting it back down. "I saw Byron before I came in."

She sat and dived into her lasagna dish. It was in a carton of some sort. Everything seemed to come in a carton lately. "Oh."

"I don't want you to see him anymore."

She stared surprised. "Why not?"

"I don't trust him."

"I do. He's defending my brother."

"I know. That doesn't mean you have to see him outside of court."

She boldly met his eyes. "I'll see him if I want to."

"I'm your husband and you promised--"

Brenna clenched her fork, her voice low. "I promised you my loyalty, not my heart. What about your promises?" Brenna covered her mouth and looked devastated as though she knew how much she'd hurt him. "I'm sorry. You didn't deserve that. Especially from me." She rose to her feet exasperated. "This is all wrong. I don't want us to hurt each other." She bit her lip and stared at him, sadness in her eyes. "Maybe we should—"

He knew the tone and the look. Angie had used them when she'd asked for a divorce. He didn't want to go through that again. He stood. "It will get better," he interrupted then began to walk away.

"Where are you going?"

He spun around and threw up his hands. "Dammit, not far! We live in an apartment the size of a toothpaste box. If I fell off the balcony the worse I could do is break my ankle. Where the hell could I go?"

Brenna shook her head. "It's not that bad."

Hunter rested his hands on his hips and stared at the ground. "I know I haven't fulfilled my promise to you," he said in a cold, flat tone.

"I said I was sorry."

He met her gaze. "But you're right. I know why you married me."

Brenna smiled sadly. "And I know why you married me, but I'm not much use to you now, am I?"

"Things will change." He turned.

"Why wait until then. If I left, you wouldn't have to see her behind my back."

Hunter stopped then looked at her confused. "Who?"

Brenna went into the kitchen and pulled a pair of stockings from the drawer. She held them out to him. "They're not mine."

Hunter sighed resigned and took them from her. "I know. They're mine." He saw her expression change then burst into laughter.

Brenna frowned. "I don't see what's so funny."

He laughed harder. He staggered into the living room and fell on the couch.

Brenna stood in front of him. "Hunter!"

"I'm not wearing them," he gasped some of his laughter subsiding. "They're for my company."

She sat beside him. "What company?"

He hesitated then said, "It's called FreedomWear. We supply diabetic hose. The company hasn't picked up as fast as I wanted, but it will. We're working on a new line of the product that will--"

She snatched the stockings from him and shook it in his face. "Why didn't you tell me?"

A remote expression entered his eyes. "I wanted to make it a success before I told you."

Brenna stared back at him with amusement. "The fact that you own it already makes it a success to me."

Hunter paused. She didn't see him as a failure? She trusted him?

He seized her shoulders his mood suddenly buoyant. "I don't care who you give your heart to as long as you remain loyal to me. Okay?"

Brenna nodded, but even as she did so Hunter knew he wanted more. He wanted all of her. He didn't expect her to love him, but he didn't want her to love anyone else. He wanted her completely. He wanted to be the only man in her thoughts. His lips captured hers with passion near desperation and a command that was fierce. Tonight he would make sure she thought only of him.

"Tell me you're mine," he demanded in a deep husky tone.

"I'm yours."

He peeled away her clothes, pressing his lips to the areas he exposed. "Say it again."

She wrapped her arms around his neck, pressing her body against his. "I'm yours."

Her breathless words made a possessive hunger grow within him. He couldn't remove their clothes fast enough. Having her warm, soft form melding itself against the length of him wasn't enough. Even as he found solace between her thighs it only took the edge off his need. He wanted her to know her words were a promise to him. She belonged to him and he wouldn't surrender her to anyone no matter what the price.

He didn't speak for a long time after it was over, his body limp with pleasure, but his mind filled with unease.

Brenna rested her cheek against his chest. It felt right to be with him. He didn't want her heart, but she didn't know how to claim it back from him. "Hunter?"

"Hmm?"

"Tell me you're mine."

She waited, her body filled with hope and fear, her pulse beating erratically. She shut her eyes promising she wouldn't cry. Then she felt his large hand against her face, his touch tender and he said, "I'm yours."

THE SUN SHONE through a cloudy haze the day the defense began its argument. Byron called Stephen to the stand.

It was a risky move, but Byron was confident that with his quiet reserved manner and good looks he could charm the jury. They'd practiced for this and now it was time for the stage. As expected, Stephen answered Byron's questions calmly and he could see the audience softening towards him. The DA however, had not softened and once Byron finished his question he prepared to cross-examine and approached Stephen as the suspected murderer he was.

"Why were you at Mr. Seaborn's residence that night?"

"I went over to talk to him about his house. I wanted to help him with his lighting and other things. "

"A stranger you'd only just met?"

"A lot of clients start out as strangers. He seemed like a nice guy."

"So you spent all day with him." He paused. "The first time you met him was in a grocery store. Is that correct?"

"Yes."

"Is it true that you bought his groceries?"

"Yes."

"Are you in the habit of buying people's groceries?"

"No, but he looked a little short on cash. I was just trying to help him out."

"Help him out," the DA repeated the statement slowly for effect. "Is that why you also offered him a ride home?"

Stephen nodded. "Yes. It was cold and he'd missed his bus."

"Are you in the habit of driving men home?"

"No. Like I said, I was helping him out."

"How do you feel when people break your trust?"

Stephen shrugged. "I don't like it, but I wouldn't hurt them."

"As long as they don't make you work for them without compensation first."

Byron raised his pen. "Objection. The DA assumes facts not in evidence, Your Honor."

The judge nodded. "Sustained. Watch yourself counselor."

The DA tugged on his cuffs. "Strike the statement." He smoothed out his mustache. "Has a man ever betrayed your trust before?"

Stephen shifted in his seat. "He just stole from me. You're making it sound like it was more than that."

"That wasn't the question. Has a man ever betrayed your trust before?"

"No."

The DA paused confused. "That's strange because I have a witness ready to testify that when you were eight a male relative molested you. Isn't that a betrayal?"

Stephen stiffened. "That was different."

"How was it different?"

"It's just not the same. Stealing and...that."

"But both people were individuals you trusted and they took advantage of you. It sounds the same to me, don't you agree?"

"No, I don't. Molestation is something else."

"Did you learn that in counseling?"

"I never got counseling."

"I see. So you never got counseling for what must have been a very traumatic experience?"

Stephen glanced at Brenna then his mother. "No."

"Did the incident make you angry?"

"Yes."

"And you've held in that anger all the time?"

Byron stood. "Objection. Misquoting the defendant's statement, Your Honor."

The judge nodded. "Sustained."

The DA turned to the jury. "Without counseling, were you able to handle the anger you'd experience then?"

"Yes."

"You were able to deal with an older person, you trusted, basically stealing your innocence, is that correct?"

"Yes."

"Isn't that what a thief does? He steals from you."

"Yes." Stephen sighed. "It was a long time ago."

"Do you still interact with that individual?"

"Sometimes."

"Does that bother you?"

"No, and we don't talk about it."

"Is it true that your family doesn't like to talk about certain things?"

Stephen nodded. "Yes."

"So you're in the habit of keeping things to yourself?"

"Yes. I don't need to talk about things."

"Still it must be stressful to meet with someone who violated you like that and have to pretend nothing happened. If that had happened to me, I'd be upset. But you're fine about it right?"

"Yes. I said it was over," Stephen slowly repeated his patience thinning.

"Right." He glanced at Brenna. "Is it true that you have a disabled sister?"

"She's not disabled. She has a limp."

The DA smiled. "More than a limp I'd say. More like a deformity. Isn't it true that she had a lot of surgeries while you were young?"

"Yes."

"Did you have to look after her?"

"Yes, sometimes when she came home from the hospital."

"Did you mind having to look after your big sister?"

"Objection," Byron said annoyed. "Your Honor, the defense fails to see the relevance in this line of questioning."

The DA spun around. "If the defense will give me a chance to finish--"

The judge said, "Both of you please approach the bench."

Byron spoke first. "Your Honor, while I respect the DA's position in this courtroom I do not see the benefit of exposing my client by discussing past molestation and his sister's disability."

The DA countered. "Your Honor, there is no doubt that the

defendant has led a good life. That is not why he is in this courtroom. He is a man of hidden anger and I think that it is important for the jury to see the possible state of mind he was in when he visited Percy Seaborn that evening."

The judge looked at both men then said, "Overruled." Byron returned to his seat and the judge instructed Stephen to answer the question.

"No, I didn't mind."

The DA nodded. "Isn't it true that at times you had to protect her from bullies?"

"Sometimes."

"And is it true that there were times that you resented her?"

Stephen shifted awkward. "I was young."

"Is that a yes or a no?"

"Yes."

"Isn't it also true that you helped your mother? You worked odd jobs to help support the family after your father left, correct?"

"Yes, I liked to help."

The DA nodded again. He walked to his table then turned. "It appears that it is in your nature to help people. You like helping?"

Stephen scratched the back of his neck. "Sure."

The DA rested against the table and folded his arms. "Always?"

Stephen shrugged. "Sure."

"Even when you don't have a choice?"

"Yes."

The DA slowly approached the stand and rested a hand there. "Stephen, I think you're a decent young man and I do believe that you like to help people. I also believe you graciously helped Percy Seaborn pay for his groceries and when you saw his house thought that you could help him fix it up a bit. I believe you did go back to his house to talk about improvements and stayed later because he was sociable and you liked him. You both went out for drinks then returned to the house. You could have left, but you decided to stay for your own reasons. I think you discovered him stealing from you then. Am I right so far?"

"Pretty much."

"Isn't it true that at that moment you got angry?"

"No."

"The memory of all the times you've been taken advantage of and betrayed came forth in a rage and you killed him?"

Stephen's voice remained soft. "No, I didn't kill him."

"But he did steal from you, breaking your trust?"

"Yes, but it was no big deal."

"And what did you do when you found him swiping your credit card?"

"I stopped him."

"By hitting him."

Byron jumped to his feet. "Objection."

"I withdraw the statement. How did you stop him?"

"I got up and left," Stephen said.

The DA raised his hands surprised. "That's all?"

"Yes."

"A strong young man like you. You just got up and calmly left?"

"Yes."

"A man takes your credit card and basically steals all your private information, a man you trusted, considered perhaps a friend. You just left. You didn't get upset?" the DA said with disbelief.

"I didn't kill him."

"You just left."

"Yes."

"In a hurry."

Byron jumped to his feet again. "Objection calls for speculation."

The judge agreed. "Sustained. I won't warn you again, Counselor."

The DA addressed the judge. "No further questions."

The judge looked at Byron. "Would you like to re-direct?"

"Yes, Your Honor." Byron approached the stand inside knowing the risk he'd taken by putting Stephen on the stand, but determined to make his strategy work. He could see Stephen was tense, but he was handling things well. "Could you explain why you choose to help Seaborn?"

"Because he looked like he needed it. No one really paid attention to him at the grocery store and when I saw his house; I knew I had the skills to help."

"When you found out what Seaborn was up to did you two argue?"

"No."

"Would you say you have a temper?"

"No more than average. I'm pretty easy going."

"Were you teased in school because of your sister?"

"Yes."

"Did it make you angry?"

"Yes."

"Isn't it true that there was an incident where a kid tripped you in the hall and you fell and got a bloodied nose?"

"Yes."

"What did you do?"

"I left."

Byron paused to let the reply linger in the air for the jury to remember. "Even though kids were laughing at you? You didn't turn around and fight him?"

"No, I thought he was stupid and I wanted to get home."

"So you left?"

"Yes."

"Just like you left Seaborn's house?"

"Yes."

"How was Seaborn when you left him?"

Stephen thought for a moment. "Sad, remorseful. He wanted to know if I'd come back."

"What did you say?"

"I said he was a thief."

"Did you plan to come back?"

"I don't know."

Byron turned away. "No further questions."

"Re-cross?" the judge asked.

The DA rested back in his seat. "Is it true that at sixteen you discovered that same relative who molested you had once touched your sister and another cousin of yours?"

"Objection."

"Overruled," the judge replied he nodded at Stephen. "Answer the question."

Stephen paused then said, "Yes."

"And isn't it true that made you angry?" the DA pressed.

"Yes."

"What did you do?"

Stephen sighed resigned. "I hit him."

"Isn't it true that you hit him so hard that you nearly killed him?"

He blinked. "No."

The DA raised his brows. "Didn't he suffer near fatal head injuries and need over fifty stitches in his jaw and left eye?"

Stephen swallowed feeling the threat of prison looming closer. "Yes," he said.

The DA nodded pleased. "No further questions."

Chapter Twenty-Six

"You shouldn't have put him on the stand," Brenna said to Byron in his office.

He ran a tired hand over his face. "I had to. This isn't a slam-dunk case on either side. It's best to introduce as much information as possible."

"I'm not talking about a case. I'm talking about you letting some DA emotionally rip my brother to shreds."

"Brenna—"

"No, you should have stopped him. Didn't you know he was going to use that argument?" She read his face and her anger grew. "You knew and you set him up. You didn't even prepare him."

"I wanted a natural response. I wanted the jury to see how he acted under pressure and I succeeded."

"No, you made him look ridiculous."

He grabbed her shoulders. "Brenna—"

She stepped away. "Don't touch me. It was wrong."

"It's a close case. I want to establish reasonable doubt. That's all."

"But he's innocent."

"I can't prove innocence. All I want is not guilty."

"At all costs?"

"There's no other choice. Please trust me." He seized her arms, his face close to hers, his voice low with simmering emotion. "Brenna, I'm going to do whatever I have to in order to make sure that he walks out of that courtroom a free man. This isn't about truth or lies it's a game of persuasion."

"I don't like the game you're playing."

"I feel the same way about the one you're playing. Do you think it's easy for me to have to let you go home to that cold bastard you call your husband?"

She yanked herself free. "Don't say that."

"Why not?"

"Because I love him."

Byron released her as though she'd grown thorns. "You don't mean that," he said in a hoarse whisper. "You just want to hurt me."

"No, this has nothing to do with you. I didn't mean to love him, but I do."

Byron shook his head unable to believe her. "You're just grateful that he married you."

"No, that's not it."

"How can you respond to my touch and say you love him?"

"I respond out of memory not out of love."

"I don't believe you. You want to be with me." He gathered her close again, pleased to feel her tremble. "You still love me, but you're afraid to admit it." He caressed her cheek then stopped and frowned. "You're burning up."

"It comes and it goes."

"How long have you had this fever?"

She shrugged. "I don't know."

"I've seen you rubbing your leg a lot. You're hurt."

"It's nothing."

"With you it's never 'nothing'. Have you seen a doctor?"

Brenna hesitated.

"You can't afford it?"

"I can afford it, it's just that some of the out of pocket expenses are—"

"I'll take care of it."

"No."

"You can't fight me on this Brenna." Byron grabbed his coat. "We're going to the emergency room."

STEPHEN BLINDLY STARED at the black TV screen trying not to remember how bare and exposed he'd felt on the stand. Trying to think of how he could have responded differently. Fiona came into the living room and sat on the couch. She pointed to the TV. "You know that's not on."

"I know."

She bit into a chocolate bar. "So who was it?"

"Who was what?"

"The male relative who molested you?"

He swung his head around and stared at her, amazed. "Why? So you can picture it in your mind? So you can point him out at family bar-b-cues?"

"It was just a question."

He would never have thought a simple question could bring back such emotions. Guilt, sadness, anger, disgust. The emotions were bad, but the memories were worse. He remembered how it started and how it stopped. He remembered how he and his Uncle use to wrestle all the time and he used to tickle him. Then he remembered the time he'd put his hand down his pants. How he'd been forced to forgive his Uncle because he was a good guy. How his family had been so ashamed and made him feel bad for saying anything. Brenna was the only one who truly believed him. How could it be so long ago and yet so clear?

"Where are you going?" Fiona demanded when he grabbed his coat.

"I'll be home later."

"Stephen, talk to me."

"I don't feel like talking."

"Maybe the DA was right. You have to learn to talk more."

"Or maybe I just don't want to talk to you." He closed the door.

Stephen didn't remember driving to Brenna's place. But a half hour later he was standing at her door ringing the doorbell. Hunter answered the door. "Is Brenna home?" he asked eager to speak to her.

"No, she went to run errands."

His face fell. "Oh."

"Come in," Hunter said. "I could use the company."

Stephen halted, surprised at the invitation. "Okay." He went into the living room and saw cut up pantyhose on the table.

"I'm just experimenting with a few ideas," Hunter explained scooping up the evidence. "Like anything to drink?"

"No."

"Sit down. Make yourself comfortable."

Stephen sat on the couch then slid to the floor and glanced at Hunter. He'd never been alone with him before. He'd always assumed the experience would be awkward and it was. Hunter didn't seem to feel the need to say anything. He didn't ask him how he was or how the trial was going. Stephen drummed his fingers on his knee trying to think of something to say—then realized he didn't have to say anything. That was a relief. He soon felt himself relax. He got up and went to the kitchen. Hunter didn't say anything. He poured himself some orange juice and grabbed a bag of chips. Hunter changed the channel.

Stephen sat feeling relaxed. This was just what he wanted. It amazed him that Hunter understood him. Too bad he couldn't say the same. He still wondered why Hunter had married Brenna. He didn't believe what Byron had said, but had nothing to counter that opinion. "Do you ever have memories you don't want to remember?" Stephen finally asked him.

"Yes, some I've blocked out."

"How did you do it?"

"I don't know. Denied their existence I guess. I get flashes sometimes, but try not to pay too much attention." He closed the window blind then sat. "Brenna told me what happened today."

Stephen set the bag of chips aside. "Oh."

Hunter spread out his arms the length of the couch.

Stephen waited for questions, but nothing came and soon he wanted to share. "We told Dad and the first thing he said was, 'What did you do?'" Stephen smiled without humor. "They always used to say how pretty and sweet I was. They talked about me like I was a damn girl or something and I..." His words trailed off when Hunter shook his head.

"You don't need to explain," he said. "It wasn't your fault. I know how it feels to be betrayed by the people you trust." A look of pain crossed his face. "By the men you trust. The men you look up to. I used to wonder why my father didn't like me. Was it something I did? Was it because of my mother? I don't know why. Perhaps I never will, but his feelings are beyond me and I accept that." Hunter rested a hand on Stephen's shoulder. "You were a little boy and it shouldn't have happened. And since your father hasn't the sense to tell you this I will. You're a good man and I'm proud of you."

Stephen shrugged Hunter's hand from his shoulder. "Yea, thanks, but you want to know the truth? I'm not a good man. Growing up I was ashamed of Brenna and did resent her. At times I wanted her to disappear. When Percy stole from me, I was angry and I could have hurt him and at times even Fiona makes me mad and I want my marriage to just end."

Hunter stared at him. "You're a good man and I'm proud of you."

Stephen drew up a leg and rested his elbow on top. "And I hate my father for leaving and my mother for letting him. I hate him for making us struggle and inviting my Uncle over night after night and I hate what he did to me and the others and I hate the family for not caring."

"You're still a good man and I'm proud of you."

Stephen leaped to his feet and stared at Hunter with rage. "Stop saying that. You don't even know me."

"I know you're a good man."

He clenched his fists, not wanting to hear the words. Not wanting them to matter. "I'm out of here."

Hunter shoved him against the wall and wrapped a hand around his throat like a noose. Stephen struggled; Hunter tightened his hold. His eyes clashed into Stephen's, his tone held a steel edge. "I'm bigger than you, stronger than you and older than you. So go ahead and get angry but listen to what I have to say. A good man can get angry. So you go ahead and hate everyone you want to hate. You let the anger burn, you let it fester, you let it simmer then you let it boil until you want to shatter the plastic smiles of everyone that crosses your path. You let it settle and you let it rot and then you let it go. I don't care who you hate. It could be me. It could be anyone, you just need to let yourself feel the pain and anger for a while. First you have to say his name."

"I can't," his voice cracked.

"It's his shame not yours. Say his name. I don't care how it makes you feel, you have to say it."

Stephen shut his eyes feeling the energy of mounting rage.

Hunter shook him. "Say it!"

Hunter's words fueled him. Stephen swallowed then said, "Uncle Jerome."

"Good," Hunter patted him on the back. "And it's okay to be angry because your Uncle shouldn't have touched you and Percy shouldn't have stolen from you and your father should have been there for you, and your mother should have too. You have a right to be angry because sometimes your wife doesn't understand you or your sister or anyone else you care about. Go ahead and be angry because you had a right to beat up the man who touched you, because you're fighting for your freedom." Hunter released him.

Stephen felt something pushed into his hands. He opened his eyes and looked down at a glass.

Hunter nodded at the object. "Go ahead."

Stephen gripped the glass and threw it against the wall. Then he grabbed a dish and did the same. He attacked the couch pillows, the lamp and a few pictures until the rage dimmed to a cool simmer. He stared around at the damage and the anger slipped into regret. "Brenna's going to kill me."

"I'll deal with her," Hunter said. "Personally, for the longest time, I've wanted to do that myself." He picked up a pillow and tossed it on the couch. "Feel better?"

"No."

He patted him on the back. "It takes time. Trust me, you will eventually."

It was a casually affectionate gesture and Stephen was oddly touched by it. He sat in front of the couch. He still couldn't predict Hunter, but he felt an affinity. He liked him. "People don't understand you either, do they?"

"No, they don't."

The phone rang before Stephen could reply. Hunter answered it and Stephen watched Hunter's face change. "I'll be right there," he said then hung up.

"What's going on?" Stephen asked as Hunter grabbed his keys.

He headed for the door. "Brenna's in the hospital."

Hunter paced outside the waiting room. He'd been asked to leave because he was making everyone nervous. He had to pace or he would need to break something, preferably his grandfather's hands.

"Mr. Randolph?"

He spun around and saw a dark skinned woman wearing a white lab coat with a tag that said 'Dr. Brice'. "How is she?" he asked with more force than he meant to.

She hastily stepped back.

Hunter sighed and softened his tone, trying to take control of his worry. "I'm sorry. I just...how is she doing?"

Dr. Brice gave him a look of sympathy. "I'm afraid your wife is very sick."

"What does that mean?" Bryon asked, coming up to them with Stephen close behind.

She looked at the three men and chose her words with care. "It means she's going to need a lot of help."

"I brought her in," Byron said. "Do whatever you need to do cost is not a problem."

Hunter shot him a glance. "Whatever bills need to be paid will be sent to me."

"Even if you can't afford it?" Byron smirked.

"I can take care of my wife."

"She wouldn't be here if you could."

Stephen stepped in-between them. "Brenna's the issue right now. We can worry about the money later." He turned to the doctor. "What do you have to do?"

Dr. Brice folded her arms and turned to Hunter. "Your wife has a fever of one hundred and two and the X-rays show the pain she was experiencing is the result of a fractured pelvis."

He groaned. "I probably made it worse."

Dr. Brice smiled gently. "It's not likely that you did her any harm. The location of the fracture would not have prevented you from engaging in intercourse." She sighed. "When your wife fell, she should have come in sooner. Hers is a special case because of the deformity she has. Adequate blood flow is crucial, and for a number of weeks it has been compromised."

Hunter folded his arms, trying to understand what the doctor was 'not' saying. "What is really wrong?"

"There is a possibility that your wife may lose her leg. Her temperature is an indication that she has septicemia, which is caused by the spread of bacterial infection in the blood. We are also very concerned that she may be in the early stages of gangrene."

He flexed his hands. "Can I see her?"

"I'm afraid not. Right now she is being prepped to go into the OR. The surgery will take several hours so I'd suggest you relax in the surgery waiting room. The nurse will call you to let you know when the operation is over. By the time you come back she should be coming out of anesthesia."

"Thank you."

The doctor smiled then left. The three men stood in silence then Stephen said, "I can't imagine Brenna without her leg."

Byron turned to Hunter. "Do you know how much a surgery like that will cost?"

Hunter kept his voice cool, his gaze a piercing onyx. "I can take care of it. This is none of your business."

"Brenna is my business. I love her. You just own her for a while," he said with disgust. "I know her. Have you ever seen her cry?"

"No," Hunter said softly. "But I've never made her cry either."

"That's because she doesn't love you."

"Brenna is loyal to me."

"But she loves me."

Hunter paused, a raw pain gripping him. He folded his arms then let them fall. "Did she say that?"

"She doesn't need to."

"That means no," Stephen said.

Byron shot him a glance then returned his gaze to Hunter. "She feels sorry for you and that's the only reason why she'll stay by your side. Why don't you do what's best for Brenna instead of yourself?" He shook his head then walked away.

Hunter stood—the whites of the floor and ceiling seeming to blend together. Did she still love Byron? Was he being unfair?

"Sometimes I wish I could get a different lawyer," Stephen said.

Hunter slowly walked towards the waiting room, feeling as though his legs were made of wood. "No, you wouldn't want that."

Stephen looked at him confused. "Why not?"

"Because he makes a good argument."

Stephen didn't want to leave Hunter alone. He didn't like how calm and detached he seemed, but he couldn't avoid going home. He groaned when he opened the door and saw Fiona sitting on the couch surrounded by a box of tissues. "Hello," he said.

She sniffed.

He pet Lillian and made sure she'd been fed then sat next to Fiona and stroked her back. "You're not going to talk to me?"

"Oh? So now you want to talk?"

He gathered her close. She rested her head on his chest and whispered, "You know it really hurts me when you leave without telling me where you go."

"I just had to get away."

"From me?"

"From everything."

"Why?"

"Just because." He brushed her tears away. "Don't you ever just want to get away?"

"No. I wish you'd talk to me more."

"I want to talk to you, but...you judge everything I say."

She sat up. "I do not."

"You don't like any of my ideas."

"That's because they don't make sense. Look where your latest idea got you."

He stood. "Brenna's in the hospital," he said tired.

"I'm sorry. Is she going to be okay?"

"I don't know." He headed to the bedroom. It was the only other way of escape.

Lewis Yancey prided himself on the seventeen years of service he'd given to the Randolphs. The latest affair had been organized with every detail in mind from the shine of the crystal chandelier to the table setting. The scent of the glazed salmon and thinly sliced russet potatoes in cream sauce filled the air. He listened to the light sounds of ice in glasses, a baby's cooing and the low murmur of polite conversation, pleased that everything was perfect. What he hadn't prepared for was Hunter Randolph slipping into the room as silently and quickly as a shadow. His appearance was so unobtrusive that a few moments had passed before his presence was seen and little by little the polite chatter died.

"Isn't this nice?" Hunter said watching the group with a malicious grin.

Lewis made a move ready for action but Orson shook his head. The older man calmly lifted his drink. "I don't believe anyone invited you."

"I didn't need an invitation."

"Are you drunk?" Angelina demanded.

"No. I don't have the same tendency as some."

She hung her head embarrassed.

"You're not welcome here," Daron said.

Hunter physically removed Daron--chair and all--from the head of the table, took a chair from the wall and sat facing Orson. "I don't care."

Daron sat outraged then stood and approached Hunter. Hunter sent him a look of such venom that Daron took a step back, grabbed his chair and squeezed between Angelina and Ruby.

Hunter rested his hands on the table. "I wanted to share with everyone what Grandfather's been up to."

"No one is interested," Curtis said.

"It's not about me. Everybody knows about me. Grandfather made sure of that. I'm a lesson. It's best to keep yourself in line or you'll end up like me. Not a pretty picture I know."

Orson set down his utensils and clasped his hands. "The moment you learn to behave yourself you have a position waiting."

Hunter reached for a roll as though Orson hadn't spoken. "No, I'm here because of my wife."

Curtis glanced at his father then said, "If your wife wants to leave you it's no one's fault but your own."

Hunter broke his roll in half. "True, but I didn't put her in the hospital."

A chilled silence whipped through the room.

Orson looked bored. "You've got your mother's flair for the dramatics."

Hunter pinned him with a stare. "I haven't started yet."

Ruby grasped her chest appalled. "What happened?"

Hunter kept his gaze on Orson. "He made her fall."

Orson shook his head. "She tripped."

"You took her cane and made her fall. She is in the hospital now because she fractured her pelvis and may lose her leg."

"That has nothing to do with me."

"You made it happen."

Orson signaled to Lewis. Hunter noticed the signal and said with deadly patience, "I will leave once I've said my piece not before." He rested his palms on the table. "Why did you visit my house when I wasn't there?"

"You mean my house. You don't live there anymore."

Hunter raised a brow. "Afraid to answer my question?"

Orson bristled at the suggestion. "I wanted to have a private chat with your wife."

"Why?"

"She was meddling in family business, calling places she shouldn't and other things. Did you know she was trying to find out about your mother?"

"No."

"Did she tell you what I told her?"

"No."

Orson grinned. "I'm not surprised."

Audrey finally spoke up, staring at her husband with fear. "Orson, please—"

"No, he wants answers. Let's give him some."

Ruby rushed up to Hunter and grabbed his arm. "It doesn't matter now. Leave. Forget about us." She lowered her voice so that only he could hear. "If you need money—"

"Curtis, get your wife under control."

Curtis glared at her. "Ruby, sit down."

She gripped Hunter's arm tighter. "You don't belong here. You never did. You—"

"Ruby!" Orson bellowed his voice rattling the glasses.

She reluctantly released her grip and returned to her chair, looking much older than Hunter had remembered.

Orson met Hunter's gaze across the elegant dinnerware, his gaze sharp enough to cut the distance. "Here's your family history. You had a brother. You killed him by strangling him to death when he was an infant. Your mother found you and saw what you did and she went crazy."

"That's not true," Hunter said. He turned to his father and Ruby, desperate to hear them deny it, but neither would meet his gaze. Angelina stared at him with pity and Daron with triumph. He swallowed suddenly feeling sick. "You told Brenna this?"

"Yes, she was so shocked by the news that she lost her balance and fell."

He felt his throat closing. "But she told me—"

"She was trying to protect you from the truth."

He couldn't believe it. It couldn't be true. Did Brenna see him as a murderer? Did she fear that he would go crazy too? Did they all already think he was crazy? He stared at Angelina and Daron and thought of Brenna and Byron. Would people always be planning and whispering behind his back? A rage so fierce he could nearly see it flooded him and he pushed himself away from the table. He glanced at Angelina again and saw the fear in her gaze that had always been there when she looked at him. He gripped his hands into fists. Brenna was different even after she found out about his past; she'd never looked at him like that.

He took a deep, steadying breath. "Brenna didn't trip. She wouldn't lie to me."

"She doesn't lie?"

"She doesn't lie to me."

Orson shrugged. "What if she did fall?"

Hunter paused then moved which such speed he nearly reached Orson before Lewis could act. Lewis fired a warning shot that whizzed past Hunter's ear. Hunter spun around. Lewis pointed the gun at his chest.

Hunter stared down at the gun. He'd forgotten that all of Orson's help carried weapons. He had a lot of enemies to look out for.

Orson slowly rose to his feet, his tone cordial. "Hunter, there's no reason to be so stubborn. I admit that I miss having you around. We were good friends. You just let a woman get your priorities all mixed up." He walked up to Hunter and rested a hand on his shoulder. "How would you like your old life back? You could be sitting at the head of this table one day. Isn't that what you'd always dreamed of?" He turned and rested his arm on Hunter's shoulders as he'd done when Hunter was younger. "Think of all the power you could have," he said in a soft coaxing voice. "Power is a wonderful thing. You could guarantee that Brenna's brother gets off, you could give Brenna the best medical care in the world." He lowered his voice to a whisper. "And you could wipe that smirk off of Daron's face once and for all. You'd like to do that, wouldn't you?" He turned to him. "We haven't always seen eye to eye, but I'm willing to forget that. You just have to be willing to trust me and trust what I say. And I say Brenna tripped." He smiled. "What do you say?"

Hunter's gaze slowly surveyed the room. With a few words he could be a part of this again, he could have the money, the prestige and the power. All he had to do was obey. He met his grandfather's gaze and said with quiet defiance. "I say she fell."

Orson stepped away from him, barely controlled fury in his eyes. "I could crush you like a bug."

"Yes, but I've learned that people always try to crush the things they're afraid of."

"I know about that little company you're trying to run."

"And I know all about yours."

Curtis stood. "I think it's time you left."

Hunter looked at his father for a long moment until the tension in the room grew unbearable then said, "Yes sir," and walked out as quietly as he'd entered.

Ruby met Hunter in the foyer as he opened the door. "You've caused a lot of fuss in there."

He raised a mocking brow. "Did you come here to scold me?"

"No," she said quickly. "I'm sorry to hear about Brenna. Send her my love."

His dark eyes bore into hers. "She'd probably prefer something more genuine like a basket of fruit."

Tears welled in her eyes. "I'm sorry about all that's happened. You're better off without us."

The sight of her tears softened him and he lowered his gaze. "What he said about me, was that true?"

"Just leave."

He glanced up at her. "I guess the only one who'll tell me the truth is my mother. How can I find her?"

"Forget about her. Forget about all of this."

"How can I find her?" he repeated.

She spun away. "You can't."

He grabbed her arm, forcing her to face him. "Why not?"

"Because she's dead."

Chapter Twenty-Seven

"What did you say to him?" Curtis asked as he and Ruby drove back to their ranch in Virginia.

"I told him his mother was dead," she said in a quiet voice.

"What else did you say?" he pressed.

"Nothing."

Curtis nodded. "Good."

Ruby was silent a moment then said, "We have to tell him the truth."

"He knows what he needs to."

Her tone became more adamant. "He doesn't know what's important."

"Do you really want him to find out about us?" he demanded in a tight voice. "When you married me you knew what would be involved."

"I didn't expect it to come to this. I didn't think Orson would toss him out like that."

"Hunter's always been an outsider."

"He shouldn't be. He's part of this family. He's your own flesh and blood."

Curtis shrugged without empathy. "He didn't play by the rules."

Ruby turned her face to the window, staring at the bright red and white of car lights rushing past. "And Orson sets the rules, right?"

Her husband sent her a callous glance. "You should know. You helped him set them."

"Things can change."

"Not in this family."

Ruby looked down at her hands that she held clasped in her lap. "Do you think Orson hurt that girl?"

"I know he did. But there's nothing we can do. There's no way to prove something no one witnessed."

Ruby shivered from an inner terror. "He went too far this time. There wasn't hurt in Hunter's voice, there was rage."

Curtis shot her an uneasy glance. "Are you afraid of him?"

"I'm not sure who to be afraid of."

"Hunter can't do anything to us, Orson can."

"But Hunter still deserves the truth."

"He doesn't deserve anything."

Ruby took a deep breath then said, "If you won't tell him then I will."

Curtis checked his rearview mirror then glanced behind him before he merged into another lane. He then rested his arm on the back of Ruby's chair. "No, you won't darling," he said softly. He lifted a strand of her hair. "Because that would be a big mistake."

"Curtis—"

"I have a lot more to lose than you do. Don't push me."

Ruby looked at her husband amazed then resigned. "You still hate him, don't you?"

Curtis turned on the radio letting classical music fill the air.

Brenna rarely allowed herself to cry, but as she lay in her hospital bed sorrow welled up inside her. And for the first time in years she pitied herself and her husband. She felt like a burden and she knew that her love could not compensate for that. Tears leaked from the corners of her eyes as she stared at the doorway that Hunter hadn't enter in the last two days. She would be released tomorrow. The fracture wasn't as serious as everybody thought and a minor procedure had fixed the damage, but she knew the damage to their marriage had already been done. She could already see the hospitals bills piling up at their door.

She remembered Orson's words that she wasn't like other women and no matter how hard she tried, she had to face that reality. She angrily brushed her tears aside and replaced her pity with an inner resolve. She could handle this. She could handle anything. She had to be strong. She would be at Stephen's trial tomorrow and she would be his support. Her problems were minimal compared to the future he faced. She swallowed back any remaining tears and turned from the door.

***

HUNTER PACED OUTSIDE of Brenna's door. He'd barely slept the past two days and hadn't been able to face her. He'd killed his brother. A brother he didn't even know he had. He'd made his mother leave, just as his love had made Angelina leave. And now his past would make Brenna leave him too. But he couldn't lose her; aside from Daniel she was the only family he had left.

"Excuse me," a voice said behind him.

He turned and saw Byron with a bouquet of flowers. "What do you want?"

"I want you to move," Byron said. "You're blocking the door."

"How much longer will this case last?"

"Closing arguments start tomorrow."

Hunter stepped back from the door. "Good."

"But I don't know how long the jury will take," he said and walked into the room.

Hunter growled then followed. He saw Brenna's face light up as she held the flowers. He sat in the far corner and watched the pair, resisting the urge to remove the smile from Byron's face.

"How are you?" Brenna said.

It took Hunter a moment to realize she was talking to him. He flexed his fingers on the arm of the chair. "I'm fine."

She waited as though she expected him to say more and he watched some of the light in her face grow dim. His gaze grew sharp. "Are you in pain?"

"No, I'm fine." She plastered on a smile, but he didn't believe her and continued to watch her. She made a face. "Stop that."

He blinked. "Stop what."

"Staring at me like that, it makes me nervous."

"Oh." He moved his gaze to Byron. "He said the case should be over by tomorrow."

"The closing arguments," Bryon clarified.

"How do things look?" Brenna asked.

When Byron hesitated, Hunter said, "Let me guess. It doesn't look good for Stephen."

Byron sent him an ugly look. "It wasn't an easy case from the beginning. There's a witness that saw him meet with Seaborn. Another witness who saw them at the bar and the house. And there's the woman across the street and the man next door with his wife. They all say they saw him enter and leave the residence at the time of the murder. No one else. There was no break in, nothing. The next day Parkov noticed something was wrong, but went inside because of watery eyes."

Hunter folded his arms. "Why did he have watery eyes?"

"He didn't say. Perhaps he had a cold."

"Or an allergy."

Byron and Brenna both stared at each other as a possibility came to their minds. Brenna's hopes lifted. "I hadn't thought of that."

Hunter shook his head. "It could be nothing."

"But it could be something."

"It's a far leap."

Byron headed for the door. "It's all we have."

Chapter Twenty-Eight

"The defense would like to recall Ralph Parkov to the stand," Byron said.

Ralph approached the stand with a self-important air. "Mr. Parkov," Byron said, "Is it true that you previously stated you saw the defendant leave the house that night?"

"Yes."

"And the next morning while you were cleaning your car you noticed the victim's morning newspaper in the mailbox?"

"Yes."

"Why were you cleaning your car?"

"As I said, I was expecting visitors."

"Isn't it true that as you were cleaning your car that you had to go inside because your eyes were watering. Does that happen often?"

"No."

"What do you suppose caused it?"

"I don't know."

"Is it true that you emptied out the vacuum bag that day?"

"Yes. I hate dirty bags."

"Hmm. So unfortunately, we won't know what caused your eyes to
water, right?"

He shrugged. "I guess not."

"Isn't it true that your daughter who is visiting out of town also developed watery eyes that day?"

"Yes."

"Who does the laundry in your house?"

The DA stood. "Objection. Your Honor where are we going with this line of questioning?"

Byron said, "Your Honor I am getting to the reason."

The judge rested his chin in his hand. "Overruled, but please get to the point."

"Isn't it true that your daughter has the same allergies you do?"

"Yes."

"Do you own a cat?"

"No."

"Why not?"

"I'm allergic to cats."

"That's interesting because your daughter is willing to testify that there were cat hairs in the lint dryer that caused her to start sneezing and we found cat hair on a hat of yours. Where did the cat hair come from?"

"I don't know."

"I'll tell you. It came from your neighbors' house. He doesn't own a cat either, but the defendant owns a long haired cat that likes to travel with him in the front seat. So anyone who sits in the passenger seat usually ends up with some cat hairs on them. So cat hairs were on Mr. Seaborn and on his couch."

"I don't see how--"

"I have an expert willing to testify that the cat hairs from your hat are an exact match to the defendant's cat. If you weren't there that night, how did the cat hairs get on your clothes?"

"I don't know."

"Isn't it true you wanted Seaborn to sell his house?"

"Yes, that's no secret."

"Why?"

"Because our property value would go up, but he was a stubborn old man. Yes, I remember now I got the hairs from the other day. The first time your client came by. I went over to talk to Seaborn."

Byron shook his head. "No, it wasn't the first time you saw him that night. I know this because the cat hairs from the sample were from a flea treated cat. She hadn't been treated that first day. I think after my client left you went into the house and killed Seaborn knowing you had the perfect alibi and scapegoat, isn't that right?"

"The damn bastard wouldn't sell!"

After the DA and Byron made closing arguments it took the jury less than seven hours to reach a verdict of Not Guilty.

Stephen slumped forward relieved. Moments later his mother hugged him then his wife and sister. A little distance away, Tima caught his eye and winked. He now had a chance at a new life and he meant to take it. The courtroom quickly emptied and Brenna stayed behind as Byron shook the DA's hand then closed his briefcase.

"We did it," she said.

Byron held out his arms to her feeling buoyant and renewed.

Brenna hesitated then went into them, but drew away before he could make it more. "Thank you."

He grabbed her wrist before she could leave. "This isn't over Brenna."

She tried to free herself. "It has to be."

"No, it doesn't. I can't deny what's in my heart. I love you. I haven't stopped loving you. Letting you go all these years was a big mistake."

She briefly shut her eyes, his name a whisper. "Byron--"

"Let me finish. Run away with me." His eyes clung to hers. "I'll take care of you."

She turned away. "No."

He cupped her chin and forced her to look at him. "You're not happy with Hunter and either rich or poor you never will be. Hasn't everything that's happened proven that? I know you're afraid, but you don't have to be. I realize it will take time for you to trust me again, I have the money and you'll be with me. Remember how you dreamed about a house near a carnival where you could hear the sound of a carousel every spring and summer? Brenna, I'll build one myself. I can make your dream come true." His eyes lowered to her lips then returned to her eyes. "Randolph isn't the man for you. You can't make this work and you shouldn't have to. No, don't say anything yet. Think about it. I'll wait for you."

Days later, Byron's words still echoed in Brenna's head. There was nothing between Hunter and her now. She did not want to be just some mother figure to Hunter or a burden. Byron was better for her. He was steadfast. He never wavered. He didn't have Hunter's unpredictability. She knew what to expect from him and he loved her. Loved her! Her father was right, she deserved to be loved. There was nothing to keep her here.

"Brenna, do you know where my cufflinks are?" Hunter called.

He was preparing for an important meeting today. She didn't know what it was for, but he seemed excited.

She sighed. How could a man not know where things were in his own home? He'd have no idea where anything was without her. He'd probably go around naked and starve to death. She shoved the suitcase further under the bed and went to the living room. She picked them off the bookshelf. Why he had a habit of leaving his cufflinks there she had no idea.

She walked up to him as he searched the living room. "Here."

He turned to her. "Thanks."

She grabbed his sleeve. "Stand still." She put them on him then smoothed down his shirt. "Did you iron this?"

"Of course I did," he said offended. That was one thing she'd forced him to learn. To her relief he didn't mind it and even ironed her clothes (although she had to explain he didn't need to iron bras).

She looked at his shirt critically. "Did you turn the iron on?"

"The shirt is fine."

"It's not fine. Take it off."

He grabbed his jacket. "I don't have time."

Even the jacket looked crinkled and as she adjusted his collar she figured out why. He'd lost weight. Clothes hung on him now. Damn. Orson was right. He could slowly kill a man by taking away all that he cherished.

But she wouldn't let him do that to Hunter. With her gone, he'd be free. Without her there would be no more medical bills, no more sleeping side by side without touching, no more pretending. Of course she'd miss the scent of cinnamon that seemed to cling to everything he wore, the distinctive sound of his footsteps, his energy, his drive. She hoped the meeting would go well. He hadn't shown this type of enthusiasm in months.

"Good luck," she said.

"Thanks."

She kissed him on the cheek. "Goodbye."

He opened the door. "Bye."

She listened to his footsteps pound down the stairs then closed the door. She rested her forehead against the door, imaging the relief he'd feel when he returned home and she was gone.

Chapter Twenty-Nine

"Did you get it?" Fiona asked as Stephen came through the door.

"No." He bent down and patted Lillian as the cat greeted him by wrapping around his leg.

She stretched her legs out and sighed. "I knew you wouldn't. You should have waited. It's crazy for you to think that just because the case went well everything else would."

Stephen sat beside her and looked at her with a probing query in his eyes. "Couldn't you believe in me just once? Just once couldn't you be on my side?"

Fiona cupped the side of his face and smiled into his troubled eyes. "I am on your side. I don't want to see you get hurt."

"Do you think it doesn't hurt that you have no faith in me?"

"I'm just afraid—"

"Afraid of what? That I might fail or that I might succeed?"

She moved away and tucked her feet underneath her. "Why can't you just be happy with the way things are? Why isn't anything ever enough for you? You're just an ordinary guy, Stephen. Like my Dad and that's okay. He worked for the same company in the same position for thirty years then retired."

"I'm not your father."

"I know—"

He rose to his feet feeling a desperate need to get her to understand. "I don't want to just exist. I want to live, feel alive. Take risks."

"Why?"

"Because."

"I don't know what you're looking for."

"A different life. Something more exciting. Brenna really likes my lighting ideas and thinks I should start my own business. Perhaps someone would see my designs and –"

"And what?" she sneered. "Make you rich and famous? That's not going to happen. If you were truly special you'd have been discovered by now. You've tried things before and they haven't worked out. You didn't get the fabulous job that certificate program promised you or even a promotion. You're just a dreamer, Stephen, but this is the real world."

Stephen stared at her, letting her words sink in. He loved her. No. That was the trouble. He didn't. That was the truth he'd been afraid to admit for years. Afraid to admit that he'd loved her once, but not anymore. That he felt a fleeting fondness, a responsibility and nothing more lasting. Perhaps he was a dreamer, but he didn't plan to change. He suddenly felt a sinking feeling of inevitability. He knew what he had to say.

"It's not going to work." He rested his hands on his hips. "We need to divorce."

"Don't be silly. You're upset."

"No, I'm—"

"If you want time apart that's okay. We've separated before."

"Fiona it's different this time. We're only hurting each other. We'll grow more and more apart. This is for the best and you know it."

"But I—"

"I've always wanted the best for you and the best isn't with me. Before I was afraid to let go, I was afraid of a lot of things, but I'm not anymore. It's time to say good bye."

She jumped up and ran into the bedroom. Stephen sat expecting a feeling of relief instead a deep pain filled him as he faced his loss. He buried his face in his hands.

HUNTER BALANCED A BOUQUET OF FLOWERS, chocolates and his briefcase as he tried to open the door to his apartment. The meeting had been a success. Mylar Industries wanted to buy them out for thirty million! His strategy had worked. Brenna would never have to worry about money again. He stepped inside and paused surprised that the lights were off. Brenna must have gone to bed early. He dropped the chocolates and briefcase on the couch, left the flowers on the kitchen counter and raced into the bedroom ready to tell her the good news. He turned on the lights. The bed lay empty, a note on the pillow. He stared at it as though it would suddenly attack him. He didn't have to read it to know what it said. She'd made her choice. He crumbled it up and stormed into the kitchen.

Maybe Brenna had made the right decision. She had no reason to stay without his money. He was of little use to her. If only she'd waited. Why couldn't she have waited? And why did she have to do it this way? Was he some monster they all felt they had to run away from: His mother, Angelina, Janice, Brenna. Was he such a monster that he didn't deserve a chance? He pressed his fists to his eyes. Then grabbed a knife by its blade and squeezed until drips of blood fell on the counter. A searing hot pain shot through his arm. It felt good. He wanted to feel the pain to dull the ache in his heart. He didn't want to miss her. He didn't want to believe that he still needed her, that their marriage had become real to him.

He dropped the knife onto the counter, when he heard the front door open. Brenna walked through the door. She turned to him and gasped. She tossed her bags aside and came towards him. "What happened? You're getting blood everywhere. What were you doing?"

He stared at her tongue-tied.

"Never mind." She gently cradled his hand and examined it. "We need to clean it."

She led him into the bathroom and cleaned the wound. He stared at her bent head confusing clashing with an unfamiliar joy. "Where have you been?"

She carefully wrapped a bandage around his hand. "Errands. I left a note on the bed so you'd see it when you changed."

He remembered the crumbled note with embarrassment. "Of course."

Once finished she stood and went into the kitchen. "What were you doing?" she called over her shoulder.

He followed her. "Cutting."

"I can see that." She picked up the knife curious. "What were you trying to cut?"

Hunter glanced around searching his mind for a good response. "Umm."

Brenna suddenly smiled. "I know."

"You do?"

"Yes." She picked up the bouquet. "You were trying to cut the flowers for me. You should have known I could have cut them myself when I got home." She lifted the bouquet to her face and smelled them. "Hmm, they're beautiful. Thank you."

He made a noncommittal sound not knowing what to say. At that moment all he noticed was her. How the yellow lily petals looked against her cheek, the highlights in her hair.

Brenna laid the flowers down and grabbed a vase. "I guess your meeting went well?"

Hunter shifted from one foot to the other. "Um, yes." He had so much he wanted to tell her, but the words wouldn't come. He watched her spread the flowers on the counter and fill the sink with water.

"So what happened at this meeting?"

He told her all that he'd been working on and how things had progressed. She threw her arms around him. He held her close, brushing his cheek against her hair. "When I came home I thought you'd left me," he said.

"I did."

A sheet of ice spread through him. He drew back. "Oh."

"I left you for a full ten minutes. Then I came back."

"Why?"

Brenna took a deep breath then said, "Because I love you." It felt good to say the words. It felt good to admit that he'd swept into her life and shredded all past feelings she'd tended for Byron. Those feelings had been light superficial longings. Her feelings for Hunter were deeply embedded, flowing in her veins. Saying goodbye to him forever felt like her skin was being torn from her--leaving her raw and vulnerable. It felt scary too. But this was the moment she'd been afraid of. Being completely real with no pretending, trusting someone else to be kind, expecting them to be kind and not knowing if they would be. Why? Because Hunter felt no need to rescue her, no need to pity her.

When he didn't respond, for a moment she wished she hadn't come back. Wished she hadn't revealed herself.

Brenna lowered her gaze and returned to the flowers. "These really are beautiful."

Hunter spun her around to face him. His eyes intense, his voice deep filled with an emotion that awakened some foreign emotions in her. "I'm glad you came back."

He captured her mouth with his own; his lips both persuasive and demanding. It was more than a kiss. It was more a secret not spoken between two people making the invisible visible. When his lips touched hers, she could see loyalty, she could feel honor, as though it was just within her grasp. She knew he could see her love for him as though it were twinkling in the dark sky.

As he held her she realized how much she'd blocked him out.

How much of life she'd blocked out. How many feelings and experiences she had kept at a distance. And how much she had lost by doing so. She'd denied herself this moment. This terrifying, frightening yet freeing moment for years. Never had his touch felt so tender, his lips so gentle. Never had she felt this alive. She felt more alive than Byron had ever made her. "I'm--"

"Shh, we'll talk later."

But they were talking now and saying so much more. His lips were a warm, wet tantalizing invitation for more. Igniting vivid desires. She soon lay naked in his arms, the length of him on top of her. She could feel him sinking between her thighs, stirring emotions, once dormant now like a hurricane mingling passion and pain. A sweet, savage pain that needed to be brought forth in order to heal. Tears sprung to her eyes as she let go of the old Brenna and allowed the new one to emerge: This wife, sister, friend. This woman who would no longer hide from her feelings.

She cried and he let her, gently brushing away tears, freeing her to lift off the weight of her mask. He pulled the couch throw over them and she snuggled in his arm. He tightened his hold and lowered his arm to her waist.

"I'm so happy," she said.

Hunter absently stroked her thigh. "Just wait until the Randolphs hear about this."

Brenna turned to him and saw a look on his face that worried her. "Why should we care what the Randolphs' think?"

His eyes met hers filled with a darkness that paralyzed her with fear. "Because I plan to make them care."

Chapter Thirty

Brenna's fears were realized a month later when she glanced over to the other side of the room and noticed Hunter in the corner reading a series of papers. For the first time she noticed how his weight loss had given him a hard, edgy look she didn't like. "What are you doing?"

He glanced up. "Randolph Medical is in trouble. Their sales are low and they've overextended themselves. They are prime for a takeover." He flashed a cruel grin.

She inwardly shivered at his expression. "I hate when you smile like that."

"I thought you liked my smile."

"I do. Just not that one."

"Why?"

Because she thought he looked like Orson. "Never mind. So what are you going to do about it?"

"About what?"

"Saving the company."

He frowned. "I'm not planning to save the company."

"You're not going to let it fall, are you? This is your family legacy and a lot of people depend on its survival. I'm sure you'll try to save it."

Hunter looked down at his papers. "You've made a poor assumption," he said in a quiet tone.

"What assumption?"

His eyes met hers. "You're assuming that I am a kind man."

Brenna licked her lower lip, choosing her words carefully. "I know they betrayed you, but destroying the company isn't going to make it right."

Hunter stared at her amazed. "Why are you defending him?" He gestured to the couch. "Do you remember what he did to you? Trust me, this is about much more than betrayal."

"I know what he did to me was wrong, but--"

He narrowed his eyes. "There are no buts. Your loyalty lies with me."

"It is."

"Then don't get in my way."

"Hunter, please listen to me. Your revenge won't just hurt him, but everyone else. Think of your grandmother."

He shrugged nonchalant. "She's lived a long life."

Brenna paused at his cold disregard. "Let me help you get what you want, but--"

His eyes darkened as his voice turned to acid. "I will settle for nothing less than the sight of his blood dripping on my hands."

Brenna stared back at him, although it took all her courage to do so. She could feel his anger and his need for revenge, but she knew that what he was thinking of could destroy him too. "I won't let you."

"You can't stop me."

"Then I'll fight you."

Hunter stared at her as a cool anger began to gather in his mind. It was an anger he'd never felt before. It didn't grip or seize him, but whispered calmly. Quiet thoughts he could never utter aloud. For a moment he wondered if he had inherited his mother's madness, because as he looked at his wife he felt a dangerous anger fill him. An anger that her loyalty meant everything to him, that her opinion mattered and that gave her a certain power over him.

"Don't get in my way, Brenna."

"I will if I have to."

"You know they say I killed my brother."

"I don't believe that. When I have time again I'll find your mother."

He threw down the paper and stood. "You can't because she's dead."

"Did they tell you that too?"

"Ruby wouldn't lie to me."

Brenna shook her head and looked at him in sympathy. "I wish I could believe that."

"It doesn't matter anyway." He turned to the window. "They'll all get what they deserve."

Brenna came up behind him and wrapped her arm around his. "He made us both suffer. Are you any better if you make others suffer because of the actions of one man?"

"At this very moment I don't care about being moral or decent. To Orson power is all that matters."

"That may be so but Orson possesses something a lot more important than his power, which is why he has been able to succeed all these years and destroy and control people's lives including yours. Hunter, true vengeance is discovering a man's weaknesses, not trying to take away his greatest strength."

Hunter reluctantly listened. "Go on."

"What does Orson value more than his money, his power, his position? What is the one thing you're willing to protect with your life?"

He looked down at her for a long moment then glance away. "Orson isn't like me." He removed her arm. "This is my fight and I'll do it alone."

BYRON NEARLY SWALLOWED his tongue when Hunter burst into his office like an avenging warrior. He held up his hands in surrender. "Whatever you think I did, I didn't," he said.

Hunter raised a brow.

"Okay, so I asked her to run away with me, but she decided not to. That's all, nothing happened. I swear."

Hunter sat, looking suddenly amused. "Yes, I know."

Byron let his hands fall, relieved. "Then why are you here?"

"Are you still in the mood for a little revenge?"

Byron began to smile. "Keep talking."

"Orson was responsible for putting Brenna in the hospital. I have decided that I would like to thank him personally."

Byron stilled, a look as dangerous as Hunter's, coming into his eyes. "So would I. If you want to destroy his company I have just the information you need."

"I already know it."

Byron's face fell. "You do?"

"Yes. However, I could still use your services."

"Fine. So do you know everything?"

"Yes, the embezzlement scheme of my father is no secret to me."

"Do you know about Victor Erickson?"

"No, who is he?"

Byron rubbed his hands together. "Our winning card."

ORSON SAT in his study trying to figure out the best way to get Randolph back on track. He glanced up when he heard a knock on the door. "Come in."

Two officers entered the room. "Orson Randolph?"

"Yes."

"Please stand."

He casually did so. "Why?"

"You're under arrest for the assault and battery of Brenna Randolph."

"What! There must be a mistake. That bastard." He called out his wife's name. "Audrey! You get my lawyer on the phone now. You can't do this to me. Do you know who I am?"

"Yes, sir." They ushered him towards the front door.

"I'll have your jobs."

"You have the right to remain silent..."

ORSON RETURNED HOME HOURS LATER. He marched into the sitting room and poured himself a drink. He turned to Audrey who sat on the couch. "That boy has gone too far." He took a long swallow then set the glass down. "He thinks he can play the game, my game, but I'm bigger than he is. He'll find out. Why are you looking at me like that?"

"Curtis called."

"So what?"

"He needs to see you at the office."

"I don't care. He'll see me tomorrow."

"He said it was urgent. Apparently there are two men who want to invest in your company."

Orson's interest peaked. "Fine. I'll change and get over there right away."

HE WOULD DEAL with Hunter later. If that boy thought a little jail time would rattle him, he was dead wrong. He chuckled to himself as he strode down the hall to his office. Here he was in the company he'd made. Created on his own. Nobody could defeat him. He opened the door to his office and halted. Hunter sat at his desk. He glanced at his son and the two other men in the room.

He slammed the door. "If you value your life, you'll get up out of my chair."

Hunter clasped his hands. "If you value yours, you'll take a seat."

Orson looked at Hunter with contempt. "I don't listen to orders I don't give."

Byron pushed him into a chair. "Think of it as a suggestion."

Orson glanced at Curtis who stood near the wall like the weak, coward he was. "You knew about all this?"

"No, he didn't."

"Don't blame him," Hunter said. "He called you under our direction."

"Why are you here?" Orson said.

"To do a little negotiation."

He began to smile. "What do you have to offer me?"

"Your reputation."

"I already have one."

"Yes, but you could lose it. Think of how it would look if it were known that the president of Randolph Medical Supply attacked not only the spokeswoman for the company, but a disabled individual, who has used his products for years, causing her to be hospitalized."

"I didn't attack anyone."

"You made her fall."

Orson looked bored. "She tripped. Her cane got caught on something and she fell."

"She said you took her cane."

"That's because she's a liar. You think I don't know what you're trying to do? You're trying to frame me for something I didn't do. Too bad you can't prove this little story of yours. It's her word against mine."

"You lying son of a bitch." Hunter leaped from his seat; Miles grabbed him before he lunged at Orson. "She nearly lost her leg because of you, and you're not even man enough to admit it."

Miles patted him on the back. "Don't let him get to you."

Hunter sat, his eyes filled with rage.

Byron tugged on the cuffs of his jacket. "In reality, the truth of what happened is immaterial, it's what we can get the public to believe or more importantly the press. They would love a story like this. I am sure it would sell a lot of papers, but I doubt it would do you much good."

"I can pay them to keep quiet."

"I'll pay them even more to speak," Hunter countered. "Imagine if this went viral."

Orson felt perspiration rise on his top lip. "What do you want?"

Hunter spread his hands on the desk. "Right now I'm sitting where I want to be." He shoved a paper across the table. "I know you're an old man, but I hope you still know how to spell your name."

Curtis suddenly laughed. "You can't get rid of us that easy."

Byron folded his arms. "Do you know a man by the name of Victor Erickson?"

He blinked. "No."

"Of course you do," he urged. "You've been paying his mortgage for over twenty years."

Curtis glanced at his father, nervous. "I don't know what you're talking about."

"That's why you've been embezzling money from the company, right? You needed the extra cash to keep your friend satisfied."

"That's my business not yours."

"So you admit it's true?"

Curtis just stared back mute.

"Why don't you just live with him?"

Orson pounded the arm of his chair. "Because it's against nature."

Curtis jerked his head in Orson's direction. "Because of him," he said with feeling. "He's made me feel like a freak my entire life. Like there was something wrong with me. No matter what I did he treated me like a dog." He glared at Hunter. "Then you came along and he pushed me aside."

"But I'm your son."

"I don't have a son."

"What?"

"You're not my son." Curtis glanced at Orson. "You're his."

Hunter sat frozen. "I don't understand."

"What's not to understand? I'm not your real father."

Hunter stared at Orson. "Is it true?"

Orson leaned back his face impassive. "Is it true that your mother was a whore? Yes."

"She wasn't a whore," Curtis said.

"How would you know? Did you ever get a chance to find out what she was like?"

Curtis' mouth twisted into a cynical grin. "You seduced her and you're still proud of it. Why don't you tell Hunter everything? Go on Dad, tell him how you took her from me. Tell him how you shamed me. You want to talk about unnatural? What about a father that sleeps with his son's wife?"

"That's because she wanted a real man."

"I tried to change, but I couldn't. I couldn't give her a baby, so you did that for me. Twice." He looked at Hunter. "I hated you the first time I saw you. Every day you reminded me of the control Dad had over my life. When Lionel came..." Curtis briefly held his hands over his eyes. His voice lowered with regret. "I didn't mean to do what I did. He just wouldn't stop crying and I lost my temper. I shook him hard. He stopped crying.

"It didn't take me long to realize what I had done. All I thought about at that time was that I didn't want to go to prison. So I staged a scene. I used a child--you. I wrapped a scarf tight around Lionel's neck and told you to hold your brother. You liked to hold your brother while Lionel slept. But when Ruby and Marlene came into the room they knew right away."

"Ruby was there?" Hunter said.

"Yes, she was your nanny. She knew everything, but kept it quiet. We covered up the incident, but your mother couldn't take the pressure and tried to kill herself. You probably don't remember this but you found her and thought she was tired from painting. Blood soaked your pants and shirts as you hugged her. But she never recovered completely.

"I blamed Dad for everything and that's when I started stealing money over the years. I threatened to come out if he said anything. I wanted him to pay for making me keep my secret and his too. I wanted him to pay for the life he forced me to lead." Curtis sighed. "I know none of this was your fault, but I still can't stop myself from hating you. From seeing you become everything I tried my whole life to become. I envied you. You had your mother's love, and your father's respect. Orson wanted to groom you to replace him, he saw himself in you."

Hunter looked at Orson. "Pity."

Orson leaned forward. "It's true you know. You have a lot of me in you. That's what gives you that fire. We could work together," he said in a coaxing tone. "We are of the same mind and the same blood. Think of what we could create. How much we could dominate. Wives are just ornaments, I'll pay for whatever damages you've suffered, but don't let her stop you. No man should be too dependent on a woman. They're fickle, flighty creatures. But you can depend on me. I know people. I can make you great."

Hunter came from around the desk and held out a pen, experiencing no feeling towards the man he now knew was his father. "It's too late."

Orson whipped out a gun and pointed it at him. "It's never too late." He grinned. "You should have known better than to try to beat me."

Curtis moved forward. "Dad, don't."

"Stay where you are. I've covered up murder before and this won't be any different. I'm finally going to do what you should have done years ago." He aimed and fired. Curtis rushed in front of Hunter then fell back as the bullet made impact. He crumpled to the ground. Hunter dashed over to him and cradled him in his arms. He put pressure on his chest but blood continued to seep through. "Dad, you've got to be strong now."

Curtis slowly shook his head. "But I'm not—"

"Yes, you are. You're the only father I've known."

His breathing grew more labored. "All this time I thought I hated you, but what I hated was me. I'm sorry."

"I forgive you Dad," Hunter said, holding him close although he could feel the life quickly leaving his father's body. "Do you hear me? I forgive you. You have to hang on." He squeezed his eyes shut but tears slipped from underneath his lids. "I forgive you please. Please, Dad don't leave me."

"He's gone," Orson said.

Hunter slowly turned his heated gaze to him. "You killed him."

"Pity. I wasn't aiming for him." Orson lifted his gun again then his head seemed to explode and his body fell to the ground. The men stood stunned then noticed Orson's wife Audrey standing in the doorway. She lowered her weapon then fell to her knees and sobbed. "God forgive me, but it's all over now."

Chapter Thirty-One

Hunter walked along a strip mall as the summer wind howled through the alleyways hinting at the coming of autumn. Although four months had passed, the confrontation with his grandfather—he still couldn't call him his father—and his father continued to replay in his mind. He now worked with his Uncle Walter, who he'd appointed president, and Doran to help restructure the company. He didn't care if Doran eventually became CEO; he no longer desired the position. He enjoyed being a consultant with FreedomWear and investing in other companies and working on new inventions. He and Brenna had looked at possible new homes, but weren't eager to move. He'd accomplished a goal he didn't even realize he had. He now had someone to come home to. Someone who cared whether he came home or not. It was a satisfying feeling.

He was about to turn around when a carousel horse in a gift shop window caught his eye. He went inside and stood in front of the display case. He turned when he saw wispy brown hair in the corner of his eye. "Pauline?"

She turned with a welcoming smile. It fell when she saw him. "Yes?"

He pointed to the display case. "Which one do you think I should choose? The horse or the carousel?"

Pauline looked at him stunned then wary. "Excuse me?"

"It's a gift for Brenna. I'm not sure which one she'll like."

He was so focused on the objects he didn't even sense her animosity towards him. "I'm sure it doesn't matter," she said ready to leave.

He nodded. "You're right. Both are nice." He smiled faintly. "But Brenna really likes carousels. Perhaps I should get both."

Pauline stared at him uncertain. She couldn't match the doting husband in front of her with the arrogant, cold man she'd met earlier. The man who'd stormed into Brenna's office and convinced her to enter into a marriage of convenience. She remembered Brenna telling her how he'd saved her niece's puppy's life, but she hadn't seen it, so she hadn't thought much about him. She couldn't imagine him caring about anyone but himself. She didn't understand him, would never try to, but she knew one thing his faint smile couldn't hide. He loved Brenna—a lot. And maybe if she'd let herself admit it, he'd saved Brenna's life, as he had the puppy, saving her from a life of isolation and enriching it somehow.

"The carousel," she said. "She'll like the carousel."

"You don't think I should get both?"

"No."

"Yes, I suppose two gifts show a sense of indecision. Thank you."

"You're welcome." She hesitated. "Tell Brenna I was wrong."

He nodded then approached the counter. Pauline watched him with a heart full of joy and regret.

HUNTER STOOD in the living room, wondering where he should set the gift. When Brenna came out of the bedroom he wanted her to find it in the perfect place. He'd set it on the shelf, the dining room table, and the windowsill. He was about to put it in the kitchen when

Brenna came out of the bedroom. He was surprised to see her in a business suit. "Where are you going?"

"To an emergency meeting."

"Do you want me to take you?"

"No, I'm fine."

He held out the box. "Here. I bought this for you."

She glanced at her watch then the box obviously torn. "Is it important?"

His heart fell. "No, I just—"

"Then I'll open it later." She crooked her finger, inviting him closer. He leaned toward her. She kissed him. "I'll see you when I get back." She glanced at her watch again then raced out the door.

Hunter sighed and set the box on top of the TV. He picked up a magazine and flipped through its pages. He was on his third magazine when the doorbell rang. He swore, tossing the magazine aside, then answered.

An older woman with a short gray Afro in a flowery dress stood there holding a peach colored note.

Hunter pulled out his wallet. "Which charity is this for?"

"I'm not a charity."

He put his wallet away, curious. Perhaps she was a neighbor in need of sugar. In TV shows people always seemed to ask for stuff like that. "How can I help you?"

Tears sprung to her eyes. "I can't believe it's you."

He took a step back. Great. He'd opened the door to a nutcase. "I'm sorry, but you must have me confused with someone else." He began to close the door.

Her tone firmed. "Hunter Matthew Randolph, don't you close that door on me."

His heart stopped as he stared at her. "Shit."

She smiled, showing off her dimples. "That's not the kind of welcome I'd expected, but I know what you mean."

"They told me you were dead."

"I was dead to them. I know this is a shock." She tugged on one of her earrings. "I was shocked when your wife found me."

"Brenna?"

She raised a sly brow. "You have another wife?"

"Uh, no," he said lamely. He couldn't believe Brenna was behind this. He began to smile, then again, he wasn't. At least now he understood her 'emergency meeting'.

"I wasn't sure if I should come, but your wife assured me this would be a good idea." She rested her hands on her hips. He noticed two large gold bracelets circling her wrists. No doubt they covered her scars. "So do you want to hug, kiss or shake hands?"

"I don't know."

"I'll make up your mind." She hugged him and at first he stiffened then allowed himself to relax. He wrapped his arms around her, fighting against the tightening in his throat and the threat of tears. He abruptly pulled back and cleared his throat. "It's nice to see you."

"Can I come in?"

He took a hasty step back. "Yes, come in. Would you like anything to drink?"

"No, I'm fine." She sat down and looked around the room with appreciation. "You have a lovely home."

Hunter shoved his hands in his pockets and followed her gaze. Strange, but he'd never considered the apartment a home before. He'd never considered any place he'd lived a home, but suddenly it seemed true. From the window he could see the sun spreading its golden rays on the lake, the bookshelf crowded with Brenna's books, his sketches scattered on the couch and the faint scent of lilac lotion Brenna loved to wear. Yes, he and Brenna had a home. They always would no matter what size.

He saw his mother staring at him as though she could read his thought. He grew awkward and took his hands out of his pockets. "Are you sure you wouldn't like something drink?"

"Yes."

"How about something to eat?"

"No, thank you."

"So you're sure you don't want anything?"

"I want a lot of things, but right now all I want is to talk to you. You've become a fine young man."

He felt his ears burn, and then became annoyed that her praise mattered to him. "Thank you."

"So what did they tell you about me?"

Hunter sat down rubbing his hands against his trousers. "Does it matter?"

"You're not even curious?"

"No."

"I'm sure it's because they've said horrible things and you're afraid they're all true. Well, they probably are. Yes, I was Orson's mistress. I'm not proud of that, but he gave me the attention I desperately needed and he was a very determined man. He wanted me and he got me. He was so charismatic and in charge. Your poor father didn't have a chance. No matter how he tried he couldn't measure up to Orson's rigid standards."

"Did you know—?"

"That he was gay?" she guessed. "No, not originally. Then one day Orson insulted him and hinted to the fact. We should have divorced then, but we decided to fool ourselves. We convinced ourselves that we could live with the charade. When I got pregnant, that was the beginning of the end. He knew the child wasn't his."

"He said he hated me the moment he saw me."

"He also hated himself. Ultimately, it was the choice he made that destroyed him. The choices we all made. Lionel died because of my indiscretion, Curtis' spirit slowly crumbled because of his secret and Orson's choice to rule us caused his downfall. Even Ruby made a fateful choice. She married Curtis for the status and riches and paid the price of keeping secrets. There's a certain freedom in living truthfully. It's not easy, but it's worth the risk."

"They told me you were crazy."

She laughed. "I was for a time. It took me a long time to crawl out of the abyss. I had to find myself again."

"For years I've been trying to live up to a lie. It seemed everyone kept expecting me to fail and now I know why. There was no way to succeed."

"You've forged your own path. You threatened Orson even when you were young. You had a will all your own. Only you could have broken the ties the way you did."

They talked for hours, getting reacquainted, getting past the lies. They didn't try to recapture the years lost but instead built a foundation for the years to come. Eventually, she had to go. They exchanged addresses and phone numbers then Hunter walked her to her car. He hugged her again this time without reservations, and then watched her go. She was no longer either a goddess or demon, but an ordinary woman. Someone he would like to have in his life.

Brenna arrived home an hour later.

Hunter pretended to focus on an action movie on the TV. "How was your meeting?"

"It was great."

"Good. What was it about?"

"Oh, nothing interesting."

"You sure left in a hurry."

"Yes," she said vaguely. "Well, there was something that needed to be addressed."

"Oh."

She affected a casual tone. "So what did you do?"

"I read some magazines then watched a movie."

"That's it? Nothing happened?"

"No."

"No one called or stopped by?"

He turned to her curious. "Were you expecting someone?"

"No, no I just...well I'm glad you had a quiet evening."

She headed for the bedroom looking depressed. Hunter slapped his forehead as though he'd forgotten something. "Oh, there is one thing. My mother stopped by."

She picked up a pillow and threw it at him. "You jerk! You knew I was waiting to hear that."

He laughed. "I couldn't resist. Since you wanted to be clever I thought I'd respond in kind."

She sat beside him eager to hear the details. "How did it go?"

"Next time I want you to be here."

She clapped her hands, thrilled. "There's going to be a next time?"

"Probably." He rested an arm behind her head. "How did you find her?"

"Daniel's grandmother. She knew all about her brother's secrets and helped me track your mother down. It wasn't as hard as I thought." She looked down at her hands, a sly smile toying with her lips. "Now if I remember correctly you have a gift for me."

He clasped his hands behind his head, stretched out his legs and stared at the TV. "I've changed my mind."

She unbuttoned his shirt. "You'd better change your mind back or else."

He glanced at her a glint of amusement in his gaze. "Or else what?"

"Or else I'll stay married to you for the next fifty years."

He retrieved the box and handed it to her. "Make it sixty." He sat down and rested his arm on her shoulders. "We tend to live long in my family and I'd hate for you to go before me."

She sat there stunned, surprised by his words. "Do you love me?"

His eyes caressed her face. "I could no sooner name all the stars in the sky than tell you how much I love you."

"I love you too."

"Yes, I know. Even though I'm not your Prince Charming."

"That's true."

His brows furrowed. "What do you mean by that?"

"Byron was my Prince Charming, but I needed a real man."

He frowned. "I'm not sure I approve of that statement."

"Too bad."

He groaned. "I knew the moment I walked into your office you'd ruined my life. There was nobody else for me, but you."

"You're a perfect match."

"Are you going to open the box?"

"It's a carousel, isn't it?"

His eyes widened. "How did you know?"

"Because you always give me what I need."

In one motion, she was in his arms and his lips were on hers. Her body tingled with a bottomless feeling of joy. She felt the power and strength of his love and returned it in kind. She cupped the side of his face. "My own true love."

———

A YEAR later they welcomed Martin Randolph who decided to arrive two weeks early on a winter day. The year after that during a summer rain they welcomed Edward Randolph.

In the hospital room, Brenna noticed Edward's left leg was a little bent and felt a tinge of sadness. Hunter, however, balanced Martin on his lap while he held his second son with pride silently vowing to be all that his father couldn't be to him. With eyes full of joy and a voice full of amazement he said, "He's perfect."

About the Author

Dara Girard, an award-winning, national bestselling author of more than fifty novels, from romance to suspense, loves telling stories.

Born in the US to immigrant parents, Dara enjoys pulling from her Jamaican, British, Nigerian heritage and exposure to various cultures to bring what reviewers and fans call "vivid emotional stories" to life. She is best known for her popular Henson Series, the mysterious Clifton Sisters, and the fun Black Stockings Society.

You can write her at:
contactdara@daragirard.com
or
P.O. Box 10345
Silver Spring, MD 20914
If you'd like to receive a reply, please send a self-addressed stamped envelope.

Visit her website to sign up for her newsletter and get sneak peeks, monthly updates on new releases, and special offers.

For more information visit
www.daragirard.com